NYPHRAZI

GODS + MONSTERS

NYPHRAZI

GODS + MONSTERS

MINKY ST ANNE

PAPERBACK ISBN 978-1-991321-23-7

A catalogue record of the paperback which contains this full series is available from the National Library of New Zealand.

GOD of the WOODS

1

Annoyance floods me as I check my watch for the umpteenth time in the past twenty minutes. My younger brother's MIA for the third time this week! "What a pain in the ass!"

I know he hasn't forgotten me. It's just that he doesn't want me stinking up the cab of his new truck. But what he doesn't know is I'm so tired I'd let him lash me across the hood like a deer carcass. Sure, there are washing facilities at the plant, but hot water is always in short supply. I'd rather put up with the stench of fish for another hour than suffer a cold shower.

Damn it! The sooner my truck is out of the shop, the better. I hate having to rely on my brother to get me to and from work. I stamp my foot, pain shooting up my leg, reminding me I've spent the past twelve hours on my feet. That my arms are like noodles is a testament to wielding a filleting knife for almost as long.

Still, it could be worse. At the height of the season, we were pulling sixteen-hour days, meaning I had to sleep in the

dormitory with all the other women. As soon as the hours had dropped enough to allow for it, I was back home.

I still can't believe I'm living with my folks. The global downturn had seen me made redundant from my security job in Seattle, with people seeming to think their stuff wasn't worth guarding anymore. How stupid was that?

With nothing other than minimum-wage crap on offer, and my credit card debt through the roof, there had been nothing for it but to move back home to "Shitka", Alaska.

Obvious drawbacks aside, at least here I could live rent-free and get work that paid better. Not that I'd choose to work in a fish processing plant, but beggars can't be choosers and all that.

This isn't where I thought I'd be at this stage in my life. After finishing the arts degree that my folks had said was a waste of time, I'd struggled to find work. In the end, I'd had to give up on my dream of working in a gallery and settle for a job with a security firm. There were bills to pay.

What had started out as a stopgap had turned into an okay job when management realized I had more brain cells than all their other employees put together. Not that those same brain cells had done me any good when contracts started dropping like flies.

All I had to show for the job when I left was a cardboard box full of dinky desk ornaments, a letter of recommendation, and a propensity to swear. More than someone with an arts degree should.

I had to hand it to my folks, though; they hadn't once pulled any of that "we told you so" crap. I think they knew I was taking care of that myself.

With thoughts of failure continuing to run through my tired brain, I stare without focus at the spectacular view before me. Growing up amid all this beauty, I don't see it anymore.

Even paradise wears thin when you'd rather be somewhere else.

As I stood there fuming, I faced a simple enough question. "Forward or backward?"

I'd already walked a couple of miles toward home to reach my brother's prearranged pickup point. This meant my options were to walk back to the plant or push on. I'd call and abuse Josh, but a pathetic signal meant my phone was only fit for selfies, and I wasn't indulging in those when I was a hot mess.

Just three more miles to my folks' place and a home-cooked meal; less if I take the shortcut through the forest that pops out opposite our driveway. Thankfully, it's summer, or as summery as it ever gets in Alaska.

Resigned, I swung toward home. My feet hurt, my legs are tired, and the rest of my body is ruined too. It's this exhaustion that has me deciding ahead of time to cut through the forest. It's not that it's dark and spooky—there's still plenty of light. It's more that I'll need to keep my wits about me to make sure I don't get trampled by a moose or taken out by a bear.

As I walk along, I scan the side of the road, soon spotting what I'm after. The branch is small enough to carry but, if I sling my jacket over it, large enough to make any bear think twice about attacking me. Well, that's the theory, anyway.

I swing off the sealed road and onto the narrow gravel track that is all that's between me and a moose casserole. With no chance of being run over, I drop my lump of tree on the ground, ditch my backpack, and shrug out of my jacket. There's no missing the coolness of the day, leaving me thankful that along with heavy-duty jeans, I'm also wearing a long-sleeved T-shirt and a hoodie.

I put my jacket on the branch, shoving twigs into each

sleeve before closing the zipper to hold it in place. Luckily, the branch has heaps of little twigs in all the right places, allowing my jacket to achieve a human-like silhouette.

"You'll have to do," I say to my new walking buddy and self-defense device while threading my arms through the shoulder straps of my backpack. After slinging the branch over one shoulder, I strode out along the track with fake enthusiasm.

Given how bone-tired I am, I make pretty good time, all the while scanning the forest and keeping an eye out for any movement. Nothing's happening other than the leaves shivering in an almost nonexistent breeze. All is quiet apart from the twitter of birds and the loud crunch of gravel underfoot.

When the crunching stops, my senses go on high alert. I've walked down this track enough times to know the gravel goes all the way through to the other road. Sure, the undergrowth is trying to overtake it in places, but there's always that base of rock to make it suitable for quad bikes. It's also perfect for the dog teams who use the area to practice during the summer months.

Looking down, it takes a moment for me to comprehend that I'm up to my ankles in mud. Given it hasn't rained in days and there's no other water source around here that I know of, this shouldn't be possible.

I turn back to face the way I've come, but it does me no good. The track I've just crunched my way along has disappeared and been replaced by a river of mud.

Despite swiping my hand across my eyes, the scene before me doesn't change one iota. "Damn it, I need a vacation," I mutter before turning back to continue home.

Well, I would if there weren't a man standing in my way.

"What the hell?" I stagger back, unable to comprehend what I'm looking at.

For one thing, the guy is naked, although not entirely. The bits that should be covered are, but it's how they're covered that takes my breath away. No loincloth for this guy. Instead, his cock and balls are encased in what looks to be a custom-made leather condom of sorts.

The mid-tan hide is a perfect match to his skin tone and is tooled all over with intricate patterns. It's too snug a fit to be called a codpiece, being as it is lashed together in a herringbone pattern along the underside of his cock.

As though to add extra emphasis to its extraordinary length, there's a leather cord threaded through a loop on the end that then wraps around his muscled waist. The setup is both tidy and intimidating in turn. Just like the man himself.

The guy's like a mashup of National Geographic and Cosmo centerfolds.

It's only when he coughs that I stop my detailed examination of his equipment. However, it still takes me a while to look him in the eye, given I have to devote some further attention to what I encounter on the way up.

He's covered in tattoos, with swirling vines and leaves covering his muscled torso like a living chest plate.

When my gaze clashes with his, I'm further stunned. To call his eyes green doesn't do them justice. They'd give spring leaves a run for their money, and I'm sure it's only a trick of the light, but they seem to glow.

These luminescent orbs are edged with dark brown lashes that make mine appear moth-eaten by comparison and are topped with eyebrows that hint at a quick temper. His hair is long and also deep brown.

After sniffing the air, he took a step in my direction. It's too

close for comfort, with my sense of self-preservation kicking in just as my self-defense instructor said it would.

I jump back to give him room to crumple in a heap at my feet, but he does no such thing. I'm still wearing my steel-capped work boots, so for him to remain standing after I've introduced one to his leather-encased cock and balls is of major concern.

Of even more concern is the anger that springs to life in his eyes, changing them from leaf green to something altogether more reminiscent of sludge.

"Subdue and have her washed." He sniffs the air again. "Make it thorough."

It takes a heartbeat for my tired brain to work out he's not talking to me. But before I can react to the new arrival, a large hand lands atop my head, and my brain buzzes like a bee caught in a mason jar.

Not that this slows my reaction. I twist, ready to introduce my footwear to some more reproductive organs, but the palm stays where it is and the buzzing increases to the point things get blurry.

I'm sinking in an ungraceful heap on the ground when I hear Green Eyes say, "No, wait! I think I'll wash her myself."

I black out to the sound of rich male laughter.

2

My regaining consciousness is a slow process. It's like I'm trying to claw my way out of some bizarre dream. Then I realize that what I'm experiencing is bizarre, but it sure as hell isn't a dream. More like a nightmare.

I think I'm in a cave, but only because of how the place smells. There's light streaming down on me, blinding me and making it difficult to check out my surroundings. Above me is a hole through to the sky or the world's largest light bulb. I'm opting for the former.

After shaking my head to clear it of any residual haziness, I squinted both to the left and right of me. Nothing. I can't see a thing with that light shining in my eyes.

As the grogginess drops away, my anger ramps up, and I know it won't be pretty, but I don't care.

If they think I'll lie here like a good little girl, they are in for a hell of a surprise. Three months working in a fish processing plant has only added more muscle to my already athletic body, making me no shrinking violet.

I'm more akin to violence than violet. And there'll be lots of it if they try keeping me here against my will.

However, the very act of thinking about where I am has me pausing my nefarious thoughts of revenge. I'd thought the track turning to mud and then disappearing was down to sheer exhaustion. Whereas, it'd seem I'm stuck in some weird alternate reality or parallel universe. Either that, or I've lost my mind due to the long work hours.

Wherever I am, it's a hell of a lot warmer than it was outside. More than that, it's toasty. Hot enough that I need to ditch my hoodie.

I tried to struggle into a sitting position. Only I can't. I'm being held down.

This has me lifting my head to see what's got me stuck in place. It also has me discovering that I'm naked as the day I was born, and that what's holding me down shouldn't even be possible.

I'm lying on a wooden table made up of what seems to be hundreds of carved hands, palms up, to form a surface solid enough to support me. Now and then, a wooden hand would claw its way free and wrap itself around one or the other of my limbs. I try kicking my leg against the hand that is clasped around my ankle, but rather than letting go, it tightens to a point of pain.

Panic claws its way up my throat, and I throw myself to one side, desperate to escape. The table of hands has other ideas. More and more of them detach themselves from the surface to hold me firm. When I continue to struggle, I'm pinched hard on the ass. It hurts enough that I lift myself off the table as much as I'm able to get myself away from the evil digits.

"Cease!"

This yelled instruction scares the living daylights out of me,

stopping me cold, but still arched away from my tormentor. Fortunately, this command also has the hands that had squirmed all over me settling back onto the table. Back until I'm down to a single hand holding onto each of my limbs. Only then do I sense it's safe to drop my ass.

When Green Eyes comes to stand next to the table, I let him have it.

"You bastard. What the hell do you mean by holding me here? And where the hell are my clothes?"

Unable to move, I put every bit of hate I can into the gaze I nail him with.

It doesn't faze him in the slightest. "They are being washed. They stunk."

He has me there. "That's no reason for you to take them away!"

A single raised eyebrow tells me what he thinks of this sentiment as he moves closer to the table and reaches out to touch my face. I yank my head away from him until my neck muscles are at their limit.

I don't understand what he says next. It's not a language I'm familiar with and is more akin to a series of clicks, hums, and whistles than speech.

Whatever he says, I soon have what I suspect are a couple of wooden hands clasping my head between them. They force it back into alignment with my body rather than skewed off to the side, away from my captor.

Try as I might, I'm unable to move when he once again reaches for my face.

The temptation is to squeeze my eyes shut, but I refuse to back down. It's not my way. I glare at him while waiting for him to do whatever the hell it is he has in mind.

Rather than hurt me, he peels something off my face and holds it up for inspection.

It's a fish scale.

After flicking it away into the dark, he clicks and whistles again. For a moment, nothing happens. Then the surface of the hands dissolves, apart from the four that I'm thinking of as my handcuffs. I'm lowered into warm water with the edges of the table forming a wooden pool.

I can't stop myself from struggling, thinking the bastard is about to drown me. Then I hit the bottom and realize it's not deep enough for a bath, let alone murder. The water only reaches partway up my body, with my front still high and dry.

His gaze roamed over me, dwelling on my breasts and pubes. I can tell he likes what he sees by the way his pupils dilate and the thong that ties the leather condom around his waist pulls tight.

"You wash the hair. I'll take care of the rest."

"What? How am I supposed to wash my hair when I'm being held down?"

He ignores me. Instead, he disappears into the gloom outside the circle of light illuminating me. I can hear him moving around with the occasional clatter. He returns holding a cloth and a wooden jug that has a leather handle on one side and a narrow spout on the other. This too has swirling vines carved into it.

I'm still pondering how the hell I'm supposed to wash my hair when the hands on either side of my head move. Thinking I'm about to get my head freed up, I tense my neck muscles. But they don't let me go. Rather, they make room for more hands to get on with shampooing my long, blonde hair.

The air is soon fragrant with the scent of spring flowers. Unable to move my head, I squint, trying to see who's in

charge of rinse and repeat. It doesn't take long to understand that I'm alone with my captor.

I'm still looking back behind me when liquid is poured all over my body. Upon snapping my gaze back to see what he's up to, his expression of naked greed has me in panic's grip. After dipping the cloth in the water next to me, he lathered me from head to toe.

He's thorough, I'll give him that. No crease, dip, or crevice is missed, with the roughness of the cloth ridding me of any lingering fishy smell from work. Wooden hands even lift me to the side so he can wash my back and ass.

This had him sliding the rough cloth back and forth between my cheeks and causing me to flush with embarrassment. By the time he's finished, I'm clean as the proverbial whistle and tighter than a drum.

It's only when he stops his ministrations that I notice how tense I am, and I exhale with a shuddering moan. Then, after shutting my eyes, I concentrate on quelling the sensations zipping around my body. The last thing I want to do is go off like a firecracker when I'm at the mercy of God knows who.

My eyes ping open when a stream of water hits my stomach, getting my undivided attention. Or rather, the person responsible for it does. He looks me dead in the eyes and indulges in a wicked smile when he moves the jug he's holding even higher above my body.

"Don't you dare!"

Oh, but he does.

I think I'm as relieved as he is disappointed when he runs out of water before he's able to move far enough down my body to hit his target.

My relief is short-lived when I hear him click and whistle and the wooden hands come to life again. Those holding my

ankles at either side of the pool move my feet closer to my ass until my knees are sticking up in the air. I clench myself tight, gripping my knees together with all the strength I can muster. It's only after a third pair of hands have applied pressure to the inside of my thighs that I succumb.

I'm spread wide, with the water lapping at my core, causing me to struggle. Once again, all the hands get in on the act, and I'm soon spread even wider, leaving me vulnerable.

All the while, I've been getting the best head massage ever. Better than the lame job the local salon does. If only I could relax and enjoy it, but hearing the jug being refilled next to me has me tensing. This time he doesn't waste the precious water by starting at my stomach and working his way down.

He empties the whole thing bang on target, although I avoid the worst of the damage by squeezing myself together as hard as I can. Not easy when you've been exposed to the elements.

While my clit is beside itself with glee, I'm less impressed.

Sure, I haven't had sex since moving home, but this is not how I expected to break the dating drought.

When he tuts several times, my first thought is that he's talking to the wooden hands again, but then I realize this admonishment is directed at me.

"Stop fighting it."

I have trouble concentrating on these instructions. "Get your hands off my tits!"

He ignores me, instead tugging first on one nipple and then the other until they're hard enough to take someone's eye out.

"If you think I'll just lie here and take it, think again, buddy."

"Vyran."

"What?"

"I am Vyran, Nyphrazi God of the Woods." That he follows

this with a questioning lift of one eyebrow lets me know that this is where I'm supposed to introduce myself. Tough.

As if realizing I won't respond, he again chats to his grabby pals swirling around in the water next to me. They act enthusiastically.

"What?" I spat out at Vyran. "No!"

There's no mistaking his intentions. The only thing I'm unsure of is whether I want him to proceed. Or not.

3

None of my yelling stops two of the hands from sliding up between my thighs. They're soon buried deep in my cleft and make quick work of spreading me to the sides. One of them even gets in a quick flick to my cherry pit that has the dirty little slut humming away to herself as though we're separate entities. While I'm still fighting it, she's already rolled over.

We're reunited when another rivulet of water rains down on her. I mean me. The thin stream of water drills into me, but when Vyran lifts the jug higher still, the water separates into droplets. Each of them was a small bullet of pleasure.

This time, I'm as disappointed as Vyran when the water runs out.

"You like?" His voice is deep, his words are as much a statement as a question.

I'm too far gone to fight it, and only an idiot couldn't see I'm ready to explode into a million pieces. "Oh, yes!" I choke out.

While refilling the jug, he chatters away in that strange language of his. This results in two of the hands sliding up each side of my chest and cupping my breasts before rolling and tugging my nipples. That they have the dexterity of human hands is freaking me out. If I weren't so damn aroused, I'd lose it.

As it is, I don't know which part of my body to focus on. If nothing else, my hair is the cleanest it's been since I started work at the fish plant. My clit is soon fighting for supremacy on that front when he tips more water over it.

One drop at a time.

I can't believe this; I'm out of my mind with ecstasy and arch and buck when he slides first one and then two fingers deep inside of me. He spreads these wide, filling me, stretching me, and applying pressure to the small nub nestled just inside. I disintegrate, with the climax strong enough that it has the water rippling around me.

About now, most dates would expect me to return the favor. It seems Vyran is different, leaving his fingers buried deep inside me until the last of my spasms die away. He then moves them again, pulling them almost free before plunging them back in again as deep as he can go, and wiggling them for maximum effect.

This in-and-out is a poor imitation of what I'd like him to be doing to me, and the next climax is slower to tighten. But it does until I keen for release. This is achieved when Vyran presses my clit until I explode, with every nerve ending in my body screaming right along with me.

After a thorough rinsing, the hands that had been plastered all over my body slid down to once again support me. They raise me out of the water before forming themselves back into

a table where Vyran helps me sit upright before swinging my legs over the side.

"I hope you don't expect me to walk?"

He chuckles before sliding me to the edge of the table, where he tucks my ankles around behind his back. I hook them together without thinking, his leather-clad cock snug in my cleft, filling it from top to bottom. His hands, cradling my ass, pull to each side so that I'm even more open to him.

I reach around his back, trying to untie the leather cord that is the only thing between me and what I hope will be mind-blowing sex. I'm still struggling with the knot when he carries me out of the light and into the gloom of what proves to be a cave.

The dark is absolute after the brightness of the pool of light, and because I'm looking over his shoulder; I don't know where we're heading.

We walk between curtains that appear to be made out of animal skins and into a cavern that is lit by smoking tapers; the bed I see out of the corner of my eye is massive and covered in animal pelts. The sight of this has me forgetting the cord, my core tightening in anticipation at the thought of lying on all that fur with Vyran.

After using a chamois to dry me and wrap my hair, he lays me back on the bed where I luxuriate in the pelts, rubbing against my naked skin. I slide when he drags me far enough down the bed that my legs hang over the end. He then kneels on the ground and settles himself between my thighs.

Hell, it's like he can read my mind.

It's only when he licks his lips that I realize he's not human.

His tongue is far too long and comes to a wicked point. When I see the control he has over it, I'm both horrified and aroused in turn.

After pushing my knees apart, he dropped his head and attacked my sex like a starving man. Any reservations about him being an alien, or whatever the hell he is, gasp out of me. Oh, good God, that tongue might be foreign, but it's also magic. I try grabbing hold of the surrounding fur to anchor myself to the bed, but it's too thick and I can't grip it.

After running his tongue up and down my slit until I'm arching up off the bed, he pokes it right inside of me. The tip twists around, exploring every inch of me until my juices run more freely than they ever have.

"More," I groan, "More."

I'm lucky he seems to know what I want more of because he sucks hard on my nubbin while plunging his fingers into me over and over. This sends me over the edge, again and again.

And here I was thinking multiple orgasms were an urban myth.

But it's official; I've had more orgasms in these caves than I have in all my years of dating. I'm not counting the faked ones that were necessary when a date was so far off the mark that it wasn't happening. And all I wanted to do was go to sleep.

I'm like sex personified, lying there with legs spread wide, arms flung high above my head. All I can think about are the sensations that leather condom will impart with each plunge. At least, I hope to hell he keeps it on. Just thinking about it has my sex twitching in anticipation.

It's therefore like having a bucket of cold water chucked over me when, rather than joining me, he covers me with furs and leaves me on my own.

"What the hell? Where are you going?"

"You must rest before we carry on."

"I don't need a rest!" I yell at him as he disappears back through the pelts that cover the door. "I need you to fuck me!"

Damn it all, what is wrong with me? While my libido has never been what I'd have called rampant, now I'm at the other end of the spectrum. All I have to do is think about Vyran and my sex lights up along with any other erogenous zones on offer.

Thumping my hands down on the bed in frustration doesn't bring him back and only leaves me angry as well as horny and hungry and thirsty and needing to pee. I'm suffering from all the wants and needs, but horny wins out.

Damn him to hell.

I think about having a scout around to see if there's a way out, but there's the minor fact that I'm naked. I'm looking at the hide curtain that covers the doorway as a viable solution when I hear footsteps. I lean up in bed, ready to give him a burst for abandoning me, but it's not him. Rather, it's an old woman who looks to be human, although I'm reserving judgment until I see her tongue.

Dressed in a sheath dress that looks to be made of chamois, she's holding a wooden platter. The dress seems to irritate her, with her tugging at the neckline as if it doesn't fit right.

The other thing that I find unusual is that her posture is too straight for someone doing menial work. There wasn't a chance I could have stood like that after a shift at the fish processing plant.

Without looking at me or even speaking, she crossed the chamber and placed the tray on a small table that sat next to the bed. The way she sets it down is careful, almost ceremonial, rather than the practiced efficiency of actual serving staff.

She's turned to leave and is close to running when I yell, "Wait!"

She skids to a stop in a move reminiscent of a cartoon character before turning back to me. Her head is bowed, while her body shakes—though something about her trembling feels more like suppressed irritation than fear. For a split second, I catch her shooting me a look that's almost... calculating? But then her eyes dropped again.

"Bathroom?"

She shakes her head, but still won't look at me. While her gesture had started out sharp and authoritative, she'd soon appeared to catch herself, making it more deferential. I'm now unsure if her initial response was because she hadn't understood, or because there wasn't a bathroom.

"Toilet?" I'm unable to keep the desperation out of my voice this time, causing her to lift her head.

After realizing I'm wasting my time with English, I jumped out of bed. I then cross my legs and hop around in what I hope is the intergalactic signal for needing to use the bathroom. My bladder is now full enough that I'm not faking this charade, and I'm relieved when she nods and shows that I should follow her.

As we move toward the doorway she'd entered through, I notice her glancing back over her shoulder. If I didn't know better, I'd think she was checking to see if we were being watched or followed. Reinforcing this are her movements are quick, almost nervous.

I'm right next to her before she realizes I'm naked and holds her hand up. She disappears through the curtains a second later, but not before I catch her muttering something under her breath in a language I don't recognize.

I hope to hell she's coming back. Otherwise, I'll have to pee in a corner or risk streaking through the caverns until I find something that resembles a toilet. At this point, even the bowl on the tray that's overflowing with berries would work in a pinch.

4

On hearing movement on the other side of the leather curtain, my relief was immense. Although I don't relax my pelvic floor muscles just yet, knowing it wouldn't be a good look.

The old lady hands me a pile of soft chamois, and I waste no time in pulling the dress on. After tightening the leather thong above my breasts, I gestured for her to lead the way.

She shows me to a small room off the chamber where I'd been washed earlier and nods at a hole in the ground with footplates on either side. It's the first squat toilet I've seen since a whirlwind trip around Europe in my gap year. Though it's a hell of a lot cleaner than any I used back then.

I waste no time making use of it and am soon back in the bedchamber where I fall on the food and drink with zeal.

Replete and my nakedness covered, I'm free to wander back through to the bathing chamber. Despite having a good look around, I didn't find any doorways other than those I'd already used. The old girl is nowhere in sight either, which is weird.

My examination of all the walls is thorough, but it doesn't reveal any hidden entrances. How the hell did she get to me? Maybe she teleported through the hole above the table of hands because I doubt she walked through solid rock.

With nowhere else left to check, I lie on the bed and wonder when I'll see Vyran again. I'm not as aroused as I was, but I'm not ready to sleep either. I can't help but wonder what he is, too. While it's obvious he's humanoid, there isn't a chance he's an actual human.

Does he come from this planet or from somewhere else? Given the primitive living conditions, it seems hard to believe he arrived here in anything as sophisticated as a flying saucer. Then there's the way he can control wood. Just thinking about that makes me shiver with remembered passion.

In the end, I fall asleep, but my dreams are disturbing and nightmarish. The one where I discover the end of Vyran's cock is similar in shape and abilities to the end of his tongue has me aroused enough that I wake. Fevered as I am, I have to relieve the pressure myself.

The next time I wake, it's because of the pleasure being exacted on me by Vyran. He's kneeling beside the bed, his face buried in my mons, and he's pulling on my clit like he's a drunk and I'm the last drink on the planet. And who am I to leave him thirsty?

I thrust my hips to give him better access. He groans before spinning me around, dragging my legs over his shoulders and plunging that wicked tongue of his in and out until I'm frothing.

But rather than let me reach fulfillment, he kneels back so he can look at me, leaving me on the edge of climax even though he's no longer touching me.

His cock appears to be straining for gratification as much

as I am. Maybe it's the dim light, but it looks as though the patterns and ridges on the leather condom are swirling as if alive. This is something that's confirmed when he lowers himself onto me so he can rub the length of it up and down my furrow.

"Do you plan on taking that off?" It's only when I've asked this out loud that I admit to myself what I want the answer to be.

"You mean my fettyr?" He says, kneeling back and tapping his cock for confirmation. This has it bucking hard against the waist cord like a wild beast. "I never remove this. Ever."

I know my eyes have gone a little deer-in-the-headlights as I explore the possibilities of sex with it still in place. With all those ridges and patterns, it could be mind-blowing, if a little scary, on the length and girth side of things.

Despite these reservations, I can hear my girly bits chanting, "Keep it on! Keep it on!" in the background.

When I see a knife in his hand, it cuts through my haze of arousal. But rather than a stab of pain in some weird alien love act, he hacks through the leather thong around his waist. Freed, his cock snaps away from his body and the swirling of the bumps and lumps of the engravings speeds up.

"Oh, my."

Other bits of me aren't as subdued in their response. My sex thumps in time with my heart, which is beating nowhere near as slow as it was before he cut that restraining cord.

I don't hesitate before wrapping my legs around his waist and propelling him forward. However, rather than lie down and plunge himself into me, as I've been hoping, he unhooks my legs and rolls me over. He then stands and drags me up onto my hands and knees, and close to the edge of the bed.

This isn't what I want, or how I want him. I try to turn

around so I'm facing him, but his hands on my hips hold me in place.

I'm still squirming when he leans over and whispers in my ear. "Hold still! It has to be this way for the fettyr's lacing to work."

I'm still trying to work out what he means when he spreads me wide with his fingers and enters me without pause. My relief that he's entered my sheath rather than where I thought he was aiming for is soon forgotten.

The lacing clatters its way over my G-spot, winding me ever tighter with each row of eyelets. This, along with the ridges and patterns of the fettyr swirling and undulating, makes it feel like his cock is trying to burrow its way into my depths.

The sensation is overwhelming.

When he slides his hands around in front of me and strokes and flicks my pearl, I'm a shuddering mess in an instant. An orgasm rips through me and I'm unable to stop slamming myself back into him again and again, my body jerking out of control.

We drop onto the bed in a heap, but he holds my hips high, so he stays embedded in my depths. I wait for him to soften and withdraw, but it doesn't happen. It takes a second or two to realize he's burrowing deeper still. And yet his body is tight against mine.

What starts out gentle enough soon speeds up. The ridges and patterns of his fettyr are now more pronounced than earlier, hitting all the right spots and nudging at my womb. As my breathing snags, so do the patterns, causing Vyran to laugh in my ear.

"Why don't you try panting or humming?" he suggests, his voice thick with passion.

I don't need to be told twice.

I keep control of the embellishments for as long as I can. However, this proves impossible when I lose my ability to breathe with any semblance of rhythm. Vyran pulls himself free with agonizing slowness before flipping me over and back down onto the furs.

In what I suspect is a practiced move, he slides right back in and up to the hilt, with his leather-covered scrotum now hard up against my ass. This fullness and contact only increase when I put my feet over his shoulders.

"More?" he says?

"More!"

He withdraws until he's close to pulling out, then plunges in again and grinds for all he's worth.

He keeps up this slow fuck until I'm panting like a Lamaze student to prolong my ecstasy. When he takes things up a gear and thrusts ever faster, I shatter harder than I ever have before. I'm losing consciousness when I hear his roar of release.

I wake alone. Again. This is becoming tedious. The only difference this time is that my clothes, washed and folded, sit in a neat pile at the end of the bed. When I lean over the side, I spot my boots sitting on the floor. They've been polished. Hell, I don't think they were this shiny when new.

Grabbing my chamois sheath off the floor, I slip it on and pop through to use the bathroom. Back in the bedchamber, I make use of a bowl of water and a cloth to wash myself down before dressing. It doesn't seem worth it.

"Now what?" I said to the empty room.

It isn't empty for long. The old lady from the previous day arrived and showed that I should follow her and be quick about it. Good, I'm craving Vyran's presence again. The man is like a drug to me.

I followed her first through the bathing cavern and then through an archway that hadn't been there when I'd surveyed the cavern the day before. The next chamber is bare of any furniture, but leather curtains cover an arch opposite where we've entered. Stepping to one side, she bows again and again, all the while gesturing at the hides hanging from a pole set over the head of the arch.

"Okay, okay, I'm moving."

I skip across the room and flip the curtains to one side, and rush through the archway in anticipation. Therefore, I'm confused when I find myself outside. On swinging back to the curtains, I'm stunned to find them missing.

Instead, I'm looking back along the gravel track I'd trudged down a couple of days earlier. My backpack and the branch, with my jacket still wrapped around it, lie abandoned in the middle of the track.

While this is a relief, given how the weather can turn in an instant, I'm pissed that Vyran has ditched me without so much as a goodbye. Talk about being abandoned like a used tissue. However, my anger is soon replaced by an unwelcome sense of loss.

5

With no obvious way of getting myself back into the caves, I throw my backpack on and then toss the branch along with my jacket over one shoulder. The weight feels different now. Everything feels different. My body hums with an energy I can't identify, like electricity running just beneath my skin.

How do I explain my absence to my family? After being missing for two days, I'm coming home cleaner than I have been since I started that disgusting job. Hell, I'm cleaner than I've been since before I started that job. Even my fingernails are no longer dirty and chipped.

While the angle of the sun tells me I've been freed at a similar time of day to when I was captured, how do I explain where I've been? I pause, looking out at the familiar landscape of my home state.

The ocean, the snow-covered mountains, the surrounding forest. It all looks the same, but somehow smaller. Diminished. Like I'm seeing it through fresh eyes.

Vyran's eyes.

"That bastard!" I mutter, but even as the words leave my mouth, I know they're a lie. My anger is a thin veneer over something much more complicated.

The way he'd looked at me every time he left me on my own, as though memorizing me. As though he never wanted to let me go. I'm sure of it.

Despite this, he'd still let me go.

With nothing to be accomplished by staying put, I continue crunching down the trail with each step loud and unnatural in the afternoon quiet. However, there's nothing quiet about my mind, with it racing as it attempts to construct a believable story.

Food poisoning? No, that wouldn't explain two full days. And there's not a snowball's chance in hell my family would believe I got lost. They know these woods almost as well as I do. What about a freak accident?

My stomach chooses that moment to growl, reminding me I've eaten nothing but those sweet berries for days. The memory of their taste makes my mouth water. They'd been unlike anything I'd ever experienced, bursting with flavors that seemed to change with each bite. Otherworldly, just like everything else in that place.

Just like him.

I shake my head, trying to dislodge thoughts of Vyran's hands on my body. The way he'd commanded those wooden appendages with nothing more than clicks and whistles. The way he'd made me feel things I didn't know were possible.

The late afternoon breeze picks up, carrying the fragrance of pine and wildflowers, and for a moment I smell that spring-flower fragrance from the cave. My body responds in an

instant, a flush of heat that has nothing to do with the walk and everything to do with muscle memory.

Focus, Jasmine. Family first. Explanations first. Everything else... later.

On exiting the trail and starting down the hill toward home, I'm surprised to see my parents' trucks parked in their usual spots. I thought they'd be out scouring the countryside looking for me, not hunkered down for the evening.

Rather than being in the throes of anguish over a missing loved one, everything looks so very normal. In which case, why do I feel like an imposter approaching a life that no longer fits?

I take a deep breath and commit to my story. I'd twisted my ankle on the trail, found shelter in an old hunting cabin, and spent two days waiting for the swelling to go down to a point I could walk. It's plausible enough and explains not only my absence and the fact that I'm not limping now, but that I'm famished enough I could eat a moose. On my own.

What my cobbled-together excuse doesn't explain is why every cell in my body is singing with an energy that feels divine.

"That bastard," I repeat, but this time it comes out as a whisper. This time, I'm not sure if I'm cursing Vyran for what he's done to me, or for kicking me out before I was ready.

I square my shoulders and carry on toward explanations and casseroles and pretending that the last two days were just some weird wilderness adventure instead of the most intensely erotic experience of my life.

But even as I rehearse my lies, I can feel that something fundamental has shifted. I'm not the same woman who took that shortcut three days ago. The question is, will anyone else notice the change in me?

"That bastard!" This refrain continues as I stomp down the road. But with each step, the refrain loses its bite and gains something else altogether.

Longing.

After ditching my ultra-clean boots in the mudroom, I opened the door to the living room, bracing myself to be pounced on by my folks. I'm opening my mouth to spout the lies I've been working on, but I don't get the chance.

"You're home early," says my mom, not bothering to take her eyes off the huge casserole she's stirring. The aroma has my stomach gurgling in anticipation after only eating berries for a couple of days.

"I've just made your brother drive back into town to pick you up," says my dad, his gaze remaining riveted on the TV.

It takes mere seconds to realize I haven't lost time or been missed, but if either of them sees the non-fishy state of me, they'll smell a rat.

"I got sick of waiting and walked," I say, before scooting through to my bedroom and ditching my clothes before anyone sees them. I then stand in the shower long enough to fake my unexplained cleanliness and long enough to have my dad banging on the wall.

Dried, I drag on my evening sweats and make it to the table in time to have a plate of casserole put in front of me. I've already gobbled down a couple of mouthfuls when my brother gets home, bitching about not being able to find me. On seeing how annoyed he is, I struggle in vain to keep the smile off my face. Something he doesn't miss.

"How the hell did you get home?"

"When you didn't show, I ended up walking." I avoid any mention of when I'd started out because, while he's not a rocket scientist, neither is he stupid. The last thing I need is for

him to work out that my story doesn't add up time-wise. I mean, how do I explain something I don't understand myself?

After helping Mom clean up after dinner, I fake a few yawns so I can escape to my room. "I'm off to bed. It's been a long day."

A chorus of good-nights follows me down the hall as I head to the bathroom to brush my teeth. In the mirror, I catch sight of my reflection and pause, toothbrush halfway to my mouth.

Josh is right—there is something different about me. My skin has a subtle luminescence, like I'm lit from within. My eyes seem brighter, the blue more vivid than usual. Even my hair appears shinier, the blonde strands catching the light in a way they never have before.

I lean closer to the mirror, studying my face. The changes are subtle—nothing that would alarm a stranger—but obvious enough that even my obtuse brother picked up on them.

I can't help but feel relieved when I shut my bedroom door and climb into bed without the events of the past two days having been discovered. I hate lying, especially to my folks, even if only by omission.

But what choice do I have? How do you explain to your parents that you've been intimate with a god? That you've traveled to another realm? If I were to come clean about that, I'd risk being locked up wearing a jacket that did up the back.

In the silence of my room, I'm free to think about my experience with Vyran. My body responds to the memory in a heartbeat, a flush of heat spreading through me like wildfire.

I can still feel the phantom pressure of those wooden hands, still taste the sweetness of those berries on my tongue. The way Vyran had looked at me—like I was precious, powerful, necessary. No one had ever looked at me that way before.

I roll onto my side, pulling my pillow against my chest. The cotton feels rough against my sensitized skin, another reminder that something fundamental has changed.

Everything feels more intense now—colors are brighter, sounds clearer, sensations amplified. It's like I've been living my life in black and white and now it's technicolor.

But it's more than just physical changes. There's an energy thrumming beneath my skin, a power I don't understand. When Josh had been interrogating me at dinner, I'd felt this strange urge to... do something. I'm not sure what, but the feeling had been there, coiled and ready. It had taken conscious effort to tamp it down, to appear normal.

It's useless. My body remembers every moment in that cave, every touch, every sensation. The wooden hands manipulated me with impossible dexterity. The water cascaded over my skin. Vyran's leather fetters created friction in places I'd never imagined.

And after relieving some of the sexual tension that this brings on, I get back to thinking about him.

The relief is temporary, though. Even as my breathing slows, even as my body relaxes, I can feel something building inside me. Not arousal this time, but something else. An anticipation. A knowing.

What if I never see him again? The thought hits me like a physical blow, leaving me gasping. Given how bizarre my popping into that parallel world of his had been, the likelihood of it happening again seems slim.

But even as I think about it, I know it's not true. Whatever connection we'd forged in that cave, it's not broken. I can feel it humming in my veins, see it in the subtle glow of my skin, taste it in the enhanced flavors of my mom's cooking.

I close my eyes and let myself drift, but even sleep doesn't

offer escape. Now I know the truth. Vyran hasn't just marked my body.

He's marked my soul.

And somewhere, in the space between waking and sleeping, I can swear I hear the distant sound of clicking and humming, like a promise whispered in the wind.

6

The next two weeks passed in a blur. I walk home from the plant when it's fine, taking the shortcut, hoping to crash through that invisible barrier again. But it doesn't happen. It also doesn't seem to matter how early I get to bed. I wake up exhausted. My dreams of Vyran are vivid and erotic, leaving me in a constant state of arousal with no respite.

By the end of the third week after my visit to the Nyphrazi caves, I'm running on empty. I'm therefore pleased when the shifts get shorter due to a lack of fish. In the past, I'd have been pissed about missing two days' work and the subsequent drop in pay. Now, the thought of a decent break has me close to weeping with relief.

The joy of going to bed without having to set the alarm for four thirty is a simple pleasure. It's not the only pleasure I indulge in as I scratch the itch that has been tickling me since I last saw Vyran.

Nor is this the first time in the past couple of weeks I've

had to scratch myself either. I've never been aroused around the clock before.

I'm not sure what time it is when I'm woken by someone climbing on top of me. I lash out with closed fists, but don't encounter anyone. This has me scrambling for the lamp on my bedside table and slamming my hand down on the switch.

Rather than facing an intruder, I'm alone.

And yet I can still feel a weight bearing down on me. When I see a shape forming under the blankets, I'm unable to stop the scream that pierces the quiet of my room. It's loud enough that my dad opens my bedroom door moments later, his favorite shotgun locked and loaded. His appearance has the blankets dropping back down to hug my body.

It's official; I'm freaked out.

He propped the shotgun in the corner by the door and dropped onto the edge of my bed. "What's wrong, baby girl?" he says, pulling me into a firm embrace and stroking my hair.

"Sorry, I guess it must have been a nightmare." And I guess it must have been, because nothing else explains what just happened.

Once he's convinced I'm okay, Dad struggles to his feet, collects his gun and pulls the door shut on his way back to bed. I soon heard the muffled tones as he told my mom what it was about. I tried settling down, hoping to get back to sleep, but I'm sure as hell leaving the light on.

This also means I'm able to see the blankets taking shape once more.

I fill my lungs, ready to scream for my dad again. But all the air in them hisses out when whatever is beneath the covers gives my nipples a good, hard tug. I lift the blankets and look at my naked breasts. There's nothing visible apart from two very erect nipples.

When I sense rather than see a hand on my breast and one of my nipples stretches before my very eyes, I think I'm going nuts. But then Vyran's image flickered into focus before my startled gaze.

"I didn't want you to go," he whispered, "but the extra power you gifted me has allowed me to visit you."

All the rejection and loss washed away, and I can't help but curve myself up against him. He doesn't need any further prompting and is soon moving down my body with that clever tongue of his darting all over the place as he goes.

"Huh, what power?" I ask him after my scrambled brain has had time to process, but he's already dropped between my thighs and I no longer care. I hold the covers up so I can watch the master at work, but then his image flickers like a television on the fritz, and he fades.

The sensations don't stop, though. If anything, they intensify, forcing me to shove the corner of one of my pillows into my mouth to gag my cries of ecstasy.

While Vyran might not care that my folks are a couple of doors away, I sure as hell do. Especially when he buries his ghostly self in me up to the hilt. It's when he withdraws in readiness for driving into me again that I put a stop to things. Although not for long, and not until we're on the floor. Funny, but up until this point, I hadn't even realized my bed squeaked.

It's only when I close my eyes that any of it makes sense. Without my sight to confuse me, I straddle him while he kneels and leans back over his heels, allowing his cock to stand tall. But when I glance at my reflection in the mirror on the closet door, it's as if I'm suspended in mid-air. As weird is seeing the lips of my sex peeled back, exposing me to the cool night air.

Once we get into a hard pumping rhythm, I'm unable to

tear my eyes away from the mirror and my wanton reflection. Vyran picks up on this fascination of mine and pulls and twists my clit. Being able to both witness this and surrender to the sensation is mind-blowing.

I'm about to sob my release when he stops cold and places his hand over my mouth just enough to muffle my frustrated whimpering.

"We need to go back to the cave," he murmured. "I want to hear you scream."

Before I can nod my consent, we're there.

I'm still straddling him, but now he's sitting on the edge of the bed and sliding me out along his legs and then back in again. I'm mesmerized by the sight of his leather-clad cock disappearing into my depths and his thumb mashing my clit. Soon enough, all those sensations come crashing down on that one small part of me before exploding in spectacular fashion.

I scream his name over and over as he's wanted me to, and am soon rewarded when he finds his own release and roars out my name.

"How do you know my name?" I ask as soon as I've got my breath back.

"I've watched you throughout the years of our time."

I have trouble comprehending this from a physical point of view, but also because I'm lying spread out on top of him. His ever-ready cock nudging for entrance again does nothing for my concentration.

"I never wanted you to go. It was Gaiya," says Vyran, lifting his hips and gaining entrance.

"The old lady?" I think back to her behavior—the way she'd kept looking around, as if worried about discovery. How she'd led me to that portal and tricked me into walking through it.

"Old, but powerful. She was once... favored by my father.

That favoritism allowed her son to walk among us as an equal rather than being relegated to the lesser ranks." His expression darkens. "It also gave her ideas about her son's importance that don't match reality."

Looking back, everything made sense now. Why Gaiya seemed so uncomfortable in that servant's dress, why she'd kept glancing around as if fearing discovery, why her movements had that authoritative edge she kept trying to suppress.

Hell, she hadn't even been Vyran's servant, and all that cringing and trembling had been an act. The bitch had been playing with me from the moment she walked into his sleeping chamber, and I'd fallen for it completely.

I should have known something was off when she knew where to take me, when she'd moved through those caves like she owned them.

I have to take some calming breaths before I'm able to continue my conversation with Vyran.

"What did you mean when you said I'd gifted you power?"

"When I achieve Nysa, I draw power from the source. It's an effect that appears to interest the God of All Desire."

When he falls silent again, I wait for him to continue.

"It's power that lasts," he murmurs, frowning. "Praedytus has been asking many questions about it."

"Huh?" I don't understand how that can be. I'm not drained after he's climaxed. Tired, yes, but drained, no. In which case, where does the power that he talks of come from?

I'm readying myself to ask him yet another question, but before I can, the pelts to his bedchamber are thrown aside and five large men walk in. Rather than being put off, Vyran lifts me free of his length and pops me next to his side while they line up across the end of the bed.

Meanwhile, I drag as many furs over my naked form as I'm able, but this still doesn't stop me from feeling exposed. I'd like to avoid their ravenous gaze, even if, as a group, they're magnetic.

While their dress and bodies might be comparable in form to Vyran's, there all similarities end. Whereas Vyran is hewn from nature, the men standing at the end of the bed are more akin to precious metals.

"Will you not introduce us to your new toy?" says the man on the far left. Everything about him smacks of silver, from his hair and eyes to his glistening skin. That the fettyr covering his cock is fashioned out of this metal seems appropriate.

With my attention captured by his question, I can't help but notice that the pattern on his fettyr is more straightforward and military in design than that of Vyran's. The entire surface is covered with small, round-headed cones. That these are undulating up and down its length while he stands there with arms folded and legs astride is enthralling.

"You like what you see, acolyte? Imagine it buried deep inside you."

I'm readying myself to abuse him for daring to call me an acolyte, when my words stall as I give thought to the very picture he's painted. And he knows it, with the undulations on his silver fettyr breaking into a random pattern that mesmerizes me.

God, I'm such a slut.

"Jasmine, these are my brothers. The lecherous bastard on the end is Seolfer," says Vyran, nodding to the silver man. "Then we've got Ciprus, Axel, Aurum, and Marlo."

I nod to each of them in turn, marveling at the fettyrs they're all wearing. Ciprus's fettyr is copper and matches his coloring. Axel's is reddish silver that I'm thinking might be

made of nickel. Meanwhile, Aurum's is glittering gold and thin enough that I can see his veins pulsing through its unadorned simplicity. In contrast, Marlo's is a dark, unforgiving iron.

When my gaze latches onto Marlo's fettyr, he takes it as an invitation to lean on the bed and grab my foot; the only part of me not covered in several layers of fur.

I squeak and try to pull it out of his grasp, but he holds on tight, despite a filthy look from Vyran. What starts out as a gentle buzz on the sole of my foot soon gains in intensity as it works its way up my leg. Even after Marlo lets go of my foot, the buzz continues its journey before circling my sex twice and then going in for the kill.

I'm unable to stop the gasp of surprise at the strength of my response, something that has Vyran looking sideways at me and Marlo chuckling aloud.

"She's a keeper," says Marlo, his fettyr bouncing against the iron chain that secures the end around his waist. "Vyran, Praedytus made it clear, and you agreed, that we could all have a turn. Right now suits me."

"You what?" I splutter out before turning on Vyran.

"That was before," he says, his tone subdued.

"Before what?"

"Before I attained Nysa with you."

This statement has the five at the end of the bed gasping and booming out "No!" in turn.

"Is that right?" says Seolfer, his gaze cold and calculating as he stares at me.

At my questioning look, Vyran says, "I ejaculated."

"Damn it," says Ciprus, of the copper hue, "our father's directive means we're duty-bound to at least try."

"Now hang on just a second," I shouted into the hubbub of

assertions from the brothers that they should all get to have a go at me. "Don't I have some say in this?"

"They're right," says Vyran, his expression bleak. "Praedytus, the God of All Desire, insists balance is maintained. He requires that all his sons attain Nysa, though I don't understand why."

What follows is a flurry of fur and flying fists, but it does no good. Soon enough, I'm lying uncovered in the middle of the bed. Marlo's dark iron-colored hand holds one ankle while the other is held tight by Aurum's golden paw. While they spread me wide, they're gentle about it.

Axel then positions himself between my feet, and the gaze he rivets on the juncture of my thighs is raw enough that I tighten in response. When Vyran sees what's happening, he gives his all to get free of Ciprus and Aurum, who are holding him back. But they prevail.

"I want to go first!" says Aurum. "I'll ruin her for the rest of you."

There's a buzzing in the soles of both feet at the same time. I'm still roaring "No!" at the top of my lungs when one ball of energy attacks my clit while the other has my honeypot vibrating out of control.

My eyes snap open in time for me to see Axel lean forward and hold a hand over the top of each of my thighs. I'm too far gone to fight it and arch my sex, trying to get as near to him as I can. He needs no further enticement and slams his hands down inches from my mounting climax.

I'm getting close to shattering when a hand hits each knee as Seolfer and Ciprus get in on the act at the last minute. I'm shaking and my core is rippling, leaving me only just aware when Vyran drops on the bed beside me.

"It's not safe for you here." He placed his hand on my

forehead, and my brain was soon buzzing as hard as the rest of my body.

I know I'm back in my bedroom when the bedside lamp blinds me with its brightness. My girly bits are still whirring, and I'm on the brink of a mind-blowing orgasm. This sees me chewing on my blanket as the throbbing of my sex starts a pulsing pattern that has me rigid with anticipation.

The vibration in my knees works its way up the front of my legs, its slow pace filling me with both dread and hope in equal parts. The closer the quivering gets to the apex of my thighs, the harder I have to chew on my blanket.

While one ball of energy goes to join its brother deep inside me, the other drops between my legs. There it burrows its way up between my cheeks, and there's nothing I can do about it despite concerted clenching.

No sooner would one spasm died away than the next engulfed me. As each peak thrummed through my body, I'd hear one or another of the brothers' voices inside my head. They were as clear as if they were on the bed next to me. Each whispering promises of what they'll do to me when it's their turn for real, with this only stoking my lust.

By the time they've finished with me, I've been energy screwed by all of them, and come five times in a row. Once for each brother. Now limp and compliant, my entire world is centered between my legs.

On succumbing to sleep, I know I'm forever changed. Whether this is for better or worse, only time will tell.

EPILOGUE

Three weeks later...

I'd slept sixteen hours straight after that multiple orgasm, and on waking, my energy levels had still been shot. This had seen me waiting until I was strong enough to get out of bed.

Time spent realizing I didn't understand what Vyran had meant when he'd said something felt wrong about that Praedytus guy's insistence on maintaining the balance of their realm.

Even now, if I shut my eyes, I can still see the worry on his face when he'd said, "He's never cared about such things before."

For now, the dreams have stopped, nor have I had any late-night visits from Vyran, waking to find my body humming from phantom touches. I should be relieved, but instead I feel hollow, like I'm missing a vital part of myself.

I'm walking from the fish processing plant to my truck when I catch my reflection in the side window. My hair looks

different in the late afternoon light. More ash than blonde. I pause, running my fingers through it, and that's when I notice my silver bangles catching the light in a way I've not noticed before.

They feel warm against my skin, something that's at odds with the late afternoon temperature.

"Damn it," I whisper, because I know what this means. The balance Vyran talked about. It's not just about him anymore. His brothers are waiting their turn, and from what I remember of that night in his cave, they're not as patient as he is.

When I reach for the front door at home, there's no missing my bangles pulsing against my wrists like a heartbeat. Or a warning.

Inside, my family chats over dinner, unaware that their daughter has been marked by the gods. This has me smiling and nodding at the right moments, but my mind is elsewhere. I'm remembering silver eyes and the promises Seolfer had made when I saw him last.

As thoughts of those pulsing silver domes that covered his fettyr filled my mind, I had to excuse myself. I wouldn't be able to swallow if I tried, preferring to be alone when worrying about how sex with the God of Silver would be.

Would I fight him, or would I succumb?

Would I even be given a choice?

GOD of SILVER

1

Have I gotten over my infatuation with Vyran, my God of the Woods? Nope! It's been close to six weeks since I last saw him. It should have faded by now, shouldn't it?

But I'm like an addict when it comes to him. Despite no longer having dreams about him screwing my brains out, this doesn't stop me from staying awake and thinking back on that wicked tongue of his. It's the same tonight, with me once again staring at the ceiling, dreaming of what could have been.

Unfortunately, I've also spent a good amount of time worrying about his siblings and the whole balance issue that Vyran had hinted at. I'd been busy dealing with a mind-blowing orgasm at the time, and he'd zapped me home before I could ask him about it.

It's his brothers who are no doubt responsible for his not having visited me since. He'd had his turn, and now it was theirs. In particular, Seolfer, whose presence I'd felt last month when my bangles pulsed, although nothing since then.

Even thinking about all five of Vyran's brothers in their almost-naked glory as they stood at the end of his bed has my sex twitching like a rabbit.

In hindsight, they would have been less alluring if they'd been naked. But thinking back on those industrial-strength condoms, or fettyrs as they called them, has my imagination in overdrive.

Each brother's fettyr had been made of a different material and each with a unique pattern, doubtless for the sole purpose of exacting pleasure. That is, apart from Aurum, God of Gold, whose fettyr seemed to be all about looks.

I found the whole thing about them stimulating me until I climaxed over and over to be a little odd. Don't get me wrong, I wasn't complaining. But other than the occasional guy who pretends to care that you get satisfaction, it's all for show until they've shot their wad.

With Vyran, he'd seemed to get a real kick out of me coming so hard I couldn't see. Likewise, his brothers, with those pulses of energy they'd slammed into me. I was having trouble seeing what was in it for them.

Lying in bed trying to sleep, I do my best to rid myself of memories of the demonstration Seolfer had given me. What his silver fettyr, with its round-headed domes, wasn't capable of, didn't rate a mention. His ability to control them by thought alone was erotic beyond belief. I guess this made him the Nyphrazi God of Silver.

Unlike Vyran, with his leather fettyr and natural coloring, Seolfer appeared hard and unforgiving. Maybe it was because of his silver hair and eyes and that shimmering skin of his.

Shutting my eyes doesn't help. This has me replaying the psychic promises they'd all whispered to me after Vyran had

transported me back home from the Caves of Nyphrazi. But he'd been too late.

Far too late.

You try having five orgasms in a row when your folks are a couple of doors away. I came close to eating my pillow to stop crying out as those balls of energy pulsed away. I might well be old enough to look after myself, but to my parents, I was still their little girl, and little girls didn't have multiple orgasms.

"You look like crap," says my younger brother when I stumble into breakfast the following morning.

"Thanks!" I spear him with a withering glance that does nothing to soften the glee he's experiencing at my ill health.

"Still suffering from insomnia?" says my mom, her face a picture of concern.

"Yeah. Thank goodness I'm finished at the plant." I sip at the mug of steaming hot coffee she's put down in front of me. Yuck, decaf. I know she's doing it for my own good with the sleeping problem and all, but it tastes like crap. Crap that doesn't even give me a buzz.

Ah, the plant, my own personal hell for the preceding three months. Twelve-to sixteen-hour days spent gutting fish. It's been a couple of days since I finished my contract, and despite scrubbing myself every day, I'm still aware of a faint fishy odor. Thankfully, I'm not planning on dating in the near future.

"What will you do now?" says my dad.

"I'm not sure. I need something if I want to nail those credit cards."

"There's a job going at the gold mine," says my brother.

"Doing what?" I ask, doubting it will be anything I'm trained for.

"Working in the cafeteria."

"Really?" Now this I could do.

"You should get in soon, though. I only heard about it late yesterday."

Knowing how quickly jobs got snapped up, I hurried through breakfast before dressing as I thought someone interviewing for a job in a cafeteria would. This has me on the road, not far behind my brother. The site office is easy enough to find, although the mine boss is a little surprised by my appearance, given that the job hadn't even been advertised.

"Do you have experience scrubbing pots?"

At first, I think he's teasing me, but soon see he's serious. Lucky I hadn't given him a smart-ass reply as I'd been tempted to.

"Ah, yes. Over twenty years," I say, hoping I've kept the incredulity out of my response.

He nods before rocking back in his chair and looking at me through slit-eyes as though to check for homicidal tendencies.

His chair slammed back down. "There's a drug test!" He throws this at me like a gauntlet.

"No problem." Hell, I haven't even had caffeine in a couple of weeks.

"The hours are long."

"I'm used to that."

"Dang, I thought I could smell fish." He chuckles away at my expense. "Okay, if Glory likes you, you're hired. Save me a heap of trouble, that's for damned sure."

"When do I start?"

He looks at his watch and then at me. "You're late already. Every five minutes, we dock fifteen."

I'm running by the time I reach the cafeteria. There I report

to Glory, a woman who looks to have been boiling the hell out of anything green for nigh on forty years. She's hard-boiled herself, but I like her and thank my lucky stars that the feeling is mutual.

I'm washing my first dishes within minutes of her giving me the job and after a week working at the mine, I no longer smell of fish. Now I'm an enticing mix of dishwashing liquid and over-boiled greens.

I settle into the new routine, and while the hours are long; the work is light compared to the fish processing plant. Sure, we're run ragged at break times, but we get to rest up a little in-between. And I'm working with an experienced crew, some of them having been there almost as long as Glory. When she tells me she thinks I'll be there for a long time, too, I don't know whether to be flattered or depressed.

Just think of the money becoming a constant refrain.

One thing I do have trouble with at work is all the guys hitting on me. As far as the cafeteria crew goes, I'm the youngest by around twenty-five years and so it's not like I've got a lot of competition. I wouldn't mind if they seemed to be interested in me, but it feels more like a Pavlovian response to anyone under fifty.

It has now been a couple of months since I saw Vyran, and he hasn't tried to contact me. Not once. Despite this, I'm having difficulty looking at another guy without comparing them to him. He's a hard act to follow.

If I take errant thoughts about his brothers into account, the highest ranking of the guys at the mine, in the men-I'd-like-to-fuck stakes, is position number seven. Only Gary, Alan,

and Ross make the grade, and I'm keeping them at arm's length. With difficulty.

In the end, my horniness and Gary's leaving to work in the lower forty-eight resulted in the perfect night for a date. This way I can screw his brains out, and then it's goodbye, baby. Even better is that I don't have to work the following day either.

2

Gary is the perfect gentleman in front of my folks when he picks me up for our date. This doesn't last. No sooner are we in the cab of his truck than he turns to me. Without preamble, he says, "We can go to dinner and then I can fuck you sideways, or we can forget about dinner."

His cheeky grin is the only thing that stops me from slugging him. But who do I think I'm kidding? This is what I want him for.

"I've already eaten." My grin matches his.

A slight lift of one of my eyebrows is all it takes for him to floor it, with him distributing a fair amount of gravel in his haste. In looking over my shoulder at the rooster tail of dust behind us, I knew I'd get grief about it from my dad in the morning.

Gary's been staying with his folks too, but he has the advantage of staying in a guest cabin a short distance from the main house. This also means there's no indoor plumbing, and

so I know I'll have to use an outhouse at some stage during the evening. We haven't had one of those at our place in forever.

Again, Gary plays the part of the gentleman until we're inside. Then he's peeling my clothes off me before I've dropped my purse. I take a moment to relax into what will be a fast fuck, but once I do, I make quick work of his clothes, too. Less than five minutes after entering the cabin, and we're both standing naked.

He devours me with his eyes while I'm examining him with less enthusiasm. I find him wanting after Vyran and his brothers. Damn, I knew this would happen. He's big enough, all right, but rather white bread when compared to the exotic gods of Nyphrazi.

Oh well, it's this or my hand, and his taking a small step forward is all the encouragement I need. In seconds, I've slapped a condom on him because, even though I'm on the pill, it's safety first with me.

As luck would have it, I'd done a bulk buy of condoms not long before my life in Seattle disintegrated. There was no way I'd buy them up here. Everyone in town would know before I'd opened the first packet.

"Bed or counter?" he says, before his eyes skitter between both.

However, there's no mistaking his gaze dwelling on the counter just that little longer. I could ruin his night and say the bed, but to hell with it, the counter height looks as though it'll make things interesting. My response is obvious when I, too, look at the counter before smiling.

With a whoop of joy, he grabbed me around the waist and swung me up.

"Arrrrgh! It's freezing." This is no understatement. It's as though my ass has just been plonked down on a slab of ice.

"Half the fun, baby," he says, while sliding me forward so my cheeks are damned near being cut in half by the edge of the counter.

He wastes no time in foreplay. Instead, he buries himself, although nowhere near as deep as Vyran had. It's just as well I've been in a perpetual state of arousal since my visit to the caves; otherwise, the condom would have been in tatters after that maneuver. As would I. He pumps away, and to be honest, I'm numb to his presence, but then everything changes.

The first thing I notice is my silver bangles vibrating. Then it's as though they've got a life of their own. They tighten around my wrists, and an unknown force drags them and my hands high above my head.

Gary takes this as an invitation to suck hard on my nipples. One and then the other and then repeat until I'm arching in search of his questing mouth and moaning deep in the back of my throat.

By now, the bracelets have attached themselves to cup hooks set on the underside of the shelf high above the counter. I'm stunned when I see the hooks crush closed, locking me in place.

That's when everything changes.

Gary goes rigid, his mouth still latched onto my breast but no longer moving. I can feel his breath coming in gasps and cooling my nipple as though he's fighting for air. When he lifts his head, his familiar hazel eyes are wide with confusion and something that looks like panic.

"Jas... what's..." His voice sounds strained, different somehow. He blinks as if he's trying to clear his vision. "Something's wrong. I feel..."

His words are then cut off, and his whole body convulses,

although not in a good way. No, this is something else altogether. Something that makes my blood run cold.

"Gary?" I try to reach for him, but my silver bracelets hold me fast. "Gary, what's happening? Are you okay?"

He yanks himself free of me before doubling over and clutching his head as if in pain. When he straightens, there's no missing the change taking place. It starts with his eyes, with the familiar hazel flickering like a dying flame before being overtaken by liquid silver. But it's not just the color. The shape changes too, becoming deeper-set and predatory.

"No, no, no," I whisper, yanking at my restraints. Because I know those eyes. I've seen them in my dreams, in my nightmares.

Gary's sandy brown hair shifts next, lightening strand by strand until it gleams like polished metal. Next, his cheekbones become more pronounced, jaw more defined. Even his skin takes on a subtle metallic sheen.

But the worst part is watching Gary fight it. I can see him struggling, his human consciousness flickering in and out like a bad TV signal. One moment his face is twisted in fear and confusion; the next it's cold and calculating.

"Gary, fight it!" I scream, but even as the words leave my mouth, I know it's too late.

He draws himself up to his full height, and when he looks at me again, there's nothing human left in his expression. The smirk that spreads across his lips is pure predator. Cruel and satisfied in a way that Gary could never be.

"Gary's stepped out," he says, and the voice is all wrong. Still Gary's vocal cords, but the cadence, the tone, the arrogant confidence—it's all Seolfer. "This was the only way I could reach your realm and fuck you until I achieve Nysa."

The man I'd arrived at the cabin with, the man I'd trusted

enough to get intimate with, is gone. In his place stands something wearing his face like a mask, and the realization hits me like a physical blow.

I'm trapped. Alone. And at the mercy of a god who's already proven he doesn't understand the word.

"Ready, acolyte?"

I yank at my restraints to free my hands from my mangled silver bracelets. "And if I'm not?"

"You soon will be."

I'm abusing him for all I'm worth when he nudges himself inside me. That the domes on his fettyr are rotating at some unspoken command only adds to the surreal horror of the moment. He grinds himself into me as far as he can, then stands still and lets all the little domes on his fettyr do the work for him.

Despite his body not moving an inch, it still feels like he's drilling himself into me as the domes pump in and out along the length of him. Meanwhile, he stands there and watches my reaction.

Rather than satisfy his apparent need to see me lose it, I think about doing mountains of dishes by hand, vacuuming and cleaning toilets. It works until he speeds up before folding the lips of my labia back with the fingers of one hand and licking the thumb of his other. I know where it's headed, but my scream of denial soon turns into something altogether different when he grinds his wet thumb into my clit.

He leaves my wrists hooked above me while he fucks me for what feels like hours. I climax so many times that I lose count, with each response more wanton than the previous. He, however, looks more and more frustrated as time goes by, with no sign of his being anywhere near achieving the dreamed-of Nysa.

He gives up on the bumps of his fettyr doing the work for him and slams himself into me again and again, desperate to come. Every thrust he smashes into me is more desperate than the last, his face contorted in passion and anger as he tries to reach his elusive goal.

I'm in the middle of going off again when my wrists are released with shocking speed. My arms drop to the counter on either side of me and a vicious case of pins and needles kicks in soon after.

But the physical pain is nothing compared to what's happening in my head. The moment Seolfer withdraws from Gary's body, reality crashes back over me like a tidal wave.

I can't breathe. Can't think. I can't process what just happened to me.

The most terrifying part isn't that Seolfer possessed Gary. It's that when those silver eyes looked down at me, when that arrogant smirk curved Gary's lips into something cruel and commanding, part of me responded. Part of me wanted it.

Even knowing it wasn't Gary. Even knowing I should be horrified.

Gary's hair shifts back to brown, his eyes clear to hazel, and it's just him again. Confused, disoriented, and unaware that his body had just been used to awaken something in me I didn't know existed.

He looks muddled and shakes his head as though to clear it, and the innocent bewilderment on his face makes everything so much worse. This is Gary, with his wicked sense of humor. He wouldn't hurt a fly unless it was really bugging him.

But his body... his body just gave me the most intense experience of my life. And it wasn't even him.

"Are you okay?" My question comes out as a croak. I don't know why I'm asking him. I don't know why I'm talking at all.

Never mind angry, I should be outraged. Instead, I'm fighting the urge to ask Seolfer to come back.

What the hell is wrong with me?

"I think so?" Gary doesn't seem too sure, rubbing his temples like he has a headache. "I feel like I lost some time there. Did I black out?"

I stare at him, and something inside me just... breaks. He has no memory of what Seolfer did using his body. No understanding that I had just experienced something that's rewritten every fantasy I've ever had.

How do you explain to someone that a god possessed them? How do you make them understand that while they were gone, something else was wearing their skin like a costume? And how do you admit you liked it more than you should have?

You don't. You can't.

Instead, I lie.

"You're fine," I whisper, even though I'm anything but fine. "We're both fine."

But as Gary moves to pull out of me, as he goes to remove the condom that isn't there anymore, I know that whatever Seolfer has done to me, whatever he's awakened in me, this is only the beginning.

Gary's eyes widen when he realizes the condom is missing. "Fuck, where...?"

He laid me back on the counter, pushed my thighs apart, and started searching for the missing rubber with his fingers. That I can't control my response to his touch only adds to my confusion. My body is still hypersensitive, still craving the intensity that only Seolfer seemed capable of providing.

"It's not here," he mutters, reaching for a flashlight. "Maybe it's just... deeper?"

He has me hold myself open while he shines the light inside me, and what he finds makes his voice tremble with terror.

"It's turning silver. Your... your pussy. It's like it's made of silver."

I lift my head to look at him, and the reflected metallic gleam on his face confirms what I already know deep down. When he reaches out to touch the silvery surface, it reacts in an instant—snapping at his finger like it's alive, pulsing with energy that sends shockwaves through my entire body.

Shockwaves that feel good in a freaky way.

Gary staggers back, his face white with horror, and drops the flashlight.

That's when the full scope of what Seolfer has done hits me. He's marked me. Claimed me. Left a part of himself inside me like a twisted promise.

And the worst part? My body is still humming with satisfaction, still responding to what was done to it. I hate myself for wanting more, for longing for the darkness he showed me, for being attracted to something I know I should fear.

For craving a monster.

I'm now glad Gary is leaving town at the break of dawn, with less chance of him blabbing to anyone. As it is, it's a battle to get him to drive me home, given he's looking at me like I'm some sort of alien life form. I'd only just shut the door of his truck when he roared away as though the hounds of hell were after him.

The only plus in all of this is that everyone at home seems to have turned in for the night. I would have had trouble facing

them now that I'm the proud owner of a silver-plated Delta of Venus. Fuck, that's something I never thought I'd say.

3

After sneaking in as quietly as I can, I brush my teeth and am soon lying in bed shivering as the reality of what's happened sinks in. When things move down below, I close my eyes, hoping to blot it out, even though I know it's futile. I also know it's not my imagination when something covers my clit.

Despite being worried about what I might encounter, there's no way I'm not shoving my hand down there to see what the hell is going on.

"Oh, for fuck's sake."

If I ever get my hands on Seolfer, I'll... I don't know what I'll do. Part of me wants to knee him in his silver balls, and part of me... No. I'm not going there.

As it is, not only am I the proud owner of a silver-plated cleft, but, yay, I've got a clit to match. Talk about your family jewels. I pick at the river of silver that runs from my clit before disappearing deep inside of me to see if I can peel it away.

Big mistake.

The whole thing vibrates, and it's not long before I'm doing the same. It's only when the first climax rolls over me that I hear Seolfer's voice inside my head.

"Any time you want me to bury myself deep inside of you, just tap it."

I'm about to tell him to fuck off and take his silver with him, hoping he can hear me, when he says, "Or I can do it."

The laughter that follows does nothing for my peace of mind.

On waking the next morning, I stared at the ceiling for a good long time. After a deep breath, I let my hand stray south to confirm that what I thought had happened last night had. I'm not even close to my bits when the vibration starts.

My animosity toward Seolfer for saddling me with this doesn't survive when I have some of the best sex I've ever experienced.

On my own.

My biggest worry is that I'll spend every waking moment tapping the hell out of that lump of silver. And how do I go about washing myself?

I soon found out in the shower when the silver shucked to the side to give me access before melting its way back into place after. Clean and dressed, I walk down the hall to the kitchen, but when the vibrations start again, I'm rooted to the ground while I'm rooted in the hall.

What the hell does he think he's doing? I sure as hell didn't set it off that time. Feeling weak in the knees, I continue through to breakfast and a chorus of good mornings.

"Are you all right?" says my mom. "You look a little flushed."

"I'm fine."

"Maybe you're coming down with something?" says my dad.

While tempted to inform him I'm coming—but just not down—I keep my thoughts to myself and concentrate on my breakfast. I'm close to finishing when the vibrations start and stop several times in a row before settling down into a steady pulsing.

I can't get out of the house fast enough and have put several miles between myself and home before the pulsing stops. I think Seolfer's session is over, but then the silver that coats my sex goes ballistic.

I'm sitting there, hands gripping the steering wheel like it's a lifeline, when a truck pulls up next to me. It takes every bit of effort to turn my head to look at the occupant. It's old Harry from next door.

"You okay, girly?" he calls to me through his passenger window.

"Fine," I grit out.

"Are you sure?" he says, not looking convinced.

"Yes!" I say with a lot more force than is appropriate for such a response, but it suits the orgasm roaring through my body. "Yes!"

When I open my eyes, he's driven off. It's a couple of minutes later before I can do the same.

The first snow of winter has fallen, and still Seolfer has possession of my body. I'm not sure if it's a coincidence or not, but the blasted silver seems to go off at the most inappropriate times. I'm now a master at masking rip-roaring orgasms,

telling anyone who asks about my breathing that I'm an asthmatic.

But then my body becomes so used to them I keep my head, even at their peak, and they don't affect me as much. Unfortunately, Seolfer's voice inside my head is as strong as ever. Maybe even stronger.

And that's the problem. It's not just his voice that I'm hearing anymore. It's the memory of how he felt, how he moved, the way those silver eyes had burned into mine with such intensity. I replay moments from the night he possessed Gary, remembering the weight of his presence, the commanding way he'd taken control.

And this only makes me hate him more. It also makes me despise myself.

I hate that sometimes, when the fascinum pulses to life, I don't bother resisting. Sometimes I close my eyes and pretend it's him touching me instead of some supernatural piece of metal. Sometimes I imagine what it would be like if he came to me, without possessing someone else, without tricks or deception.

Just him. Just me. Just the overwhelming darkness that calls to something deep inside me.

But then reality crashes back, and I remember that this isn't a choice. He's controlling me, manipulating my body, invading my thoughts whenever he pleases. And no matter how much my treacherous body craves what he can give me, I can't let him win.

"Are you sure you won't come?" says my mom, standing next to the mudroom door.

"You always have a good time at the Fergusson's parties," says my dad.

"Come on, you guys. If she wants to stay home, let her," says my brother, before herding my parents through the door and shutting it with a resounding bang.

After hearing Dad's truck crunching down the driveway, I give it half an hour to make sure they're well and gone, and then I strip off and get into bed.

There's no need for soft music and candlelight to get me in the mood. Rather, I tap Seolfer's silver clit cover half a dozen times to get things moving.

And boy, do they ever.

The orgasm is more like a fit. It's so strong I faint.

I come around to discover my body is purring and that I can still hear Seolfer's voice inside my head. I hear him only when I'm at the height of the climax. That's when he hits me with how hard he'll fuck me next time. He seems to think if I climax hard enough, I'll get that buzzing in the brain and bam —I'll be at his mercy in his cave.

Well, to hell with that. Never let it be said that I let others rule my life. It's with this in mind that I tap the clit cover again, twice for good measure.

His voice sounds strained. "What are you doing?" he gritted out. "You only need to tap it once."

Now, this is an interesting development. "Why?"

"Because the fascinum I've gifted you with has been used to execute people."

"Gifted? What? Hang on—execute?"

This snippet makes me wonder about my plan for revenge. Then I think about how my life will be if I continue to let him rule me like this.

I'd gotten my idea for payback from a book, although the

scene in the story is different from how I plan on playing it out in real life. It's a simple concept: if he wants to play games with my pleasure, I'll play games right back. I'll give him what he doesn't want to hear.

The plan is risky, maybe even dangerous. But I need to know if I have any power in this twisted relationship, or if I'm at his mercy.

Of course, it'll only work if Seolfer can hear me as clearly as I can hear him. Even as I steel myself for what I'm about to do, part of me whispers that I'm taking an enormous gamble.

And why? Because I'm not sure I want him to stop. And that terrifies me more than anything else he could do to me.

I don't allow myself to think about the ramifications any further.

A quick double-tap to the fascinum and I relax into the sensations that are soon flooding my body. It's only when it's as though I'm floating above the bed that I think I should have waited longer between that last session and this one. And maybe tapped it just the once, as he'd suggested.

Every nerve in my body is vibrating, with even the hair on my scalp standing on end. Then, as though on an unspoken command—although I know who's behind it—the buzzing in my extremities heads for my core. My clit is soon overpowered, throbbing as the energy engulfs it

The explosion is such that the rest of my body jerks in response. But I keep my wits about me enough to go in for the kill.

"Oh, Vyran! Yes! Yes! Yes! Vyran, you're the best lover I've ever had!"

I hope I haven't gone too overboard, aware that even to me I sounded like a B-grade porno. But I figure it'll be damned

hard for Seolfer to achieve Nysa if I'm screaming out his brother's name.

When I hear the God of Silver roaring inside my head, I know two things: he can hear me when I orgasm, and he isn't a happy camper.

"Every time you take over my body, I'll scream Vyran's name. I don't care where I am!"

In response to my threat, he hit me with everything he had. "You will shriek my name! You will!"

But still, I scream Vyran's name. When my voice gives out, I continue screaming it inside my head, all the while conscious that the bastard's trying to do me serious damage.

"Vyran! Come for me! Come to me!"

I think Vyran is as surprised as I am when he flickers to life beside me in the bed.

I croak out, "Help me," before surrendering to the orgasm that's rolling through me without pause.

4

Feeling fur under my body, I know I'm no longer in Alaska. I can hear labored breathing from someone nearby.

"Vyran?" I don't bother opening my eyes when I speak. I don't think I could.

"Remove the fascinum!" barks Vyran, his voice vibrating with anger.

When Vyran's request is backed up by others, I force my eyes open so I can see what's going on. Axel and Marlo are holding Seolfer while Ciprus attacks the chain that holds the God of Silver's fettyr around his waist. As freaked out as I am, I wonder at the bolt cutters Ciprus is wielding, with these out of place in the natural setting of Vyran's sleeping chamber.

"No!" roars Seolfer, struggling to free himself.

His struggle falters when Marlo slaps his hand on the top of Seolfer's head. A second later, the God of Silver's eyes glaze over, and the fight goes out of him.

"I don't know that you should have done that, Marlo," says

Aurum, from beside the head of the bed where I hadn't even seen him.

"He deserved it. He's ruined her for the rest of us!" says the God of Iron, scowling.

"What? What does he mean?" I stare at Vyran, pleading for an explanation.

He doesn't look like he wants to answer me, but I don't let up in my silent plea, and he relents. "The fascinum can kill off your nerve endings. Forever."

He doesn't need to explain further. "You bastard!" I scream at Seolfer, despite the rawness of my throat. However, he's out for the count thanks to Marlo having fried his brain. The guy's more like a zombie than a god.

During this exchange, Ciprus has continued sawing away at the silver chain around Seolfer's waist. The minute the sound of metal against metal ceases, Ciprus announces Seolfer is ready.

I'm unable to stop the dread that creeps into my next question. "Ready for what?"

"It's the only way," says Vyran, before nodding to Marlo and Axel in some unspoken command.

They drag Seolfer over and dump him on the furs next to me, and I scramble off the edge of the bed. I tell myself I want to put as much room as I can between myself and the monster who's made the last couple of months an orgasmic hell for me.

But seeing him like this—unconscious, helpless, with that perfect silver hair disheveled—does something unexpected to my chest. Something that feels a lot like concern.

I shouldn't care that they're manhandling him. I shouldn't feel this twist of... what? Sympathy? Protection? Whatever it is, I hate myself for it. My legs hold me up, but only just.

"I'm not going near him," I say, dragging a fur off the bed

when I realize I'm still naked. But even as the words leave my mouth, I know I'm lying. It's not fear that's making me resist. It's the treacherous part of me that wants to get closer to him, that remembers how it felt when those silver eyes burned into mine with such intensity.

What if touching him again awakens something I can't control? What if I don't want to be free of what he's done to me?

"You have to. It's the only way to remove the fascinum," says Vyran, pulling me into his arms. His touch is gentle, comforting, but it's not what my body is craving. And that terrifies me more than anything Seolfer could do.

"He's right," says Ciprus, coming up behind me and resting his hands on my hips.

"I'll make it easier for you," says Marlo, who's walked over to join the three of us.

Before I can fathom what he means, his hand rests on the top of my head and bang—it's like I've just downed half a dozen vodka shots.

I know what's going on, but I don't give a damn when the fur I've been using to cover myself drops from my nerveless fingers.

Ciprus runs his hands all over my ass, squeezing my cheeks before sliding a hand down to rest between them. I'm unable to stop myself from moving my feet apart to give him better access. But he can't plunge his fingers into me while I'm being guarded by the God of Silver's fascinum.

No sooner had Vyran dropped his head and sucked one of my nipples into his hot, hot mouth than Ciprus tapped the fascinum. It flares with a short-lived burst of energy that makes my legs buckle. I'm only half aware of the two of them carrying me over to where Seolfer lies on the bed.

I'm now so out of it and aroused that I don't think twice about straddling the God of Silver and sinking down on his fettyr. The moment our bodies connect, even through the metal of his fettyr, something electric shoots through me that has nothing to do with Marlo's influence. My body recognizes him, responding to him in ways that feel both familiar and dangerous.

I then still, expecting him to do the rest as he had when he'd possessed Gary, but because he's been zonked by Marlo, he did nothing. Part of me is relieved. Another part, the part I don't want to acknowledge, is disappointed.

"You need to move," whispers Vyran in my ear.

Weird, I didn't even feel him crawling onto the bed next to me.

"Up you go," says Axel, putting his hands under my ass and lifting me before letting me settle again.

When it becomes obvious that I'm past the point of moving, he continues to help me slide up and down on Seolfer's rigid length. Any sensation now is because of my movement, with the domes on the silver fettyr frozen and the rippling of the fascinum having faded away to nothing.

"That bastard, the poor girl. She's as good as dead to us," spits out Ciprus.

"Rouse him," growls Vyran to Marlo.

Once again, Marlo rests his big iron-colored hand on Seolfer's head, but this time, instead of his eyes glazing over, clarity returns to the God of Silver's gaze. The moment awareness floods back into those molten silver depths, my breath catches.

I can tell when he grasps that he's buried deep inside of me because the domes move in that now familiar pattern, but

more than that, his eyes lock onto mine with an intensity that makes my heart race.

For a split second, it's just us. Not the brothers surrounding us, not the ritual, not the fascinum that needs to be removed. Just him and me and this connection that I can't deny, no matter how much I want to.

The silver in his gaze seems to burn straight through me, and I have to fight the urge to lean down and...

No. I won't give him the satisfaction.

I think all the brothers are as disappointed as I am when, although I continue to get more and more aroused, I don't climax.

"Do I have to?" I say, shuddering weakly in response to the latest internal massage.

"Yes!" Vyran's response is unforgiving as he leans close to whisper in my ear, injecting urgency into this one word.

I'm aware of the fascinum having dropped away from my clit when the coolness of the air puffs over it each time I plunge down onto Seolfer's cock. "Has it moved enough?"

"You need to find release before it can be removed," says Vyran.

"So close," I gasp out as my climax builds higher and higher, refusing to break.

What follows is a grab-fest as first one nipple is rolled between eager fingers, then the other, then both together. My eyes drift open in a sensual haze as I look at the brothers crowded around me. While I'm way beyond counting, I can see that Ciprus with his copper locks is missing. That's when someone behind me slides their hand between my cheeks and spreads me wide.

"Are you ready?" says Marlo, the only one not connected to my body in some way.

I'm unable to articulate either a question or an answer, but he takes my silence as consent and reaches out with both hands. One he places on Seolfer's head, the other on my uncovered pearl. What follows is a sexual overload.

This only increases when whoever is behind me pushes something sleek and hard into my back passage, adding to the sensations coming from Seolfer's cock. It's enough, with me crying my release, my head thrown back and every erogenous zone screaming as they shatter.

Upon waking, it doesn't take long for me to realize I'm in the wooden pool that Vyran had bathed me in when I first visited the Caves of the Nyphrazi. He rubs me all over using a soft leather cloth. While his movements are supposed to be relaxing, they're not.

Maybe that bastard Seolfer hasn't ruined me for sex after all. Thinking about him and his damned fascinum has me jerking one of my hands down to explore myself, to see if I am free of his silver.

"Thank God!" This response is both because I'm free of metal and also because my clit doesn't seem to have been ruined altogether.

But even as relief floods through me, there's something else. Something that feels akin to... loss? Losing his mark feels wrong somehow, like a piece of me is missing. I should celebrate my freedom, but instead I wonder what it would have been like if he'd come to me of his own volition, without tricks or possession or force.

I push the thought away. I'm free. That's what matters. Even if part of me feels empty without his silver claiming me.

. . .

"How do you feel?" says Vyran, rubbing the cloth in circles on my stomach, the motion hypnotic.

"Okay, I think. It's just that..."

"What?" His brow furrowed when he looked at me, as though trying to spot some change.

"It's as though there's still something inside me."

"That will pass. But it can take some time."

"No. Not there." I stumble to a stop, words failing me.

I can see comprehension spring to life. This is followed by his clicking and humming to the table in a language he seems to use for that sole purpose. As before, the wooden hands that make up the table in its solid form swirl around in the water next to me.

Then they crowd my lower half, with me soon ready for the woodland equivalent of a gynecological exam. No longer am I laying back relaxing. Rather, my legs are in the air and my bits are on display for the world to see.

It doesn't take long for Vyran to find the problem. I hear him muttering about Ciprus before he retrieves what looks like a solid copper butt plug.

"No wonder your release was so great," he says, dropping the plug into a bowl that rests on the edge of the pool.

With the problem sorted, I expect to be lowered back into the water, but Vyran has other ideas. After dipping his cloth into the water, he stroked it up and down my cleft, all the while clicking and humming.

Before long, some wooden hands peeled the lips of my labia back like a flower to give him greater access. I'm powerless to stop myself from curving toward the sopping wet chamois.

"All is not lost, my lovely."

5

I'm no longer restricted to the sleeping and bathing chambers after Vyran created another archway with the merest wave of his hand. I've explored as far as I dare, with the cave system being a labyrinth of similar-looking passages that has me worried about getting lost.

Looking out of the main entrance of the caving system, I take in the unfamiliar territory. It wouldn't take a lifetime subscription to National Geographic to know that I'm no longer in Alaska.

I hadn't realized just how different the landscape was when I'd first stumbled upon the Nyphrazi realm. I don't recognize any of the trees. The birdlife is different, and it's a lot warmer than my home state.

"How long will I have to stay?" I say to Vyran when he joins me.

He put his arm around my shoulders and pulled me close. "Only until you've healed."

"But I'm fine." And I am. After weeks of uninterrupted

sleep, good food, and fresh air, I'm myself again. I'm even aroused without stimulation. Something I thought would never happen.

"Until I can make you come by blowing on your clit, you're staying right where you are."

I pull away and punch him in the arm, hard. "That isn't fair! I wasn't that sensitive before Seolfer..." I trail off, not wanting to finish the thought. Because the truth is, part of me misses the intensity he brought to my body, even if his fascinum came close to destroying me. "Before he marked me with that damned thing."

That lump of silver was the last thing to be up there, too. Vyran had refused to touch me since washing me down after he and his brothers had rid me of it.

Vyran rubs his arm where I've punched him, but I know I don't have the strength to hurt him. His smile says more than words, that his show of pain is just that.

"Your lessons begin soon."

After dropping this bombshell, he turns and vanishes into the depths of the cave. I know he's heard the "What lessons?" that I yelled after him, when I hear him laugh in delight. It's full of promise and has my sex tightening in an encouraging manner.

"Rest well. You'll need it," soon echoes back along the tunnel he's disappeared down.

"Like that'll help!" I bellowed back at him.

My bedtime routine that evening is different, with Vyran still missing since dropping his news about lessons. On entering

the sleeping chamber that I share with him, it's not my God of the Woods waiting for me. His place has been taken by Ciprus and Marlo, who stand next to the bed.

"God, what now!" This must be part of the lessons Vyran was talking about.

When the two brothers understand what I'm thinking they're there for, they burst out laughing. So much so that there's even some knee-slapping and crying. All this does is ramp up my anger.

"Fine!" I stomp over to the bed, rip my chamois sheath dress off, toss it on the ground and then throw myself onto the bed. Flat on my back, I yell, "Ready!" as loud as I'm able.

Not that I assume the position. There'll be no closed eyes for me. Instead, I death-stare the pair of them, challenging them to have a go. The bastards call my bluff when they both climb onto the bed with me, one on either side. I thought if there were two of them, I'd somehow be safer. That had been the reason for Vyran's decree that no single brother, other than himself, could be with me at any time. It would appear that these two missed that particular memo.

Marlo holds his dark hand above my left breast, so close that I can feel the heat beating down from it. But rather than settle, he sweeps it up to my forehead and places it there with surprising gentleness. The buzzing has only just started when he whispers in my ear, "Sweet dreams, Princess."

Even so, I'm not under when both my nipples are tweaked to the boom of more male laughter.

I wake moments later, but the brothers are nowhere in sight.

I'm also no longer on the bed. I'm suspended in a body harness of some sort. That it's made of soft leather lets me

know Vyran is behind its construction. This gives me some small measure of comfort, although when I examine it, I can see it's been designed with one thing in mind.

"How the hell?" I was only out for seconds. They didn't have time to do this to me. I struggle against the straps that hold me in place, causing the harness to swing and creak. It also has parts of the apparatus grinding into my cleft, which only makes me writhe more.

"Oh, no you don't," says Vyran, coming to stand before me. He tugs on a couple of straps hanging from the ceiling, and my feet are pulled out to the side. This removes any leather from the mounting dampness between my thighs. My arms are also held out to the sides so that I'm sure I look like Leonardo's Vitruvian Man. Though I doubt Da Vinci had this in mind when he'd first sketched it.

Vyran moves closer, and I'm transfixed when he stretches up and that sharp tongue of his shoots out to its full length and flicks one of my nipples. This is easy enough, given they're poking through holes cut in the leather. After a slight swivel of his head, the other bud receives attention too. Lord, I hadn't realized just how long that tongue of his was. I'd squirm, but I can't in this position.

Vyran's lips part again and I'm expecting more of the same, but rather than licking my nipples into hard points, he clicks, whistles and hums. I can't help a squeak of surprise when the leather harness shoots me up in the air, with me now looking down on the top of his head. I keep forgetting how much power this godly lover of mine has.

"Oh, my."

From up here, there's no missing that his tongue is inching ever closer to my very core. I twitch to move myself toward him, but it's no good. I'm stuck fast where I am. No doubt

exactly as he's designed it. I'm whimpering before the glorious organ wraps itself around my clit and squeezes. Hard.

I moan, close my eyes and drop my head back so I can concentrate on the sensations swirling through me. But no sooner do I adopt this position than Vyran stops what he's doing.

"Don't stop," I gasped out.

I wait, but when nothing else happens, I open my eyes and peek down. He's not there.

"Vyran!" I can't believe he's left me like this. Hanging and horny as hell.

I've yelled for him half a dozen times before he returned. He's got Marlo with him. For once, the God of Iron doesn't appear threatening. Of more concern is his compassion.

My internal alarm systems go haywire at the expression he gives me as he walks to stand in front of me, his mouth level with my mons. "What's wrong?"

"You are, Princess," he says, looking up at me.

"What? I'm fine."

"No. You're not," says Vyran. This disturbing comment is followed up with some of his clicking and whistling.

This time, I'm not surprised when the leather harness lifts me. What surprises me is Marlo positioning himself between my legs so that when I'm lowered, my core is the target of his outstretched tongue.

It takes only the smallest glance to see that it's not as sharp as Vyran's and is instead wide and thick and gleaming with spit. I fight as much as the harness will let me, but Vyran walks behind me and puts a hand on either of my hips. He stills them, forcing my sex ever closer to Marlo's glistening tongue.

"Marlo is our healer. The enzymes in his spit will help you.

We all have them, but Marlo more than any of us. We need to do this." His tone tells me he's not happy about it.

"You cannot be serious?" I grit out, while still keening when Marlo drags his tongue through my slit.

"When I wrapped my tongue around you before and squeezed, it shouldn't have been pleasurable. But it was," says Vyran, as my shoulders are lowered into his outstretched arms.

Now I'm parallel to the ground. Vyran supports my head and shoulders, while my legs are slung wide over Marlo's shoulders. Meanwhile, his pulsing tongue slicked up and down my furrow without letup. The longer he licks, the more sensitive I become, until I'm whimpering for release.

This is achieved when he plunges the full length of his tongue in and out of me a dozen times or more, with the end exploring every inch of me.

As the shudder dies down, the harness takes my weight again.

"Thanks, Marlo," says Vyran to the healer who's already leaving the chamber.

"Right, let's get back to it," says Vyran, before once again wrapping his tongue around my clit.

"Owwww! That freaking hurt!"

"Good. Now we can proceed."

6

The joy of sex returns as Vyran trains my body to once again respond to his every whim. After each session, my desire mounts rather than diminishes, as it had when I'd been coated in silver courtesy of Seolfer. My nerve endings are once again singing their little hearts out.

After another enticing lesson, Vyran and I lie replete on his bed of furs, toying with each other's bodies.

"Not that I want to see him, but... where is Seolfer?" The lie comes without thought, but the truth is I want to see him, and that bothers me more than his absence.

"Banished! Axel, Marlo, and I sent him to live with Gaiya in the Fields of Obadyn." Vyran's tone is unforgiving.

"For how long?" I ask, but I'm unable to stop a brief twinge of guilt. I'm uncomfortable at the thought that someone, no matter how odious, has been cast out of hearth and home on my account.

"Life!"

"Life? Isn't that a little extreme since there was no lasting damage?"

Vyran pulls away so he can look at me, his disbelief easy enough to recognize. "Axel, Marlo, and I were furious. Seolfer came close to sacrificing everything, and our father wouldn't act." As if realizing I'm still not convinced, he leans forward until our foreheads touch. "Jasmine, he could have killed you."

I'm unable to respond, although my mouth hangs open, ready to do so.

"If we hadn't removed the fascinum, the peaks would have increased in intensity and frequency until your heart gave out."

"But... how?"

"After a little, ah, persuasion from the three of us, Seolfer admitted that if he couldn't achieve Nysa with you, then no one would, especially not me."

"In that case, fuck him!" But even as I say it, something twists in my chest. The thought of him being banished forever, of never seeing those silver eyes again, leaves me feeling hollow.

"That's better," says Vyran, settling himself back next to me.

"So, what's the deal with the gift of power? Why was he so desperate for it?"

I know Vyran's heard my question by the change in his breathing, but I think he's ignoring me before he responds.

"We've all heard the stories, but none of us believed them."

I wave my free hand in the air to show he should continue.

"When I achieve Nysa with you, my body is flooded with energy. Far more than if I couple with a Nyphrazi. It's even more than when I achieve Nysa with a goddess. And rather than dwindle over time, it remains." He pauses for a moment, his brow a crisscross of worry. "Seolfer was furious when he found out. But there was something else. He claimed Praedytus

had promised him he would achieve Nysa with you and be powerful beyond his wildest dreams."

"Ah. No wonder he was so ticked when he possessed my date and still couldn't come!"

"He possessed your date?"

I look sideways at Vyran, and there's no need to be a behavioral scientist to work out he's furious. The only thing I can't decide is whether it's because Seolfer possessed Gary or the fact that I went on a date.

"If he'd achieved Nysa in your realm, he would have siphoned all your energy, and you would have died. In an instant."

"That mother-fucking asshole!" Though even as the words leave my mouth, I remember the intensity in his eyes when he looked at me through Gary's face, and part of me shivers with something that isn't anger.

Despite this, if I ever saw him again, I'd castrate the bastard, using a tin opener if I had to. Only after I calm down and run out of expletives to describe Seolfer do I relax against Vyran so I can mull things over.

"Hang on a second. If he's living with Gaiya, does that mean she's banished too?"

"Most certainly."

"Because she tricked me into going home?"

"That, and because she's his mother. When we banished Seolfer, I sent her with him as a punishment for interfering." Vyran's expression grew darker. "She had no right to spirit you away without my permission."

It takes only a glance to know he doesn't wish to discuss the matter any further. This is a pain because I'm nosy and want to know whereabouts they've been banished to.

Another place?

Another realm?
Another time?

The next evening, after I've finished my simple meal, Vyran strolls into the chamber I think of as my own private dining cave. Without a word, he grabs one of the tapers off the wall, takes my hand, and leads me out of the cave.

In the past, this sort of high-handed behavior would have had me digging my heels in, refusing to move without further explanation. These days I trust my God of the Woods to lead me where he will.

We pass through the cavern where the brothers congregate at the end of each day, with some good-natured ribbing sending us on our way.

Other than a couple of young serving girls, I've seen no one other than the brothers in the weeks I've been living there. They either live apart from the rest of their society because of their status, or the Nyphrazi people are the smallest tribe in history.

In which case, they must be in danger of dying out if there are only two young females available? Where are all the ordinary citizens—the farmers, builders, cooks? Every society needs worker bees. The grunts.

We walk hand in hand up a long tunnel I've not explored before, with its gentle curving slope telling me we're heading higher into the mountain. The tunnel opens out into an enormous cavern, the lattice of tree roots above showing us to be close to the surface. Vyran lets go of my hand and walks around the perimeter of the cavern, lighting tapers as he goes, until the cave is aglow with their flickering.

"Are you ready?" says Vyran, his eyes dark with passion.

"For what?" I think I've got an idea, but my squirming girly bits want to hear him say it out loud in that husky voice of his.

"The ceremony, to see if you're ready to return home."

This isn't what I was expecting him to say at all, and thoughts of going home stopped any squirming on my part with my core cooling.

"Leave?"

"There is no other way. Our worlds are so different. If your visits here are too long, you'll age in your own time. Faster than is natural."

"Why can't I just stay here, then?" I'm unable to keep the element of begging out of my voice and know I sound a little on the whiny side. Oh, how I've changed.

"Because, in the end, you'd die. And I don't think I could face that."

"You'll grow old too. We all do."

The sadness in Vyran's eyes is answer enough.

"Oh."

Rather than speak, he pulls me into a crushing embrace and holds me tight until he's ready to proceed. He's still squeezing me when I hear him clicking, whistling, and humming up into the cavern.

There's a quiet rustling that soon increases in volume. I look up when I see fine dust falling around us. The tree roots are no longer a tangled mess at the very top of the cave and instead have dropped to us. We're trapped in the center of the cave, in a living jail.

Stepping back a little, Vyran makes quick work of the thong that holds my chamois dress in place, with it dropping in a liquid puddle at my feet. My nipples don't need any encouragement from him and are soon hard little buds.

They tighten even more when he bends down and blows on

them. I tried to take a step to get myself closer to him, but he put his hands on my shoulders and stopped me.

"No, once the ceremony starts, we can't touch. You'd best get used to it."

"What?"

"Shhh, this is how it has to be." Vyran lifts my arms out to the side and then puts his knee between my legs and nudges them apart.

It's all I can do not to ride his thigh to my release.

While I'm doing the Da Vinci thing again, Vyran has a chat with the tree roots surrounding us. They sway from side to side, with tendrils slapping against my body. I'm unable to stop a squeak of surprise when, almost simultaneously, most of them wrap themselves around my limbs and lift me into the air. They then maneuver me to Vyran's liking, if his smile is anything to go by. Meanwhile, I'm thrilled when I see how close his mouth is to my jewel.

Some finer roots get in on the action, and I soon find my nipples lassoed and the lips of my sex spread to the sides. When a puff of warm air washes over my clit, I twitch my hips to come into contact with something more solid. Although the roots allow me to sway, my search is in vain. Even when I sway, I find the only things touching me are the roots and the warmth of Vyran's breath.

I collapse back into the roots' embrace and give in to the sensations. But when the huffing turns to puffing, my core opens to Vyran, with my body desperate to swallow him whole. I know it's not my imagination when I hear his breathing speed up, with each puff of his breath now like a soft tongue poking at me.

"When you come, I'll get the roots to lower you so I can drive into you." This is followed by the unmistakable sound of

him hacking through the leather thong that secures the end of his fettyr around his waist. "Again and again."

My moan is one of arousal and a wanton need for him to fuck me until I scream his name over and over.

But still, he doesn't touch me.

With his breath sweeping up and down over my clit, Vyran soon has my arousal centered on my sex, crowding my bud and bullying it into submission. True to his word, he has me coming without his having to touch me. I close my eyes against the dust falling on me, caused by my spasms yanking against the roots that are holding me up.

As promised, Vyran has the roots lower me in readiness for him to enter me. But rather than looking at the roof of the cave, I'm flipped in mid-air so that I'm now looking at its floor.

With my legs spread wide and my core tilted up, he nudges for entry. I soon felt the crisscrossed laces of his leather fettyr pummeling the nub just inside of me. In and out he plunges, taking his time, with every inch of him a delight.

He walks forward while still deep inside me, and I find myself angled up so I can once again see the stalagmites that dot the cave. That some of these look very similar to the organ that's filling me is a visual turn-on in its own right.

And because of the angle I'm hanging at, Vyran only has to push me forward for momentum to have me settling back on his length. We settle into a rhythm of push and pump until I'm again whimpering for release.

I don't have to wait long before waves of feeling are rippling through me. Still, Vyran keeps up the pattern, and rather than die away, the sensations in my body build even further. I'm ramping up for a third time when I hear Vyran clicking and humming to the tree roots.

They pull me clear of him, resulting in a cry of frustration

on my part. I'm threatening to attack them with a weed eater when they flip me over and lower me again.

After guiding me back onto his glorious, leather-clad length, he slips in and out of me, slow and steady, while rolling my nipples between his fingers. When these same dexterous digits drop to the juncture of our bodies, I'm soon shaking to the point the roots come close to dropping me. My screaming and his roar of release echo back at us from the walls of the cave until all is silent.

When I'm able, I look at Vyran to see if I can see any of this power he talks about. He seems unchanged until he opens his eyes. They're glowing. When my gaze drops, I know it's not my imagination that his already impressive cock has grown a little.

Vyran has to carry me back to our sleeping chamber, with my legs no longer able to support me. Even now, my body is still vibrating from the strength of the orgasm that had ripped through the pair of us.

He lays me on the bed, lies beside me and then pulls the furs over us until we're covered. I'm close to falling asleep when Vyran shatters my peace.

"You must return home soon," he says, rubbing a length of my hair between his fingers.

I take some pleasure in him not sounding happy about my leaving, but thoughts of doing so have me feeling down.

"Already?"

"Yes, if you don't leave soon, you risk not being able to return to your own time and place."

"If I stayed, what would happen?"

"You'd age. You'd die."

His response is blunt, perhaps on purpose, as though to stop the conversation dead.

Ignoring his unspoken request, I asked how long, expecting

him to respond with something like fifty years or the like. More if I'm lucky.

"A year," he says, his hand splayed across my back as if to protect me.

"A stinking year?"

"Yes, a year before you withered and died. Maybe less."

"Oh." I can't think of anything better to say. I'm having trouble grasping the enormity of his answer. I have no trouble with the tears that are soon trailing down my face. I hide these from Vyran by rolling on my side and snuggling my back against his firm chest.

Sleep doesn't come, and by morning, my eyes feel as though they're full of grit.

I allow Vyran to bathe me one last time to prepare for him sending me home. A gentle climax is still thrumming through me when I realize I'm back in my own bed. I lie there, listening for sounds of the household getting ready for the new day, but all is quiet. Too quiet.

After crawling out of bed, I pull the curtains back, expecting light to stream in, but it's still dark outside. A quick check of the clock on my bedside table shows me it's only five minutes after I'd left all those weeks ago.

This entire space/time continuum thing is doing my head in.

I get back into bed, but once again, sleep eludes me. I know I haven't seen the last of Vyran, but because we've been as good as glued at the hip for weeks, his absence is cruel.

"Come on, sleepyhead," says my mom the following morning as she crosses my room to pull the curtains back. "Time you were up."

I'm tempted to respond with "What for?" but I know the interrogation I'd receive as a result would be thorough.

"My goodness, what on earth have you done to your hair?" My mom stands beside my bed, looking down at me, her eyes wide with horror.

"My hair?" I grab a strand off the pillow so I can look at it. "Oh, I, ah, put some henna through it. For a change," I stumble out in reply.

"I hope it's not permanent."

"Hmmm, me too."

With my mom off to the kitchen to get breakfast underway, I stagger out of bed and look at my new hair color in the mirror on the wardrobe.

It's red.

No, not red. Copper.

And that can only mean one thing. Ciprus must be next in line!

When my gaze drops, my eyes are soon as wide as my mom's had been.

My nipples are encased in little copper pasties, until Ciprus decides otherwise, by the feel of things.

"Oh, for fuck's sake!" Copper pubes? That's my social life fucked right there.

EPILOGUE

Two months have passed since I woke up with copper hair and Ciprus's "gifts" adorning my body. Eight sessions with hair dye remover that have done nothing to extinguish my flame-red locks. Sixty days spent trying everything to remove the copper pasties from my nipples and failing.

I'd even attempted an at-home Brazilian wax, but my pubes just grew back overnight, more luxuriant than ever. Ciprus, it seems, is thorough in his marking.

However, other than these outward signs of his claiming me, the bastard has been quiet. Too quiet. No possessions, no voices in my head, no silver-style torment. Just everything copper marking me as belonging to him while he bides his time.

In the normal part of my life, I'm still working at the cafeteria at the mine and have even been promoted to cooking duties since Judy retired to Hawaii. Picturing that lily-white

and shriveled old girl lying on the beach, plastered in coconut oil, is still a head-shaking experience.

Glory, of course, continues to rule the place with a cast-iron oven mitt.

The major change at work is that with my new over-the-top copper locks, I'm being hit on less, with whole days passing without a single proposition. Pavlovian or otherwise.

But I can feel something building. There's a tension in the air, like the calm before a storm, because I know the God of Copper isn't done with me yet.

Just like Seolfer before him, he'll want his chance at achieving Nysa, if for no other reason than to maintain the balance of power.

GOD of COPPER

1

As I add yet more salt to the humongous pot of soup I've been tasked with preparing, I can't help wondering about Vyran.

I've seen no sign of my God of the Woods since he sent me home all those months back. No more erotic dreams, nothing. Just like before, it's as though there's a barrier between us.

Coming to stand next to me, Glory sniffs the steam rising from my cabbage soup.. "Mmmm, mmmm, mmmm, that smells good!" she says, with genuine enthusiasm.

I wish I could agree. The stench of boiled cabbage isn't one I'd call good. Tenacious is more apt with most of the clothes in my closet now reeking of the stuff. Yep, what's left of my pitiful dating life is being killed off, one pot of soup at a time.

Still, I'm enjoying the extra money that my promotion has resulted in, and my credit card balances are dropping, albeit not as fast as I'd like. Not that I'll stop there. If I can grit my teeth and hold out for another year, then I'll have a decent chunk of change in the bank and can look for work further

afield. Part of me still hopes I can get a job where I get to use my arts degree.

"Hey cutie," says a deep voice from somewhere behind me. I ignore it. My orange hair, sweat from stirring fifty gallons of cabbage soup, and the resultant stench, means whoever it is sure as hell isn't talking to me.

"Hey, Red!"

I can't believe I'm going on a proper date—copper hair, eau de cabbage, and all! As soon as I'd spotted Ben leaning over the counter that separated the kitchen from a dining room full of miners, I'd known we were a match made in heaven.

The guy's hair is redder than mine; if such a thing is even possible. Still, he's cute for a ginger, in a Prince Harry kinda way. It also helps that he's freckle-free.

On pulling into the parking lot of the nicest bar in town, I'm relieved to see the place isn't heaving like it would be on a Friday night. This is more than likely due to Christy Weaver's engagement party. It's as close to a society event as you're going to get in a town like this, and I'm still pissed I didn't receive an invitation.

It doesn't take long to spot Ben sitting in a booth near the back of the bar. Even with a hat pulled low over my ears, I'm sure I stand out just as much. These days I also favor darker colors, hoping to compensate for my hideous orange hair. Damn Ciprus.

Not long after I've slid into the booth opposite him, he leans over and strokes the side of my face. I have to admit to being a little love-struck by the tenderness he shows to me, although that's quashed when his hand veers upward. Soon

enough, he pulls my beanie off and sets it down on the bench seat next to him.

"How can you hide that gorgeous hair of yours?"

I open my mouth to reply, but realize there's no easy way to tell a redhead that you, personally, loathe the color. In the end, I shrug, and this seems answer enough for him.

The evening is pleasant and, as it progresses, Ben makes no secret of the fact that he'd like to take things further. While I'm tempted, I can also feel those cursed copper pasties nudging against the inside of my bra. This has me ignoring his less than subtle hints that we should go back to his place.

As it is, I've had to leave my jacket on to hide the twin peaks that are in danger of ruining my best sweater. Not something you want to explain on a first date.

Standing in the gloomy parking lot next to my truck, Ben pushed me back against the cab and, leaning in, gave me a toe-curling kiss. It's the first kiss I've had in ages, and it is bliss. On my disastrous date with Gary, he'd been more interested in sex than romance, while Vyran seems to prefer using his tongue on other parts of me. Just thinking of the superb head he's capable of has my girly bits squirming and seeking the nearest male.

Ben takes this as encouragement.

His hands skim up inside my quilted jacket and knowing where they're heading has me pushing on his chest to put some distance between us. I don't want him reaching his goal only to find my nipples aren't so much hard as industrial.

He holds his hands up in the air in surrender, but this doesn't stop him from moving back in for another kiss. While that dexterous tongue explores my tonsils, I rummage in my

bag for my keys, finding them at the very bottom of a side pocket.

"It's been fun," I get out while his lips are still plastered to mine.

He pulls back until he can look at me. "You're going?" I can hear the surprise and disappointment in his voice.

"Ah, yeah, I need to, ah, yeah. But it's been fun."

I have to feel sorry for the poor guy; he looks like someone's just chucked a bucket of cold water over him, which I have done as far as sex goes.

It's only when I'm out of town that I scream my frustration at not being able to take things further. Ben is a nice guy, and if it weren't for the accessories adorning my nipples, I'd have been all over him.

"Ciprus, you bastard, get these damn things off me!"

The only response is long, rumbling thunder. It's loud enough that I can't hear the noise of my truck crunching along the snow-covered road. A second later and the world was lit up, with everything around me visible in the bright white flare of lightning. Crap, I hate driving in weather like this. The quicker I'm home, the better.

It's a miracle I don't have an accident when lightning hits the road right in front of my truck. Instead, I stomp on my brakes, skidding to a stop and sideways to any oncoming traffic. I'm still humming with adrenaline when I realize the truck is surrounded by a soft, white glow. Even from inside the cab, I can smell ozone.

"Weird."

Headlights further down the hill, is enough to have me putting my truck into gear, and then inching off the side of the road and out of the way. I also need to get my heart rate under control before I tackle the zigzag that's between me and home.

Winding my window down, I wait in readiness to speak to the driver of the other vehicle. No Alaskan would drive past a stationary truck without checking that everything is okay.

I needn't have bothered when they steamed straight past me without slowing. When I realize it's my brother's truck, I'm confused. No way would he leave me sitting here. I hunt through my purse and find my mobile, itching to abuse him, but a quick check on my phone lets me know I'm in yet another dead zone. No, scratch that. The phone is lifeless. Maybe the lightning strike fried it altogether?

I'm about to pull back out onto the road when the whiteness encircling my truck condenses until it's inside the cab and smothering me. While the smell of ozone is overwhelming, so is the sensation that I've just been hooked up to a generator.

My truck's engine then stops without so much as a shudder, and I'm stunned by the eerie lull that follows. It's quiet enough that I can hear the cloud of white that coats my body humming away in pulses. Any sense that this is soothing is smashed when my copper-coated buds are tugged and teased.

It says a lot about my experiences with the Gods of Nyphrazi over the preceding months that this doesn't strike me as odd. Rather, I accept that some unseen force is having its way with my body.

The cloud swirls over me before dipping down between my legs, and I'm unable to stop myself from spreading them wide to give it better access. I'm not disappointed.

The pulsing purr on my clit is outstanding and has me scooting down in my seat as though to give the strange cloud better access. Not that access seems to be an issue if the way it

vibrates up into the very depths of me, both front and back, is anything to go by.

It's only when it builds inside me until it's hard and unforgiving, rather than soft and ethereal, that I freak out.

"Seolfer!"

So much for that asshole having been banished for good! I'm still having nightmares about that bastard brother of Vyran's... though sometimes they're not nightmares. Sometimes I wake up disappointed it was only a dream."

You always imagine death by orgasm would be a good way to go, but trust me, the novelty wears off after the first week. It had taken hard work on Vyran's part for me to get my sensitivity back after the experience.

Even though I know I can't outrun that silver asshole, I'll be damned if I'll sit here and take what he's handing out.

I'm relieved when the truck starts the first time, with me soon jamming it into gear and flooring it as though a hoard of demons is after me. That the white cloud stays with me in the cab is disconcerting as hell. As unsettling is when its inherent sensations also remain.

This has me stopping every half mile or so while I ride out another orgasm. They start out small, but by the time I pull my truck into the barn at home, they're rip-roaring and I'm struggling to swallow my cries of ecstasy.

Timing will be everything.

2

Slumped in my truck, the orgasm built, and only biting on the strap of my purse stopped me from screaming the roof of the barn down when it exploded. I'm still buzzing when I throw myself out of the cab and come close to collapsing.

When I slam the door, it's as though the connection between me and the white cloud has been broken. However, I can still feel a hard presence jammed deep inside me.

Even walking is tricky, and the only way I can do so without going off every half-dozen steps is by walking like someone out of a Western. Of course, this is okay while I'm out here, but as soon as I get inside the house, I'll look like an idiot. I keep the cowboy stance up until the moment I open the door from the mudroom and step into the house proper.

The relief at seeing both my parents engrossed in books is immense. My brother isn't in sight and so he's already gone to bed. Damn, I could have given him grief for ignoring me.

"Did you have a fun time?" says my mom, looking up at me.

"Yes, it was lovely, but I'm exhausted. Goodnight." I try to sound as nonchalant as I can and puff out a sigh of relief when I get away with it.

With the hallway door shut behind me, I'm John Wayne again, hoping to keep the sensations to a minimum. The sound of the shower shutting off is all the incentive I need to barrel down the hall to the safety of my room.

Even with legs wide apart, because of all the movement, I'm ramping up for another orgasm by the time I shut my bedroom door. Collapsing onto my bed, I let it tear through me, once again gagging myself with the strap of my purse.

Waking some time later, I become conscious that the white cloud is now in my room. Fuck it all. I thought I'd locked it in the truck. It doesn't take long to realize it's this that's woken me.

There isn't an erogenous zone in my body that isn't being hummed, with that hard presence pumping in and out of me without letup. I have to give it to Seolfer. He's come up with a different trick than last time. There's no missing when the presence leaves my body but for the tip, before plunging back in again.

Before the sensations get the better of me, I wait until it leaves my body, and then shove my hand between my legs.

"Ha! Gotcha, you cock." The irony isn't lost on me.

I yank the intrusion free of my body and hold it up to the light, expecting to see the sparkle of silver.

"Copper?"

Not only is the dildo copper, it's also beautiful in its own way. It's as though someone has stuffed half-a-dozen golf balls into a copper condom. All dips, curves, and dimples. No wonder the sensation had been so mind-boggling. I'm admiring the workmanship when I'm filled again. This time

when it moves, the sensation is something else. Not so slick and a little rougher.

"Fuck you, Ciprus," I hiss over the sounds of slurping and suction.

Tossing the first dildo on the bed, I make quick work of grabbing its replacement.

Again, it's beautiful, but the swirling ridges that spiral along its length look as though they're designed to screw the recipient.

"For fuck's sake!"

I dropped the copper screw and put my hand between my legs in readiness to grab my next probe. I don't have to wait long with it, only managing one thrust before I snag it.

One thrust is more than enough.

There's nothing pretty about this one. It's ugly, with enjoyment being the last thing in mind with its design. Sure, it's ribbed, but not for pleasure, being as it is devoid of any soft edges. It had been like a rasp when it pumped in and out of me just then. If it had been any faster, it would have ripped me to shreds.

On realizing the dildos will only become uglier and escalate in the pain department, I grab the first dildo and shove it back in as quickly as I can. The thrum of pleasure that shoots through me lets me know I've done the right thing.

I'm scaling the dizzy heights again when what I'm presuming is a copper butt plug comes to life inside me. It throbs in time to the domes that cover my nipples and the dildo that's juddering its way in and out of my cleft without let-up. I hold on to the orgasm as hard as I can, keeping it hovering on a knife's edge and not allowing it to crest. However, the overwhelming fusion of stimulation soon wins out, and I disintegrate.

. . .

In the morning, I'm relieved to find I'm free of the copper dildo and butt plug, although my nipples are still bulletproof. Knowing my mom's fondness for barging into my room first thing to open the curtains, I rummage around on my bed, searching for copper dildos. I can't find any.

Hopefully, it's the last I'll see of them, although I suspect I'm hoping in vain. No sooner had I confirmed my bed's a copper-free zone than Mom knocked on my door.

"Morning!" Her tone is breezy and full of energy. "Don't forget we're off to the Carter's today. You need to be up and dressed. The floatplane's booked for ten."

"What's the time now?" I asked without opening my eyes.

"It's eight-thirty."

It takes the merest of calculations to appreciate that if I want to have breakfast, I'll have to move it. Even so, I wait for her to leave before I throw the covers back. I doubt any explanation I could come up with would convince my mom that my breast accessories are a good idea. She'd given me hell for getting my ears pierced.

It's only when I swing my legs over the side of the bed and sit up that a twinge comes from amongst my pubes.

"What the hell?"

I peel myself back with dread, something that's well-founded when I see the small copper dome that covers my clit. I tug at it to see if it's removable, but all that does is shoot a series of spasms throughout my body.

Fuck, I thought the pasties were bad enough.

My shower, while brief, is one of the most stimulating I've ever had. By the time I've rinsed, I'm leaning against the wall with my knees locked to stop my legs from buckling under me.

The drive down to the bay is one of pure, rapturous agony for me. The only thing in my favor is that my brother isn't on this trip with us, meaning I'm in the back seat on my own. I'm having trouble hiding my reactions to every bump and hollow we encounter. The plane trip isn't a joy either. Well, it is, but hiding the mini-explosions that are rocketing through my body isn't easy.

By the time we're safe at the Carter's place, it's as if I've been wrung out. I'm thankful when everyone leaves me on the deck to have a snooze in the weak sun. It's as though I've just nodded off when my sleep is interrupted by a deep male voice.

"Well, who do we have here? I don't think I know any redheads."

Whoever he is, he's standing between me and the sun, forcing me to open my eyes to see who the obstacle is.

"Cole? I didn't realize you were back home."

"Sure am. You up for a ride?"

That's weird. Cole's never come onto me before. I'm still stuttering for a response when he continues.

"Dollar and Amber need a good run."

"Oh, right? Sounds like fun."

"Come on then, give me a hand with the saddles." He grabs my hands and drags me to my feet. It's only then that I think about what a dumb idea getting on a horse is. If I'm a shuddering mess after my dad's truck and the floatplane, what the hell will riding a horse do to me?

I soon found out.

Nothing.

Nada.

Not a damned thing. I don't know whether to be relieved or disappointed, although I err on the side of the former. Kind of hard to explain to a childhood friend why you're slumped

over the front of your saddle, moaning in ecstasy. I know I've dodged a bullet when we finish the ride with me still intact. It's as though I'm being manipulated by remote control, with Ciprus deciding when and how I'll come.

If I get my hands on him, I'll ... My evil thoughts stumble to a halt when I smell ozone and hear a distinctive humming. "Okay, okay, I'm sorry. I didn't mean it," I whisper inside my head, and sure enough, the buzzing dies down.

I waste no time going to my room when we get home. Having spent the duration of the plane trip and the drive in a constant and peaking state of arousal, I'm once again close to collapse.

3

The next morning I'm still half asleep when I notice Ciprus's presence.

First there's the smell of ozone, then my nipples tingle, then my sex. Before you can say copper dildo, I'm full to overflowing with dimples, dips, and curves. The copper beast then gives me the perfect early-morning fuck. Long and slow, in and out, until my body is drawing in the length to take it even further. Something I'm able to do when it increases in size.

I'm shaking with passion when the buzzing in my sex moves up my body, stimulating everything in its path. Then it fills my head and blinds me to my bedroom.

I know even before I've opened my eyes that I'm no longer in my room, or Alaska, for that matter. The sun beating down on my back is hot, while a warm breeze puffs over my naked body.

My eyelids flutter open, and I look down at a smiling

Ciprus. I'm straddling him, the narrow copper-clad plank he's lying on, allowing my legs to dangle down on either side.

"At last, it is my time," he says, his smile holding a hint of satisfaction and a weird sign of relief. "Events must happen as Praedytus decrees."

While his statement smacks of being a royal decree, there's nothing regal about my current position. I'm impaled on his erect length and, if anything, he's even bigger than the dildo he's been pleasuring me with for the last few days.

With a sharp jerk of his hips, he embeds his copper-clad cock even deeper.

It's not unpleasant.

It's anything but.

However, it leaves me vulnerable and open to being hurt. Not only are we a long way off the ground, but there's also a decent thunderstorm developing, and it's heading our way at what looks to be supersonic speed.

Rather than worrying, Ciprus scrubs his hands together before holding them near my breasts. A small arc of electricity jumps across the gap and zaps my nipple caps. Without wanting to sound corny, the sensation is electric.

With his hands discharged, he rubs them together again before holding them lower down my body. This time I welcome the sensation and am unable to stop myself from grinding into him and urging him on like I had Amber, the strawberry roan. The temptation to yell "Yeehaw!" at the top of my voice is strong and one I give in to. Hey, he set us up like this; let him deal with it.

I squawk in surprise when he sits up, rocking me backward. I put my hands behind me to steady myself, but all I encounter is thin air. I'm sure the only thing between me and the ground below is his hands supporting my ass. It's

something he shows when he lifts me almost clear of his length before letting me slide back down on it again.

This allows me a quick peek at his copper fettyr.

Holy hell, it's not the one he'd been wearing when I'd first met him. Rather, it's the same as the dildo he'd been screwing my brains out with only moments before. I suspect sex with Ciprus will be just as good as it had been without him, or even better.

The thunderstorm is now overhead, and I can't stop another squawk when a couple of bolts of lightning slam into the ground at the base of our copper plinth. The smell of ozone that I now equate with mind-blowing sex is building, and there's a swirling cloud of white building up on the ground. This soon coalesces into a tight, glowing band that encircles the plinth; a band that's rising.

"Should we be worried about that?" I gasp out between thrusts. I have good reason to be cagey about the white cloud.

The crazy bastard laughs before whispering, "Better hold on."

I don't need to be told twice and am soon gripping him so hard he's only able to achieve a small thrust and grind movement. But none of this matters when we're engulfed in white. Then, every nerve ending in my body is tingling and my hair drifts out in a copper halo of static. When I realize this will be the only effect, I loosen my death grip.

His shout of elation lets me know it's what he's been waiting for.

He lifts me again before once again plunging me back down until I engulf every copper inch of him. But it's not enough, and he once again jerks his cock and pushes down on my hips, driving himself in even further. He keeps this lift-and-pump action up until I'm screaming for release.

Each time he drives into me, small sparks of electricity arc between his copper fettyr and the copper dome that covers my clit. Each time he's sheathed, a surge of electricity zaps through the pair of us, with every bit of copper on my body arcing.

I'm a fucking hazard! In the literal sense.

He seems in control while I'm getting to a point where all my circuits are ready to blow. But the closer I get to exploding, the more annoyed he gets.

"It's... not... going... to... happen," he gritted out, in time with his deep thrusts. His face is a picture of frustration.

He placed his hand on my forehead, and I'm pissed on several counts.

A) He sent me packing before I've come.

B) I just scorched the sheets on my bed and

C) I'm glowing enough that you could use me as a night light.

I need to get rid of the charge, or I'll incinerate something. It's only by getting out of bed, putting on some rubber-soled shoes and giving myself a good hand-job that the glow dissipates. That prick.

On the bright side, I'm free of all my copper accessories.

"Hey, Red." Ben's tone is friendly.

This has me crossing my fingers that he hasn't been put off by my weird behavior on the Friday night just gone. Who knows, maybe it's a case of treat them mean and keep them keen. I damn well hope so.

I pause in my stirring of a toothless chili con carne. "Hey, yourself."

He beckons me over, but I know if I turn my back on the

beast I'm stirring, any remaining flavor will be burned to a crisp. "Can't stop." I nod toward the cauldron for clarification.

"What time does your shift end?"

"Four."

"I'll meet you at your truck."

True to his word, at the end of my shift, he's waiting for me at my truck.

"Holy hell, Ben. You look frozen. Jump in."

It's only when we're both sitting in the cab and I've got the engine running and the heater cranking that I'm self-conscious of sitting so close to him. This is especially true after I'd left him standing in the parking lot at the bar on Friday night.

But I needn't have worried, because rather than grill me about my weird behavior, he chatted to me about his day and asked about mine. His day sounds more exciting, that's for damned sure, but it doesn't take long for us to run out of small talk.

The yawning silence does stupid things to my mouth, and before I'm conscious of doing so, I've broached the subject we've both avoided up until this point.

"Ah, sorry I had to race off on Friday night, I ah ..."

Because I haven't thought it through, I'm now panicking because I don't have an excuse.

"I'm sure you had your reasons."

This response has me stopping mid-panic. I can't believe I've gotten away with it.

Then my stupid mouth takes over again.

"Maybe we should try it again?"

Rather than say yes, he raises his eyebrows in question and leaves the decision to me.

"Ah, well. I was, ah, thinking we could go for another drink."

Now that I'm the one asking, I'm nervous about what his answer will be.

"I've got a better idea. How about we head up to a cabin I know about on Saturday? Just for the day. Fire up the grill and enjoy the view."

"That sounds like fun. What do I need to bring?"

"Nothing, I'll sort it all out. I'll pick you up at eight on Saturday."

After Gary being reluctant to drive me home when he'd seen my silver cleft, I'm gun-shy about relying on guys for a ride home.

"Or I can meet you there?" I said before that he's out of the truck.

His response is a gentle shaking of his head. "It's all good. Just text me your address." After closing his door, he then mouthed "eight o'clock" at me through the passenger window.

4

Because of our shifts, I don't see Ben until he pulls into my driveway on Saturday morning, bang on time. I know when he arrives by his headlights flashing across the wall of my bedroom, with the sun not due to appear for another half hour at least.

Wasting no time, I grab my jacket and backpack and am almost running by the time I hit the living room. There, I yelled goodbye without slowing, leaving my parents sitting in stunned silence at the breakfast table. The last thing I want is them asking to meet Ben. I'm having enough trouble explaining away my own hair color without going into why I'm dating someone who's sporting a similar hue.

The drive up to the cabin was completed without much talking, music filling what could otherwise have been an awkward silence. The higher we climb, the colder it gets, with Ben tweaking the heating. I'm glad I've brought one of my thicker jackets, as the cabin will be icy until we get some sort of heat going.

. . .

"Oh, wow, this place is amazing."

The cabin is of the traditional log variety, with a pitched roof to stop snow from building up. The front of the place comprises glass, double or triple glazed, if we're lucky. A matching outhouse sits a reasonable distance away, letting me know the place has no indoor plumbing. God, I hope there's something set up inside too, because I figure my ass would stick to the seat with temperatures as low as they are now.

There's an open-ended shed to the right, and it is there that Ben steers, nosing into the space until the truck is out of the elements. After turning off the engine and pulling on the park brake, he gave me an old-fashioned key on a length of chain. "You head inside and I'll grab everything out of the truck."

"Are you sure I can't help?" I'm having difficulty playing the fragile flower role that seems to have been foisted on me. I'm used to pulling my weight.

"Nah, I'm good."

Short of standing there fighting over the gear, I give in and trudge to the cabin. Unlocking the door, I'm expecting the inside to be musty and cold, but I needn't have worried. The place smells dry and, while not super-hot, it isn't freezing either. Even so, the embers inside the wood burner are as good as dead.

Yet when I put my hand on the beast, I can still feel some residual heat. I'm standing close to this behemoth when Ben staggers inside, loaded down with an assortment of bags. At my questioning glance at the lump of iron, Ben confirmed he'd been out at the cabin the day before getting everything ready.

Now I'm nervous. No one's ever gone to this sort of trouble before.

After lunch, cooked on the propane stove due to the weather having turned so foul, we settled back on the big couch, wine in hand. We're supposed to be taking in the view, but the snow swirling outside is making this close to impossible. And to be honest, the guy sitting next to me is far more attractive. My gaze therefore travels in his direction rather than to the large windows in front of us.

"It's cooling off," says Ben, before putting his glass down on the coffee table and getting to his feet. "Be back in a second."

I get that he's going outside when he pulls on his jacket, gloves, and a beanie. This is soon backed up by the blast of freezing cold air that slams its way into the room when he opens the door. It's getting nasty out there. At this rate, we could be stranded, and I'm not sure if that prospect sits well with me.

I'm lost in my thoughts about what this could mean when there's a thump at the door. I dive to my feet, race across and open it, allowing Ben to stagger in under the weight of a ton of logs. Given how many there are, I suspect he's thinking we'll be stranded for a while, too.

I put my full weight against the door to close it. But when it rattles hard enough that it might break the lock, I snap the bolts into place, top and bottom. That done, I close the heavy-duty drape that's designed to help block any of the more persistent drafts.

While I've been dealing with the door, Ben has chucked more logs on the fire and set the vents, so the thing is going like a blast furnace. He then grabs the matches from the shelf above the fire and sets about lighting the candles that are dotted around the room. It's not that dark in the cabin, and so I'm wondering why he's doing this until he closes the drapes.

At my questioning look, he says, "It's going to get a lot colder, and this'll help keep it out."

"I already figured we're stuck here for a while."

"At least a couple of days, I'd have thought."

"Days!"

This is so weird. I'd checked the forecast before we set out, and there was nothing to show we'd encounter this type of weather. Having grown up in Alaska, checking the weather before leaving home was second nature to me.

"Yeah, so we'll need to conserve heat." That his eyes are already darkening with passion and his smile is seductive has my body temperature ramping up in no time.

"What do you suggest?"

"We could stay here, or we could head up into the loft. That's where all the heat will be."

I know what else will be up there, because pretty much everything else in the cabin is visible except for a bed.

"Ah, before we do that, I need to use the bathroom."

Now, I'm hoping there's something set up inside because if I were to use the outhouse now, it'd take a spatula to get my ass off the damned seat. I let out a sigh of relief when he pointed me to a door off the kitchen at the back of the cabin.

My relief only gets greater when I see that the small bathroom not only has a composting toilet, but a shower and a tiny basin. With running water! It's something I'll ask him about in the morning, because I'm sure as hell not going to ruin the mood with a discussion on sanitary ware now.

Back in the main part of the cabin, I do a quick scout for Ben, but it doesn't take long to realize he's already in the loft. I rummaged through my bag until I found the "foil ravioli" I'd

stowed there earlier that morning. It doesn't take a brain surgeon to know Ben and I will do more than stay warm up there. I stuff the condoms in the back pocket of my jeans before scurrying up the solid wood ladder.

I'm expecting to find a mattress on the floor, but once again, I'm surprised when I see Ben reclining on a bed lush with high-end linens. The thing is enormous and looks to have been crafted out of entire tree trunks. I take a running jump and bounce into place next to him, where he drags me into his arms.

Rolling me onto my back, he slides one of his legs between mine, nudging them apart, all the while kissing me with mind-blowing expertise. His free hand runs up and down my side before claiming one of my breasts, massaging it through the layers of clothing I'm still sporting. His hand is moving down my body when the cabin is lit by lightning. This is accompanied by a deafening clap of thunder.

I know I'm in trouble when I smell ozone and am thankful when Ben pulls away, just as all those hated copper pasties and the clit cover pop into life. How do I explain all this to him?

"Damn, I was hoping this wouldn't happen," says Ben.

"Ah, you were?"

I look down at my chest, but there's no outward sign of my pasties. I'm wondering how on earth he knows when he climbs off the bed, stands next to it and starts stripping. With the removal of his thermal undershirt, I see his nipples are pierced with small copper barbells.

By the time he's naked, I can see not only is he rock hard and ready for me, but that his cock is pierced in several places. Among the hardware are curved and straight copper barbells, one of which goes sideways straight through the head.

"Ouch!" I can't think of anything more intelligent to say.

"Not so much. I was out cold when it was done to me," says Ben, with chagrin. "And it doesn't hurt when they pop up now."

It takes only a moment's hesitation before I speak. "The Nyphrazi?"

Ben's face floods with a mixture of surprise and relief, and then he nods.

"I didn't realize Ciprus played for both teams," I say, unsure how I feel about this.

However, rather than appear embarrassed, Ben's brow is wrinkled in confusion. "Ciprus?"

"Yeah, their God of Copper."

While pulling me to my feet and peeling my clothes away, Ben explained that his own experience had been with the Goddess Cuprum.

"Sister?"

"Not sure."

Once I'm as naked as he is, he experiments with flicking my nipple covers with his copper-studded tongue until the pasties are humming with electricity and my breasts are tingling.

Not wanting to be left out, I tugged on the small barbells that pierced his nipples and even tried a gentle twist. This has him groan deep in the back of his throat. Even more amazing is that if we get close to each other, sparks arc between the copper piercings on the two of us.

"Whoa, are you sure you're not one of them?" I asked him, eyeing his bright copper locks.

"I was about to ask you the same," he said, doing likewise.

I take only a moment to think about this fresh development.

"Ben, if your experience is anything like mine, we don't have long before one or the other of us is zapped outta here."

He gets the hint when I drop back onto the bed, with my legs wide. I'd be a little more decorous, but needs must.

No further encouragement is required, and he positions himself between my thighs. I think about the condoms sitting in the back pocket of my jeans, but I doubt anything that flimsy would last five minutes. Not when faced with the copper hardware he's been fitted with. He's closing in when an arc shoots between the barbell that pierces the end of his cock and the cover on my clit. Both of us gasped.

"This is going to be staggering," he says, before inching his way into me. That all of his adornments are fizzing in the same way as mine makes for incredible sensations. Even when he's deep inside me, it feels as though every piece of copper on both of us is connected by thin streams of electricity.

It's the first time I've experienced my nipples pulsing in time with a guy pumping into me. It's fucking outstanding. It's outstanding fucking.

I chuckled to myself at the old joke before locking my ankles together behind Ben's back. I curl up off the bed as I try to draw him in deeper and deeper. This encouragement is enough to have him scoop me up off the bed. After grabbing the hard-backed chair that's been doing duty as a bedside table, he sits upright. I doubt he could go deeper if he tried, and I love it.

I grind myself into him, which has the curved barbell at the base of his cock zapping my copper-plated pearl from both sides. Meanwhile, the arcing taking place between his nipples and mine has both my breasts now humming. The pleasure is incredible, and I see by the glazed look on Ben's face he's in the zone, too.

I'm about to blow and can only hope it happens soon because the white cloud that surrounds us is getting thicker all

the time. A sure sign that one or the other of us is about to disappear.

I'm about to crest when the buzzing from my breasts rises through my body, leaving them feeling bereft. On feeling the hum settle deep inside my brain, I rock my head and dislodge it. This buys me another minute of the glory of pumping up and down on Ben's hard length. I'm screaming my release when the buzzing fills my head.

5

On realizing I'm draped backward over a large copper barrel that's slung end-on between two posts, I scream some more. My legs are spread enough that my hips are feeling it, but when I try to pull my knees together, it becomes apparent I'm being held in place.

There's a dark cloud hovering overhead, with the God of Copper's expression every bit as thunderous. Perhaps asking Ciprus where Ben was hadn't been the brightest move on my part. Still, if I'd ever wanted to know if the gods ground their teeth, the answer was standing right in front of me.

"You were chosen for this," he spat out. "And yet you waste my gift on a mere human!"

I take a second to realize he's talking about all those copper do-dads.

"Gift! Gift! Why, you, you—"

I'm still trying to find an appropriate adjective when he throws his hands up in the air, fingers spread wide at the storm

cloud brewing above us. The cloud changes from threatening to electrified in a matter of seconds. Oh, crap.

"I don't think that's a good idea," I yelled at him over the clashing thunder.

He looks down at me before going back to his jazz hands.

I struggle against my restraints, but it does nothing more than hurt my wrists and ankles. I lie back and wait to be electrocuted.

What happens next is just as shocking.

Two bolts of lightning explode out of the flashing cloud and into Ciprus's hands. That the drum gets some of the residual electricity he doesn't absorb has me pulling away from it as far as I'm able. This makes it easy for Ciprus to roll the drum, and me along with it, toward him so he can spear me with his cock.

While the sex I'd just experienced with Ben had been mind-blowing, this was otherworldly. Every hair on my body sizzles with static, while every nerve ending crackles. Wherever Ciprus's hands stray, I sizzle and hum. And he runs his hands everywhere.

He starts at my shoulders, then goes down over my breasts, before circling my sex and repeating the cycle. Over and over. All the while screwing me stupid with the drum rolling back and forth, as if of its own free will.

Then, when I'm thinking it can't get any more surreal, the copper of the drum undulates underneath me. My cheeks are spread and a buzzing presence soon makes itself known in my ass. That this hums in time with Ciprus's copper-clad member and the sensations rippling through my body is awe-inspiring.

"Faster," I gasp out. "Faster."

While the pulsing speeds up, Ciprus doesn't, maintaining

his rhythm, although he seems to go deeper with each slow thrust.

To hell with this. I squeeze my muscles tight, and this sends me over the edge. The sound of Ciprus roaring "no" is still ringing in my ears when I pop back into the mountain cabin.

I'm alone.

I must have come back around the same time as I popped out because the cabin remains toasty and warm. The wind roaring around the cabin also lets me know the storm is still in full force. There's nothing for me to do but wait for Ben to return.

If his goddess was as ticked off as Ciprus was, then he could be in for some serious payback if she's the jealous type.

Pulling the blankets back reveals fluffy sheets on the bed, which is a relief. If they'd been cotton, I'd have had to put my clothes back on, because everyone knows how cold those can be. As it is, I slide in, still naked, pull the covers up and am soon asleep.

It's dark when I stir, and there's still no sign of Ben. There's a faint glow from downstairs, letting me know the candles continue to burn, but the fire must be dying down as the cabin is cooler.

After a few quick pants, I throw the covers back, pull on the barest requirement of thermals and clamber down the ladder. Boy, it's a good thing Ben brought all those logs in earlier. If he hadn't, I'd be forced to search out more wood. Not a pleasant thought, if the howling of the wind is anything to go by.

I'm getting close to running out of firewood before Ben pops back into the here and now. He's sitting on the wooden

chair next to the bed as he had been when I'd been zapped away by Ciprus.

While he looks tired, he's smiling, so he mustn't have gotten too much grief. He's also still sporting all of his copper adornments, making me realize I am, too.

After throwing the covers back, I patted the bed beside me.

Ben is soon next to me, snuggling up and letting us both know that the arcing we'd experienced earlier is even crazier now. It gets to the point we have to pull away from each other to avoid setting fire to the bed.

"So, when were you first taken?" I'm lying on my side, looking at Ben over the pillows we've jammed between us. The storm outside is too bad for us to risk burning the cabin down.

"It was a couple of years back now. I was out hunting and, bam, next thing I know, this crazy redhead has me strapped to a board and my cock's bristling with copper hardware."

"Best sex ever?"

"By far, although she didn't seem that moved by it. I thought she was just interested in making sure I had a good time."

His "but" hangs heavy in the air above the bed.

"Go on," I urged.

"I know this sounds weird, but have you ever seen them eat?"

While my habit is to answer without thought, I stop myself, thinking back on my time with the Nyphrazi gods. "No. Now that I think about it, I haven't. I always seem to eat my meals at different times than they do."

"Meals?" splutters Ben. "Cuprum just screws my brains out and then sends me home."

I don't bother correcting Ben in his assumption that my only experience has been with Ciprus. Even I'm feeling uncomfortable with all the action I've seen in the past five months. Both human and godly.

"So, what's your theory?" I say, steering him back on course.

"Well, I'm thinking that maybe they recharge themselves somehow when we come. Cuprum is always fizzing at the end of one of our sessions even though she never comes herself."

"Are you drained after?"

"Fucked!" is Ben's bald reply.

It takes only a second before we're cracking-up at his no-frills response.

"When I saw your red hair, I wondered if you were in touch with them too," says Ben, reaching over the pillow barrier so he can twirl a length around his fingers.

"I can't say I'm a fan of the color, even if it has cut down on the number of guys hitting on me."

"I'm used to the color now," he says, continuing to play with my hair.

"Damn it. I'm stuck with this for life?"

"Hey, it's not all bad," he says, laughing. "Admit it! The sex earlier was staggering."

"It's just a shame the cabin's so much cooler. There's no way I'm getting out of bed to use the chair again." Despite the drop in temperature, remembering how amazing that had been, has me shivering with remembered delight.

I know Ben's recovered from his session with Cuprum by the amount of energy he uses when jumping out of bed and dragging on his clothes. "Get some rest. You'll need it."

"Hah, as if I can after you've said something like that."

Ben sees my hand snaking down under the blankets so I

can deal with my sudden horniness and smacks the covers to stop me.

"Oh, no, you don't. The hornier you are, the better it'll be."

"Hurry, then."

"On it!"

I have to give him credit. He doesn't waste any time because I hear the front door being unlocked not much later. Even under a mountain of blankets up in the loft, there's no missing the gust of frigid air that blasts its way into the cabin. I don't hear him come back in for what seems like ages, to the point I'm thinking about getting dressed and going in search of him.

This time, the blast of cold air is accompanied by Ben swearing and cursing at how arctic it is outside. Half an hour later and I'm aware of the heat from the re-stoked fire swirling up into the loft in waves. It's not long before I'm pushing the covers back because the place is stifling. All the banging and crashing downstairs gets the better of me and on hearing furniture being moved, I'm unable to just lie there any longer.

6

I look down at him from my spot at the top of the ladder. "What on earth are you doing?"

"I want to fuck you so much right now, and this looks like the only way I can do so without incinerating us."

This bald expression of longing makes my sex squirm for release and makes my trip down the angled ladder a risky endeavor. I'm about halfway down when Ben grabs me from behind, holding me in place.

"Argh, your hands are freezing!"

"Turn around," he says, before nipping me on the bum.

True to form, my girly bits are chanting, "Turn! Turn! Turn!"

I do so with difficulty, and it's only because Ben is keeping a firm hold on my hips that I don't slip. Now I'm leaning back against the rungs of the ladder with my mons level with his mouth. It's something Ben takes immediate advantage of, with his hands swooping in from the sides. His fingers feel like icicles as they peel me open to his questing tongue. But when

there's a zing of electricity from his tongue stud to my copper-clad pearl, I no longer care.

"Oh my God, oh my God, oh my God." After that, I'm incoherent as he runs his scorching hot tongue up and down my cleft, its barbell flicking back and forth on my clit for good measure. The rungs of the ladder digging into the back of me, fade into oblivion. All I can concentrate on is his tongue driving me closer and closer to the edge.

I'm shuddering and near to release when he pulls his mouth away and slams the palm of an ice-cold hand down over my sex, stopping me in my tracks. My eyes fly open, and I'm about to give him grief for being so mean, but his expression stops me.

"Are you okay?"

"Yes," he grits out, "but when you come, I want to be so deep inside of you I touch your heart."

It's only after he's helped me to the ground that I realize there hasn't been any more arcing during our session on the ladder. A quick look down shows me I'm no longer copper-clad, and yet the oral sex Ben had given me was right up there with Vyran and his alien tongue. While I might be free of adornment, Ben's still sporting all those barbells of his.

"Hurry, I can't wait much longer." He leads me over to the setup in front of the wood fire. There, two kitchen chairs, with a plank between them, form a makeshift bench. The whole setup is covered with a silver space blanket.

"We don't need to bother."

He stops in the middle of straddling the plank and gives me a questioning look. I point at my breasts and see when comprehension makes itself at home in his gaze.

"Don't know about that. I'm sure I've got enough of a

charge for both of us." In saying this, he lies back on the bench, a leg over each side. "Ride me, baby."

I straddle him, grab that adorned cock of his and lower myself onto it, and then grind back and forth until he's as deep as possible. If I lean forward, this brings my already swollen pearl into direct contact with the curved barbell at the base of his cock.

"Oh, good God." It's as though a small bolt of lightning has just pierced my clit, but rather than be painful, the sensation has my nub humming with pleasure. As good as it is, I want Ben's hard length with all its adornments pumping into me again and again. This makes me straighten my legs. After pulling free, I slam back down again, sheathing him. Again, I'm rewarded with another zap of electricity under the hood.

I hope my legs are up to the challenge I'm about to set them.

They hold up to a point before giving out, but by then I'm so close to coming I no longer care. On realizing I'm spent, Ben sits up and holds my ass, drawing me closer to him and thrusting in as deep as he can.

The little barbells that pierce his nipples zap both of mine with electricity, when snakes its way down through my body to where we join. My sex vibrating and Ben grinding himself into me are more than I can hold out against. Maybe the gods haven't ruined men for me after all.

We're snowbound for three more days, by which time we're close to running out of food and have fucked each other in ever more inventive ways. My favorite is me leaning over the fire-protected arm of the couch and having Ben take me from behind.

I love him filling me to the hilt and plunging into me so deep he touches my heart. That he can reach everything in front while he pumps away is a bonus.

On waking on the fourth day, the silence was deafening. All I can hear is Ben's quiet breathing. The storm has passed. A snuffled breath heralds Ben waking up, too.

"Morning," I whispered so as not to blast him.

"Morning back," he mumbled. "Sounds like we'll be able to get out of here today. I hope you like shoveling."

"I've done a bit in my time."

"Once we've backed the truck out, I can attach the snowplow."

It takes the best part of the day before we make it out to the road. It hasn't been graded, but neither is it covered in heaps of snow.

"Now that's just plain weird," says Ben, looking at it.

The trip home is one of easy camaraderie, with both of us at ease in each other's company. Fucking another person's brains out for three days will do that for you.

I call my parents as soon as I get a signal on my phone. But rather than be in a lather about my having been missing for four days, my mom asks me if I'm having a nice day.

"That's strange."

"What is it?" says Ben.

"We haven't lost time. My mom asked me if I was having a nice day."

"I'm thinking that storm was ours alone."

I twist in my seat so I can look at Ben. "Where were you when you first got taken?"

I can see him thinking back. "Out the back of the cabin."

"Boy, are we in for some long weekends!" I find it hard to contain my glee about day trips that last four days. "More food next trip."

"And maybe some toys to pass the time," says Ben, when swinging his truck through the gates at my folks' house.

"Don't say that when I'm about to face my mom and dad." I gave him a playful punch on the arm.

"See you at work on Monday," says Ben, after a chaste kiss on my cheek.

Not wanting to sit around and chat with my folks when I'm conscious I reek of sex, I feign a headache and escape to the shower. I'll be able to take longer than the glorified bird baths that were on offer at the cabin when we didn't want to run out of water.

By the time I've soaped myself all over, I'm aroused long before I'm ready to rinse. As I run my hands all over my body, I think of Ben and the days we've just spent together. It takes a second for me to realize the water is moving up and down my body and keeping pace with my hands. The showerhead then switches to the massage setting with no help from me, and small balls of water are soon bombarding my body.

I open my eyes to find the showerhead snaking around in the shower cubicle like a cobra. Inch by inch, it drops ever lower until the pulses of water are pounding away at my cherry.

Any eroticism falls away, and my blood runs cold when I see that the fixtures and fittings have changed from stainless steel to bright, shining gold.

I'm not sure if my shivering is because I ran out of hot water before Aurum, the Nyphrazi God of Gold, had finished

playing with me. Or was it because there's another orgasm waiting in the wings?

With a towel still wrapped around my head, I stumble into bed and wait to warm up or climax, whichever happens first. I don't know whether to be relieved or disappointed when, rather than climaxing, I fall asleep.

The following morning, it's as though I've been put through a wringer. I didn't sleep well with Aurum strutting through my dreams, his golden fettyr tugging against the gold chain that held it around his waist. This told me more than words that he was ready to plunge himself into me.

As if to prove a point, he'd unhook the chain and then lay back on what looked like a golden altar. There he'd strike a Cosmo pose that had his cock jutting upward and leaping each time he jerked his hips. It was as though I were already skewered on its hard, luxurious length.

God, that guy is such a poser. Even in my dreams.

It takes a second after I've rolled onto my side to comprehend that it's already after eleven. I never sleep this late. The towel is no longer wrapped around my head, and a quick exploration with my hands lets me know my hair is sticking out at all angles. I'd wash it again, but I don't think my legs are up to another going over with the showerhead. They're shaky when I stand.

When I pick the still-damp towel up off the floor, shock hammers through me when I see it's covered in what appears to be blood. This has me spinning to the mirror on the wardrobe door, expecting to see a head gash or something, and I'm relieved to find nothing that requires stitches.

Even better is seeing my hair is back to its usual dirty

blonde. I wonder what Ben will think about the change. He quite likes my copper locks because they match his own.

A quick glance down and I see my pubes are no longer red either. What I see is even worse, with them missing altogether. We are talking way past a Brazilian wax, without so much as a landing strip to keep me warm.

EPILOGUE

It doesn't matter how many times I check, my pubes don't reappear. Aurum, God of Gold, had doubtless obliterated them because they were bright orange and clashed with his aesthetic. They were also a reminder that his brother, Ciprus, God of Copper, had already claimed me.

Despite all this, I can't shake the feeling that my being marked by the gods is part of a larger pattern. My accidental meeting of Vyran, Seolfer's attack, then Ciprus's electrification of me, and now Aurum marking me as his. It's almost too convenient, too orchestrated.

As I ponder their endgame, I again catch sight of my mons, my lip curling in disgust. Aurum's ministrations have me looking more like a porn star than a glorified kitchen hand at a gold mine.

I'd rather have my pubes back even if they were green or purple or whatever because without them, my girly bits are feeling the cold. On the plus side, my shoulder-length hair is back to its natural dirty blonde.

Today will be my first day back at work in the cafeteria since I lost my redhead status, and I know I'll get grief from the miners. It won't matter to them that my hair is pulled up in a no-nonsense bun, its very blondeness having a magnetic quality.

I'm still surprised Aurum didn't change it to a bright shining gold so it would be more in keeping with his own. Perhaps he didn't like the idea of the competition?

While dressing, I catch sight of myself one more time. How the hell am I supposed to explain to Ben why I look like I'm ready to be mounted in a display case?

Which, knowing Aurum's narcissist tendencies, might be the very thing he had in mind.

God of Gold

1

My fears about the miners being attracted to my blonde locks were well-founded. It's not even six a.m. and I've already been hit on four times. I'd forgotten how oversexed they were, so when I heard someone grabbing a tray at the counter behind me, I waited for the next round of innuendo or lurid offer, my back stiffening in readiness.

"What happened to your hair?"

Even without turning from the pot of brown stuff I'm stirring with a glorified oar, I know it's Ben, and the tension seeps out of me. His tone is neutral, so I can't tell whether he's keen on my natural color.

Looking at him over my shoulder, I'm none the wiser.

"Can we talk about it later?" I say, raising an eyebrow for emphasis.

I can tell by his expression when he realizes the change in my hair color might be courtesy of the Nyphrazi.

"Oh, sure. What time do you finish today?"

"Four. I'm on early shifts for the next couple of days."

"Damn, other way for me. What about heading up to the cabin at the weekend?"

"Sounds good," I say, failing to keep the excitement out of my voice. If the coming trip is anything like the last one, it'll end up seeming like three days, and "coming" is all I'll be doing. "I've got Sunday off."

It's only after Ben's finished his lunch and disappeared with his co-workers that I receive a good-natured ribbing from my fellow kitchen crew. When Glory, my septuagenarian boss, starts reminiscing about past lovers of her own, the chat grinds to a nauseated halt. This is followed by everyone rushing back to their stations, working to block out her more X-rated memories.

The rest of the week drags, and I only see Ben when he's in the cafeteria for lunch. By the time I clock off late on Saturday evening, I'm shattered and so keen on retiring that I pass on dinner, opting instead for an extra-long shower.

I'm relieved that the shower at home is no longer being possessed by Aurum, and I've seen no other signs of him either. Unless you count the erotic dreams that crowd my head each night and have me twisting and turning enough to tie my sheets in knots.

I turn the shower off only when I run out of hot water. My brother will be furious, but I've needed the time to think.

Tucked up in bed, I continue mulling things over. It's now very obvious that all of Vyran's five brothers will try for orgasm—or Nysa, as they call it. Just as they'd promised; the

power-hungry bastards. I still find it weird that such sexual beings have an issue achieving orgasm. Not that they have any problems handing them out.

Vyran is still my favorite of all the brothers, although Ciprus had his moments. The only brother I hope never to see again is Seolfer. If I saw him, the only reason I'd go near him would be to smash the asshole's nuts to a paste with one of my knees. My plan is to keep telling myself this until I rid myself of the strange craving I have whenever I think of that silver jerk.

By the looks of things, Aurum won't cause me too much grief. He struck me as too self-centered to be interested in making my life hell like Seolfer had.

Axel, God of Nickel, also looks like he'll be easy to deal with, but I'm nervous about Marlo. That fettyr of his is made of iron and doesn't appear designed with pleasure in mind, unlike his tongue. I've already savored the delights of having him slurping away at me, and I wouldn't mind enjoying it again.

As I think back on how he'd used that glorious organ, with its miraculous enzymes, to heal the nerve damage caused by Seolfer, a frisson of pleasure burst to life. And for once, it's not at an inconvenient time. I yield and am rewarded with my sex warming. I'm thinking about giving myself some light relief when I hear Aurum's voice inside my head.

"No. You shall not. You shall achieve Nysa only with me."

There's something different about his voice this time. It's more confident, as if he's following a script he's rehearsed. Like he knows how this is supposed to play out.

I'm wondering what the hell he can do about it when it feels like hot liquid has been poured over my mons. Whatever

it is, it seeps down between my legs, and by the time I get my hand under the covers, it's set hard. I know without getting out of bed what color it'll be.

Not that this stops me flicking the covers back to check out my latest adornment, courtesy of the Gods of Nyphrazi. The only god who hasn't saddled me with any unwanted hardware is Vyran. I wouldn't have minded a souvenir from him.

There's nothing dull about the glittering gold that covers my whole pubic mound like a botched wax job. Not that I'll need one of those in a long time, thank you very much, Aurum.

A quick exploration also lets me know I'm not getting any sex this weekend. That bastard Aurum has even covered my asshole with a setup similar to one of those stupid C-string bikini bottoms.

I can only hope the stuff disappears when I need to wash or answer the call of nature. That had been the case with the fascinum that Seolfer had lumbered me with.

I pick at the edge of the gold to see if I can slide my finger underneath it, but it's as though it's been glued to my skin. I can't even get my fingernail in there.

"Do not remove the mantle, Jasmine. To do so would be foolish." I hear Aurum's caution as clearly as if he's in the room with me.

Mantle? Is he fucking joking? It's a chastity belt; that's what it is.

Lying back down, I pull the covers up and wait. If Aurum is anything like Ciprus and Seolfer, his metal-aligned brothers, he'll now play fast and loose with my body.

But I wait in vain, and my arousal fades enough that I can fall asleep.

. . .

My bedside lamp is still burning bright the next morning, and a quick grope lets me know it wasn't all a bad dream. I hate to think about how I'm supposed to explain this to Ben when he picks me up in an hour.

After a quick shower, in which the gold covering shucks to the side, allowing me to wash myself, I'm none the wiser. I'm glad it's Sunday and everyone else is still in bed because it wouldn't take a session with Mr. Freud to see I'm struggling with something. I'm still struggling with it when I walk out to Ben's truck.

Inside the cab, it's warm and intimate, and the kiss I get from Ben has my toes curling. Pulling back, I find him holding onto one of my braids.

"Does this mean you're free of Ciprus?"

"I guess it does," I say, not wanting to update him on developments just yet.

"So," says Ben, tugging on the braid, "do the curtains match the carpet?" His gaze drops to my lap, letting me know what he's asking about.

"Ah, yeah, about that," I say, shrugging out of my jacket.

"I won't mind either way."

I tried several times to spit it out, but each time my throat closed on me and all I manage is a pathetic squeak. This is so not like me.

"Never mind, I'll be able to check for myself soon enough," says Ben.

His tone is full of promise when he puts the truck into gear and drives out onto the road.

My own lust overpowers any worries I might have about how this will play out, and I soon feel the gold mantle warming. I'm settling in to enjoy the ride when I again hear Aurum inside my head.

"No. You shall not. You shall achieve Nysa only with me."

No doubt contrary to his intent, this psychic reminder about some of the mind-blowing Nysa I've received only has me getting hotter.

"Pull over."

"What? Why?" Despite his questions, Ben does as I ask.

Luckily, we're away from any houses, and so there's no one around to witness me undo my seatbelt and shimmy forward on the bench seat. Only then can I undo my jeans and push them down around my thighs. I haven't bothered with underwear since there didn't seem to be any point, and so the sparkling gold is visible.

"Wow." Ben taps it with his fingernail. "Is that gold?"

"Solid."

Ben runs his hand down between my legs and, while I can sense him against my inner thighs, that's it.

"God of Gold?" says Ben, his brows raised in query.

I nod in response. "I'll understand if you want to drop me home," I say, dragging my jeans back up.

"I don't give in without a fight, so I'll need to stop by my office at the mine."

"You have an office?"

"Did you think I was there because of my muscles?" says Ben. He follows up by striking as good a bodybuilder's pose as he can in the confines of the cab.

"Ah, well, yeah, I did."

"Nope. I'm a qualified metallurgist. I know how we might be able to get rid of that."

"I'm game."

. . .

Stopping by the mine only delays the start of our trip by half an hour. But after I see the bag of tricks Ben drops on the seat between us, I decide I'm okay with the delay. There are some loud metallic clunks that don't inspire confidence and have me thinking of him going at me with an industrial-sized can opener.

"Not long before we've rid you of that chastity belt of yours," says Ben, before laughing at his own joke.

We're creeping up the driveway to the cabin when the snow on either side of the truck explodes, creating an instant whiteout. By the time Ben reacts and slams on the brakes, we're already through it and into clear air again. Not that Ben can move the truck forward, because the driveway is no longer there.

The cabin is though. But rather than being surrounded by mounds of snow as it was seconds ago, it now sits in the middle of a field of flowers. The weather's different too. The sky is no longer a solid, leaden gray, but rather an endless expanse of brilliant blue.

"What the fuck?" I can't think of anything more intelligent to say.

"What you said," stammers Ben.

You'd think both of us would be used to being ferried around by the Nyphrazi by now, but transporting two of us together—and a truck!

We sit in stunned silence until we see someone walk out of the cabin.

"Cuprum," says Ben, recognizing the voluptuous redhead who sways down the stairs before threading her way through the flowers to join us.

The Goddess of Copper is sex incarnate. Dressed in a

skimpy onesie made of articulated copper discs, she doesn't so much walk as undulate her way over to Ben's side of the truck. Her nipples, which are poking through holes, are pierced with large rings from which hang small lengths of copper chain. These sway from side-to-side, the action hypnotic.

It's enough to have Ben and me resembling a couple of dogs watching a tennis match.

2

The closer Cuprum gets, the faster Ben's breathing becomes. No surprise with her sex glistening in readiness, and all on display due to her outfit's design. The chains that run through her cleft are pulling her open to the world.

I can't imagine how uncomfortable that must be.

But isn't it typical that while the gods get to cover their organs with those fettyrs of theirs, this goddess has all her parts on show? Still, if Ben's hyperventilating, rather than being a weakness, Cuprum is working the outfit to her advantage.

Spotting movement behind her, I swing my gaze back up to the cabin. "Aurum!"

My outburst breaks in on the trance-like state Ben's achieved from looking at the goddess. He turns toward me and slurs, "Who is it?"

I know I'm not imagining it. He sounds drunk.

Before I can respond, he swings back around to continue his visual groping of Cuprum.

"I'll tell you later," I say, although I doubt he can hear me over the roar of blood rushing to his cock.

As if by an unspoken command, both of us opened our doors at the same time and climbed out. It's only when I'm outside that I realize how hot it is, but I guess the Nyphrazi won't enjoy standing around in the snow naked.

Hell, if I could change the weather like this, I'd be living in a permanent summer, too. As it is, the jump in temperature is overwhelming, and I'm glad my puffer jacket is in the truck rather than on me.

Cuprum is now right beside the truck and wastes no time placing her hand on top of Ben's head. They disappear a second later.

As focused as I've been on them, I get a fright when my breasts are fondled through my hoodie. Without conscious thought, I smash my elbow backward into a set of very hard abs, but I don't get the smallest of grunts to show I've done any damage. Damn it, these gods are tough.

As though I hadn't just assaulted him, Aurum takes my hand. Since I don't know where—or when—I am, I allow him to pull me to the cabin.

Rather than walking up the front steps, he veers off to the right and down the side of the building. There he leads me along a path that disappears into the nearby woods. I tug my hand free of his so I can ditch my hoodie before tying it around my waist; the last thing I need is to pass out from heatstroke. I caught up with him just as he disappeared into the trees.

The darkness formed by the dense canopy soon forced me to push my sunglasses up onto my head to avoid tripping over

the tree roots that littered the pathway. This also means that when we break into an open glade, I'm blinded by the bright sunshine.

Something else that is blinding is the golden altar that sits right in the middle of the clearing. It's the one that has featured in my recurring erotic dreams of Aurum.

"Tradition and Praedytus say your time to live up to your legacy is now." And if that nonsense isn't enough of a turnoff, he then strikes a pose that has the end of his fettyr-sheathed cock pulling hard against the restraining chain around his waist. "I'll fuck you, and you will love it!"

I'm about to drawl, "Oh, will you?" in the most bored tone I can manage, when I realize he's given me an instruction rather than stated a fact. So that's how it's going to be, is it?

Aurum removes my sunglasses and tosses them on the ground. I'm itching to retrieve them because they cost me an arm and a leg. But he's now got me backed up against the end of the altar and is stripping me. I think about fighting it, but let's see what's on offer first. Maybe he's got a reason to brag?

It doesn't take long before I'm naked apart from the golden mantle that guards my sex. He bends down so he can run his tongue over my nipples. Back and forth, over and over, until they've scrunched up into hard little buds. I might not need to fake it after all.

Grabbing me around the waist, he lifted me up to sit on the altar. Rather than being warmed by the sun as I'd expected, it's borderline hot. This not only burns my ass but also heats the mantle and the very core of me.

Aurum pushes me back, and I'm surprised when the hard surface of the altar ripples under me like a living thing, pushing my hips high. If it weren't for the god-damned golden chastity belt he's saddled me with, I'd be on display right now.

No sooner had this thought popped into my head than my hips were raised even further and Aurum nudged my thighs apart. When he runs his finger from my mons all the way around to my ass, the solid gold of the mantle opens, dragging any soft tissue with it.

First, the lips of my labia are pulled to the sides, leaving my clit bared to the world. Then it's as though I've had a funnel inserted into my sheath and ass, so wide are they spread. When Aurum runs his finger down my slit again, holy hell, he's everywhere.

What follows is a piece of pure theater, with Aurum's actions done as though for an audience. Every movement is exaggerated, though I can only see this when I lift my head.

He runs his tongue down the inside of one thigh, then skips across my mons, tweaks my clit, before sweeping up the other thigh. And repeat.

It's as if he's performing for an unseen audience, with every gesture calculated for maximum effect. I'm wondering who'd want to watch this when I find myself mesmerized by his back and forth, counting down the seconds between each pass. This proves impossible when I surrender to the sensations that are engulfing my body.

Every time he closes his lips on my clit, my core twitches against the gold that's holding it wide. The same thing happens with my ass. When Aurum slides a finger into each of these while sucking hard on my nubbin, I yield to the orgasm that rushes through me. It works hard against his fingers that he's rubbing together through the wall of flesh that is all that separates them.

I'm still limp when the table flattens beneath me. Sensing a dimming in the light, I open my eyes and am confused. I'm now looking up at a shimmering roof of gold rather than a

clear blue sky peppered with wispy clouds. There's been none of the usual brain buzz to let me know I was being zapped somewhere else.

A quick turn of my head confirms I'm in a cave, but it's like no other I've ever seen. It's not just round; it's a perfect dome down to percentage points. The floor is ballroom-flat, while the curve of the ceiling is smooth without a single opening to mar its perfection.

Every surface, even the floor, is covered in gleaming metal, meaning that the tapers that stand at regular intervals around the altar have their light multiplied in brightness. The golden ceiling, walls, and floors have been buffed to a high polish, so my reflection is everywhere, even if it is a little soft.

It's while I'm looking sideways that I see Aurum's reflection, enabling me to watch him climb onto the altar. Turning back to face him, I see he's looking very pleased with himself.

"That was nothing. You will scream your release over and over when I fill you. As will I! Nysa will be mine," he says, his tone trespassing into Crazy-land.

He crawls forward like something out of a cabaret show until my legs are spread wide. Then, as though out of my dream, he unhooks the chain that holds his fettyred-cock snug against his stomach, and it bounces free. The merest touch to my golden-coated sex, and I'm spread even wider.

Aurum leans forward on his forearms before burying himself deep inside me with a simple twist of his hips. Being as open as I am, I'm only conscious of him when he's already partway inside me, meaning every time he thrusts, he nudges my G-spot.

This nudge and thrust keeps up with my hips now rising to meet his, although it's still not enough, and so I wrap my legs

around his waist. The faster we fuck, the more my golden coating ripples until my ass pulses while my clit is being squeezed from the sides.

When I open my eyes, I'm put out to find Aurum looking off to the side rather than down at me. It takes a second to realize he's looking at his reflection in the golden walls. I'm about to give him grief over it when he takes all his weight on one arm and places the other on my head.

The familiar buzzing overtakes my brain, and a second later, I straddle him, the golden altar taking care of thrusting his hips up and down. It's as if I'm riding an X-rated mechanical bull. With his arms clasped behind his head and a smug grin marring his beautiful face, he's what I'd describe as showboating.

But fuck, it feels so damned good, and I can't stop myself from grinding away at him to reach orgasm. And I'm close, oh, so close. I need help, but when I move a hand to my clit, Aurum's face darkens with anger, and I freeze.

"No. You will not!" he yells, loud enough that I lean away from him.

Feeling movement, I look down and can see my clit is being squished outward by the gold that surrounds it. When I see Aurum unhook one of his hands from behind his head, I'm expecting some manual stimulation. But he's far too much the showman to make it that simple.

Instead, he swirls a couple of fingers in mid-air, and I'm surprised to see streams of gold shoot out the roof of the cave before zooming straight for my pearl. They tangle around it, pulsing with energy and moving me ever closer to the edge.

As if sensing I'm not there yet, Aurum unhooks his other arm. This time swirls his entire hand in the air. Rather than streams of gold, a solid ball of the stuff drops from the roof of

the cave. This hits me dead on target, buzzing with enough energy to shove me straight into multiple orgasms.

It's only after the third climax that I notice applause. When I open my eyes, I'm disturbed to see that the smooth walls are no longer smooth. Instead, golden ledges now jut out at regular intervals, with each of them having a naked stranger sitting on it.

But glancing around, I realize not everyone in the audience is a stranger. Ben is there with the Goddess Cuprum, although with her straddling him, I'd almost missed him.

Since she's facing away from him, she's able to look me straight in the eye. It's something she takes advantage of when she pumps herself up and down on his hard length like it's an Olympic event.

I wouldn't say she looks bored, but rather than being lost in the throes of passion, it's more like she's chowing down on a big, juicy steak. Maybe Ben is right about the gods feeding off our sexual release.

The sight of Ben's copper-studded cock plunging into Cuprum's slick depths over and over does funny things to me, and I'm unable to look away. That the chains that dissect her depths pull tight each time she drops herself on him only adds to the allure.

By now, Ben is gripping the goddess around her waist and jerking his hips up in hard thrusts, with any sense of control long gone. When he comes, I welcome the small shudder of release that also shimmies through me, much to Aurum's disgust when I tighten around him and he realizes what's happened.

He wastes no time yanking himself free of me.

A woman, who looks to be coated from head to toe in gold, surges to her feet. "You didn't come close to achieving Nysa!

The legend speaks of a genuine connection, not this theatrical nonsense. Praedytus will be disappointed." She clicks her fingers and disappears without warning.

She's hit a nerve with Aurum. Damn, he looks pissed. Before I know what's happening, he drops his palm on top of my head and, bam, I'm back in the clearing behind the cabin. The altar's gone, and so are my clothes. The one thing that's back with a vengeance is the snow.

A second later, Ben appeared next to me.

"Fucking hell, we'll freeze if we stay out here," he says.

I don't need any encouragement from him, and as we stumble toward the cabin, I can't help but wonder if that golden audience was planned. The way Aurum kept posing, like he were following directions. And that woman who criticized him. She spoke as if she knew what was supposed to happen.

It's hard going for me, with the gold mantle doing nothing to protect my sex from the elements. There's also something different about how it's sitting, leaving me walking like a duck.

However, there isn't a chance I'm checking what's wrong out here. Not with hypothermia waiting in the wings. This has me throwing one arm across my breasts to lessen the jiggling, and cupping my mons with the other to keep the worst of the cold at bay.

When we stagger into the cabin, my girly bits are doubtless suffering from frostbite, and I'm giving a good impression of a wet dog. Ben isn't in much better shape, although he takes time to toss a pile of logs into the wood fire. Meanwhile, I stagger up the ladder into the sleeping loft, the fit of the mantle not making this easy.

I'm snuggled under a pile of blankets, doing my best to control my shivers when Ben joins me, wrapping himself around me. I'm not sure whether it's an improvement. If anything, it's like cuddling a snowman, although this soon changes, with his core fiery compared to mine.

There's nothing sexual about our embrace. This is about survival. But that all changes when Ben runs his hands over me, checking for damage. When his questing fingers hit my core, it's confirmation that Aurum had left the mantle wide open in his haste to dump me from his stage show.

I don't have to wait long for Ben to stroke me again, and thanks to that all-access pass, the sensations soon coursing through me are mind-blowing.

"Whatever you're doing, don't stop." I gasp out. "It's amazing."

"I'll bet it looks that way too," says Ben, before whipping the covers back.

Thankfully, the temperature in the loft is now pushing boiling point, and so this is no hardship. Neither is the look I get from Ben when he settles himself between my legs.

"Wow, that's weird."

I poke my head up and look at him over my breasts. "Is that weirdly good? Or weird bad?" Experience has taught me it's never a good idea to assume anything when the Nyphrazi are involved.

"There's what looks like a gold ring embedded around your G-spot. Can you feel it?"

I'm ready to say no, but instead force myself to concentrate, to see if I can sense what must be a new ornament. "No. I can't feel anything."

"Hang on a sec."

Ben slides a finger inside me, and I can tell when he's

touched my G-spot because of the vibrating that starts deep inside of me.

"Fuck me," is all I can stutter, with my capacity for rational thought shattered by the vibrating that is gaining in strength with each passing second.

Ben takes my oath as a command, and he's soon balls-deep inside of me.

"Fucking hell," he stutters out.

"Can you feel it too?"

"Hell yes," says Ben, before withdrawing only to slide back in as though savoring every inch.

We don't last long, being unable to fight the overwhelming spasms that rock the pair of us. And all this even though Ben's cock is free of studs, since they had disappeared by the time we made it back to the cabin.

"I think I'd like to keep this one," I say, my voice softened by my recent orgasm.

"Yes! Yes! Yes!" says Ben, although I can't tell if he's agreeing with me or coming again.

3

No longer in a sensual haze, I have to ask Ben about our shared experience in the cave of gold.

"So, what did you think of my performance with Aurum?"

Ben raises himself up on an elbow so he can check me out. "What performance?"

"The one where he screwed me on the gold altar."

"Gold altar?"

I can tell by his confusion that he doesn't know what I'm talking about.

"But I could see Cuprum pumping herself up and down on your cock like her life depended on it."

"You could?" Ben rotates his hand, showing I should continue.

"Yeah, one minute Aurum was screwing my brains out on the altar in a clearing behind the cabin. The next minute, we're in a cave that looks to be made out of gold. It was empty when we first got there, then bam—it's like Nyphrazi X Factor, with the emphasis on X."

"Huh?"

"Applause, audience feedback and then I got voted off by Aurum. I think I was ruining his act."

I explain Aurum's weird behavior, his posing and bragging.

"Sounds like my roommate in college. Fucking narcissist."

Ben sums up what this meant for him and, more importantly, any girls unlucky enough to date this self-proclaimed expert in the sack.

"Aurum wasn't even that good. I had to finish for him," I say, unable to keep the disgust out of my voice.

After Ben stops laughing, I continue. "There's not much chance of him achieving Nysa if I don't get off."

"Nysa?"

Damn it, I'd forgotten he knows nothing about this or my experiences with Vyran and Seolfer. After taking a deep breath, I unburden myself, hoping Ben can see I haven't had a lot of choice in the matter.

"Fuck," says Ben.

I lie frozen, waiting for him to get up and leave.

"That is so hot!"

He shows me just how hot he thinks it is by climbing on top of me and burying himself as deep as he can. The ring vibrates a second later and builds in intensity until my whole pelvis is humming and tingling.

Ben continues driving himself into me, but he's not deep enough to satisfy my heightened needs. When I swing my legs up and around his waist, I'm rewarded when his next thrust almost pins me to the bed. I'm thinking it can't get any better when the vibrations from the ring fan out through the rest of my body until I can even feel my nipples buzzing.

"Oooh, don't stop. Whatever you do, don't stop!"

The next morning was fine and clear, which was just as well, since the clothes we'd been wearing the day before were lost in space and time. Luckily, there are enough odds and ends for us to dress in without freezing our asses off—clothes left behind or forgotten by people over the years.

"I'll have to remember to pack some spare clothes if this becomes a habit," I say, fighting to do up the pair of jeans Ben has handed me. They're more than snug—they're intimate, and I suspect their previous owner was a twelve-year-old boy or a supermodel.

“I don’t know, I quite like them,” says Ben, running his thumbnail up the straining zipper and causing all sorts of reactions from my clit.

Ben’s truck is still sitting where we’d abandoned it the day before, although it’s now under a ridiculously tall pile of snow. But we're not complaining—we're pleased to see it's out there at all and not stuck with the Nyphrazi like our clothes.

By the time we’ve dug it free, including clearing some snow out of the cab itself, it’s late afternoon. I'd had to stop because the jeans rubbing against my still-swollen clit had me climaxing all over the place.

It's dark when we arrive at my folks' place—well, as dark as it can be with every light in the place blazing. Visible from space if someone cared to look.

“See you at work tomorrow,” I say before planting a kiss on Ben's lips.

“Later.”

I’m in the mudroom ditching my borrowed size ten boots when the door to the living room is wrenched open.

“Where the hell have you been?” says my dad, his face an interesting mix of anger and relief.

“At the cabin with Ben, my, ah, friend from work.” I still haven’t let on to my parents how advanced our relationship is.

“You said you were going for the day,” says my mom, coming to peer around my dad, her eyes brimming with tears.

Crap. How much time have I lost? I can’t ask and so I hope to hell I’ll be able to fudge my way through it.

"Uh, the weather closed in. We were stuck. My phone doesn’t work up there." Out of excuses, I trail off.

“We were so worried,” says my mom, pushing her way past my dad so she can hug me and bursting into tears in the process.

I’m closing my bedroom door when I hear my dad on the phone to the Sheriff’s office telling them I’ve turned up. They'd reported me missing? Talk about an overreaction. However, a quick glance at my bedside clock makes me realize why they'd been so worried.

“Four days!” I peer at the digital readout and squint. Yep, four days. “Hell, I hope I’ve still got a job.”

No wonder my folks made no mention of my wearing someone else's clothes. Nor had they noticed I was walking like someone who’d just spent days on a horse. It was to be expected after my having been missing for four days.

Searching through the pockets of my backpack, I located my phone. It's close to dying, so I plug it into the charger before calling Ben. He picks up after one ring.

“Four days,” I hiss, although I want to scream.

“Huh?” says Ben, letting me know he’s still under the

impression we've been zapped home the same day as in the past.

"Those bastards sent us back to a different time. We've lost four days. My parents were freaking when I walked in under my own steam rather than being rolled in on a gurney."

"Crap," says Ben, once the impact of this development makes itself known to him.

"I just hope I've still got a job!" I say, thumping myself down on my bed.

"You and me both, sweetheart."

I wake early the following morning, disoriented, as though suffering from jet lag, with my body desperate to settle into a new time period. Which isn't that far from the truth. Damn Aurum for stealing four days from my life.

I like it a lot more when I'm gifted the days. Which has me wondering about another gift. Interesting. I'm still spread wide, something that has me plucking my clit to see if I'd imagined how epic it had been with Ben.

I hadn't, with my body firing in response to this small action. I was settling into a rhythm when Aurum hissed, "Not until I say so," inside my head.

A second later and the mantle is snapping like a gold-plated rat-trap. I was mid-pluck when it happened and came close to losing my fingers. Damn it, it would appear my sex is once again off limits to all but Aurum.

However, an experimental touch proves this isn't altogether true. Since I was tugging on my clit when the mantle snapped shut, that part wasn't covered—it's now exposed, sitting in the center of the gold like a grape on a platter. The mantle formed

around what I was doing, leaving my clit accessible while sealing everything else.

Further investigation tells me the mantle hasn't closed in other areas, which is a relief. I hadn't been looking forward to waddling around the cafeteria.

On getting dressed, it doesn't take long to realize that a skirt will be my best option. With my clit sticking out, wearing jeans is too stimulating, with the bottom of the zipper working hard against my pearl. Poor thing would be rubbed raw by the end of the day.

After a decent amount of rummaging, I found my old ice hockey Jill strap. I'm then relieved when I get it sitting in such a way as to protect me.

Despite my daybreak fiddling, I still arrive at work early, hoping for Glory's mercy and, with luck, keeping my job. I've still got too much credit card debt to tell her to shove it if she doesn't like it.

"Where in blue blazes have you been?" Glory punctuates this demand by burying a cleaver in the lump of meat lying on the chopping board in front of her.

Not the most auspicious start to negotiations, but I have to at least try.

"I was out of town on Sunday with Ben for the day, but we got snowed in. I couldn't call because there wasn't a signal."

I assume a meek stance but have to resort to wringing my hands and squeezing out a few tears before she relents.

"Could happen to anyone," she says, her tone begrudging.

After thanking her to the point of groveling and perhaps too much, I swing around to go put my bag in my locker. I'm

stopped in my tracks when she mutters, "But I'll expect you to work doubles to make up the time."

I nod my acknowledgement of this before leaving the room. Phew, that's a relief; I only hope Ben's gotten away with it, too.

Back in the kitchen with an apron on and hair tied back, I revise my position on how lightly I've gotten off. Rather than continue her icy treatment of me, Glory is now demanding a blow-by-blow account of what Ben and I did to pass the time.

I don't think she buys how many games of cards I said we played. But I must be convincing enough that she doesn't feel she can call me on it. My relief when the dining room fills with miners is palpable. Anything to divert her attention away from my sex life.

I see Ben at lunchtime but can't speak to him because Glory is working me hard. She's determined that I make up for my absence for the best part of a week. Anyone would think it had been she who'd covered for me rather than the rest of the crew.

I clock off sixteen hours later. I'm shattered, and the thought of having to keep this up for another three days has me shrinking into myself. But when I see the note under my windshield wiper, I can't help the lift in my spirits, and when I get a strong enough signal, I call Ben.

"How goes it, Goldie Box?" says Ben, before I can speak.

"Hah! Hilarious." I try to keep my voice stern, but I too have a laugh at my own expense. Although he's not laughing when I tell him of the latest development.

"We can have another go at getting rid of it if you like," says Ben, annoyance clear in his tone.

"Just so long as it doesn't involve an acetylene torch!"

"Would I do that to you?" Ben doesn't give me time to answer before suggesting Sunday, the first day that either of us will see daylight.

"Yeah, but let's give the cabin a miss. I don't think I could keep up these double shifts if we get trapped in another time warp."

4

Driving out the front gates of my folks' place, I turn to Ben. "So where are we going?"

"My room at the hostel is out, so I'm using a friend's place while he's out of town."

It feels good when we hit the main road and head away from the cabin. I'm too shattered to keep working all hours. My relief is short-lived when I see how primitive the shack is, with the place looking like a powerful gust of wind would flatten it. If anything, the outhouse looks to be in even worse shape. With luck, Ben will be able to remove the gold without my having to use the facilities.

Fortunately, the inside of the place isn't as bad as I'd feared, although it's freezing cold and smells damp. In our favor is that there's a decent pile of wood next to the fire, and Ben soon has it roaring.

And because the cabin is so small, the temperature rises apace. The cabin becomes so stifling that when I strip so Ben can get to work, I'm not uncomfortable at all.

"Might be best if you lie on the table," says Ben, before throwing a threadbare blanket over its scarred wooden surface.

"I hope that's thick enough to save my ass from splinters," I bitch, while easing my way up onto the rickety structure.

Once I'm in place, I freeze, scared that if I move, the whole thing will collapse in a heap on the floor with me sprawled on top of it.

"Right then, if you'll lie there, I'll remove this for you in a jiffy."

Ben's hokey bedside manner does nothing to ease my fears. Not when I see him pull a couple of heavy-duty, laboratory-style glass bottles out of the cooler he'd retrieved from the back of his truck. I don't need a science degree to know the sticker with its symbol of a half-eaten hand means the contents are corrosive in a big way. When a small eyedropper follows, I'm hit with a wave of nerves.

"What if you spill some? You could wipe me out!"

"If I'm right, one drop will be enough."

I'm still looking at him with a healthy dose of skepticism when he removes the glass stopper from the larger bottle. Angling it over, he's able to put the dropper in far enough to draw up a good amount of the liquid. With that complete, he squeezed it into a mason jar that he'd found in one of the cupboards. He repeats the process with the second bottle but adds less of whatever that is.

I'm expecting him to dump a dropper-full of this mixture straight onto my golden covering, with my girly bits quivering in dread. They're relieved when he instead grabs a bag of cotton swabs and pulls one out.

"I was getting worried there for a moment."

"I'm thinking that if the gold can materialize out of thin air, it can disappear the same way if we attack it with some aqua regia."

"Aqua what?"

"Royal water," says Ben. "It's a mixture of acids that dissolves gold. If this stuff is actual gold, even magical gold, it should eat right through it."

He dips the cotton swab into his solution and is about to apply it to the mantle when I hold my hand up to stop him.

"What if the gold ring disappears, too?"

"Damn, I hadn't thought about that." Ben puts the swab back into the jar and carries the lot over to the slab of wood that's doing duty as a kitchen counter.

"What's your preference?" he says, back at the table. "Slow or fast?"

"Fast. Slow would be too dangerous." At his look of inquiry, I held up my hand to show him my bruised fingers.

Rather than putting him off, he gives me a wicked grin. "Like sexy Russian roulette? Okay, I'm in. Well, I soon will be." And true to his word, he is. All the way.

It takes longer than expected for the pair of us to get the thought of losing the G-ring, with its fabulous vibrations, out of our systems. There's no sign of Aurum. Nor does the mantle snap shut on us to the point where we relax enough to enjoy a slow and steady session against the kitchen counter.

It's getting dark when I inch my way back onto the table. My legs are still wobbling from the last orgasm, and my bits are as battered and bruised as my fingers. But I don't regret any of it for a second.

After dragging his clothes back on, Ben retrieves the jar from the counter, and then swipes the swab across the gold, right above my labia. For a second nothing happens, but then I hear loud fizzing. This is followed by Aurum shrieking inside my head. He does not sound happy.

“Oh, crap!”

“What!” says Ben, yanking the cotton swab away. “Is that hurting?”

"No, I can't feel a thing, but I can hear Aurum screaming."

“The gold’s still there, though. Let me try again.”

Ben pushes my legs apart and dabs more of the mixture on the gold. When I hear even louder fizzing, alarm floods me, although this is eclipsed by Aurum’s howling. Moments later, and every bit of the gold evaporates, leaving me feeling more vulnerable than usual.

"Can you check if everything is okay? Something doesn't feel right."

After stowing the last of his bottles in the chiller, Ben is soon back next to the table, leaning forward and checking me out. His examination is thorough, with his head torch as bright as any operating theater.

“That’s weird.” Ben’s tone doesn’t fill me with confidence.

“What is?” I ask, pushing myself up onto my elbows to see if I can spot what he’s on about. I do, and I have to agree with him. Wherever the gold had been, my skin still shimmers. Even though the metal that surrounded my clit is gone, it remains swollen, sticking out.

This, combined with a lack of pubic hair, has me looking more adult movie star than ever. It’s something I’m not happy about. What if I don’t return to normal?

However, it doesn't appear to bother Ben, who whoops and then bends over to taste me. This has me shuddering so hard

that the table bucks underneath me, and Ben scoops me up before its legs fail.

"Are you okay?" says Ben, holding me tight.

"I don't know. No," I stutter out.

Even though Ben is no longer touching my sex, being pressed against him is doing strange things to me. Everywhere the gold had been is supersensitive, and even my own skin rubbing against itself is more than I can bear.

But the pleasure soon becomes pain, and it's not long before it's as though I'm on fire. I'm unable to stop myself from whimpering, causing Ben's face to crease with concern.

"We need to get you to a hospital," he says, while putting me down on the battered and bruised couch. I fit right in because that's how I feel, too.

"I can't go to a hospital like this," I say, waving my hand toward my crotch. "Vyran will know what to do."

"He's the wooden guy, right?" At my nod of confirmation, Ben carried on. "Can you get in touch with him?"

"I've done it before. I can do it again."

"Well, what are you waiting for?"

I don't need any more prompting with the burning between my legs escalating. I'm on fire and not in a good way.

"Vyran. Come to me!"

It's not so much a polite request as a screeched summons, and a direct result of the pain I'm in. Thankfully, it works.

Vyran glances at me before turning his attention to Ben.

"What have you done to her?" Vyran's dark eyebrows were drawn together in a frightening scowl. However, there's genuine fear in the God of the Wood's voice, not just anger.

Ben is still struggling for a response when I interrupt their standoff.

"Not him. Aurum."

Vyran goes ballistic. I don't understand what he says, but I get the idea. He bends down and scoops me up off the couch, and I'm unable to stop my hiss of pain.

"Sorry. The quicker we get you to Marlo, the better."

"Marlo?" says Ben, unsure who this is because I'd kinda glossed over the God of Iron's involvement in my adventures. Technically, he hasn't fucked me. Yet.

"Our healer," says Vyran.

There's a buzzing in my head a moment later, and the world blurs around us. The cold, damp air of the shack disappears, replaced by warmth and the earthy smell of Vyran's chamber. My stomach lurches as reality settles, and he lays me on the pile of furs that sits in the middle of his bed. "Where's Ben?"

"I'm not bringing your lover here!"

Vyran is the epitome of male outrage, and if I weren't experiencing stinging and burning between my legs, I might be tempted to laugh.

Leaving me on his bed, Vyran disappears through the skins that cover the archway that leads to the rest of the cave system. No sooner had the pelts dropped back into place than I heard him bellowing for Marlo to present himself.

Again, the pain ruins my enjoyment of his actions. What—does Vyran think those skins are soundproof? I continue to hear him yelling for Marlo, with the sound getting fainter the farther away he gets. When silence descends, it rids me of any distractions, and all my focus goes on the pain.

Maybe some of that stuff Ben daubed on me spilled after all, though this seems unlikely since he'd been super careful and used a cotton swab. I'm hurting so much that he might as well have dumped the contents of both bottles right over me.

That's how it feels, with the burning sensation now

spreading over my torso before scorching its way up and over my breasts. It's as though my body is being swarmed by fire ants.

I'm alternating between panting and whimpering before Vyran returns with Marlo. I've never been so glad to see the God of Iron and that magic tongue of his. Unfortunately, he's followed by Aurum, the narcissistic fucker. I'd rearrange that fettyr of his if I wasn't in so much pain.

It's only after Marlo sweeps his tongue over my breasts, soothing them, that I look more closely at Aurum. He looks to be in worse shape than I am, his flawless golden skin now tarnished and pitted like corroded metal. Dark patches spread across his torso as if the damage to the gold mantle he'd lumbered me with has somehow transferred to his divine form.

Not looking so pretty now, is he?

"What the hell did you do to me?" he spat out with enough venom that saliva spotted my face.

Before I can respond, Vyran answers on my behalf. "It wasn't Jasmine. But mark you well, you'll pay for harming her. Praedytus will see to that."

"If it hadn't been her, then who was it? Look at me!" he gestured to his damaged body, his eyes full of pain. Not physical pain, by the looks of things, but pain from the damage to his ego. It would appear his stage show will be canceled for the foreseeable future.

"Stop bitching and help me here," says Marlo, looking up from running his tongue over my torso. "This is your fault. You can help fix it!"

Even in the instant Marlo lifts his head, I can feel the burning spike again.

It's not until Aurum, Marlo, and Vyran are all working

away that the burning sensation subsides. While Marlo is their healer, it would appear all the gods carry the same healing enzyme in their saliva to some degree. Their combined efforts are enough to have me go from writhing in agony to writhing in ecstasy in under ten minutes.

5

Vyran is the first to pick up on the change in me. This results in his going from licking away the pain in my breast to tweaking and teasing the nipple with that prehensile and wicked tongue of his.

Aurum, deducing the change in his brother, works away on my other nipple with equal skill, no doubt hoping to surpass Vyran in the pleasure stakes. Desperate to increase the sensations, I don't know which one to lean into first, eager for both of them to work their magic.

Marlo, having finished with my torso, runs his powerful tongue across the top of my mons, where Ben had first applied the acid to the gold coating. It's as though a cooling balm has been spread there, and I can't help a heartfelt sigh from escaping.

"A little help, brothers," says Marlo.

I'm not sure what he means by this, but Aurum and Vyran respond. Their fingers swoop into my cleft from either side so

they can spread me wide, allowing Marlo to slide his healing tongue everywhere I still hurt.

Any residual pain vanishes in seconds, my body opening to him and wanting his tongue to go deeper. When he flips my legs over his shoulders, he's able to plunge it into me as deep as any cock, setting the gold ring vibrating in the process. But he pulls that superb tongue of his out again, leaving me whimpering in longing. I want it back, even though all traces of pain are gone.

"Aurum," says Marlo, smacking the God of Gold on the back of his head and causing his teeth to graze my erect nipple, "get rid of it."

"You bastard," says Vyran, taking his mouth away from my nipple so he can smack Aurum around the back of the head, too. "You know the rules."

"What?" I'm unable to be any more coherent than this as I'm still buzzing from all the tongue action. "No, not the ring," I gasp out when I realize what they're talking about. But it's as though I haven't spoken for all the notice they take of me.

"Fine," says Aurum, his tone saying otherwise, as he slides off the bed. He waits while Marlo moves and then takes the God of Iron's place between my thighs. I'm expecting more sucking and slurping, but instead Aurum spreads me wide and then drives his golden length deep inside of me without preamble.

Because of the thinness of his gold fettyr, he feels much more like a human cock than his brothers do. Then the gold ring that surrounds my G-spot vibrates more wildly than it ever has before. At first, I thought he must have some nodules on his fettyr for the sole purpose of stimulating the ring, but when he withdraws his cock, it's smooth as glass.

He's shoved to the side by Vyran, who slips two of his

fingers deep inside me and has a good grope around before grunting in satisfaction. Not that he removes his fingers. Rather, he leaves them where they are, massaging my G-spot. I can tell the gold ring is gone by the lack of vibration.

"Go!" Vyran barked this command at Aurum before turning to Marlo. "I owe you, brother. Thank you."

With the slightest nod, the healer followed Aurum's strutting form.

The moment we're alone, the atmosphere in the chamber shifts. The urgency of healing me is gone, replaced by something more intimate, more about us.

"Now, where were we?" says Vyran, pulling his fingers clear only to plunge them back in again the second the skins over the archway stop flapping.

"I've missed you," I gasp between his fingers, sliding in and out of me. And I have. While I love having sex with Ben, my bond with Vyran is special.

"And I you," says Vyran, sliding his muscled body up next to mine while continuing to stroke me. "What would you like?"

"I'd like to have that gold ring back in place," I griped.

"Fun for you, but dangerous for us. I promise I'll make it up to you tenfold."

His eyes darken with passion, and I soon forget about the loss of the ring, instead thinking about what could be ten times better. This has my sex throbbing with eagerness and my imagination going loopy on me. I'm not sure some of my wilder fantasies are even possible, but never say never when you're dealing with someone like Vyran.

I'm still working on my list of finalists when Vyran ruins my rosy glow.

"I cannot risk Nysa, though. Praedytus has forbidden it

until... until the right time. When my father speaks, his word is law."

Father? I'm not sure I'm keen on his discussing our sex life with some crusty old dude! Talk about creepy. However, with his piece said, he drags his fingers free and runs them up and over my clit in a move that has my hips arching of their own volition. Father? What father?

"But I have an idea," says Vyran, before getting to his feet and leaning over to take my hand.

It's only once we're outside and a good way down the path that leads to the woods below the caves that I speak up.

"Ah, where are we going?" I hope it's nowhere too public because I'm wearing less than Vyran with that leather fettyr of his.

"Shhhh," he says over his shoulder.

Annoyed at being shushed, I stop in my tracks and yank my hand free of his. I'm about to give him a blast, but quick as lightning, he's next to me and slaps his hand over my mouth.

I've already gotten a good amount of palm between my teeth when he whispers in my ear.

"We are not alone."

After dropping this bombshell, he takes his hand away from my mouth and pulls me just off the path before stopping dead. Fast enough for me to bump into him. I'm about to ask him why we aren't making a dash for the trees when I hear someone stomping our way. I shift positions so that I'm behind him because there's no way in hell I want some stranger checking me out.

"Remain still and silent until I say it's safe," Vyran whispered over his shoulder.

I'm puzzling over this crazy instruction when, a moment

later, four men clomp out of the trees and up the path. Besides being armed to the teeth, they're also sporting fluoro orange vests, labeling them as hunters. They're also the first men I've seen in the Nyphrazi realm who are wearing clothes. I have never felt so naked, in both senses of the word, in my entire life.

I plaster myself against Vyran's back, hoping to hide as much of me as possible. If I can get propositioned in my ugly work clothes, God only knows what it'll be like when I'm in the buff. Even Vyran might be pushed to fight off four armed men.

However, my fears dissipate when, despite walking straight at us, they don't react to our presence at all. Instead, they trudge their way up to where we are and straight on past us in single file. Not one of them looks in our direction, even though we're within touching distance.

It's as though Vyran and I are invisible, yet I can see the four men as clearly as I can see my God of the Woods. But there's no missing the muscles in his back twitching as he fights to keep himself still.

Relaxing a little, I peel away from his back, and my gaze drops to his perfect ass. It's like my hands have a life of their own, and I'm soon exploring it, though he stiffens when I do. When I've got a hand splayed across each flawless cheek, I'm unable to stop squeezing them and breathing out a small moan of satisfaction.

It isn't loud, but it's enough to have four guns trained on us, and it doesn't take Vyran squeezing my leg hard to know I have to remain motionless. I doubt I could move, even if I tried.

"Do you see anything?" says one of the hunters, staring straight through us at the trees behind.

“Nothing,” says another, after also staring hard in our direction.

It's not until they disappear and we can no longer hear them crashing around that I risk a deep breath. I don’t move until Vyran relaxes his stance and unclasps my death grip on his ass.

"How come they couldn't see us?" I keep my tone low, just in case.

Vyran turns to look at me, his puzzlement clear. "Who?"

"The hunters." I know my own expression is now matching his.

"You could see them?"

"Well, yeah."

Vyran's expression flips from puzzlement to worry in an instant, and I can't say it fills me with confidence.

"What?" I'm unable to keep my own mounting worry from coloring this one word.

"Ah, nothing." Vyran shakes his head as though to clear his thoughts. "It's just... as a mortal, you shouldn't be able to see through to your realm from here. That you can..." He trails off, frowning. "It's unusual, that's all."

I'd question him further, but he's already taken my hand and is urging me back onto the path. Once there, he storms off at a pace that has me trotting to keep up and bemoaning the fact that I'm not wearing a bra, let alone a sports bra.

We don’t stay on the path for long, with Vyran taking a sharp right-angle into the woods and dragging me right along with him. What at first looks impenetrable soon changes. With the merest wave of his hand, the trees pulled back, allowing us to walk between them. They don’t stay that way for long, and I can hear them swishing back into place behind us.

We hadn’t gone far when we came across a tree that was

ailing. I'm no green thumb, but even I can tell when something's half-dead. Vyran places his hand on the bark and begins a series of clicks and whistles—his tree-speech that I remember from my first ever visit to the Nyphrazi realm.

The conversation is brief but intense, and I can almost feel the tree's gratitude in the way its leaves rustle with no wind. By the time we pass, the tree is bursting with fresh growth, and the scars that had marred its trunk have all but disappeared.

Vyran repeats this process a couple more times with other trees and plants before he stops at a solid cliff face that blocks his way. Dropping my hand, he placed both his palms flat against the stone's smooth surface. I feel the vibration through the ground as he begins his deep communication—not just clicks and whistles this time, but a low humming that seems to resonate through the rock itself.

The stone responds with a groan that I feel in my bones before it splits with a loud crack. It's loud enough that my heart has missed a couple of beats. It's like the trees all over again, but much more impressive.

"Come," says Vyran, grabbing my hand. "It won't stay open long."

Nothing puts a spring in your step quite like the possibility of being crushed by several tons of rock.

"Go, go, go!" I urge him forward and follow right behind so that we move as one. When I hear the rock rumbling behind me, I press myself against him even harder while yelling, "Move it!"

It's only after we arrive in daylight on the other side that I'm able to relax enough to realize what a stupid maneuver it was. We weren't all gods. This results in me punching Vyran in the chest. Hard.

I don't know who's more surprised when he staggers back, his hand straying to his chest to rub it.

"That's unusual," says Vyran, still massaging his chest.

"What is?" I held my hand up to stop his reply. "And if you say nothing, I'll thump you again."

"It's just that..." His response stumbles to a halt, forcing me to wave my hand in the air to urge him on.

"You're stronger than I'd have expected by now," he says, and I don't know whether to be worried about the words themselves or the wonder in his voice. "Things are as foretold, but..."

I go to ask him to elaborate, but he's already moving between the stone pillars we'd faced when we'd escaped the Rock of Doom. Rather than risk being lost, I hurry to follow him into what turns out to be a maze.

We zigzagged for ages before breaking into the open. The outer edge of the space we're standing in is ringed by more of those damned pillars, though in this context they look more like Grecian columns. But it's the rock pool in the center of the space that takes my breath away.

It's at least thirty feet across, and while shallow at the edges, the bottom drops away after that. The deeper the pool gets, the darker the color of the water, until in the middle it's a startling sapphire blue.

Even though it's a warm day, there's steam curling off its surface, showing it's hot enough to cook in. I'm therefore surprised to see Vyran walk into it until the water is up to his chest. Once there, his face was a picture of ecstasy. A moment later, he shudders.

"Oh, by the gods, that is good. Come join me."

6

I walked to the edge of the pool where the ripples caused by Vyran sluiced over the edge. The blue of the water is spellbinding and enticing.

"How hot is it?"

"Very," he grits out before another tremor wracks his body, "but worth it."

I dip my toes in to check if what's boiling for a god isn't fatal for a mere human. No sooner had my foot touched the water than it's as though my blood had been replaced with Champagne.

The water is indeed hot, just as Vyran said, but it's not scalding, and so I inch my way in. The deeper I go, the more my body fizzes, and I need no further encouragement to immerse myself.

"God, this is amazing."

And it is. Every time I move, it feels as though I'm being massaged by zillions of tiny bubbles, both inside and out. I'm

unable to stop a sigh as I give in to the pleasure of having them kneading and stroking my body.

Vyran moves through the water to my side and after the merest touch from him, the bubbles speed up. Now they're zooming in to focus on erogenous zones I didn't even know I had. My whole body is soon humming with pleasure.

My breasts feel as though a multitude of small mouths are suckling them, with my nipples getting extra special attention. Stabs of desire ripple out from them and down to my buzzing sex.

"Float on your back for me," says Vyran, his voice thick with pleasure, letting me know he's experiencing the same sensations as I am.

I glide onto my back and surrender to the bubbly goodness that engulfs me and, when one of Vyran's hands supports me, I relax. I'm rewarded for my trust. With his free hand, he nudged my legs apart before splashing water over my clit until the effervescence was eating away at me, fizzing me ever closer to orgasm.

I'm hovering on the edge of sensual oblivion when Vyran's supporting hand drops away, but it's soon replaced by smooth rock when he pushes me into the shallows. When he moves from my side, there's a sense of loss, but this is replaced by anticipation when he slides between my legs.

For a moment, nothing happens, so I lift my head to see what he's doing. This means that not only do I feel him run his tongue through my slit, but I get to watch it, too. The combination is overwhelming. I'm shuddering in response when I see him take a mouthful of water and squirt this straight onto my exposed clit, courtesy of Aurum and that blasted mantle of his.

I'm screaming my release when I'm surprised to hear Vyran join me. His cock is nowhere near me, so how the hell could that happen? The orgasm is still ripping through me when the air fills with steam. A second later and I lay high and dry on the hard rock, with there being no water left to support me. There's not a single drop in the pool, although it's so deep that I can't see the bottom.

Vyran is also nowhere to be seen.

I called his name until my throat was raw.

After it sinks in that I'm on my own in the middle of God knows where, I freak out. Well, who wouldn't? I'm alone, naked and lost, and with all the water having evaporated, I'm as thirsty as hell. Panic wells up, and I have to take a lot of calming breaths to keep it at bay.

"Come on, stupid, don't lose it now."

My pep talks to myself are always blunt.

Because of my constant muttering, I don't hear the voices until they're quite close. Torn between salvation and preservation, I dart behind the nearest column until I can check things out. I'm glad I had when I spotted two men I've never seen before entering the space around the pool.

Rather than being naked like the gods, or wearing fluoro like the hunters, these men are dressed in baggy leather pants. These are paired with a wraparound-style top made of the same tanned hide.

They stagger to a halt after a few steps, and their horror becomes clear, even though I can't understand a word they're saying.

I'm still tossing up whether to appeal to them for help when they disappear. Not through the columns, but in a puff of steam. I leave it a moment before I go out to investigate, but the only signs they'd even been there are an empty bowl and a

lone sandal. The bowl would show they were here to collect water, so I hope someone will come looking for them.

People do, but with the same result, to the point I'm facing a reasonable pile of mismatched sandals and bowls.

I jump in front of the next pair before they can step into the open space, hoping to stop them from being vaporized, or whatever the hell is happening. I'm over being naked by now but figure I must look scary because they high-tail it out of there, taking the bowl and their sandals with them.

I don't have to wait long for someone else to come by. But at least this time I know them.

"Axel! Am I glad to see you."

Axel, God of Nickel, doesn't look pleased to see me at all.

"Jasmine. What are you doing here?"

I chatter away about everything that had led me up to this stage, but am conscious of his gaze veering to the pool. When I get to the point about Vyran and me being in there together, he puts a finger on my lips to stop me. This is okay with me because I didn't fancy going into details.

"Where is Vyran now?"

"Gone," I wailed. "He disappeared in a cloud of steam when the water evaporated. I've called and called, but he's gone."

"Oh, brother. What have you done? Our father said the pool was out of bounds. You've ruined everything."

Despite my constant nagging, Axel won't spill. In fact, the more I ask, the quieter he becomes. It's only after a nerve-stretching silence that he speaks. "We need to see my father."

"Do we have to?"

"Well, no one else can fix this." He waved his hand in the general direction of the bottomless hole in the rock that had once been their beautiful pool.

I'm waiting for him to put his hand on my head and zap me

to wherever, but he stands there and says, “Father, come to me.”

When the father of the gods appears in a cloud of steam, I stagger back. The guy is hot! Not steamy hot, but if George Clooney went to the gym, hot! Hair streaked with silver never looked so good. Perhaps the most interesting development is that he’s naked, with no fettyr covering his remarkable length.

Nor does he appear to have need of one of these, with his cock pointing skyward without help.

“Father, this is Jasmine. Jasmine, this is Praedytus.”

"So, I met the one worth fighting over," he says, before stepping forward and rolling both my nipples between his dexterous fingers. "But I can see why. Her power, her response to my touch." His smile doesn't reach his eyes as he continues. "Yes, she's as I expected. The rites are very specific."

Something in his tone makes my skin crawl even as my body responds to his touch. The way he says "rites" is like he's speaking of something ancient and sacred—and with the potential to be lethal. " She's almost perfect."

I'd ask him to tell me more about my near perfection, but the minute his hands touched my body, my mind turned to mush. I couldn't think with my clit humming and my body curving, begging for release.

It’s something he gives me by touching my clit with a single finger. My body turns to liquid, and if I were any hotter, it would be me disappearing in a cloud of steam.

Then, as if he hadn't just reduced me to a quivering mess, he carried on as if nothing was amiss.

"Things must continue. Vyran was first, and Seolfer's failure only made her more resilient—as I predicted. While Ciprus purified her energy, Aurum tested her limits..." He

paused, his gaze growing distant. "Each trial strengthens the offering. Each god's power adds another layer."

The word "offering" sends a chill through me, though I can't say why. There's something ceremonial about the way he says it, like he's discussing a religious rite rather than my relationship with his sons.

"Axel, I believe you are next," he says, glancing at his son, before laying me on the ground so I can finish twitching. "You must be careful. More careful than Vyran has been."

"Where is Vyran?" I gasp out, fighting against the pleasure that's rolling over me in waves.

"Safe enough," says Praedytus before laughing.

Unfortunately, his wicked laugh is enough to give me pause.

"I'm wondering if it's worth it, to be honest," says Axel, looking down at me in a way that has me annoyed, him finding me wanting on some level.

"Oh, it's worth it," says Praedytus, followed by what I'd describe as a dirty grin. "Without question."

"Will you fix the Opelythe?" Axel says, looking at the empty basin with genuine worry.

Rather than speak, Praedytus glances in the pool's direction and, boom, it's once again full of that gorgeous dark sapphire water. I'm impressed.

"Axel, go now. I will escort Jasmine back to her home. Everything proceeds as decreed. Soon enough, her reason for living will be known by all." His voice carries a note of satisfaction that makes me uneasy. "The texts speak of one who can bridge the realms—not as a savior, but as a key."

"What do you mean, a key?" Axel and I said in unison.

"Nothing for you to worry about. Your part in this is to be

yourself—powerful and passionate," says the God of All Desire, ignoring his son.

Nor is the God of Nickel given a chance to ask again, with him disappearing in a puff of steam, leaving me alone with his father.

"Let's get you out of here," says Praedytus, holding his hand out to me to help me to my feet. I don't think twice about taking it.

I had expected him to deliver me back to the shack with Ben. At least this is where I'd asked him to send me a moment before he placed his hand on top of my head. It would seem he has other ideas.

There's nothing cave-like about the room I now find myself in, with the design being more Roman than anything else. Here the columns are smooth and look to be made of marble, as is the bench that Praedytus has just placed me on. I'd steeled myself for it being cold, but the stone is as warm as human skin and almost as soft.

"Where's Vyran?" I say, still worried about what has happened to him.

"You concern yourself far too much about that boy of mine. Relax," says Praedytus, cupping both my breasts and rolling the nipples in a way that tells of practice. A lot.

My traitorous body soon forgets about Vyran, and all I can focus on is the sensations now churning through my body. What the hell is it about this guy that his touch has me wet and ready in seconds?

I sink back onto the marble bench with little care for how my legs fall open. No, that's not true. I care. I spread them

wider, my core open to Praedytus's fiery gaze in hopes he'll soon fill me with that amazing cock of his.

"Alas, that is not possible," he says, as though reading my mind.

Or maybe it's that my eyes are locked onto his organ, to the point I can't focus on anything else.

When he claps his hands together twice, it breaks my concentration, and my gaze once again meets his. I'm wondering what he's clapped for when a young woman dressed in a chamois sheath runs in. After putting a small earthenware jug on the ground next to the bench, she wasted no time in leaving again.

Praedytus lowers himself to the ground between my thighs, and I slide myself down the length of the bench until my ass is hanging off the end. I don't care how desperate I look. I just want him to fuck me more than anything I've ever wanted. It's as though my life won't be complete without it.

I'm therefore disappointed when, rather than do so, he picks up the small jug and tips the contents of it over my mons before putting it back down. With his hands now free, Praedytus massages the oily substance into every crevice and fold, and I ready myself to take him. My body heats whatever it is, and the air is soon full of a sweet perfume.

"Ah, nectar and the taste of a woman," says Praedytus, as if to himself. He then bends forward, spreads me wide and feasts on me like I'm a ripe peach. He takes his time about it, too, and is thorough.

I'm thinking he's finished when he says, "You'll enjoy this," before plunging his tongue deep inside me in a poor imitation of his cock. Though I doubt his cock could twirl around like that!

My God, I thought his sons had cornered the market on

oral sex, but they're novices compared to this guy. The pleasure he's eliciting is borderline torture.

"What are you the god of?" I gasp out between the waves of desire washing over me, although never enough to let me come. He's a master at keeping me hovering on the edge.

"I'm the God of All Desire, the only one with the knowledge to prepare you to be pleasured, as ritual dictates." He pauses only long enough to give me a smile that doesn't come close to reaching his eyes. "Of all the gods, I am the most treacherous of all.

"Treacherous?"

"I'm addictive, whatever your preference," he says, before swiping his tongue across my protruding clit.

"But. What. Do. You. Do?" I gasp out in time with his tonguing me.

I can tell he's thinking about an answer when his tongue stills and he lifts his head. I raise myself enough to look at him, but rather than answer my question, he shrugs.

"Is this not enough?"

Without waiting for me to respond, he returns to his task, licking at my core until I'm opening myself up to him, my body begging for release.

"I'd better let you go before I ruin you for the others. Axel and Marlo still have a role to play in preparing you for the ultimate trial. Until next time," says Praedytus, before waving his hand over my body.

I'm no closer to understanding what the hell he'd meant by all of that when I bounce my arrival on the skanky couch in the hut belonging to Ben's friend. I'm looking around the cabin for him, my body screaming out for release, when I spot him out on the deck.

"Ben!" I yelled loud enough for him to hear me, and he's at my side in an instant.

I lie back and peel myself open for him, too far gone to be embarrassed by my wicked behavior.

"Fuck me, fuck me hard."

I'm frustrated when, rather than do my bidding, he sits back on his heels and stares down at my body with his gaze running up and down it several times. "What the hell happened to you?"

"What? What? Just fuck me." I'm whimpering with need because all the sensations left there by Praedytus are swirling around in my body, looking for release.

"You're glowing," says Ben, before reaching out to touch one of my nipples. He hisses as hard as I do.

"Holy fuck." He stands in a flash, coming close to falling over, but soon gains his balance and loses his clothes at the same speed.

I'm relieved to see he's hard because the need to have him buried deep inside me is overwhelming.

"Coffee table!" I grit out, and while he settles himself, I struggle to free myself from the depths of the couch. "Hold yourself ready for me, because I think if we touch before then, it'll all be over."

With my legs wide, to avoid touching him, I move forward until I'm right over the top of his rock-hard cock. I lower myself and, as soon as I'm on target, I slam myself down hard, taking every inch of him in the process. But it's still not enough, and I grind away, trying to take him ever deeper. Meanwhile, he draws hard on my nipples with his mouth and grips my ass as though to get us even closer.

But both of us are still hovering on the edge and looking around, hoping to find something, anything, that will help us

come. I'm crying in frustration when I hear Praedytus's voice inside my head. "I told you I was addictive."

That I then feel The God of All Desire's hot mouth suckling my clit is enough to have me coming so hard I see spots. Ben follows me over the precipice.

"Did you feel that?" he says when we're lying in a heap on the couch?

"Feel what?" I'm not sure I want to admit to him what I experienced.

"In the middle of all that, it was as if someone was sucking my balls."

I don't dare explain to him that this was courtesy of a George Clooney lookalike who's old enough to be all our fathers. I think it would ruin his buzz.

It's not until we're in the truck heading home that I ask Ben about something that's been niggling away at me. "So, what do you know about nickel?"

I try to be as nonchalant as I can, but he's not fooled for a second. His expression says he's worked out which god is next in line. "Um, atomic number 28, corrosion resistant, takes a high polish, can cause rashes. Magnetic at room temperature."

All I take in from this list of attributes are the rashes and magnetic bits. Damn, and here I was thinking Aurum had put me through hell and back. Now it would appear Axel won't be a breeze either.

EPILOGUE

Despite knowing it was only a matter of time before Axel claimed his time with me, I'd done my best to settle back into a routine. This had me attempting to get to work on time, going on regular dates with Ben—though none up to the cabin—and behaving as I should.

Even so, I couldn't shake the memory of being in the God of All Desire's presence when he healed me. While his touch had been gentle, underneath was something vast and hungry that made Aurum's vanity seem like a minor character flaw.

As time has passed, it's become easier to think I imagined everything and pretend it never happened. Like tonight, when I've pushed it all to the back of my mind to have a fun night with Ben.

While the shack is nowhere near as nice as the cabin, the improvements we've made over the past few months have made it at least bearable. Best of all was replacing the run-down couch with a double bed complete with a memory foam mattress.

"You okay?" says Ben, his chin coming to rest on my mons.

"Just thinking," I say, arching my hips and giving myself over to his ministrations. "About what comes next."

Ben nods. "I should imagine it's you," he says, before sucking on my clit and finger fucking me to prove his point. It hadn't always been this easy for me to climax, but my time with the gods has paid off.

I'm also sure Cuprum has taught Ben a thing or two when it comes to seduction, with her lessons still happening on a regular basis. I know I have no right to complain about his time with the Goddess of Copper, but this doesn't stop my eyes from turning green every time she abducts him.

However, until Axel claims me, I'm making the most of my time with Ben. And after the God of Nickel, I'll only have Marlo, the God of Iron, waiting for his chance to achieve Nysa with me. What happens after that is the stuff of dreams.

The only question now is when Axel will get his act together and come calling. This is the longest I've ever had to wait, and if not for Ben's company, I know I'd be going out of my mind by now.

GOD of NICKEL

1

Five months have passed since my last interaction with the gods, with no sign of Nickel, who is next in line to achieve Nysa with me. However, that's not what saddens me. It's that there's also been no sign of Vyran.

As happened in the past, all contact with him has been severed. However, this time I suspect it's as a result of his father rather than his brothers.

It doesn't matter that I've tried requesting Vyran's presence whenever I'm on my own, because it does no good. If I persevere, all that happens is I end up with a blinding headache that takes days to recover from.

When Ben found out I was trying to contact my God of the Woods, he looked so hurt that I put my search on hold. At least for now.

And yes, Ben and I are still dating, and he's even met my parents, who like him, although my mom did a double-take at his bright red hair. However, there's been no change in how we act with each other. The chief obstacle our relationship faces

these days is when and where we can screw each other's brains out.

Unfortunately, the shack is no longer an option after Ben's friend kicked over the propane heater in his sleep. The guy would have ended up crispy if it weren't for the smoke alarm Ben and I had installed.

So, with Ben living at the hostel and me at home, our moments are few and far between. I'd rather forget one athletic session in the cab of Ben's truck that had me coming close to doing the dirty with the stick shift knob.

We'd thought about heading back to the cabin in the hills, but the risk of disappearing for days on end in a weird Nyphrazi time warp was too great. Instead, we're avoiding going anywhere near the place.

Now, other than the occasional night in one of the local motels, we're having increasing difficulty in scratching each other's itches. It can't last, and neither can we.

Ben and I stand and stare, transfixed, at the properties for rent in the realtor's window. They range from straight-up hovels to palatial pads with all the bells and whistles, but not a lot in between.

"This won't be as easy as I thought," says Ben, peering at the photo of a cabin that's at the hovel end of the spectrum.

We continue looking at the cards in silence until this is broken by Ben. "The pain in the ass is that I already own the cabin in the hills."

"You do?" This is news to me because he'd always made out that it belonged to a family friend.

"Yeah," says Ben, looking sheepish. "Some girls get weird when they find out I'm not flat broke."

I don't know whether to be flattered that I've passed some test or annoyed to find out that I've been one of many females he's taken up there. On the upside, he's good in bed because of it, so I can't complain. There's also the minor point that I've been manhandled by four of the Gods of Nyphrazi now. With two, maybe three, while I've been seeing him.

I know it's only a matter of time before Axel, the God of Nickel, appears, but I'm making the most of his reticence in the meantime. Unlike his brothers, who were eager to try for Nysa, Axel doesn't appear to want to have anything to do with me.

The God of All Desire is the only one that Ben and I have interacted with since my last trip. Not that Ben realizes our amazing sex is sometimes due to the oldest god of all sticking his "tongue" in our affairs. I'd tell him, but I'm still coming to terms with it myself.

"What about this place?" says Ben, breaking in on my thoughts.

"I thought you wanted to rent." I sure as hell can't help him with a mortgage. While my credit card balances might be down to manageable levels, I won't stop throwing money at them until they're cleared. Even then, I want a decent stash of cash tucked away in the bank before I relax.

"I thought I did, but at that price I'd be crazy not to buy."

"If you can afford it, you go for it," I say, hoping to let him know that if he buys the place, he's doing so on his own. While the sex is out of this world, I'll be damned if I'll bankrupt myself for unfettered access.

Or was that unfettyred?

. . .

I looked around the parking lot again. “He said three o’clock, didn’t he?”

“Yeah, and he’s late,” says Ben, stating the obvious.

I move my weight from one leg to the other until I’m swaying on the spot, but at least it’s gotten my blood flowing again.

“Are you folks interested in The Metal Beast?” says a man, popping up next to us unannounced. Damned if I know how we missed him though, because once seen, there's no ignoring him. Not with that comb-over, those checked sports pants, and that butt-ugly orange blazer.

He'd still startled me, though, and I hadn't been able to stifle the small scream that escaped. However, it was one that soon turned into a snigger. I mean, who calls a boat The Metal Beast? While I’ve been going through this raft of emotions, Ben has confirmed that we are indeed who the realtor is looking for.

“Follow me,” he says, and we do. However, it's hard to keep up because he sets a breakneck pace across the parking lot before swerving onto a floating walkway without slowing. I keep waiting for him to take one of the walkways that branch off on either side at regular intervals.

But he keeps going until his only option other than swimming is to turn to the right. He takes the corner like a pro, and we follow.

“There she is, folks,” says Stan, according to the name embroidered on the pocket of his bright orange polyester jacket.

The Metal Beast occupies the second-to-last spot.

“Fuck me!” says Ben, after looking at the motor yacht. “Is she seaworthy?”

"Yes, indeed, the rust is superficial. Just needs a spruce up here and there."

"Spruce up?" I mutter under my breath to Ben. The photo we'd seen in the realtor's window had either been taken years earlier or had quite the run-in with Photoshop.

Seeing we aren't about to enthuse over the pile of crap, Stan nips down the floating pontoon that sits between The Beast and the luxury sloop at the very end.

It's not until all three of us are on the aft deck that he starts what is a well-rehearsed sales patter. The gist of this appears to be that The Metal Beast is bursting with potential.

Any potential makes itself scarce when we open the door to the main cabin—moving faster than the resident roach population. Never mind Roach Motels, we'll need condos to take care of this many of the little fuckers.

Stan points out The Beast has good bones, although these are hard to see under the sheer volume of crap that clutters every surface. There's even half-eaten takeout, which might explain the sheer number of roaches.

After yet another shudder of revulsion, I do my best to focus on anything but the scuttling of the current tenants. "What about storage?" I ask, assuming there isn't any given the easy-access system in use.

Stan assures me there's plenty and proves it by throwing open cupboard after cupboard, with all of them packed to the gunwales with even more crap. And roaches.

There doesn't appear to be any logic in how things have been stored either, with crumpled clothing sitting next to pots and pans and engine oil. I'm surprised there are any pots left in the cupboards, considering how many await washing in a teetering pile in the sink.

After asking if the yacht was seaworthy, Ben has been quiet, and we're back in the parking lot before he speaks again.

"And they want fifty grand for that pile of crap?" says Ben, his arms folded across his chest, his body square-on to Stan. Even from a couple of feet away, there's no missing the tic in his jaw.

Stan opens his mouth, and I think he's about to defend the quality of the vessel, but instead he says, "forty-eight," without preamble.

Ben repeats this figure, though his delivery is nowhere near as smooth as Stan's.

"I'm sure there's a deal to be done," says Stan.

Ben tips his head to the side as if to rid himself of the tension in his neck. "You better believe it, pal. But I'll need to see that tub out of the water before I part with so much as a dollar."

The catch in Stan's breathing turns into a coughing fit, and so I'm surprised by his answer when he gets his diaphragm under control. "I'm sure that can be arranged," he choked out, his voice strained.

He leaves us in the middle of the parking lot with promises that he'll be in touch. It's not until we're in the truck that Ben and I talk about the pros and cons of The Metal Beast.

"There is a lot of space," I say.

"True, but I reckon there's fuck-all chance of them wanting to stump up for a haul-out fee. And I'm not touching it without going over every inch of that hull."

"I guess that means you keep looking?"

"Yep," says Ben, with a slight drop of his shoulders.

. . .

We've checked out half-a-dozen other places without luck and are getting to the stage where Ben's coming to terms with staying at the hostel. Then, out of the blue, he gets a call from Stan—the orange jacket guy.

"It doesn't look as bad as I thought it would," says Ben, continuing to gawp at the hull that towers over us.

"Will you paint it while it's out of the water?"

"For sure," says Ben, poking the hull. That a large patch of paint and rust falls away as a result of his gentle prodding reinforces this decision.

We're wandering around underneath the boat examining it from all angles when Steve, a mechanic friend of Ben's, turned up. He gives The Beast a far more thorough check than we have, crawling over it inside and out before poking around in the diesel engine.

All the while, he's scribbling in a tatty notebook that he keeps putting down and losing. But after an hour, he declares that she's seaworthy. Just.

"He said the hull would have been worse if it hadn't been coated with a copper-nickel product," says Ben, looking at the very bottom of the boat. "That's why there are so few barnacles."

With Steve on his way with a dozen beers as payment, we don't have to wait long before Stan the realtor shows up, keen for a sale.

"So, folks," he says, rubbing his hands together, "do we have a deal?"

"Forty. Cash," says Ben, without preamble, with Stan cringing like a whipped puppy in response.

Cash? So much for me worrying I'd have to pitch in for a

mortgage. I hadn't realized Ben was loaded. At least compared to me.

"That's a lot less than the vendor is looking for," says Stan, no doubt thinking of his commission.

"There's too much that needs doing for me to pay the full asking price," says Ben, holding up several sheets of torn paper that list the fixes Steve had recommended.

Stan runs his finger down what looks to be a rather long list. "Ah, that," he says under his breath, although it's loud enough for both Ben and me to hear.

"What about full disclosure?" I say, remembering something I'd heard on one of those property shows.

Stan coughs hard rather than answer, with the silence after getting to the point of embarrassment before he says, "I'll put the offer to the vendor then, shall I?"

Like, what does he think Ben is going to say? No?

However, when it comes time to put pen to paper, Ben changes the purchase price on the contract to thirty-five thousand. That he eyeballs Stan when signing lets the realtor know Ben won't budge on the new price. Hadn't that property show also harped on about cash being king when it came to negotiating a killer deal?

In answer to Stan's unspoken question, Ben huffs out. "Your hiding the condition of the keel means I need to make sure I've got enough in the budget to cover any other dodgy crap."

Stan looks as though he's ready to argue. However, there's nothing forthcoming apart from resignation when he collects the paperwork off the hood of Ben's truck. That done, he

trundles off to a gaudy, sign-written sedan that's seen better days.

"Cheeky SOB," says Ben, as soon as the realtor is inside his moving billboard.

"Do you reckon there's enough in the pot to fix everything?"

"Yeah, not a problem. Steve said a couple of grand should sort the keel. Everything else I can fix myself."

It was just as well Stan was out of earshot, because that comment would have sparked a coronary, for sure.

2

We hear from Stan with a counteroffer of forty-five thousand, but Ben won't budge, telling the realtor he doesn't want The Metal Beast that much.

An hour later and Ben is the proud owner of a hunk of rusting boat for the bargain price of thirty-eight grand. Things moved even faster after that, with Ben taking possession in a matter of days.

"Hell, they wanted to get rid of this," says Ben, as we stand looking up at the boat that is still high and dry in the boatyard. "That they bailed as quickly as they did kind of has me worried."

After this less-than-self-assured admission from Captain Confident, we clamber up the ladder onto the aft deck, where Ben unlocks the cabin door with ceremony.

"After you," he says, standing to the side to allow me to enter first.

I walk to the small doorway but stagger to a halt after a couple of steps.

"Holy crap!"

Even from out here, I can see the cabin is still packed with the previous owner's belongings, and the moving roach circus that comes with them.

"What?" says Ben, turning to look inside. "Aww, crap."

A quick call confirmed our worst fears. The previous owners had left town the night the money cleared their bank account. They'd told Stan they were leaving a few belongings behind to help us get started.

It takes a full-sized dumpster and a team of exterminators before Ben can even think about moving his stuff in. But even after giving The Beast its first taste of disinfectant, it still has the aroma of long-forgotten takeout. We will discover the source of this soon enough.

If anything, the oven is more disgusting than the wet bath had been, with Ben resorting to cleaning that using a pressure washer. I doubt that will work with the science experiment that is the oven.

"I reckon you should buy a new one," I say, peering inside, my hand slapped over my mouth and nose. Every inch of the interior is caked in burned offerings, along with splatters of the softer variety.

"I'm with you," says Ben, slamming the door shut and trying to rip it out right then and there, using a mix of determination and sheer brute force. In the end, he had to get Steve, his mechanic buddy, back to help, with the stove stuck in place by years of grease and grime.

The mattress follows the oven into the dumpster because there's no way in hell Ben and I are going near it. Never mind a condom—the innerspring petri dish that had crowned the

master cabin would require us wearing hazmat suits to come anywhere close to having safe sex.

Our hard work soon paid off, and a month after taking possession, Ben and I were out on the water in The Metal Beast. We'd wanted to change the name to something less, well, lame, but had been told by anyone with an opinion that it was bad luck.

"I still can't believe we've got a week off," I say, twirling around and around in the captain's chair in the wheelhouse.

"You and me both," says Ben, spinning me ever faster until I have to put my feet against the wall of the cabin to stop him.

"So, where are we headed?" I say once my head stops spinning.

I assume Ben has a few ideas, given how much time he's spent flipping his way through the various charts the previous owner had left behind. I'd been worried that these looked to be out-of-date, but Ben had assured me they were only there as a back-up to the latest GPS unit he'd installed.

What is it about guys and gadgets? Not that I was anti all the gizmos Ben had bought for our trip. There were a few toys I couldn't wait to get my hands and other body parts on.

That night found us in a bay that came close to surrounding us, so narrow was the entrance. In our favor were the new depth gauge and an old chart, confirming that it was okay to proceed.

While the chart hadn't recorded the depth, there was a bright red X-marks-the-spot cross dead center of the bay. Deciding to go on this recommendation, we dropped anchor at this exact spot and settled in for the evening.

While Ben fires up the grill that sticks out over the back of the boat, I shoehorn myself into the compact galley. Stan's description, not mine. I'd call it tiny. There, I knocked together a salad and roasted some potatoes in their skins. It's not that I can't cook—it's more that it's the last thing I want to do when this is what I do all day, every day.

The other thing that feels small in the kitchen is all the pots and utensils. They're standard size but feel tiny when compared to the commercial counterparts I deal with during my working day.

With dinner over and the dishes left in the sink until morning, we retired to the master cabin to christen our new mattress. I can't help but laugh when, on entering the cabin, I see all the sex toys spread out on the bed as though ready for a catalog shoot.

"Nice lineup," I say, picking up a cock ring and spinning it around my finger before peeping through it at Ben. "You think you can fill this?"

It's all the challenge he needs, and he ditches his clothes in record time, with me not far behind him. I have to thank the Nyphrazi for one thing. At one time I'd have been self-conscious standing around naked, but not anymore.

These days, it's as natural as wearing clothes. Looking at Ben standing before me with a cock so hard I could bounce quarters off it, I'm ready to jump out of my skin.

"How do I put it on?" I say, retrieving the cock ring from the cabin floor where I'd dropped it in my haste to strip.

"Easy, it's magnetic," says Ben, taking it off me and showing me how the large ball that completes the ring pops away when he tugs at it.

"Huh, nifty."

I take the two pieces from his outstretched hand and clip the ring into place at the very base of his cock. It's a snug fit, proving he's more than capable of filling it.

"Your turn," says Ben, picking up a couple of bejeweled clips off the bed.

I can't help but suck in my breath when he snaps the first nipple clamp on. It hurts, but not so badly that I can't cope, and by the time he snaps the second one into place, I'm even liking it. When I look down and see the clips sparkling, I can't help but stand taller and stick my tits out for effect. It's something that has Ben's cock jumping for attention.

I don't see the sling until he unhooks it from the hatch above our heads.

"Spring mounted! Fancy."

It's the heat that wakes me. Damn, I must have left the oven on! I throw the covers back and stagger to my feet before stumbling my way across the master cabin and up the short flight of steps that lead to the saloon and galley.

"That's weird."

"What is?" Ben mumbled, still half asleep.

"I thought I'd left the oven on. It's so damned hot!"

I walk around the main cabin with my hands out in front of me, trying to find the source of the heat, but there isn't one. I repeat this in the master cabin with the same result.

"It's not just me, is it?" I say to Ben, who's now lying naked in the middle of the bed, having kicked all the covers on the floor and thus proving it's not me after all.

On a hunch, I go back up to the main cabin and out onto the aft deck. It's just as hot out here, maybe even hotter. That's

not the only strange thing. Leaning back through the doorway, I yell to Ben, "Hey lover, get your ass out here. You've gotta see this."

I'm thinking he must have gone back to sleep when he staggered out of the main cabin, rubbing his eyes to clear them of sleep.

Even though it's still the middle of the night, we can see our surroundings because of the unearthly glow coming from the milky water in the bay. If we can even call it that now—the entrance has disappeared.

The narrow gap we'd motored through earlier is gone, replaced by a towering cliff of what appears to be solid rock.

When the sky lightens, I revise my sense of what time it is. It's only a couple of minutes later before the sun is beaming down on us from overhead, letting me know we're no longer in Kansas.

Ben checks the instruments to see if he can pinpoint our location, but they're all dead. Even the old-fashioned compass is spinning out of control in a desperate search for true north.

"Do you think Cuprum is behind this?" I ask Ben, referring to the Goddess of Copper who energy-fucks him on a regular basis.

"Nope. Not a chance."

Turning to see why he's so sure, I'm greeted by him holding his cock. That it's not studded with copper says Cuprum isn't about to appear.

"Damn."

"What?" says Ben, coming to stand behind me and letting me know he's well on his way to being ready.

"If it's not you, then that means it's me," I say, allowing him to nudge me over to the hip-high side of the deck surround.

The height is such that my mons is pressed hard against it, and I'm more than okay with this.

"We'd better hurry then," he says, sliding his knee between my legs and cupping my breasts, making me aware I've still got the nipple clamps on.

Hell, I should have removed them, shouldn't I? Don't want my nipples falling off from lack of blood or anything like that. Bending over so I can lean my elbows on the deck surround, I know when the magnets in the clamps feel the pull of the steel boat. A moment later, my nipples clicked to the top edge of the hull, resulting in my sex being stuck up in the air and just asking for it.

"Yikes," I say, before pulling back to see what happens. The clamps release, but not without my nipples being given a good tug. Then, on the slightest movement from me, they snap back onto the top of the hull with a metallic ping.

In response to my sharp intake of breath, Ben stops sliding his fingers in and out of me only long enough to see what I'm talking about. His laugh is filthy. "Got you where I want you now."

And he does, and I squirm in delight at him entering me an inch at a time. Not that the action stays slow for long, and soon he's driving himself into me ever deeper, causing my nipples to be tugged on every time he slams himself home.

When an ethereal tongue licks my clit, I know we've got company. Ben's thrusts doubling in speed and intensity also let me know Praedytus is likely working away on him too.

My screams of pleasure echo around the bay, with them soon joined by Ben's roars when he finds his release.

3

We wake what feels like hours later in a big old dog pile on the aft deck. I think my ass might be sunburned. I'm not sure what's woken me until I hear a man's voice inside my head and know it's Axel.

"It is time."

Sheesh, he doesn't need to sound so thrilled about it! Damn, I could skip him and Marlo and go back to Vyran. But no, it's their stupid rules that they all have to try for Nysa to keep the balance. From what I've seen so far, it's stopping them squabbling like a bunch of five-year-olds. The only one of them whom it doesn't seem to bother is my God of the Woods.

I storm to my feet and look around and in so doing confirm that I hadn't imagined The Metal Beast floating in what is now a small lake. The only beach on offer is opposite the rock cliff, and it's here that I see Axel; standing with legs astride, on an immense black rock that sits to the right of the curve of pebbles that forms the beach itself.

“I'd better get this over with,” I say to Ben, who's now lying spread-eagle on his back.

He snorts before mumbling, “Have a good time,” as though I'm off to the movies with girlfriends rather than off to be fucked by the Nyphrazi God of Nickel.

What a strange world we live in.

“Cover up, or you'll burn your bits,” I warn him before stepping down onto the swim platform so I can test the temperature of the water.

I needn't have worried; it's tropical and no hardship to dive into. Even so, I surface shrieking a second or two later, with Ben landing in the water next to me, all ready to save me. His expression when he pops up is priceless. I'm relieved he's no longer wearing the cock ring, because he would have blown it to smithereens, for sure.

“What, what, what,” he stutters, but seems incapable of anything more.

“Float on your back. I'll be as quick as I can,” I grit out between the waves of pleasure that are engulfing me.

Swimming to shore while experiencing mini-orgasms is as hard as it sounds, and Axel has to help me out of the water when I get into the shallows.

His entire demeanor is one of reluctance. Unlike his brothers, Axel seems conflicted about this whole thing. There's something different about him.

“Hey, we don't need to do this if you don't want to,” I say, snatching my hand away and dropping to my knees without his support.

For the first time, I'm dealing with a god who doesn't seem eager to follow his father's script. Axel's hesitancy feels genuine, not like he's playing a role in some predetermined drama.

Instead of taking me up on my offer, he helped me to my feet and over to the large rock he'd been standing on earlier. The closer we get to it, the more my nipples are tugged on. I tried removing the clamps, but was unable to do so. They're stuck fast.

"Leave them for now," says Axel, sighing.

I've never felt so unwanted in all my life. "You know what? I've changed my mind."

For the first time, I'm dealing with a god who appears to want nothing to do with me. The others wanted the encounter, even when they had issues. Axel doesn't seem to want me here. "Screw this. I'm going back to the boat."

I reinforce this decision by stopping in my tracks. This is difficult given the pull of the rock on my nipples, resulting in my boobs looking like they're being supported by an invisible push-up bra.

Axel looks as though I've slapped him. Well, that's just tough. Let him feel rejected for a change. I turn and have even taken a couple of steps into the shallows when the water just offshore erupts in a mountain of bubbles and steam.

I'm not surprised when Praedytus blinks to life in the middle of this turbulence. His expression as he walks up the beach is one of thunder. This makes me relieved that, rather than looking at me, his ire is directed at his son.

"Axel!" roars Praedytus, with this single word conveying a wealth of meaning.

I've never heard such fury in his voice before. Whatever is happening here, it's not what he expected.

It's something that's confirmed when I turn to look at the God of Nickel. Whatever the problem is, I can see he's gotten the message loud and clear. None of this will change my mind

though, and I once again start walking toward the water, but I don't get far because Praedytus steps in my way.

He doesn't even need to touch me. Instead, he pokes his tongue out and wiggles it about, and I'll be damned if I can't feel it tickling my pearl.

"Forget it! Nothing you do will make me want to fuck him. You're wasting your time." But even as I say it, I know Praedytus won't give up without a fight. There's something about this encounter that seems more important to him than usual.

I try to stay resolute, but standing tall rather than like a toddler needing the bathroom is tricky given all the attention I'm receiving from that impressive tongue of his.

As if to prove a point, he steps closer to me, all the while keeping up with the tongue gymnastics. But I refuse to step back and so he takes another step, his rock-hard cock tapping against my stomach.

The result is instantaneous and overwhelming. There's not a single inch of my body that isn't an effervescent mess. It's the same as being in the water, but a hundred times stronger.

My legs collapse under me, and I'm soon sprawled on my back on the hot pebbles of the beach, moaning in need. I'm thinking the sensations can't get any stronger when Praedytus kneels down next to me and palms my sex.

My hips arch up off the beach, forcing pebbles to dig into my shoulder blades. But I don't care; I need more, more of everything.

At first, I think it's Praedytus who's picked me up off the beach, but when I opened my eyes, I could see that it's Axel. He doesn't look to be any more thrilled than earlier, but he's doing his father's bidding all the same. I think about struggling

against his grip, but what's the point. I may as well lie there and get it over with.

The heat of the large black rock soon brought me to my senses. What the hell does he want to do, cook me? I know the moment he releases the bejeweled clamps Ben had given me, because my nipples feel like they're on fire.

But this is nothing compared to the heat generated when Axel daisy-chains a pile of small, very magnetic pebbles around each nipple. They cling to each other, forcing my nipples up through the middle of their grip. That they're boiling hot adds to my responsiveness.

I'm still concentrating on these when Axel spreads the lips of my labia wide. A heartbeat later, and he slides more of those hot magnetic pebbles down each side of my clit. They hold together through my pearl, squeezing it hard in the process, leaving it swollen and plump. This is something that's confirmed when I raise my head to check.

He then flips me over onto my stomach, and the heat of the rock on my engorged nipples and clit is astonishing. Astonishing enough that I embrace it, plastering myself to the rock like a limpet. Not that I can move much anyway, as I'm being held fast to it by the magnets stuck all over me.

I don't know whether to be aroused or horrified when Praedytus takes a seat on a small boulder nearby and settles himself in to watch. That his cock is right in my line of sight adds to the sense of need I'm experiencing.

For someone who's reluctant to fuck me, Axel is huge when he nudges his way inside. Maybe his size is due to the nickel fettyr he's wearing. I hope I'm not allergic to the stuff after all, because it would take a lot of antihistamines to offset what's spreading me wide.

He's partway inside when Praedytus coughs, stopping

Axel's forward motion. The father of the gods then drops five round pebbles from one hand to the other. When they click together with a magnetic snap, the God of All Desire lifts an eyebrow in question.

I hear Axel sigh in acknowledgment before he holds his hand out to his father. As if in single file, the pebbles fly before clicking together again in the God of Nickel's grasp.

After spreading my ass cheeks wide, Axel feeds them inside me one at a time, with my body almost gobbling them up in its eagerness to feel their heat. He then wastes no time before driving himself deep inside me in a single, slow plunge. It's amazing, as are all the little magnets doing their best to click tight to Axel's fettyred cock through the barrier of my flesh. It's a move that proves beyond doubt his fettyr is magnetic, too.

What follows is a sensory overload. Not only is Axel pumping in and out of me amazing, so is the push and pull of all those magnets in my ass. That I get to watch Praedytus observing me with a predatory grin while all of this is going on only adds to my excitement. He's enjoying himself if the size of his cock is anything to go by.

My orgasm builds, growing stronger all the time, but still refusing to crest. My heart is hammering in my chest, blood flowing through my body, engorging anything that's in contact with a magnet. It's to the point that my breasts have grown in size and my sex is ready to explode like an overripe plum.

And burst it does, with magnificent splendor. That Axel follows me over the edge is perhaps the most shocking thing of all. Not only is he yelling his release right in my ear, but all the magnets go haywire, vibrating and clicking together with ever-increasing speed until it's a continuous jangle. But rather than dying off as I'd expected, the orgasm kept rolling along, taking both of us with it.

It's still enveloping us several minutes later, but rather than tiring me, I'm more and more energized all the time. Praedytus goes from looking interested, then bored, and last of all, onto alarmed.

"That is enough!" he shouts, and after getting to his feet, he reinforces this by bellowing, "Cease."

But the orgasm keeps working away at the pair of us.

He stalks over to the rock and slams both his palms down on it. An instant later the spasms stop, with it fast enough to shock. I'm left bereft. That Axel roars "No!" over my shoulder lets me know he's experiencing something similar.

Not that I get the chance to bitch about it to either of them because they both disappear in a cloud of steam, leaving me on my own. It takes all my effort to pry myself off the damned magnetic rock, but I'm soon free and stomping down the beach, ready to swim back to the boat.

Only there's no sign of Ben.

I made it back to The Metal Beast in super-fast time. The trip to the shore had taken twice as long. I feel so alive! Or maybe it's that I'm so pissed off.

I'm still a couple of feet off the back of the boat when I hear enough grunting and squelching to let me know why Ben is nowhere in sight. Wasting no time, I hoist myself up onto the swim platform and through the hatch at the back of the transom with fluid ease.

As I suspected, Cuprum, the Goddess of Copper, is all over Ben like a rash. I see red, or maybe that's copper, and without thought, I step forward and wait until she lifts herself clear of Ben's cock.

Then, before she can sink back down, I grab her around the waist, swing her up and around and toss her over the side with

astonishing ease. I'm disappointed in the lack of a splash when she disappears before hitting the water.

"What, what?" Ben groans, writhing around on the deck in front of me. He's out of it and in a trance of some sort. His cock is distended, no doubt due to the magnetic ring being back in place. Every time he arches his hips, his cock bounces around as though searching for the missing goddess.

"Ben!" I yelled, trying to get his attention, but he didn't respond.

"You need to finish what my daughter has started," says Praedytus, from right behind me.

"Damn!" I stagger away from him, trip over Ben, and land with a bounce on the metal deck. The magnets still around my clit and inside my ass lock me there.

"You need to hurry," says Praedytus.

"Why?" I say, trying to lever my ass off the deck.

"Because if you leave him like this, you risk him losing his mind."

It's all the incentive I need to force myself up onto my hands and knees, crawl over and straddle him. This isn't made easy by his thrashing about.

My God, he feels huge. I'm surprised he has the cock ring on at all. That magnetic clasp must be strong. I find out how strong it is when the pebbles applying pressure on my clit snap onto it with a resounding crack.

The way Praedytus watches us feels different than before. Less voyeuristic, more intense, like he's paying attention to something specific. "You need to move," says Praedytus, who's got both his hands wrapped around his cock while he stands watching me service Ben.

"I can't," I stammered out. "I'm stuck."

Praedytus grasps what I'm talking about and, after letting

go of his organ, puts a hand under each of my arms and lifts me. The tugging on my bud because of all the magnets is exquisite. There's a spurt of excitement when, rather than lift me to my feet, Praedytus lets me settle again on Ben's swollen length. He keeps this up until both Ben and I have come too many times to count before letting me settle for good.

When his hands disappear from under my arms, I glance over my shoulder to ask what gives, but he's no longer there.

"What just happened?" says Ben, clarity once again returning to his gaze. "Cuprum?"

"She, ah, went swimming."

I'm still not happy about the spurt of jealousy that had led to me tossing the goddess over the side. Ben and I are fuck buddies. Nothing more.

"Then, how?" says Ben, twitching his hips and letting me feel him hardening inside me.

I twitch my muscles in response and am rewarded by his eyes widening. That I then lean right back to test the strength of the magnets has my own eyes widening, too. Oh, that's good. It's good enough that I rock back and forth a few more times to make sure.

4

It takes a while and the judicious use of a wrench to rid me of most of the pebbles hidden in the creases on either side of my clit. Because they're as magnetic as they are, Ben has to slide them onto the tool one at a time until we're able to pull ourselves apart.

At my insistence, he leaves a couple there because the extra blood they encourage to head in their direction is doing wonderful things for my sensitivity.

Removing the butt plug is easy once Ben gets the first magnetic pebble to snap to the wrench; after that, the others tug free like a rope of pearls. He knows me well, pushing them back in twice for my sheer enjoyment while I'm doggy style on the aft deck.

"Hmmm, I might have to hang on to these," says Ben, clipping them onto the transom.

Even though the sun was as high as it had been after it had shot into the sky when we'd woken, we headed to the master

for a sleep. We end up collapsing naked in the middle of the bed when we get there.

I don't know what time it is when I wake. The sun is still at its zenith if the light pouring in through the hatch is any sign. Ben's not there and so I go in search of him, finding him on the aft deck spread out in an ancient deck chair with a beer in his hand. There's a spare deck chair next to him with a beer sitting in the shade under it.

I relax back into the canvas and grope around under the chair until I find the can, then crack it open before taking a few good mouthfuls. Damn, that's good.

"So, I was thinking," says Ben, drinking some more beer, "we should stay here."

I open my mouth to argue against this, knowing that if we stay here we risk dying young, but he holds his hand up to stop me.

"Think about it. We've got food for a week. It's sunny and warm, and I've gotta tell you that water is mind-blowing."

Realizing he's talking about a vacation rather than staying here forever, I have to agree with him. It's a perfect spot for a vacation. "We can't leave anyway," I say, nodding at the solid granite cliff where the entrance had once been.

"Oh, yeah," says Ben, unconcerned that we're trapped here.

The next few days were a blur of sunbathing, great sex, and good food, with Ben showing himself to be quite the master chef. We'd thrown lines over the side but had caught nothing, because if the water could turn humans into climaxing zombies, what hope would fish have?

It doesn't matter how many times we go swimming—the result is always the same, and it's led to us having sex on the swim platform twice because we couldn't wait any longer. I even think I've lost a few pounds because of all the exercise. I wish the gym were this much fun.

By the fifth day, even the sex has scaled down. Rather than all the bells, whistles, slings, and clamps, we're enjoying sex of the slow, comfortable kind on the top deck; with the sun beating down on our backs, fronts, or sides, depending on the position. With sex and sunbathing, there is no better combination.

Something else that's changed is that rather than superficial chatter, we talk about what matters to us; our hopes and dreams, even our fears. This makes me very nervous. Fuck buddies aren't meant to get deep and meaningful.

In my mind, it's a recipe for disaster. With what I'm going through with the Nyphrazi, emotions are best buried. It's bad enough that I wonder if Vyran is okay. If I get serious about Ben, then what about Vyran and me?

While Ben doesn't mind sharing me with the others, he's less ambivalent about the God of the Woods.

I'm once again working on my tan when the whole boat shudders and shakes. At first, I thought we must be due a visit from one of the Nyphrazi, but then it dawned that Ben's started up the engine.

On hearing the anchor chain rattling away, curiosity got the better of me and I go see what's up. After all, it's not like we can go anywhere.

"What are you doing?" I said to Ben on stepping into the wheelhouse.

"I want to check out the cliff where the entrance was, but if I swim there, I'll end up coming so many times that I'll drown."

I nod my approval of this plan because it won't be long before we face running out of food, even with our half-hearted rationing. Not that we're not down to ship's biscuits and salted pork yet.

When the anchor clangs against the steel hull, Ben puts the boat into gear, and we move. He spins the wheel, and we turn to the cliff and our search for a viable exit.

We haven't gone over ten feet when I notice it's getting colder. It's not arctic or anything, just cooler. But the closer we inch to the cliff, the cooler it becomes. It's soon cold enough that I'm thinking about clothes for the first time in days.

Then the light also fails.

Of even more interest is that the instruments flare into life, revealing that the cliff we're motoring straight at isn't there.

I'm still nervous though when Ben keeps The Metal Beast dead on course, as if to smash into the cliff face before us. Not that we can see it as we could earlier, with the sun above us fading with each second. It's as though Mother Nature is turning a big dimmer switch.

It's only when the sun blinks out altogether that I see the stars sparkling above us. On looking back down, I notice that the other thing that's gone is the cliff, and we can once again see Sitka Sound in the bright moonlight.

"Wow," says Ben, looking at me with awe.

I'm awe-struck myself by the possibilities when I check the date and time on the GPS unit.

"Let me get this right. We've enjoyed five days in a tropical paradise and don't appear to have lost more than a few hours?"

"Hold your horses," says Ben, putting his hands on my shoulders to stop my happy dance. "Remember what happened

at the cabin. What if we'd lost five days or more? What if we'd lost months? Or years?"

What his hands haven't accomplished, this dose of reality does, and all my happy evaporates in an instant. "Damn." While we hadn't lost days this time, there were no guarantees this would be the case in the future. Hadn't we been caught out like that when staying at the cabin?

"It makes me curious about the previous owner of The Beast, though," says Ben, his hand splayed on the chart. "That big red cross makes me wonder if they had a similar experience. And then there's the coating on the hull. That's an unusual combination."

"Sheesh, I hope we don't turn into rabid hoarders like the previous owners." I'm unable to suppress a shudder at the thought of getting my own TV show, and not in a good way.

We don't bother going any farther, dropping the anchor right where we are. Interestingly, the cliff we'd motored through is now back, although if we look long enough, we can see it shimmering like a hologram or mirage that it is.

"Axel must have let it drop so we'd go in there," says Ben.

"I'm not sure it was him." The moment I've said it, I had regrets. The more I think about it, the more I suspect Praedytus had something to do with us ending up in that lake. But I can't quite put my finger on why.

"If I were to put money on it, I'd say it was The God of All Desire who led us there."

Ben ponders it for a second. "Or Cuprum?"

It's a theory I jump on. Better Ben suspected the Goddess of Copper was behind our being trapped than tell him what had happened on that magnetic rock. And especially not the role the God of All Desire had played in the orgasm that came close to taking me out.

. . .

After an uneventful night, we made our way back to port so we could stock up on provisions before heading out again. This time we steer in the opposite direction, avoiding any red crosses marked on the charts.

What follows is five days of chilling out. From experience, I've always found that the first three days of any vacation are spent unwinding, and only then do I relax. As it is, I couldn't be more relaxed if I tried. Even the Nyphrazi gods seem a million miles away now.

"Here's to our last night," says Ben, raising his can of beer so I can tap mine against it.

While part of me is saddened that our vacation is almost over, another part is looking forward to a cylinder-draining, stinking hot shower. One that will rid me of the salt crystals that coat my skin.

Bed that night was bittersweet, with our sex closer to making love than it had been to date.

I'm on the very edge of sleep when Ben kisses the top of my head and whispers, "Love you."

I don't think I'm supposed to hear, and I fight to stay still and keep my breathing even. I'm unsure if I've succeeded, so it's only after hearing Ben's breathing deepen that I relax enough to fall asleep myself.

I don't know if it's the stifling heat in the cabin or the bead of sweat that's running down my side, but I know what's

happened. There's no way it could be this hot without us being back in that damned opalescent lake.

"Are you joking with me?" I say, rolling over to face Ben. Only he's not there. The only sign that he had been there was the dent in his pillow.

"Fucking Cuprum!" If I had my way, I'd weld those chains of hers together. Watch her try to fuck him then!

On realizing Ben's not even on board, I'm pissed.

"For fuck's sake!"

I stamp my foot in frustration, no doubt bruising my heel in the process. Then, as though prompted by the racket I'm making, the sun pops up over the hills that surround the lake. Once there, it zooms up into the sky like some cheesy prop in a grade school play.

Axel is where I expect, with the sunlight glinting off his polished fettyr so bright that I can see it even after I close my eyes.

"Well, screw you, buddy," I say to myself before stomping back down to the master cabin, where I throw myself on the bed.

I've just shut my eyes when I hear Axel say, "Jasmine, come to me."

Before you can say Cloud 9 innerspring, I'm lying on that rock, and I don't know who's more surprised, myself or Axel. I've never been transported before without one of the gods or their toys at least touching me. I thought they could only use the telepathic delivery service with each other.

But I don't dwell on it long. The second my back contacts the rock, it's as though someone has spent an hour licking me into submission, leaving me swollen and needy. It's so damned good that I surrender to it, writhing around on the rock like it's the best mattress money can buy.

While I lie there reveling in the tremors rolling over and through me, Axel gulps for air before stammering out, "But that shouldn't be possible. When I called you, I expected you to swim here."

He seems surprised, as if my joining him wasn't supposed to happen this way. "You shouldn't be able to travel alone without using a charm or one of the veils," he says, his forehead creased in consternation.

"Just fuck me," I grit out, my need now desperate, but still he stands unmoving, looking at me like I'm a problem that needs to be solved.

Deciding he needs some encouragement, I use my hands to gather up my breasts before thrusting them out to him, all the while squeezing my nipples hard. I'm rewarded when his eyes darken and he shakes his head as though to get rid of any nagging doubts.

The chain that secures his fettyr around his waist is gone in seconds, but it's what he does next that has my sex gasping in anticipation.

After a moment of looking at his feet, he bends down and handpicks half-a-dozen black, round pebbles from the beach. I'm expecting them to be stuck on and inside my body, but I much prefer this option.

Despite his earlier reluctance, Axel seems to care whether I enjoy this. It's a pleasant change. "Does my placement please you?" he says after he's finished attaching the small magnetic pebbles along the length of his fettyr.

Does it ever!

5

Axel inches himself into me, with the small pebbles juddering over my G-spot one after the other. His withdrawal is a lot quicker and the hammering my G-spot receives has me groaning in satisfaction.

He keeps up this rhythm until I'm begging him for release, but before he can do my bidding, he disappears, leaving me hollow and desperate to come.

"I said no more," says Praedytus, his gaze locked on the juncture of my thighs.

"You, you can't leave me like this," I say, while squirming around as though movement alone will push me over the edge. Now I know what Ben was going through after I dragged Cuprum off him.

I can tell when Praedytus realizes this too, and I'm relieved when he steps forward. I'm expecting him to fasten his mouth onto my clit like he has in the past, but he has other ideas.

"My sons are growing too independent, resisting me. I won't have it." He follows this up by leaning forward and

holding his hand out to me. Since I'm too far gone to stand, he bends and places his hand on my head.

A heartbeat later, and the softest of moss cradles my back, and I luxuriate in its lush embrace for a moment before Praedytus lies next to me.

The glade we're in is like no other I've ever seen. It looks more like a movie set than real life. It's fifteen feet across at the most and surrounded by trees that are so close together that escape would be almost impossible; not that I plan on leaving.

All around our bed of moss is a tangle of vines, their flowers a pale icy blue. Most incredible is the sun, which sits overhead, heating my skin like a soft caress.

Praedytus rolls on his side to face me, bringing his hard, hot cock into contact with my hip. After that, it's as though my body is on autopilot, and I wriggle onto my side, which brings my slit close to his fuck muscle. It's not close enough, but when I throw my leg over his hip, we make full contact.

"I need you," I say, not caring how desperate I sound. If he doesn't fuck me, I'll go nuts.

"And I you," he says, surprising me.

I don't feel him touch my head, but he must have because one second I'm lying next to him, and the next he's on top of me. Even better is that he's already edging his way into my depths.

He's big, but my need is now so great that I'd be keen even if he were twice the size. I forget how chock-full I am when a hot, wet mouth covers one of my nipples. I can see Praedytus's mouth, and it's nowhere near my tit.

Then there's another mouth on the other nipple. Both of them pull on me in harmony, and I'm unable to stop my back lifting off the bed of moss as I near the source of my pleasure.

Praedytus pushes his hard length deep inside of me until I

can take him no more. He, however, has other ideas. He withdraws, and as he does so, there's a presence between my ass cheeks. At first, I thought he's given up on my sheath, but what filled my ass was more of those small magnetic pebbles.

With them in place, he drives back into me until I squeak before he withdraws again. As he does so, the pebbles also pop out of my ass one at a time.

When he enters me next time, the pebbles again fill my ass. This, combined with my nipples both being sucked on, is almost more than I can bear. But bear it, I do, and even cope when some of the vines twirl around my ankles and then pull them up over my head. This opens me even wider to Praedytus's cock.

Now, when he enters me, he keeps going until his balls bounce against my ass and his tip crowds my womb. Three times is all he manages before an orgasm hits me hard, rushing out to my extremities and then crashing back to where we join.

I'm ready to collapse, but he has other ideas. While my body continues to vibrate, he slides in and out, over and over, those magic pebbles keeping pace. I've never been this fucked in all my life.

I'm thinking it can't get any more amazing when a phantom tongue lands wet on my clit before lapping and slurping and sucking on it. If I didn't know better, I'd think it was Marlo, the Nyphrazi God of Iron.

"Are you ready?" says Praedytus.

I'm hoping he means what I think he means.

"Hold on," he says, speeding up.

I dig my fingers into the moss next to me, but lose my grip when he moves faster and faster. Soon enough, the vibrations in my body coalesce in that one spot, and I detonate.

Even more astounding is the raw power that rushes

through my body when Praedytus signals he's also come by bellowing, his words unintelligible. His hips jerk out of control, driving him deeper than I'd have thought possible.

I'm still out of it when I recognize the sweet scent of the nectar that is Praedytus's preferred condiment when he eats me out. But I'm not so comatose that I can't spread my legs wide in readiness.

This time, he covers my whole body with the sticky liquid and, when he runs his tongue through my furrow, he isn't alone. And I don't mind being the all-you-can-eat buffet, one bit. Hell, I don't even care who he's invited to dinner.

When I wake, I'm no longer on a bed of moss. I'm on my bed aboard The Metal Beast.

Well, most of me is on the bed because my legs are hanging over the side, meaning my sex is on show to the cabin. I know from the drop in temperature that the boat's no longer bobbing about on the enchanted lake. The one thing that hasn't changed is that someone is still eating me with enthusiasm.

"Ben?"

"Who else?" he says, his words muffled because he has a mouth full.

Oh, boy, does he ever.

"That must have been some dream you were having," says Ben when he comes up for air.

"Why?"

"Because you were thrashing about like you were being fucked and screaming for me to lick you harder, so I did," he says, licking his lips. "You taste delicious, by the way."

"So, did you enjoy tonight's session with the copper cow?"

Ben's reaction to my spite is visible because of the moonlight beaming through the hatch above our heads. Rather

than reacting to my being a total jealous bitch, his face splits in a wide grin. But it soon falters.

"Hang on, what session with Cuprum?"

"When I woke before, you weren't on board and The Beast was back in that lake."

I can see he's trying to remember, because it's not unusual for him to have hazy memories of his sessions with Cuprum.

"Nope. I've got nothing."

I take some relief in the fact that he isn't pissed about not remembering either, but then I beat myself up for caring.

Fuck buddies, remember!

We putter into the harbor later the next day, but by the time we've tidied everything up and washed down the decks, it's late.

"Why don't you stay the night?" says Ben, when I'm standing on the back deck with a pile of odd-sized bags, ready to trek to the parking lot.

"I've got an early start in the morning."

This is true, but it's more that I want to spend the night at home because I need some alone time. I've got a lot to think about. I know Ben's seen through my flimsy excuse when his hand on my breast stills.

"Another time, then," he says, his tone polite. "I'll help you with your bags."

Before I can salvage the situation, he's grabbed the two largest bags and is already marching along the floating walkway. There's nothing for me to do but collect the remaining bags and hurry to catch up with him.

He's remote during our walk to the parking lot and even while we're shoving all the bags in the back of my truck.

I go from anxious that I've upset him to 'fuck it, I don't need this crap.' It's something he picks up on.

"I'll see you at work, then," he said before planting a perfunctory kiss on my cheek.

"Guess so," I say, my anger ramping up.

I don't get the chance to shoot myself in the foot before he's already on his way back to The Metal Beast, leaving me standing next to my truck.

I'm on my second trip from my truck to the mudroom at home when my mom opens the door from the lounge.

"I thought you were away for the entire week?"

"Oh, uh, we had engine trouble," I say, spouting the first thing that comes into my head. I wish the Nyphrazi assholes would send us back at the same time as they collected us. All this back and forth through time is doing my head in.

Once I make it to my bedroom, I check the date on my mobile before texting Ben to let him know so we can keep up the pretense.

On the plus side, I've still got five days before I'm due back at work. This vacation just keeps on giving. It's what I'll do with those extra days that's got me stumped, because until I sort out what I want from Ben, I'd rather avoid him.

I'm none the wiser at breakfast the next morning when Dad asks me this very question. "Don't know, Dad. I can't afford to go anywhere too far."

"What about Ron's place?" he suggests, through a mouth full of bagel.

"Is it still standing?" I'd be surprised if it were, because it had been rustic the last time I'd seen it, and that had to be well over twenty years ago.

"Believe so," says my dad. "Your uncle spent some time repairing it last summer."

"Call him and see if it's free," says my mom.

I do, and it is. Luckily, I still haven't unpacked from being out on The Beast, and so I'm on the road an hour later. My decision to text Ben when I'm on the edge of the coverage area is conscious, if rather gutless.

It takes a couple of hours to get to the cabin and half-an-hour to find the key, which isn't where Uncle Ron said it would be.

One by one, I flip the bear trap boards with their vicious profusion of nails up against the railing on the front of the deck. It'd be safer to leave them down, but a pain in the ass to tiptoe through them every time I want to use the outhouse.

Likewise, I lift the heavy boards that cover the windows at the front of the cabin. I'm sure if there's a bear charging me, I'll be able to get them in place soon enough.

Despite the cabin having been protected by these primitive bear traps, there are still a lot of scratches on the door. I'm glad my dad had convinced me to bring one of his guns.

It takes some jiggling to get the rusty key to turn in the man-sized lock that secures the place, but once inside, everything is in order. It's sure as hell looking a lot better than I remembered from my last visit here when I was a kid. Uncle Ron must have spent weeks sorting it out.

After a lunch of sandwiches, I sit on the porch and chill, even if this isn't as enjoyable as it should be. Strange how sitting on my own is boring compared to sitting and chilling with Ben.

Damn it, I don't want to spend the next five days stewing over him.

My contemplation is broken by the sound of something

very large moving through the brush, not that I can see anything. But neither am I willing to sit here until I can see if it's a bear or a moose.

My actions are frantic as I work from the outside of the deck across to the door in the middle. There, I slam the bear trap boards back down and secure the shutters. That done, I race inside and slam home all the bolts on the front door.

After double-checking everything is as secure as I can make it, I head up into the loft with the gun and a couple of boxes of shells. On realizing how crazy hot it still is, I'm glad I'd opened the windows earlier to air the place out.

On peering through one of the small windows, I watched for movement.

I see it soon enough.

It's a brown bear, and a big mother, even if it is a male. Of more concern is that he's looking at the cabin and sniffing the air, letting me know he's already worked out what I had for lunch.

He makes quick work of the distance between the trees and the cabin, and I lose sight of him when he lumbers up onto the deck. I have no trouble hearing his roar of pain when he comes across the first of the bear traps.

He reappears below me again soon enough, limps a short distance from the cabin, then turns around and sits down to stare up at me.

I'll be damned if this is how I'll spend the rest of my vacation. After sliding the barrel of the gun through the window, I take aim and slam a bullet into the dirt right between his feet.

He doesn't wait for me to take another shot and is soon hightailing it into the trees.

I yelled, “And don’t come back, either,” through the window at him for good measure.

6

Unfortunately, the bastard doesn't listen, and the next morning I have to fire another warning shot. By day three, he had worked it out. Knowing I won't shoot him, he gains in confidence, once again venturing onto the deck.

I know I'm in trouble when I see one of the bear traps has landed nails-down in front of the cabin. He starts work on the door not long after and thank fuck I'm up in the loft with a gun and ammo. Not that I want to shoot him and have to deal with seven hundred pounds of bear meat.

The door doesn't last long. On seeing the first claw poking through, I raced to pull the ladder up into the loft before picking the gun back up.

While I might not want to shoot him, if it's a toss-up between the two of us, then it's bear steaks for dinner.

Fuck, he's massive, and when he roars, the sound is deafening. Thankfully, the bacon pan from breakfast is still on the stove and proves to be far more interesting than I am.

By the time he's ripped open every cupboard, box, and bag downstairs, I'm realizing that the only food left in the cabin is the bear, or me. When I see a set of vicious claws curling over the edge of the loft platform, I put the gun to my shoulder and take aim at the spot. I know it's a matter of time before his head will appear.

I don't have to wait long, but I still take my time, squeezing my finger and freaking out when the trigger stops halfway and stays there.

It doesn't matter how many times I jam my finger against it —the trigger doesn't budge.

"Fuck, fuck, fuck, fuck!"

While I've been trying in vain to release the trigger, the bear has been clawing its way up onto the platform, using the kitchen table for leverage.

He takes a gigantic step back when I rearrange his teeth with the butt of the rifle, using it like a baseball bat to do so. This gives me a small reprieve, but I know it won't be long before he tries to get to me again.

And he does. But when I swing the butt of the rifle at his head, he swipes at it with one of his giant paws, sweeping it from my sweaty grip.

Where are the Gods of Nyphrazi when I need them? I could do with being zapped out of here.

It's not long before the bear is in the loft with me, making the space feel smaller than ever. I look around for missiles, but short of throwing foam mattresses at him, I'm out of luck.

The cold glass of the window is now hard against my back. I'm unable to retreat any further. Fuck it all, isn't this when he's supposed to shapeshift into some hot guy and screw my brains out?

As though knowing he's won, the bear roars, his mouth wide, saliva dribbling out both sides to gloop onto the floor.

I can't believe it's coming to this. I've few regrets, but one is never seeing Vyran again. With that random thought, I try one last time. Hell, it's not like I've got anything to lose.

"Vyran, come to me!"

I don't know who's more surprised when he flashes into existence in front of me. The bear or Vyran himself.

Luckily, he seized the situation, slammed his hand down on the head of the surprised bear, and then the two of them blinked out of sight a second later. Not that Vyran is gone for long.

"Where did you take it?" I say, peeling myself away from the window. It's when I take a step that my legs give out. I hope I'm never that scared again.

I'm fortunate in that Vyran can move when he wants to, and he catches me before I collapse in a heap. When his arms are tight around me, I yield to the tears that had been threatening ever since the bear disarmed me.

He lowers me onto the nearest mattress before lying down next to me. Once again, he takes me in his arms so he can stroke my back in soothing circles.

It's only when I've cried myself out that I'm able to speak.

"I've never been so glad to see anyone in all my life."

"That must be why," says Vyran, looking as though he's had a lightbulb moment.

"Why, what?"

"Because my father had forbidden it. You should not have been able to summon me. Something has changed."

"Guess I needed you more than he did," I say, plastering myself to his chest and feeling very over-dressed all of a sudden.

"Do you need me, Jasmine?" says Vyran, his lips claiming mine for the first time. He'd had them everywhere else on my body, but never on my mouth.

The kiss is different from everything that's come before. Not just because of the enzymes on his tongue that set my body on fire, but because of what I taste there. Vulnerability, and even fear. This god, who commands forests and can heal with a touch, worries about losing me.

Come to think of it, none of the gods had ever kissed me like this—as if I'm precious rather than just powerful. As if what we have matters beyond the energy exchange.

When we break apart, I see something in his eyes I've never seen from any of his family. "You're not just here for the power, are you?" I whisper.

"Jasmine," he breathes against my forehead, "you're the first thing in millennia that has made me feel alive."

"How long do we have?" I say, already pulling my T-shirt over my head.

"Not long," says Vyran, helping me with the rest of my clothes.

I want to go all wham-bam on him, but he has other ideas.

"Relax, it will take my father some time to deal with the bear."

My mouth sagged open at this revelation, but I snapped it shut before saying, "Was that a good idea?"

Vyran laughs. "It was only a little bear. He'll cope."

All the while we've been talking; he's been reaching around to collect pillows from the nearby mattresses. He puts several of these under my hips, resulting in my mons being at the perfect angle for his questing mouth. And oh, his mouth is so hot, it's as though I'm being scorched to the core.

By the time he peels me wide so he can plunge his sharp tongue deep inside me, I'm ready to blow. As always, it's as if he's everywhere, but this time it's even more wonderful and I do not know why.

"I want your cock inside me," I gasp out while he continues to tongue fuck me. It's good, but I want more. More of him.

After withdrawing, he slides up and over my body with his chest and stomach, doing an awesome job of rubbing my clit. Then the crisscross of the lacing on the underside of his fettyr comes into play, and reason departs.

The leather thong that secured it around his waist soon snapped. Although it's not until I saw how shocked he was that I realize it's me who snapped it like it was a piece of sewing thread.

"Tell me, have you seen my father of late?"

"Yes." I don't bother with anything else before attempting to divert Vyran's attention by pulling his head down so I can kiss him again. But he's having none of it.

"This is important, Jasmine. Did you complete?" There's real urgency in his voice, as if my answer matters more than I understand.

"Complete?" I say, playing the part of the village idiot.

Hell, discussing having sex with someone's dad is not my idea of foreplay.

"Jasmine, I need to know."

"Fine. We fucked. We came," I say as quickly as I can, frantic to get that gorgeous length of his buried deep inside me.

"He achieved Nysa?"

I don't know whether to be worried at the anger that floods his features, but I nod anyway.

"Where?"

I explain the bed of moss in the woods.

“What color were the flowers, Jasmine?”

I have to close my eyes to visualize them before I can answer, “Blue." Though I soon think to add, "Why?"

"Because if my father had performed with you in certain places, under certain conditions, you would have become divine. But different. Changed in ways that might not be reversible."

“What? Is that possible?”

“This is true,” says Vyran, once again focusing on my body.

I’d grill him further, but his leather-clad cock at my entrance distracts me. He enters me with a sigh of pleasure, although how he feels anything through that fettyr is beyond me. Most guys whine about standard condoms.

After that, I surrender to the sensations overwhelming my body, and every time Vyran sheaths himself, the sense of completion is overwhelming.

I’m close to losing it when Vyran’s lips once again claim mine. The instant the enzymes on this tongue hit my system, everything gets more intense. My breasts swell, with my nipples almost painful in their hardness. My clit extends until it’s being mashed every time Vyran rams home. My insides are pulsing, and my G-spot feels like it’s doubled in size.

The orgasm is blinding, with not one bit of my body left out of the experience. Waves of power slam through me before streaming out the top of my head, with my hair standing on end.

I know by Vyran’s roars he’s also achieved Nysa, but I’m still too much in the throes of passion to care much about the consequences.

It’s in seeing Praedytus over Vyran’s shoulder that I worry. The God of All Desire is angrier than I’ve ever seen him.

“Ah, Vyran, we have company.”

“I know. I was hoping he’d go away,” says Vyran, this comment adding to Praedytus’s wrath.

"I made a specific point of banning this," says Praedytus. "You've complicated things for no good reason."

"Jasmine needed me." Vyran's voice carries a conviction that surprises even me. "And I will always come when she calls, Father. No matter your divine law."

The look that passes between father and son is loaded with meaning I'm unable to interpret. Vyran has just chosen me over his father's direct orders, and we all know it. The defiance in his stance, the way he positions himself between Praedytus and me—this isn't just about tonight. This is Vyran declaring where his loyalties lie.

"I was about to be killed by a bear," I gasped, hoping to appeal to his reason.

Rather than soothe him, Praedytus goes ballistic.

“You mean this bear?” he says, turning to show me his back.

“Holy crap. Are you okay?” I say, trying to worm my way out from under Vyran, made difficult by him still being buried deep inside me.

“He’ll heal,” says Vyran in an amused tone, before withdrawing.

I think he’s pulling free, but then he drives himself back in again to the hilt. I’m unable to stop my hips from rising to take him even deeper.

It would appear Praedytus isn't keen on this development, his "Vyran, come to me" abrupt in the extreme.

A second later, I’m on my own on the mattress with Vyran now standing next to his father.

I sit up and am unable to stop my eyes from popping out when I work out what’s different about my God of the Woods.

I'm also unable to stop my hand from straying to my crotch, where I expect to find Vyran's fettyr. But it's not there either.

My actions have both gods looking down, and while Vyran appears alarmed, Praedytus seems resigned, as though the fight has gone out of him somehow.

"It is for this reason that I banned you from seeing Jasmine. Your connection interferes with the natural progression of events."

"What does that mean?" says Vyran, taking the words right out of my mouth.

Praedytus's jaw tightens in frustration at his timeline being disrupted. "Her power should develop in specific increments. It should follow a precise pattern. Your emotional bond was not something I foresaw."

He huffs in resignation before continuing. "That you, my son, are now my equal and—"

"What?" said Vyran and I in unison.

"That Jasmine has achieved demigod status," continues the God of All Desire as though we hadn't just interrupted.

On hearing this little gem, neither Vyran nor I could speak.

Praedytus looks at me with disbelief before continuing. "Have you not noticed yourself getting stronger? That we can summon you by thought? That your dreams are as real as life itself?"

Praedytus lifts an eyebrow to give this last trait emphasis, leaving me unsure if my session with him had been for real or not. But it must have been for real if I'm now a demigod.

Damn it, that's not how I ever thought I'd describe myself.

"But what does it mean?" I say, trying to understand the consequences. If life had taught me one thing, it's that there has to be a "but" in there somewhere.

"You may now travel between our worlds without need of veils or charms."

"But," I prompt again, making a mental note to ask Vyran about the veils and charms that Axel had also mentioned. Before I'd gotten sidetracked by being horny beyond belief.

"It also means he can no longer stop me from seeing you," says Vyran, rubbing salt in the wounds of Praedytus's psyche, and maybe even his back.

"But," I pressed Praedytus again.

His heavy sigh lets me know I'm about to find out.

"You'll be dead within one of your human years."

And bam, there it is, although it's less a "but" and more a "BUT". I sit numb, while in the background Vyran yells at his father for not warning him of the risk. To hell with it all. I'd avoided being taken out by a bear, only to still have a death sentence hanging over my head.

"Is divinity not enough?" says Praedytus, as though he hasn't just told me of my imminent demise.

Courtesy of a sweeping sidekick from Vyran, Praedytus is soon in a heap. Not content with this, the God of the Woods then pounces, wrapping his arm around his father's throat and choking off his words.

Loath as I am to see the God of All Desire continue breathing. I also need to hear what else he'd tried to say. "Vyran, do you want to loosen up?"

"Now, what was that again?" I say to Praedytus once his face is no longer purple.

"There is another way," he says, his voice husky.

Neither Vyran nor I spoke. Rather, we stare at him, waiting for him to continue.

"If all my sons achieve Nysa with you on the Altar of Nyph

on the eve of the Festival of Obis, your divinity can be reversed."

Something in his tone makes me uneasy, though I can't say what. Six of them in one night strikes me as being more than just a reversal ritual.

I mean... six of them!

In one night!

Oh my God, did my girly bits just tighten? What the hell is wrong with me?

Praedytus doesn't stay long after this, not because he wants to leave, but because Vyran sends him somewhere in a cloud of steam.

"I could get used to this," says Vyran, looking at the spot his father had just vacated.

"When is this festival?"

"In your time, just over a month away."

I'm not sure whether to be worried by thoughts of this ritual or aroused. In the end, I went for the latter. After lying back down on the mattress, I spread my legs wide before saying, "Vyran, come to me."

This time, I'm the one who gets the biggest surprise.

I'd thought that without the fettyr on, he'd be smaller, but oh my, he's rather the opposite. There's also nothing quite like being skin to skin.

It takes a good few hours of screwing each other in every way possible before we feel replete enough to talk. Praedytus is right. I am stronger.

"Does this mean I don't need to do the dirty with Marlo until the big night?" I say, referring to the God of Iron.

"It might be best if you didn't wait until then. He can give you the enzymes you'll need to further build your strength so

you can cope with all of us. Remember, we all need to achieve Nysa."

"Damn it, I've just realized that means Seolfer and Aurum, too."

"I'm sorry, but this is so."

"Then I need to be as strong as possible if I'm to pay them back for what they did to me."

EPILOGUE

Vyran and I have now been at my uncle's cabin for several days, with me stalling on my time with Marlo, the Nyphrazi God of Iron. I know I need the enzymes he carries on that magic tongue of his if I'm to survive the ceremony at the Festival of Obis. However, I'm in no hurry to get on with it.

The way I figure it, once I open myself up to Marlo, I'm that much closer to having to have sex with all six brothers. And all in a single night. At first, I'd quivered at the thought of it. Then I'd realized that Seolfer and Aurum would need to be part of the action, and I was dreading doing the dirty with them again.

The thing is, I'm not sure how I feel about Seolfer anymore. Sure, he tried to kill me with that silver fascinum, and I should hate his guts. And I do most of the time. But there's this nagging discomfort whenever I think about his being banished for life because of what happened between us.

Even knowing he brought it on himself, there's a twisted part of me that feels guilty? Meanwhile, there's another part of

me that tightens whenever I think of him possessing Gary so he could take his full of me.

It's messed up, and I know it. The bastard tried to control my body for months, making my life hell with those silver vibrations at the worst moments.

If it weren't for the whole demigod thing being fatal within the year, I'd stick with it. I love the heightened sensations I've been enjoying with Vyran for the past couple of days. The extra strength hasn't hurt in that department either.

I'd even consider becoming a goddess, except that this would mean I'd have to give up my family. There's also the sticking point that humans can't survive for long in the Nyphrazi realm, with the reverse also being true.

I love my parents too much for that. And while my younger brother can be a pain in the ass, I'm still not ready to say goodbye to him forever.

GOD of IRON

1

The sun beating down on my face through the open window wakes me almost as much as Vyran tongue-fucking me like a living alarm clock. It has me unfurling like a new leaf and opening myself up to my God of the Woods to give him even better access. His tongue being as prehensile as it is, he doesn't need a lot of help.

Not until my spasms have subsided does he lift his head.

"Jasmine, you need to think about your training with Marlo," he says, making me wish he still had his mouth full.

"Just one more day," I wheedle, yet again fighting against the inevitable.

"You have little time before the Eve of Obis."

"I know, all right!"

I'm being a grumpy bitch, but damn it, I don't need this first thing in the morning. It's bad enough that six gods will be devouring me like I'm a smorgasbord. Add in that I'll doubtless be spread all over an uncomfortable altar, and the last thing I need is to be hurried along.

I need time to adjust, even if only a little.

I know Vyran hasn't taken my outburst to heart when he slides up the bed and drags me into his arms. I'm thinking we're settling in for another day in the sleeping loft, but he has other ideas.

"Close your eyes," he murmured.

"They already are."

Even with them closed, the buzzing in my head and the fact that I'm no longer lying on high-density foam but unforgiving rock alert me to our having gone somewhere. I'm hoping for the blue pool with its champagne-like water.

On opening my eyes, I have trouble believing what I'm seeing.

"Where the hell are we?" I say, struggling out of his arms so I can sit up.

"The Isle of Obis. It's here we come to heal and renew ourselves."

"How?" Looking around the barren lump of rock we're stuck on, there doesn't seem to be anything that smacks of healing, let alone renewal. There's more life in the surrounding sea than on the rock itself, even including Vyran and me.

"The Isle is not as it appears," says Vyran, climbing to his feet.

He holds his hand out, and I take it. A moment later, I'm standing next to him, and the isle still looks like a big old chunk of rock.

"Patience, Jasmine," says Vyran, seeing my lack of enthusiasm.

I don't have to wait long before the rock under our feet quivers, although the vibrations cease when it dissolves and we free-fall into the space below. There's no time to freak out or even scream before we land in a large pool of gel.

Green gel that feels wonderful on my skin. It's like aloe vera on steroids. This is also the first time I've experienced something in the Nyphrazi realm that doesn't appear to have a sexual element to it. I'd be disappointed if I weren't so blissed out. Vyran, who's cradled in the goo next to me, is also looking mellow.

I'm luxuriating until I notice the cavern getting darker. It's a minute or two before I see it's because the gap high above us is closing an inch at a time.

"Should we be worried about that?" I say, kicking my feet in order to inch myself even closer to Vyran.

"No. Everything is as it should be."

I can't help an exasperated humph at this homily because, once again, I'm being kept in the dark, both in a literal and figurative sense. Is there a Nyphrazi code that says they have to be as enigmatic as possible? If so, they need to ditch it pronto.

I grab onto Vyran's hand at the exact moment the rock above finishes sealing the gap. This plunges us into a Stygian blackness that has me opening my eyes ever wider, hoping to see something.

Anything.

A minute or two passes in which Vyran answers all my questions with, "Everything is as it should be," until I want to smack him.

The darkness takes its time lifting, to the point that it's a while before I realize what's happening. The green goo is glowing like something out of a nuclear reactor. The brighter it gets, the more amazing my body feels.

It's as though every muscle has been stretched and massaged, and my blood vessels stripped of cholesterol. As if my heart and lungs have been given a tune-up and my eyes

rinsed with cooling saline. Even my skin is smoother when I run my free hand over my torso.

"Wow."

I grill Vyran on these changes, wanting to know if he's experiencing the same, but once again he silences me with the inscrutable, "Everything is as it should be."

It's only when the green goo is glowing to the point it hurts my eyes that he says anything other than this.

"Come, it is time." He stands, and in so doing, lets me know the gel is no longer as deep as it had been when we'd first dropped in.

We waded to the side of the pool and slithered on our bellies onto the ledge that encircles the pool. Standing would be tricky, if not straight-out dangerous, given we're both covered in the slippery stuff.

But that aside, I've never felt better. Even my old ice hockey knee no longer aches and I'm moving as freely as I did when I was a kid.

"Now what?" I say, while doing my best not to slide back into the pool.

"Now we wait."

I'm about to ask him what for when Marlo materializes beside us.

"Already?"

"It is time," says Vyran, having the nerve to look okay about handing me over to his brother. The sting isn't lessened when he adds, "I don't want to lose you, and this is the only way."

I didn't respond when he blinked out of sight, leaving me alone with the God of Iron.

"Come," says Marlo, holding his hand out to me.

I ease myself up onto my hands and knees, then plant one foot on the rock, moving it around until it feels less like I'm

wearing an ice skate. After that, Marlo helps me to stand, but I almost take a tumble when my hand slips from his.

"This stuff would make an awesome lubricant," I say to myself, but not quietly enough if Marlo's booming laughter is anything to go by. He then proves just how good it could be when he runs his hands all over my body, as if to memorize it. I sure as hell won't forget the experience in a hurry.

While I'd noticed nothing when he was holding my hand, when he touches the rest of me, it's as if his fingers are electrified. Not as many volts as his brother Ciprus, God of Copper, could manifest, but enough for there to be goosebumps wherever his hands had caressed.

My nipples are so tight they hurt, reminding me of Ben and the jeweled nipple clamps he'd given me. A twinge of guilt makes itself at home in my chest. I haven't thought about him in days, and I wonder if this tells me more than anything else. I don't understand my emotions when it comes to him. Or maybe it's just that there have been too many distractions?

"It tastes good, too," says Marlo, snapping my attention back to the here and now.

His gaze is one of intense hunger, and when he licks his lips with that impressive tongue of his, funny things happen to my insides. When he says, "Let's get you cleaned up," the muscles in my legs are reduced to the consistency of the green goo, and I have to lock my knees in order to stay upright.

Marlo pulls on my hand to get me moving, and I follow him, even if my first few steps are a little puppet-like. But this is a lot better than falling flat on my face.

"Where are we going?" I say, following him down a lava tube, its dimensions such that Marlo has to walk in the middle to avoid cracking his head.

"The Temple of Obis."

"Is this where the ceremony will be held?" I say, unable to stop myself from slowing.

"No."

"You don't agree with the ritual, do you?"

"No!" Despite his monosyllabic response, there's no missing its hidden meaning.

"So, you'd be happy for me to die within the year?" This time I don't just slow. I stop altogether.

"What? No!" says Marlo, his response loud in the confined space. With the echo still battering my ears, I take comfort in the fact that he also looks horrified.

"Explain, then." I've asked in a way that he can't answer with "no" again. Talk about pulling teeth.

"To strip you of unwanted divinity by using the ceremony carries some risk. More than my father has admitted."

I'm expecting him to tell me about the dangers, but instead he snaps his mouth shut and looks around, as if someone might be listening. All the while he's been urging me farther down the wormhole.

Oddly, the tunnel has gotten no darker, even with us now being a respectable distance from the glowing pool. It's only on closer inspection that I realize the walls are giving off a faint light.

"What risk?" I asked, determined to uncover the truth.

Rather than answer me, Marlo waves his free hand around in what I take to be the Nyphrazi gesture for "don't worry your pretty little head about it. It's too complicated." I swear I want to do him an injury. Was I always this violent?

I indulge in some hand-waving of my own, though he doesn't seem to understand he's just been told in sign language to go fuck himself. Not content to leave it there, I also bark out, "Not good enough!"

"If you're not strong enough, you will be overcome and succumb to a constant state of Nysa."

"Great. Either I die within a year, or I become a pleasure-zombie for eternity. Either way, I'm in a heap of trouble."

"Not all fates are equal, Princess. Some forms of existence are worse than death."

"That's a terrifying thought."

Marlo looks over his shoulder and listens before beckoning to let me know I should move closer. His lips brushed my ear when he spoke.

"When you were told you'd be dead within twelve months, it's not that simple."

Oh, what now? If there was one thing I could say about the Nyphrazi, it's that they'd make excellent poker players. Or politicians, given their propensity to bury the truth, or straight out lie.

"I suspect there's more to the ceremony than my father is letting on. That it's not just about returning you to your human form."

My gaze widening is all the encouragement Marlo needs to continue.

"He has taken a particular interest in you." His brow then wrinkles in a way that does nothing to allay my fears about what the hell this means. And I'm no better off when he continues. "I fear he wants you to take your place among the maidens."

"Among the what!?" I only realized I'd shouted when Marlo put his finger to my lips.

"The fallen maidens, Jasmine. Many consider it an honor to join their ranks—a life of luxury in the Temple, where they want for nothing and spend their days in pleasure with visiting gods." His expression darkens. "While the Temple of the Fallen

belongs to the goddesses, we gods may visit to... take our ease... but we have no authority there."

He pauses, his disquiet obvious. "But Praedytus must think you the perfect vessel to select you for such a fate."

I take a moment to work my way through his bombshell. However, there's one thing that jumps out. "What the hell did you just call me?" I know I'm still shouting, but why shouldn't I? I'm human, not some vessel for this lot to use.

Rather than answer me, Marlo patted me on the shoulder. "Come. After we've made our offering to the goddess, we need to work on your strength."

I'm dying to ask him more about the fallen maidens, but don't get a chance. Hearing voices heading in our direction, Marlo once again takes my hand, and we set off at a pace designed to leave the new arrivals far behind.

We hurry along for a good while, but we can't shake whoever it is following in our wake. That changes when Marlo veers down a side passage that's so small he has to bend double to fit. Even I have to bend down to avoid cracking my head on the rock ceiling.

But it works, and by the time we break out into an enormous cavern, the only sounds are our breathing and the bubbling of the pool located there. Rather than being full of green goo, this one is full of what I take to be water, even if it is a soft pink in color.

The girly girl buried deep inside me can't help but think it looks gorgeous.

"Can we get in?" I'd like nothing better than to scrub the remaining green goo away. While it had started out slippery, now it's drying in places and itchy.

"The pool being full, it would appear the Goddess of Obis

has decided it should be so," says Marlo, his tone one of amusement.

2

Upon looking at the pink water, I think about testing it with my foot before throwing caution to the wind and jumping in with abandon.

My glee is soon obliterated by pure, wanton lust, the likes of which I've not experienced before. I'm calculating whether I can remove Marlo's iron fettyr with my teeth before the last of the green goo has been washed away.

I've never been that great a fan of giving head. But just thinking about closing my lips over the end of his gorgeous cock has my mouth watering and my sex pulsing in need.

"Why don't you join me?"

"It is not allowed," grits out Marlo, like he's hurting.

If he won't join me, then I'll just have to join him, although I worry that when I leave the pink pool, my hunger might abate.

Once I'm standing on the side of the pool, I check in with my body. On finding my desire has heightened, I can't stop

myself from smiling. Climbing his rock-hard body like an oversexed monkey has my circuits close to blowing.

I've never wanted a man this much in my life, ever, and if he doesn't fill me soon, I'll lose all reason.

"Fuck me!"

On getting no response to this request, other than noticing his ironclad cock twitch against my slit, I add, "Please. I need you so much."

I'm not sure if it's because I've asked rather than demanded, but Marlo looks to be doing as I've requested, if not as fast as I'd like.

"Not here," he says, cradling my ass with his large hands. "Come, we have far to travel."

I'm expecting more walking, but Marlo has other ideas, and thanks to the familiar buzzing inside my head, I know he's about to zap us somewhere.

In materializing at our new location, it's almost as if we've stayed put. We're still in a cavern, but rather than being lit by eerie glowing walls, this one is lit by tapers. The pool we're standing next to is also different.

For one thing, it's not pink and there's a pedestal in the middle of it; one that's covered in phallic carvings and that looks to have been designed with one thing in mind. My juices can't help themselves and respond with alacrity.

As luck would have it for my escalating libido, Marlo keeps hold of me before walking down the wide steps and into the pool. After reaching the pedestal, he settles my ass on it, and I'm surprised to find it welcoming. There are dips for my cheeks and a gap in the rock that has my sex exposed to whatever. Just thinking about it has me forming ripples.

The water of the pool laps against me, and I have to admit

to disappointment at my lack of reaction to it when compared to the pink water. Not that I need the extra stimulation.

"Lie back," says Marlo, his voice thick with passion. I do so without thinking, and it's only when my head hits the water that I wonder about drowning. But I don't have enough time to panic before my head and torso are supported by solid rock. Weird, given the pedestal had only been big enough to fit my ass when Marlo had first sat me on it.

I'm expecting some action between my legs, but Marlo moves to stand next to me, where he bends down so that his lips can claim mine. No sooner had the enzymes on his tongue been absorbed by mine than my clit and G-spot went off like popcorn. My nipples soon followed suit.

I'm only just aware of Marlo laying one of his hands on my thigh, but the two balls of energy he pulses into me sure have my attention. I hadn't experienced these since the night I'd first met all the brothers and had forgotten how good they were.

They move up my leg before dropping under the surface of the water, where one slips inside my core while the other makes itself at home in my ass.

They explode in unison with the shock waves that envelop my body, having me screaming my release over and over into Marlo's eager mouth. I'm still screaming when he slides the first of many fingers deep inside me, stretching me, preparing me.

Soon he's nudging something else deep inside me. Something that's big and hard, something that I know is not him because he's still beside me.

"You need to build up to my size," he says, by way of explanation when our lips part.

Yikes, I already feel full to overflowing with whatever's

jammed inside me like some jumbo-sized Kegel. If I can hold that thing in once I'm standing, I'll be able to crack nuts as a party piece.

Only after I've finished shuddering am I able to contemplate standing. Once upright, I last all of twenty seconds before the iron bullet drops to the bottom of the pool with a muted clang, just missing my foot.

Marlo retrieves it and hands it to me, and on seeing the size of it compared to his impressive length, I can't help but gulp with trepidation. I've got a way to go yet.

"Come," says Marlo, holding his hand out to me.

"Are we going to make that offering to the goddess now?"

Marlo's laughter booms around in the cavern, bouncing off the walls and coming at me from all directions. It's only when he's got himself under control that he can answer me. "You already did."

"I did? When?"

He nods. "The goddess feeds off female lust. Your dip in the pink pool earlier will be enough to keep her happy for a long time."

After lifting a taper from its holder, Marlo steers me to a split in the rock that I hadn't noticed. I'm not sure where we're headed, but suspect there are a lot more of these iron bullets there. And with all of them doubtless bigger than the one I'm holding in my clammy grasp.

It's only when we walk out of the tunnel and into another enormous cavern that I realize these must be Marlo's private quarters. Where they're located, I wouldn't have a clue. Because of the Nyphrazi ability to travel through space and time, we could be anywhere on earth and God only knows what year it is. The only thing I know for sure is that it's night

because of the expanse of black outside the wide mouth of the cave.

It's only on waking the following morning that I realize I must have passed out on Marlo the night before. It's not a good look, but, damn it all, he was the one who'd overloaded my system. But damn, it had been good. I'd demand another go-around, but I'm alone.

After checking around, it didn't take long to work out where I was, with the view through the mouth of the cave being familiar. It's only when I'm sitting up that things get weird. After swinging my legs over the side of the rock ledge, I leave the luxury of the furs behind and walk out into the sunshine.

"Oh, you cannot be serious?!"

Not only can I see The Metal Beast floating in the middle of that milky lake, but I can also see myself being screwed by Axel on that damned rock. And all the while, Praedytus, the God of All Desire, looks on.

Perhaps more disturbing than being in two places at once is that I'm getting aroused watching the other me being skewered by the God of Nickel. I am one sick puppy.

My other self's screams of release break me out of the trance I've fallen into. However, I still have to shake my head to clear it before turning back toward the cave. I've got a few questions for Marlo, and my finding myself a twin is first on the list.

The cave is still empty and so I decide that now might be as good a time as any to test out my new demigod skills.

"Marlo, come to me."

Nothing happens.

I try again.

Nada.

I've not long finished with angry and moved on to furious when he blinks into being in front of me.

"You took your time," I say, unable to swallow my fury.

"Princess, the request only works when your emotions are at their strongest."

I open my mouth to call bullshit but stop, thinking back on when I'd requested one or other of the gods and, damn it, he's right.

No, hang on.

"What about when I requested Vyran at the cabin? I was calm when I did that."

"How far away was he?"

"A couple of feet."

"And were you experiencing any emotions?"

"Nope," I say with confidence, being damn sure I wasn't angry or scared at the time.

"Not even sexually?"

Rather than give him the satisfaction of admitting I'm wrong, I press on.

"But none of you guys seems to have to rely on emotions for it to work."

"We are gods. Not demigods."

"Did you just call me weak?" I say, bristling.

His only answer is to raise an eyebrow before lifting his hand so he can show me what he's holding.

"There's no way that'll fit!" I say, going weak at the knees.

Thirty seconds! Eat your heart out, Kegel. I'd learned the hard way to keep my feet clear when I relaxed my muscles, having broken a couple of toes. Not that they'd stayed that way for long after Marlo sucked on them, with his technique such that my sex twitched in rhythm with his filthy mouth. It was enough to give a girl a foot fetish.

"You are improving," says Marlo, from behind me and giving me a big enough fright that I come close to breaking another toe.

"Damn it!" I say, spinning to glare at him. "Don't sneak up on me like that."

He's grinning at my reaction like an eight-year-old who's just got one over on his little sister, rather than the greatest healer the Nyphrazi has ever known.

"You need a break," says Marlo, before taking my hand and leading me away from the cave.

I'm thrown when we walk down the path to the beach with its large magnetic rock. Axel is still screwing my other self's brains out as though on a loop. I'd asked Marlo about my twin, but he'd been vague, and even after listening to his explanation, I was still none the wiser.

Now I revel in the arousal I get every time I watch myself being pummeled by that shiny nickel cock of Axel's. If I'd thought it was a turn-on from up on the cliff, I was mistaken. Being close enough to hear all the slurping and moans of ecstasy has my bits humming in their need to get involved. It's like a mirrored ceiling, but so much better.

I take a breath in readiness to ask Marlo what gives, but he silences me with his lips before plunging that enzyme-laden tongue of his deep into my mouth.

This, combined with the sounds of Axel burying himself

deep inside my twin, has my body vibrating with need. I want Marlo inside of me so much, but I know I'm not up to it yet.

My desperation is such that even a tongue fuck would do.

As if reading my mind, Marlo stops his oral exploration before pulling away and peering at me. I'm not sure what it is he sees, but his hand lands on my head seconds later and we're out of there and back up to his cave.

Rather than still be standing, the furs caress my back while Marlo's mouth smothers my sex.

"Oh, yes! More of that!" The words rush from my lips, followed by a sigh of bliss when he obeys.

He pushes my legs to the sides before lifting them over his shoulders so I'm open to his probing tongue. He then runs it through my furrow over and over until I'm arching up off the furs. Still not content, he then spreads me wide with his fingers, tonguing me as deeply as he can.

I don't know if he has control over the level of enzymes, but this is the best session so far. There's nothing I can do to stop myself from clenching my muscles around him, to stop him from withdrawing.

I hold on for as long as I can, but when ripples run the length of his amazing organ, I'm unable to stop my own muscles from trembling in unison. It's almost enough to topple my self-control, even though this is something Marlo has been helping me with. I need a lot more practice. Damn it, don't think about the practice or it will all be over.

I'm disappointed when he pulls away, but his tongue is soon replaced by something hard, large, and fiery. Something that only just fits.

Once the bullet is in place, Marlo peels back the lips of my labia and then drives the end of his tongue into my clit over

and over. He sucks on it so hard that it pops out from under its hood.

“Oh, God. More!” I grit out and am consumed with bliss when he complies.

I know the climax isn’t far off when my core grips the iron bullet, holding onto it tighter and tighter. When Marlo slides a finger in right next to the tapered end of the bullet and presses hard on my G-spot, this is all it takes to have me disintegrate.

3

Marlo and I are lying entwined in a heap on the furs when he bursts the post-coital bubble I'm still enjoying.

"You are ready to take me."

"Are you sure about that?"

Rather than answer, he tugs on the chain of the bullet that is still sitting heavy inside me, and it pops free.

"Fuck me!" I'm unable to offer anything more articulate when I see the size of the monster he's just removed. It hadn't seemed that big a moment ago. Rather than too little or too much, it was amazing. However, it wasn't covered in rivets, now was it?

I can't help but squeak when Marlo drops the brute on the floor of the cave, the clatter echoing around the space. He then sets about removing the chain that secures that armored cock of his around his waist.

"What are you doing?"

"You said "fuck me," so I am."

"What? No! It's a figure of speech, not an instruction."

I'm unable to stop a snort of laughter upon seeing his disappointment.

"Maybe after a swim in the lake?" I say in appeasement.

"I cannot go into the lake. It would be painful."

"But I saw Praedytus in there, and he was happy enough."

"My father does not wear a fettyr."

I think about this for a minute before the implications dawn on me. Holy hell, the thought of seeing Marlo without his fettyr is doing funny things to my insides. He'd be massive, and that's no longer as scary as it once was.

"Is there anywhere I can go swimming that's colder than the lake?"

"How cold?" says Marlo, running his finger through my still-damp cleft.

"Icy!"

As the days pass, Marlo puts more pressure on me to do the dirty with him. He's never aggressive about it, but his reminders that the Festival of Obis is drawing near are constant, to the point I can stall no longer.

I'll have to take all of him to fulfill my part in the ceremony, so it's better that I deal with it now rather than wait. His size and opening night nerves would be a match made in hell.

I walk out of the cave and join him on the slab of rock that doubles as the cave's deck. "So, let's do this thing," I say, with as much enthusiasm as I can muster, but his expression lets me know I should have tried harder. "Sorry, but it's just daunting, that's all. It's the rivets."

"I am told they are the best bit," he says, looking hurt and making me feel like a complete bitch. He's far and away the

most sensitive of the gods, but I guess this is part of him being their healer. I couldn't imagine Seolfer or Aurum giving a flying damn what I thought.

"Come with me," says Marlo, holding out his hand.

I take it, expecting him to lead me somewhere. But without him putting his other hand on my head, we blink out of being, only to materialize a second or two later.

At first, I thought we must be in Praedytus's palace, what with all the marble columns. But in looking through them to the sparkling blue sea beyond, I realize we're most definitely not.

"Where are we?"

"This is my hearth. One of many."

"No. Not that. Where are we?"

I can see him trying for an answer before he gives up, and a frown settles on his face.

"Are we in Greece? Because it sure looks like Greece?"

"Greece?"

"Yeah. Part of the European Union."

The more I explain, the more his confusion grows.

"Where on the planet are we?"

At last, comprehension shows.

"Our realm is not like yours. We don't have places as you think of them."

I wave my hand at the very Greek view. "So, that doesn't exist?"

"It exists, but only to us and only now."

I thought about grilling him on this, but realized it would only be a complete mindfuck, and did it matter?

"What's the water like?" I have to ask, because there is no guarantee it'll be of the good old-fashioned plain variety. It could just as well be freezing cold, like Champagne, or the best

orgasm you could have without a tongue or cock being involved.

"It can be whatever you want it to be."

"Me?"

His nod answers my question but raises a stack more of them.

"How do I do it?"

"What do you want it to be?"

Damn it. I hate it when people answer my questions with questions. Also, how do I explain that I like it to be a little cold when I first get in, but for it to feel great after a second or two? Thinking about it, I experience a jump in my nerve endings, followed by the joy of my body acclimatizing. It's as if I'd just jumped into the gorgeous expanse of blue.

"That should do it," says Marlo, before walking out onto the patio, where he turns to look at me with an inviting expression. Not waiting for me to respond, he then walked to the edge of the cliff and, without pausing, leaped off into the water below.

I waste no time catching up, but I don't jump off the cliff as he has. It's a damned long way down.

No sooner had I thought about jumping if it wasn't so far, when it's as if the water had shot up to join me. Or maybe it's that the cliff has shrunk, but either way I line up a spot in the water next to Marlo and leap.

The water temperature is perfect, with just the right amount of shock before I become used to it.

Not that I'm cold for long with Marlo's large hands claiming my breasts. He then rolls and tweaks my nipples until they're far more puckered than they would have been from the water alone.

Knowing where this is heading both excites and worries

me, although all reason deserts me when Marlo claims my lips in a searing and enzyme-laden kiss. All of a sudden, everything intensifies, with my body responding in kind. My sex blooms, hot against the coolness of the water. Or maybe that's because Marlo has slipped one of his legs between my thighs and nudged me open.

Either way, my pearl is very at home in this particular sea.

"What do you wish for?" says Marlo, his voice choked with passion.

I think about sex on the beach, but just as soon discard it. Rivets will be bad enough without adding sand to the mix. Then it comes to me.

We swim to shore and get back up to the palace by way of steps cut into the rock face. On reaching the patio, I'm not surprised to see marble stairs leading up to the roof, just as I'd seen them in my imagination.

It's a quick climb to the top of the structure. There, just as I'd pictured it, is an enormous bed of moss, like the one Praedytus had taken me on. My imagination has even furnished the surrounding tangle of vines with icy blue flowers.

Turning to see if Marlo is impressed with my handiwork, I'm disappointed to see his expression is one of concern rather than arousal.

"Why this?" says Marlo.

"You don't like it?"

"I'm wondering how you know of this."

"Oh, I saw it when I was with your father." I don't bother telling him that his father was screwing my brains out at the time. A girl has to have some secrets.

I expect to have to clamber over the vines, but Marlo swings me up into his arms and steps into the center of the

moss. There he kneels and places me in its soft embrace as if I'm some fragile flower.

I'm waiting for him to make his move, but instead he looks at the flowers on the vines. He even picks one and examines it.

"This color, is it as you remember it?"

"Yeah, sure," I say, without giving my response any thought. If he's mucking about like this, we could be here for days.

He takes my response at face value, tossing the flower over his shoulder and checking out my body, giving it more attention than he had the discarded bloom.

The pure lust in his eyes does funny things to me, and this sensation only escalates when I see him lick one of his fingers. It's now covered with his enzyme-laden spit.

In the past, this would have been a turnoff, but knowing what that stuff can do has me squirming in anticipation. When he licks the rest of the fingers on his right hand, I become beyond excited.

My hunger is now rampant, and it's with eagerness that I watch his hand drop to my sex. I need no prompting to open myself wide, and I'm not disappointed when he slips a single finger deep inside me.

The moment those enzymes touch my insides, they turn me molten; swollen and frantic with need.

Marlo pulls his finger free, curling it in the process, riding my G-spot hard.

Then he slides two fingers in, and the sensations only get better, with the effervescence deep inside of me building ever stronger. By the time he's pumping all four fingers in and out of me in the best hand fuck I've ever had, I'm whimpering with need.

His hand is enormous, but it's still not enough.

"Please," I weep, hostage to my own growing desires.

While his expression might be one of caution, his actions show no doubt at all. This time when I hear the rattle of his fettyr chain, a thrill of want rushes through me. No doubt, just pure carnal need.

It must be something that shows on my face, because Marlo lifts one of my legs before securing it off to the side with a couple of the vines. After repeating this with my other leg, I'm left wide open for that iron-sheathed monster of his, with my sex twitching in readiness.

I welcome his hot hardness when it nudges at the entrance of my core. Even so, I'm unable to stop a few nerves from skittering through me, but I wrestle them under control. Tensing won't make this any easier.

Once again, Marlo licks his fingers but, rather than plunging them deep inside me, he massages and tweaks my clit until the ripples are close to overwhelming me. My focus on that one small part of my body is such that it takes a second for me to realize Marlo has pushed himself into my depths.

And he's right about the rivets.

Knowing the Nyphrazi as I do, I doubt it's an accident that the little metal heads are clattering over my G-spot with precision accuracy.

He's not all the way in before he withdraws, leaving me wanting more. With the next push, he goes deeper, and my little nubbin receives another glorious hammering from those rivets.

I'm not sure if he needs to take it this slow, but I love it, with the anticipation increasing with each slow pump. Not that his hand has left my clit in all this time, alternating between mashing it into submission and teasing it to come out and play.

It says a lot about the God of Iron's strength that he can

hold himself up with one arm. Just thinking about the strength behind the iron cock that's pumping in and out of me at ever faster speeds has me quivering in delight.

My G-spot is all over the action, swelling under the constant onslaught of the rivets and loving every minute. I'm having a pretty damned good time myself.

The orgasm starts out small, but doesn't stay that way for long and soon enough the muscles of my core are working hard against Marlo's iron fettyr.

I scream my release to the blue sky overhead and glory in the sun beating down on my overheated skin. I'm not sure if Marlo's having failed to achieve the elusive Nysa should worry me. What happens to me if I can't get all of them to achieve this during the ceremony to return me to my human form?

I'd ask him, but he's cleaning me up in his own unique fashion, and it's something that has me climaxing a couple more times. I have to admire his dedication.

"You must return to your own space to rest," says Marlo, letting me know more than him untying my legs that our training is over for now.

"Will you take me there?"

"You can transport yourself by wishing it so. Remember not to reappear before you left, though."

"Why? I've been in two places at once at the lake."

"What works here does not work in your world."

I guess this makes sense in some screwed-up space-time-continuum way. And so, after a soul-searing kiss from Marlo, I think of my uncle's cabin a moment after Vyran and I had left it.

. . .

On popping into being in the cabin's loft, I'm grinning like a fool.

What's not so good is that the bear is there with me. But before I get the chance to zap myself to safety, the bear's head explodes in a splatter of blood and gray matter, covering me in the process.

At any other time, this would have had me freaking out in a big way, but it was me or the bear, and that bastard had it coming.

"Jasmine, are you up there?"

"Ben?"

I shove the still-twitching carcass to one side with incredible ease before squeezing past it. When I stand at the edge of the loft and look down at him, Ben's expression is one of confusion, but it's not long before it changes to horny-as-hell.

"That new?" he says, nodding at me.

It's only when I peek down that I too notice my new adornment. The double chain that splits my furrow, in a design reminiscent of the Goddess of Copper's onesie, is then connected to a chain around my waist. After that, it's threaded through large nipple rings before snaking over my shoulders to join up at the back.

That the chain is iron does not surprise me, and the temptation to lift my arms above my head is one I succumb to, with my wanton groan heartfelt.

"Easy tiger, I'll yank your chains soon enough," says Ben, his promise doing nothing to quell my rampant lust. Then he has to ruin it by adding, "But first, we need to clean this lot up."

4

I'm not happy being filthy, sweaty, and covered in dead bear. Even with my newfound strength, getting the carcass out of the cabin had been a nightmare. But that was because I'd been trying to hide my strength from Ben. Despite being sneaky about it, I'd still surprised him twice.

After doing an awful skinning job with glorified butter knives, we got the bear down to chunks small enough to fit in the root cellar. By the time we'd done that and mopped the cabin, exhaustion had us in its grip.

The only plus about all the hard work was that it'd made it easy for me to avoid the unspoken questions that were hovering around Ben like vultures.

Despite having come out to the cabin to think about our relationship, thanks to the bear attack and my latest interlude with the gods, I hadn't had a chance. I'm no clearer on what I want now than I had been when I'd left Ben in the parking lot after our fight. To say I'm confused is an understatement.

What's weird is that while it's more than likely very fresh in

Ben's mind, for me it's been over a week since our fight. And to be honest, compared to the whole demigod-I-might-die scenario, it's lame in comparison.

Ben chucks another couple of logs into the old boiler that sits next to the beat-up hot tub out back of the cabin. I hadn't noticed it until we were in the middle of Operation Bear and can only assume it was part of my uncle's upgrades. There'd been no such luxuries when I stayed here as a kid.

"Should be hot enough soon," says Ben, closing the boiler door.

"Screw it, I think I'll get in now," I say, already ditching my clothes. That this plays hell with all the chains about my body has me hotter than Hades.

"We should jump in the lake first. If we get in there like this, the water will be filthy in seconds."

Ben has a point, but I also know from experience that the lake is cold enough to cause amnesia or a heart attack.

"Come on, chicken," says Ben, ditching his clothes and showing me that his cock is once again pierced with copper barbells.

I'm soon swamped with jealousy because I know this means he's just been with the Goddess Cuprum, or soon will be.

Well, screw how cold the lake is. I know that the redheaded cow isn't fond of water. If going into the lake with Ben will keep her away, then so be it. Freeze my tits off, it is.

"Race you," I say, already sprinting for the shoreline and all the while hoping it's as warm as that milky lake in the Nyphrazi realm.

Despite my newfound strength, Ben is no slouch and soon passes me. He doesn't slow when he hits the water and is under before I've even got my feet wet. What's surprising is that when his head clears the water, rather than screaming about how cold it is, he's whooping with delight. Crazy bastard.

It's only when I'm up to my knees that I realize the water isn't cold at all. Anything but. Could this be down to my hoping it'd be as warm as that Nyphrazi lake? There's only one way to find out.

No sooner had I thought about the temperature being what it was when I was a kid than Ben was yelling and hollering about having found a cold spot. Not wanting to take the edge off his hardness, I soon ramped the temperature back up.

I dive in, my outstretched form causing the chains in my cleft to pull tight and my nipples to be tugged on. The swim to join Ben is a sensual delight, and on reaching his side, all I can do is roll over on my back and float in bliss.

"So, who's behind these?" says Ben, tugging on the chains sitting over my stomach.

"Oh, hot damn. Do that again!"

He does so a little harder. "God of Iron is my guess."

"Marlo," I whisper, while enjoying Ben tugging on the chains over and over. The hotter I get, the cooler the water is by comparison.

"Sheesh, this water is getting cold. Enough for me," says Ben, dropping the chains and kicking hard to propel himself back to the shore, holding onto my hand so he can tow me in his wake.

On the way to shore, I can't help but notice that when my ardor cools, the water heats again. Hmmm. If I want to maintain the warmer temperatures, I need to concentrate. Okay, so no sex in the lake.

"It's not so bad here," says Ben, stopping in the shallows, but no sooner has he given me some chain action than the water temperature drops again. Weird, I'm usually better at multitasking than this.

"Come on, the hot tub should be warm by now." I flip over onto my stomach, drop my feet to the lake bottom, and am walking up the narrow beach before he joins me.

"Not so fast, tiger," says Ben, grabbing hold of the chains that dissect my back before disappearing between my ass cheeks.

The groan I make is not one of discomfort, so I keep pressing forward, enjoying it. Ben doesn't let go but rather experiments with pulling down on the chains. This has them rattling through the rings that pierce my nipples and clanking together as they run through my slit.

We reach the hot tub just in time, with my legs not so much ready to give out as no longer connected to my brain.

"In you go," says Ben, picking me up and lifting me over the side. In so doing, I notice his cock is no longer riddled with those copper doo-dads. Good, that means Cuprum won't be popping up soon.

I sink into the lukewarm water and settle on the sun-lounger-style seat that forms the bottom of the pool. Shame there's no power to run all the jets. Still, this is pretty damned good.

Rather than sit next to me, Ben settles himself on the other side of the pool, so there's no avoiding his examination of me.

"You want to tell me what was up with you on the Beast?" he asks.

Damn, I've never been great at this stuff. I think about trying to bullshit my way out of it, but taking a quick peek at

Ben's implacable expression, I don't like my odds of pulling it off. Okay, he asked for it.

"It's just that I'm so confused. I have feelings for you, I do, but it's just that." I stutter to a halt, knowing that once I say this next bit, there'll be no going back.

"Yes," prompts Ben.

"I care for Vyran too," I rush on. "And Marlo." The words tumbled out before I could stop them. "But it's different with each of them, Ben. Vyran makes me feel... free. Like I can be myself without apology. And Marlo—he sees me as more than just a power source. He cares about protecting me, not just using me.

I take a shaky breath. "But what I feel for them isn't what I feel for you. You're my choice, Ben. You're the one I want to build a life with, the one I love as a person, not as a god. You're real, as they can never be."

Oh God, did I just say that out loud? The words hang between us now, and I can't take them back. Do I mean it? Yes, I do. With my mind made up, I wait for him to explode because I have feelings for two gods, or react to my having told him I love him for the first time.

But nothing happens, and his expression is so blank that I can't tell what he thinks about my revelation.

My mouth gets the better of me, and I race on, telling him all about the demigod situation, although I gloss over the whole "I might die a bit." I tell him how it is. He doesn't interrupt me once and, of more concern, he still says nothing after I'm finished.

He's quiet for too long, the silence eating at my nerves.

"Aren't you going to say something?"

"There's not much I can say, is there? It's not like we're monogamous, is it?" His tone is an interesting mix of

exasperation, anger, and something that sounds like defeat. "Though I'll admit, competing with actual gods for my girlfriend's attention wasn't something I planned for when I moved to Alaska."

I go to respond but catch the way his hands clench at his sides and the muscle jumping in his jaw. This isn't calm acceptance—it's a man trying to process an impossible situation while holding onto the one thing that matters to him.

"I know you don't have a choice with Cuprum," I breathed. "Just like I don't have a choice with—any of this. But Ben, if I could choose—"

"Would you?" he interrupted. "Because sometimes I wonder if part of you loves the power, the way it makes you feel. And I get it, I do. What can some mine worker from Alaska offer compared to gods?" His voice drops to almost a whisper. "You said you loved me. You've never said that before."

I feel my throat tighten. "I meant it."

"Even with everything else going on? Even with them?"

"Especially with everything else. You're my anchor, Ben. You're what's real."

He stares at me for a long moment, and I can see him wrestling with hope and doubt. Finally, he gestures to the surrounding water. "It was you who changed the temperature of the lake, wasn't it?"

This throws me. While relieved he's accepted my strange reality, I'm annoyed he doesn't seem to care that I'll be screwed by six guys in a single night.

Either way, the water is nice and hot when he speaks again. "And no, I'm not happy about the ceremony, but if it means my girlfriend will be human again, I'll deal." He pauses, his voice growing rougher. "Because I love you too, Jasmine. Not the

power, not whatever you're becoming. You. And I'll fight for us, even if it means sharing you with gods."

"Ben," I whispered, reaching for his hand in the hot water. "Whatever I've become, whatever happens, my feelings for you won't change."

"Promise me something," he says, intertwining our fingers. "When this is all over, when you have choices again—promise me you'll choose us. Choose this." He gestures between us. "Choose the life we could build together."

I take some heart from the fact that he's still calling me his girlfriend, though there's no missing the strain in his eyes. The cost of what we're both enduring—him with Cuprum, me with the gods—is written in the tight lines around his mouth. For now, it's enough that he's choosing to fight for us rather than walk away.

Conscious of the vast quantity of butchered bear in the root cellar, we only stayed another night.

"I'd offer to get down there and lift it up," says Ben, looking through the trapdoor. "But I get the idea you're stronger than I am now."

So much for playing it down when I'd come clean about the whole debacle. I don't bother arguing. Rather, I strip off to avoid messing up my last clean clothes and then jump down into the cellar so I can throw the lumps of meat up to him.

They're so light, it's as if they're made of polystyrene. It's only after he staggers on catching a sizable chunk that I have to force myself to slow down. Once it's all stowed in the back of my truck, we head to the lake to wash up.

I'm horny after all the manual labor and the consequent

chain tugging that's gone on, so I'm leaving the lake just how it is. Which is bloody freezing.

That is until I'm ankle-deep in its icy embrace.

"There's no way I'm putting my cock and balls in that," says Ben with a huff, his hands crossed over them.

After getting control of my laughter, I thought about the temperature of the hot tub the night before. It isn't long before the surrounding lake is nice and steamy. If it weren't for my losing concentration every time I came close to orgasm, our washing up would have taken a lot longer.

The alarm shrieking at four thirty the following morning is a hell of a shock to my system. The return to work after a month of Nyphrazi time slips is not welcome.

I've gotten used to sleeping in and doing as I wish. The stupid thing is that I need to go to work. If I don't turn up in the current timeline, then I'll lose my job and my folks will want to know what the hell is going on. They, more than anyone, know how much my credit card debt has eaten away at me.

"Lord girl, did you get one of them spray tans?" says Glory, by way of greeting, when I stumble into the kitchen at the mine.

"Something like that," I say, balking at a full-on lie.

Despite a morning full of inquisition, I avoided most of my boss's questions. Boy, does she ever love to stick her nose into my sex life. If she only knew what it involved, she'd blow a gasket.

I come close to slipping up when I move a cauldron full of

chili from one gas hob to another. Rather than get someone to help me lift it over as usual, I pick it up and put it where I need to.

I'm about to move another enormous pot when I hear urgent coughing behind me. It sounds so fake that I turn to check what's up and see Ben looking at me, his eyes wide.

"Hi there," I say, fighting to keep the intimacy out of my voice.

"Don't hurt your back lifting anything heavy, will you?" His words sound so phony that they bring my screw-up to my attention. Lucky for me, he's the only one who's seen me manhandling the lunch.

"You finish at four?" I ask while looking around to see who can help me move the pot of rice so I don't stand out as having superhuman strength.

"Yep. You want to come to the Beast for an early—dinner?"

I'm unable to stop my chortle of smutty laughter, knowing full well what it is we'll be eating.

Glory is next to me in a heartbeat with her innuendo radar going at full belt. However, before she can give Ben or me the third degree about what we're chuckling about, I head her off.

"Great. I need help with this pot of rice. Can you give me a hand moving it?"

I turn to the range with a hand slung over her shoulder so I can steer her in that direction, too. By the time we've lifted the pot from the back to the front, Ben has done a runner and Glory's lost her opportunity. It's something that earns me a filthy look.

I'm out the door a minute after my shift ends and running to my truck. I'm on the road as soon as possible to avoid the

inevitable convoy leading to town. This also means it's only half-an-hour later that I'm hightailing it down the floating walkway on my way to The Metal Beast.

As soon as I'm inside the main cabin, I ditch my clothes like they're hot. When I walk into the master, the only thing I'm wearing is Marlo's chain onesie.

Ben's not there.

Strange, his truck had been in the parking lot.

It doesn't take long to check the whole boat, but my redheaded lover doesn't turn up.

If that copper-draped bitch has her claws into him again, I'll rip her hair out by the roots! I know my jealousy is ridiculous, given I'm not being faithful to Ben either, but I can't help it.

Damn it.

I'm thinking about getting dressed and going home when it comes to me. If I'm stronger, can heat water, and call the gods to me, then maybe I can summon Ben?

"Ben, come to me!" I say, putting as much pure love as I can into this request. Combined with how furious I am about Cuprum stealing him away, my plea is bound to be emotional enough to work.

5

A moment later and Ben materializes on the bed in front of me, writhing and moaning, his cock looking to be as hard as concrete. If I don't screw him soon, he'll lose his mind, and I'll be damned if he loses his marbles on my watch.

"You're just lucky I'm ready to go," I say to him, for all that he notices me.

This time, I'm strong enough to pin him to the bed. When I grab him by the cock, there's relief in seeing all the copper barbells are still in place. Serve the bitch right if I get some pleasure from them. I just hope my chains don't tangle in them, not that they should, because Marlo didn't seem to have any problems.

I wasted no time straddling him and sinking down onto that most luscious mix of hard flesh and copper.

I'm only a few minutes into screwing his brains out when my iron chains tingle with electricity. It's nowhere near as spectacular as when I'd been fitted with all the copper

accessories that I'd received courtesy of Ciprus, but it's still pretty damned amazing.

Each time I drop, the barbells work away at the walls of my sheath, while the chains sparkle, tingling my clit and nipples. The chain tickling between my ass cheeks has me squirming and grinding on Ben's cock, hoping to increase the sensations enough that I snap him out of his carnal trance. Not that I won't enjoy the ride, too.

I'm rewarded when I see sanity return to his eyes. I'm then further rewarded when he catches on and drives his hips up at the same time as I drop to reclaim his length. We grind into each other, pumping away, desperate to be close, desperate for what I now think of as Nysa.

I'm close to climaxing with the anticipation killing me, but when Ben yells his release, it blows all my fuses. It's like an orgasm, but so much more. The surge of energy that rages through me has all my erogenous zones awash with pleasure, but it's still more than that. The top of my scalp prickles while it's as if my skin is breathing.

I'm reeling from the overload when Ben pulls on my chains and I orgasm myself. But again, it's so much more, with a rush of power and pleasure consuming my body. After racing to my extremities, it comes crashing back, overwhelming my sex to the point I disintegrate. With love in the mix, our connection has never been stronger.

My body is liquid, with me soon dissolving in a puddle on Ben's chest, limp and compliant. It's something he takes advantage of, with his hands roaming over my body. When he pulls on the chains running between my ass cheeks, I'm spread wide, with the resultant ripple of lust leaving me begging for release again.

Before he can do anything about it, though, I get a brain

buzz and I'm out of there. I'm in a heap on the ledge overlooking the opalescent lake. At first, I thought Marlo must have requested my presence, but the feet next to my face are feminine. The copper chains around the ankles let me know I have the Goddess of Copper, to thank for being ripped away from my not quite postcoital bliss with Ben.

Rather than fight with her, I put all my energy into concentrating on The Metal Beast so I can get back to Ben.

Nothing happens.

"You cannot travel from here," says Cuprum, letting me hear her voice for the first time. There's a trace of an accent but not enough to pin down, and her voice is sultry and deeper than I would have thought was possible for a woman.

"What do you mean?" I say, scrambling onto my hands and knees.

"Demigods can enter this dominion but cannot leave. Ever!" She's still crowing when I get to my feet. Crazy bitch.

She then blinks out of sight, leaving me on my own.

What does she mean, I can't leave? I've been here before, and I left just fine that time. I try to imagine myself next to Ben, but with no more luck than on my first attempt. I then have a go at getting to my uncle's cabin, my bedroom at home, Ben's cabin on the hill, anywhere. I'm getting more panicked with each failed attempt and have to force myself to get a grip. My freaking out isn't doing jack shit.

It's only when I've calmed myself somewhat that I take in my surroundings. At first glance, it looks to be as it was before, but it's not. Axel's big magnetic rock is missing, and the cave behind me isn't the one I'd spent time in with Marlo. Most telling of all is that Ben's boat is no longer anchored in the middle of the lake.

"Where the hell am I?" I yelled at my new surroundings, not expecting a reply.

"Can you not tell?" says a man from behind me, having me spinning so hard that I come close to losing my footing.

"You!" I stare daggers at Seolfer, God of Silver. Not that he looks thrilled to see me, either and nor does Gaiya, Seolfer's mother, who's next to him. It's the first time I've seen the old woman since Vyran and Gaiya were both banished because she'd sent me home without his permission.

However, there's no hired-help vibe about her now, with the luxurious quality of her gown a match for her place in society. Gone is the supposed servant, replaced by a woman who moves with unmistakable authority. Even her face looks different without the practiced subservience.

"Damn it to hell! Does this mean I'm banished, too?"

"No," says Seolfer, not bothering to go into details. He then steps forward and fingers Marlo's body chains. "You have been busy."

I slap his hand away and know by how wide his eyes are that my strength has taken him by surprise.

"Very busy," he added.

"If I'm not banished, then what?"

"Demigods cannot be banished," says Gaiya, proving to me she can speak English after all.

"What my mother means is that only gods and goddesses can be banished. Demigods are left in stasis until they rot."

His tone is one of enjoyment and pure malice, and so I don't think twice about stepping forward and sucker punching him. Sure, my hand hurts like hell, but watching him sink into a gasping heap at my feet makes it all worthwhile.

"How dare you treat my son like this," says Gaiya, crouching down to tend to her asshole offspring.

"And you can go screw yourself, too," I say, fighting an inbuilt sense that it's not nice to be mean to old people.

After stomping off and leaving them to their mutual admiration, I wandered for hours, trying now and then to think of myself as being anywhere but where I was.

It's not until I reach the pebble beach that I come upon a solution. This has me stop in my tracks, then turn back the way I'd come. But after taking a few steps, I stopped again.

"Vyran, come to me!"

By the time I've called to Ciprus, Axel, Marlo and even that golden asshole Aurum, I'm swamped with panic. On hearing Seolfer yelling that I'll rot there, I lose it and start pelting rocks at him and his scheming mother.

I'm rewarded with more than a few yelps and roars, letting me know I'm on target and have one hell of a throwing arm. It's something that soon has the pair disappearing over the top of the hill, out of range.

A little calmer after my pitching practice, I gave my salvation one more try. It's a long shot, but I've got nothing to lose.

"Praedytus, come to me."

Nothing.

I give it another go, putting more urgency into my request.

A second later, he appears in a heap on the beach in front of me, and I'm not sure who gets the biggest surprise. Myself, him, or the woman he's sixty-nining. The way the father of the gods' cock is stretching the girl's mouth has me rubbing my jaw in sympathy.

Not that it seems to impress him, and with a casual wave of his hand, he sends her packing. The only sign of her having

been there is a tidemark of red lipstick a gaggingly long way up his shaft.

“Perhaps you would like to finish what my companion started?” says Praedytus, his tone conversational.

I’m all ready to tell him to shove it where the sun doesn’t shine when I remember he’s the only one who can get me out of this place. He must see my reluctance because, after hooking his hand behind my ankle, he runs it up and down my calf. My body’s response is instantaneous, and my legs give out on me as I’m stunned by a desire so strong that rational thought deserts me.

From balking at getting my mouth anywhere near his cock, I found my lips closing over the end. He tastes incredible. Like chocolate, like butterscotch, like toffee, like every delicious dessert you’ve ever tasted, all rolled into one.

But without the calories.

I can’t get enough of him.

I’m only just aware of him dragging my body on top of his, but there's no missing when his hot mouth closes over my sex. He sucks, slurps and bites until I’m screaming my release around his delicious cock, all the while pressing my girly bits hard against his mouth. This is one of those times I’m glad Aurum got rid of my pubes for good.

It’s only when we’re back at his palace that we talk.

“How did you end up in the Fields of Obadyn?”

“Cuprum, ah, called me to her.”

“Hmmm, that’s unusual. She should not have been able to call you from Marlo’s side.”

“I wasn’t with him. He sent me home to rest.”

“What were you doing when she called you?”

"Resting, kind of."

"And your idea of resting is?"

I told him everything up to my arriving in the fields, leaving nothing out, even my calling Ben to my side. He's quiet to the point that I get twitchy.

"What?" I say, hoping to break his silence.

"You are not like the others. You're stronger, more resistant. I'll send you back to Marlo for your final preparation. He must ensure you're ready for what's coming."

I wasn't sure which bombshell to address first. That I wasn't like the others, or that I had to be ready for what was coming. "Why am I different?"

"Because it would appear my daughter has transformed this Ben into a veil or charm of sorts. However, it's your being able to use him in this way that surprises me."

I'd heard him and Axel talk of these before, but hadn't gotten around to asking Vyran about them. I wouldn't make that mistake again. Knowledge is power and all that.

"But what are they? A veil, I mean."

"A veil is a weak spot between your world and ours. While charms are gifts, we can send through to your realm if the tie is strong enough. Things like Ciprus's copper playthings, Seolfer's fascinum, or Aurum's golden mantle. Sometimes they're small tokens we send you home with." He lifts the chain that pierces my nipples and tugs on it by way of explanation.

It doesn't take a brain surgeon to know that he's talking about things like all those copper barbells with which Cuprum pierces Ben's cock.

I am so getting some bolt cutters when I get back home. Those copper barbells are coming off Ben for good.

That's if I make it back home.

6

I've now been back with Marlo for what he calls three nyphs. They're like days, but who the hell knows how long they are or even if they're all the same length.

We've settled into a routine of sorts. We start the nyph with a simple breakfast of berries, and then he nails me to the wall of the cave with that huge armored cock of his. Even better is after when he takes away any twinges I might experience with his lubed tongue.

This morning is different. And I'm not so sure I'm keen on the change.

"What, or who, the hell is that?" I say, looking at the iron monstrosity that's as tall as I am, and that's appeared overnight on the wide rock ledge outside the cave.

"It is the Goddess of Obis," says Marlo, running his hand down the side of the statue.

Obis? The goddess we'd made a divine offering to, and after whom the isle was named? I'd thought she was dead, and yet

the way Marlo referred to her and the way he stroked the effigy said otherwise.

This has me checking her out, but there are no signs of life that I can see. This is especially so when I tap an ass cheek and am rewarded with a deep, metallic dong that confirms the statue is hollow and a goddess in name only.

"What's it for?" I say, walking around to check out the front.

That's weird. Rather than having a three-dimensional front as I'd expected, she's like an Easter egg that's been cut in half, hollowed out and that's missing a face, bunny or otherwise.

"Why don't you get in and find out?"

"Are you joking?" I say, taking a big step back.

"She will not hurt you. You might even like it."

I take some comfort in the fact that Marlo is grinning. There's also the fact that he's a healer. Does this mean he's taken a Hippocratic Oath or something that prevents him from hurting me?

After a tentative step, I stopped. "Hang on. What does it do?"

I cross my arms and tap my foot, hoping this stance will have the same meaning here as it does at home. If he thinks I'm climbing inside without a few clues about what'll happen, he can go screw himself.

"For each, it is different."

"Oh, for fuck's sake, is nothing straightforward with you, Nyphrazi?"

I stand firm. This time I'm determined to hear the full story before committing. I've been caught too many times in the past to make the same mistake again.

"For some, there is intense pleasure, the likes of which

they've never experienced before. If you are hurt, she can heal you. If you are weak, she can make you strong."

"But?" I know to ask now because there's always a "but" with these guys.

"If you are not pure of heart, then she can be your worst nightmare," says Marlo, confirming my suspicions.

"Are we talking Jennifer Aniston pure here, or Mother Teresa?"

Marlo frowns before shaking his head in confusion.

Damn, I keep forgetting these guys are more or less foreigners. "How pure does my heart need to be?"

"Pure enough that you haven't figured out my father," whispers Marlo, before looking like he's said too much. "The goddess sees all, Jasmine. She, more than any other, will know if you're ready for what is coming."

I don't think I'm any purer than the next girl. I have impure thoughts—lots of them. I can be a bitch at times, but I don't think I'm into mean-girl territory.

As if sensing my reticence, Marlo huffed out before asking, "Have you ever hurt someone on purpose?"

I shake my head, but can't help thinking about how I'd hurt Ben. But that hadn't been intentional. Had it?

Marlo places his hands on my shoulders and locks eyes with me. "Have you ever harmed another on purpose?"

"I pulled Christy Weaver's ponytail because she upstaged me in the school play in second grade." Hmm, perhaps that's why she didn't invite me to her engagement party? Vindictive bitch.

"I was thinking more of murder," says Marlo, fighting to keep a smile at bay.

"No! I only kill for food, and I sure as hell don't eat people."

Well, I do, but not with a knife and fork, and I've had no complaints.

"You'll be safe," says Marlo, steering me closer to the statue of Obis.

By the time I'm standing on the plinth with my back to the hollow, I'm having second thoughts. But before I can say anything, Marlo nudges me into the goddess's metal embrace.

At first, I noticed nothing, but then the metal heated around me. Not hot, just warm. The chains draped over my body and then dissolved but for the large iron rings that pierced my nipples.

However, I get a hell of a fright when the statue snaps tight around my body, trapping me in place while leaving my front exposed.

"Marlo, what's happening?"

"She has accepted you." His tone is relaxed and says more than his words that I'll be okay. "She has chosen you, Princess. That changes everything."

I've not asked what he means when a buzz of energy starts in the soles of my feet and weaves its way up my body. Even better is when it empowers everything in its path.

However, when it reaches my sex, I know that if it hadn't been for the goddess supporting me, I'd have landed in a heap.

There's nothing external in the stimulation. I'm being buzzed at a cellular level, and it's amazing. This leaves me throbbing with a crushing need, my sex a quivering mush. Not content with staying put, the energy then works its way up through my core before engulfing my breasts.

The nipple rings don't last two seconds after the first pulse, falling to the ground in pieces. My buds throb with pleasure, swelling in their need, my breathing stuttering in response.

When the energy hits my brain, I experience the most

intense response yet, as if every synapse on offer has fired at once. My scalp prickles and my hair floats about inside the space between my head and that of the goddess shell. My lips swell and my mouth waters in want and need.

Then, the energy recedes to coalesce in my core, forming into a tight ball before exploding and flooding me with extreme power and need.

The need is constant.

"Marlo..." I'm unable to say more than this, but my longing must be evident. He steps up to the goddess statue and caresses the sides of its legs. I know he can't touch my skin because of the iron, and yet it's as if he's just run his hands down the sides of my legs.

The goddess steps wide, taking my legs with her.

Marlo then taps behind her knees, and she bends them at right angles to the ground, flattening herself out à la Matrix. She's formed herself into a gravity-defying table of sorts, with me now lying on my back, spread wide. Ready.

The longing hasn't diminished, and I'm now craving even more of something undefinable. However, when Marlo kneels and his mouth covers my sex, the hunger only intensifies.

This is what I want. But it's still not enough.

He doesn't hold back, sucking on my clit, drawing it out and then rewarding it by licking it into a frenzy. And, oh boy, I'm overjoyed to be along on that ride.

I try arching my hips to increase the pressure that's building, but I'm held firm.

"More," I grit out, hoping Marlo will heed my wishes.

"As you command," he says, sliding a single finger deep inside me, and then swirling it around, pressing the walls and fondling my G-spot.

"More," I groan.

He gives me more, but it's still not enough.

"I cannot give you what you want while you live in the goddess."

However, it looks like the goddess has other ideas, with her spreading our legs wider than I'd have thought possible. The edges of the iron that cradles my back seep their way into my cleft, spreading me wide and open to Marlo's hungry gaze.

"I should not. Father said the final bonding must wait until the ceremony, but I cannot watch you suffer. I do not think the goddess would want that," says Marlo, conflict clear in his voice.

However, his resistance falters when he leans forward and places his hands on the plinth on either side of the goddess's hips. Or are those our hips? We grab hold of his arms and pull him forward until the end of his cock is hard up against me.

No sooner had his fettyr touched my sex than the chain holding it around his waist shattered like plastic, leaving him free to enter me.

But still, he resists.

The hunger is now so overwhelming that I'm whimpering in need. This soon turns to howling and screaming, with the craving having mutated into pure agony.

"You have to," I screamed at him. "I'm dying."

And indeed, that's what it's like. My limbs are solid with pain, paralyzed by it. I'd be rigid even without the goddess holding me tight.

Marlo has only just entered me when the agony changes to ecstasy. It happens so fast that I'm disoriented for a moment, but by the time he's balls-deep inside me, I've mastered it. Or maybe it's mastered me?

Held wide by the goddess, I'm at the mercy of his cock, but I still feel safe. And Marlo is gentle, withdrawing and filling me

in turn with great skill, driving me ever closer to whatever it is I'm longing for.

I find out soon enough.

If I'd thought my last orgasm courtesy of Ben was incredible, it proved tame by comparison to this.

I'm aroused to the point that it's as if the pain has returned. I'm aware of every inch of Marlo as I climax against him. I grip him hard enough that I've doubtless popped a couple of his rivets.

The ripples of pleasure work their way out from my very core, tingling through my body to exit through my fingers, toes, and scalp. When beyond my body, it's as though my aura is getting in on the act.

The blast when the ripples return is an adrenaline-laced rush that has my whole body vibrating inside the statue and heating until sweat prickles my skin.

So, hot.

I am the goddess, and she is me. Even when I close my eyes, I can still see Marlo, but I'm looking through her eyes with everything brighter, sharper, larger than life.

But something isn't right, with my gut telling me this is about more than the Festival of Obis because, because rather than feeling human, I feel divine.

Meanwhile, a woman whispers secrets I don't fully understand. Warnings about altars and ceremonies and seven becoming one. Seven becoming one? Didn't she mean six?

In the end, the portents of doom merge until they're nothing more than white noise, allowing me to concentrate on the magnificence of Marlo burying himself ever deeper.

I'm glorying in our connection when I once again hear the woman. "Thank you, child. Your sacrifice will change worlds."

As with everything else to do with the Nyphrazi, this leaves

me in the dark and wondering what it is I've sacrificed, or even why. I've come to no conclusions when Marlo reaches climax and all hell breaks loose.

Not only does he grow in girth and length all of a sudden, but the statue of Obis shatters into a million pieces. It's only his grabbing hold of me that stops me from falling backward to the ground. Instead, he scoops me up, and I wrap my legs around his waist before settling even more fully onto his solid length.

It's not until after we've had another bone-jarring session inside the cave that we separate and see Marlo's fettyr is missing.

There's no mistaking that he's stunned by this, even if he controls his shock in seconds. Having ridden in this particular rodeo before, I'm ambivalent about the development. Even so, Praedytus will be super pissed that two of his sons are now close to him in power.

"I need to speak to my father. He must know what's happened. You're stronger than any of us realized, and that changes everything," says Marlo, genuine worry creasing his features when he disappears.

"And I need to speak to Ben," I say to the now empty cave.

All I do is wonder if he's still on The Metal Beast, and I'm there in the master cabin watching him skewer that bitch, Cuprum.

I yank hard enough on her copper onesie that I rip her off Ben's cock and deal with a few of her pubic hairs while I'm about it.

"He is mine," I scream loud enough that she pulls away as far as she can, which isn't far given I'm still holding onto her copper slut suit.

I'm speculating on what to do with her when she twists,

slams her hand down on top of my head, and bam—we're back in the Fields of Obadyn.

"This time, my father will not rescue you. You'll serve the purpose you are destined for. The ceremony will proceed as intended," she spits out.

I'm still readying myself to slap her into next week when she disappears, leaving me on my own. Or so I thought.

"Back so soon?"

I whip around, but there's no one there. It's only when I look up that I see Seolfer standing above the entrance to the cave, looking smug. Not that he stays smiling for long when I bend down and pick up a couple of large rocks.

I wait until I see his naked ass disappearing over the ridge before I speak again.

"Praedytus, come to me!" I say, putting as much emotion into this plea as I can, but nothing happens.

Damn it all to hell. What has that bitch done that I can no longer summon the God of All Desire? It's not like I haven't tried either.

Damn it, I shouldn't have gone straight to the Beast. If I'd headed for my truck, I could have come up with a better plan.

I wish I were in my truck right now.

"Freaking hell!"

I don't know what shocks me more, that I've escaped the Fields of Obadyn or how cold the vinyl seats in my truck are on my bare ass.

I continue swearing while rummaging around behind the front seats, looking for my bag of spare clothes. After being caught naked in the snow that time behind Ben's hill cabin, I always have a bag of spare gear at the ready.

Mind you, this is the first time I've had to use it, with most of my travels having been from one naked location to another.

Once dressed, I realized I didn't have the keys to my truck. They're in my backpack on the Beast with Ben and the copper floozy.

I ran the length of the floating walkway until the last branch. From there I tiptoe, keeping as quiet as I can, inching my way closer to the boat with as much stealth as possible. With any luck, I can sneak on board, grab my backpack and get out of there without being sent back to Seolfer again.

For all I know, my escaping the gravitational force of that place could have been a fluke. I won't risk returning, even if it was fun to chuck rocks at the God of Silver and his old hag of a mother.

I'm sneaking across the back deck like something out of a Pink Panther movie when Ben pops up next to me. He gives me such a fright that I come close to having an accident.

"Ah," I garble, while clutching my throat as if he's about to steal my pearls.

"Sorry, I didn't mean to scare you," he says before pulling me into a tight embrace. "Hope you're hungry."

I'm lying in Ben's arms in the very early hours of the following morning before I have space to think about the latest developments. Due to another of those weird-ass Nyphrazi time slips, I'd ended up back on the Beast before Cuprum had even arrived.

The copper barbells had popped up on Ben's cock not long after. But I was having none of it and took to him with a pair of bolt cutters that soon made quick work of the charms. He'd been a complete girl about it, and it had taken a while to get

him hard again after I'd chucked all the copper bits into the harbor.

But it worked. No Cuprum.

I'm not sure how long I've got until the ceremony, but it can't be long, even in Earth-days. I know I've got to go back to Marlo to finish my training, and I'll have to go soon. I only hope I can time it so that he doesn't know I've been back to visit Ben while he was with his father.

Timing is, as they say, everything.

I've only just finished thinking this when I feel the familiar buzz inside my head. I'm busy freaking out that Cuprum has kidnapped me again when I materialize in the middle of Marlo's cave.

EPILOGUE

The closer we are to the ceremony, the more Marlo pushes me, though it's not all hard work and no play. We're lying back on the furs, relaxing after a strenuous coupling, when he grabbed my wrist with unusual urgency.

"Princess, there are things about this ceremony you don't understand. I've been reading the old texts, and some of the details don't match what my father described. Things that worry me..."

But before he can say more, Praedytus flickers into being in the entranceway, his timing too perfect to be coincidental. It's also something that has Marlo stumbling to his feet.

"It's not time already, is it?" I say, looking over to the God of All Desire. "Wouldn't it be better for me to recover first?"

Praedytus doesn't answer immediately. Rather, he walks over and steps in front of Marlo, invading my personal space in a way that has me leaning back against the cave wall. "No, it's not time for the ceremony, divine daughter, but there are other rituals."

His gaze when he looks down at me isn't speculative. Rather, it's triumphant, like a chess master who believes he's viewing his ultimate move—though I catch something flickering behind his confidence. A tightness around his eyes suggests that even master strategists can't account for every variable.

"Father," Marlo says, his voice tight with concern. "There's still more time—"

"No, there isn't," says Praedytus, interrupting his son as he's doubtless done a thousand times before. "There are preparations that must be completed before she faces all of you. Protocols that I must attend to."

The look that passes between father and son is so loaded that now even I'm on edge. I know I haven't imagined the friction between them when I see Marlo clench his jaw and fist his hands at his sides. This is so out of character for the Nyphrazi healer that I struggle into a sitting position.

"But Father, I haven't yet—" Marlo begins.

"The training has reached its limits, for now," Praedytus interrupted again, his tone paternal but firm. "What she needs now is knowledge only I can impart." His smile is reassuring, almost gentle. "Don't worry, I'll return her in plenty of time to finish her training."

"Father—" Marlo starts again, uncertainty flickering in his dark eyes. "There's so much she doesn't understand."

"What? What don't I understand?" I demand, looking between them. The air crackles with divine tension, and I can feel power radiating from both gods in waves.

"Come, Jasmine. There are preparations if we are to succeed," says the God of All Desire, holding his hand out.

"Don't," Marlo whispers, easing his father to one side. "Whatever preparations he has planned, they can wait until—"

Praedytus moves with divine swiftness, his hand closing gently but firmly around my wrist. The last thing I see is Marlo's face, twisted with worry and frustration, before the world as I know it dissolves.

"Trust me, child. This is for the greater good," Praedytus murmurs as we vanish in time and space, his tone warm but somehow making my blood run cold.

GOD of all DESIRE

1

After my sojourn with the God of All Desire, I'm back at my usual training spot on the platform outside Marlo's cave.

Everything feels different now. The iron bullets that once challenged me seem almost weightless in my hands. Whatever Praedytus did to me during those missing days has changed me in ways I'm still discovering.

I whoop with joy when the iron weight drops to the ground. Seven minutes!

But it's no surprise that I'm strong. I've been doing the exercises set by Marlo with religious fervor; anything to avoid joining the fallen. While the women from The People of the Mist might relish a godly all-you-can-eat buffet, the very idea horrified me.

Think of the most luxurious spa retreat imaginable, but one you can never leave. A life of pampered indulgence, beautiful surroundings, gorgeous divine lovers... and no freedom or choice in the matter. There is no way that's happening to me.

The other thing I'm having trouble with is holding back my orgasms. I'd always found them a rare and precious thing, the idea of keeping one at bay an anathema to me. It just isn't natural.

"Did I hear a whoop?" says Marlo, strolling out to join me. His hands are behind his back, with experience telling me I'm about to get another challenge. But there's worry in his dark eyes that wasn't there before his father spirited me away.

"You sure did. I lasted seven whole minutes. And with the heaviest one, too!"

Instead of the praise I'm expecting, his expression remains troubled as he hands me a miniature of the Goddess of Obis. It's heavy, and the hook atop her head concerns me. I examine this, then the chain attached to the iron bullet lying at my feet.

"You've got to be joking!"

"Not up to the task?" he says, although his usual teasing tone is strained. "Though I suspect you'll find it easier than you think."

"Piece of cake," I say with a healthy dose of bravado, though when the small statue shimmers in the fading evening light, this falters. Rather than grin as he usually would, he turns and enters the cave, his steps slow, his shoulders tense.

"Try squatting so the goddess's feet can touch the ground."

This challenge, tossed over one shoulder, has me ready to throw the statue at the back of his head. He can't be serious. Never mind cracking nuts as a party trick. At this rate, I'll be able to open bottles of beer!

"Marlo!" I call after him. "What did your father do to me?"

The question hangs between us, loaded with all my fears about what those missing days with Praedytus had involved. I can feel the changes in my body, the way power flows through

me like electricity through a copper wire, but I need to understand what price I've paid for this strength.

If there's one thing I've learned about the Nyphrazi, it's that there's always a price, even if it's not immediately obvious.

He stops but doesn't turn, his shoulders rigid with tension. I think he's ignoring me when he gives in to a heavy sigh. "Things he shouldn't have. Things that might affect the ceremony." His voice carries the weight of someone who's watched his father cross lines that should never be crossed.

Before I can ask what he means, the surrounding air shimmers just as the small statue had earlier. With it comes a presence I've sensed growing stronger since my time with Praedytus. It's as if something he did to me opened a door that can't be closed. Or had I opened the door myself?

"You feel it, don't you?" whispers the woman I'd heard after the statue of Obis shattered. "The changes he made to you. The bridge he created because of his ignorance."

I've just worked out who she's talking about when she adds, "Your increased strength since our divine bonding," with this revelation leaving me unable to move, much less breathe.

"Obis? It was you all along, wasn't it?"

Marlo spins, his eyes wide. "You can hear her?"

Before I can answer him, Obis continues without pause. "The beautification is working better than I'd hoped. Look at yourself, child. Can you not see?"

I glance down, understanding what she means in an instant. My skin doesn't just look different. Rather, it pulses with an inner light that matches my heartbeat. The power flowing through me isn't just that of a demigod, but something else.

"Goddess, she's not strong enough," says Marlo, looking everywhere and nowhere at once, his expression one of horror

"Little one, you are stronger than he knows. And more than

some are expecting," says Obis, her words laced with unexpected humor. Marlo's lack of reaction to the goddess's revelation tells me he can't hear her.

Despite this, Obis drops her voice when she continues. "Praedytus has never run the full ceremony. There are protocols, traditions... things that could go wrong if they're not followed in detail. Things no mere god would understand, but which I intend to use."

She then falls silent, as if unwilling or unable to impart more. It's this that has the weight of destiny settling on my shoulders like a mantle. My worry now is that whatever happened during those missing days with Praedytus, it was only the beginning.

Days later, when the God of All Desire returns for what he calls the final preparations, I'm ready for him. Or at least, I think I am.

"It's time," he says, his gaze holding that same triumphant gleam I've learned to dread. Ever polite, he holds out his hand to help me to my feet, but I resist taking it.

I know from experience that the moment I touch him, I'll be wetter than Sitka in October and panting for him to screw my brains out. If I'm to survive what's to come, I need to keep my wits about me.

Not to be deterred, he curls his fingers, beckoning me to take hold of them, and when it becomes obvious he won't go away, I put my hand in his.

I'm not even given a chance to stand before we leave the cave. However, when we materialize on the Isle of Obis, he's holding me in his arms, although he soon lets me stand.

That's strange.

I'm not overcome with lust.

Perhaps that's only allowed in the pink pool deep inside the Isle? I've been contemplating this with such intensity that when the rock we're standing on dissolves under our feet, it still scares the crap out of me.

Not that I freak out altogether, given I know what I'm in for. I land with a plop far below, but rather than Praedytus being beside me, I'm alone.

Unlike when I'd visited with Vyran, rather than being radioactive green, the gel is a beautiful, pale blue. The exact shade of the mystical flowers that had surrounded Praedytus and me in that enchanted glade. The memory sends a frisson of arousal through me, though this soon turns into an uneasy chill that cools my ardor.

The unease lingers as I float on my back, and I'm wondering what will happen next when I hear Obis telling me to relax. With her voice having come from right behind me, I'm now about as relaxed as an ironing board. However, when I twist around, I find I'm alone.

"Relax, child. You will come to no harm while I am here."

This time it's as though she's beside me. But when I twist back, all I can see is blue goo. It's at this moment that the rock above reforms itself and seals me in.

There's no going back now.

"Lie back, young one. Let the unguent do its work."

"Unguent?"

Instead of telling me what it is, she continues as if I haven't just spoken. "I have been waiting so long to speak with you without restrictions. There are things about this ceremony you need to know. About Praedytus' intentions and what I require, but now is not the time."

It doesn't take long to realize she's no longer next to me, or even inside my head. Despite her saying I'd come to no harm, I'm nowhere near as relaxed as I'd been the last time I was here. Back then, I'd held Vyran's hand.

As before, the absolute darkness is broken by the gel glowing brighter and brighter until I'm forced to squint. Despite this, my body has never felt better. But while the green goo had me feeling like a child, now I'm all woman.

Wanton.

Ripe.

I don't think I've ever been as aware of my womanhood before. Sure, I've felt sexy during my dealings with the gods, but this is different. This is so much more. It's sex and power, wants and needs all bound in an overwhelming package.

"You may get out now."

The disembodied voice breaks into my awareness, but it still takes me a moment to force myself to stand.

"Freaking hell!"

A glance at my boobs and I know it's not my imagination that they've gone up several cup sizes. Even more noticeable is that they're now as high as they were when I was in a training bra. Likewise, my nipples are as erect as they'd been when daisy-chained by those magnetic pebbles of Axel's.

If Ben could see me now, he'd blow.

Once I'm standing beside the pool, the woman who I have to assume is a goddess tells me to move forward. With my feet covered in the slippery balm, there's every chance I'll take a tumble. Thankfully, the fine sand on the floor of the tunnel she directs me down soon solves this problem.

A dozen rights and a couple of lefts later, and I'm more than lost. I'm disoriented. My pace slows of its own volition as

I think about whether I'll be able to find my way back to the pool.

"I will make sure you are safe," says Obis back inside my head.

She can read my mind?

"Yes, I can."

Sheesh. Happy thoughts, happy thoughts.

Fixated as I am on my secret conversation with Obis, I'm surprised when my guide and I come upon a group of women. The racket of their chatter should have alerted me to their presence, if not their appearance. Each is stunning in her own way. It's like a Miss World finale on steroids.

Cuprum is at the heart of this group, leading me to believe her companions must be goddesses, too. There's no way the stuck-up bitch would deign to mix with anyone she considered beneath her. Even so, it's been a while since I last saw this many tits in one place.

Perhaps "vacuous" is a better description.

On seeing me, Cuprum's husky laughter catches in her throat, her face turning an unbecoming red. She sure as hell wasn't expecting to see me again, and I can't stop myself from breaking into a broad grin.

If anything, she turns even redder. Stand back, she's going to blow!

"You!" she says, her eyes narrowed.

In answer to her unspoken question, I shrug because I don't have a clue how I escaped the Fields of Obadyn, either.

"You must be Jasmine," says a woman whose presence commands my attention. Unlike the others, she doesn't compete for space or volume—she just *is*. "My brother has told me much about you. I am Vyra, Goddess of the Woods."

Her appearance strikes me as both youthful and ancient,

being a lot like her gorgeous brother in this sense. She also has the type of ageless beauty that comes with divine power, and yet her eyes hold depths that speak of lived experience.

After Vyra introduces herself, the other goddesses, except for Cuprum, step forward. There's Marla, Goddess of Iron; Alexis, Goddess of Nickel; Aura, Goddess of Gold; and Seol, Goddess of Silver. She's the female equivalent of her asshole brother, right down to what I suspect is a crappy personality beneath a beautiful exterior.

After digesting their names and how closely these equate to their godly counterparts, I realize something. Praedytus has no imagination when it comes to anything other than sex. Mind you, if I could lay claim to this many offspring, I'd doubtless become a little formulaic when it came to naming them, too.

The other thing I can't miss is that I can count one, perhaps two enemies, among the goddesses. Cuprum because of her fixation with Ben. And Seol, if she knows her brother is stuck in the Fields of Obadyn because of me. The death glare I'm receiving from the Goddess of Silver says she's well aware of this.

I'm considering what this means when I once again hear the Goddess of Obis inside my head. "They cannot hurt you. You are smarter, and thanks to your ceremonial preparations and our bond, you are also stronger."

I'm preening when she adds, "But neither should you underestimate them."

"Come," says Marla, extending her hand with deliberate grace. "I will escort you to your chambers."

"Lead the way," I say, while keeping my hands to myself. Something about her measured composure puts me on alert. My gut is telling me this isn't casual friendliness.

However, rather than do as I've asked, she stays rooted to

the spot. "In the realm of Obis, there are protocols visitors must observe. Your hand, if you please."

Her tone is polite, but there's no missing the steel—or should that be iron—underneath. This isn't a request. It's a test, and we both know it.

It's with reluctance that I place my hand in hers.

The assault on my senses is immediate and overwhelming. Pure, concentrated desire floods through me like molten fire. But this isn't the wild, uncontrolled lust I've experienced with the gods.

This is precise, calculated, perhaps even diagnostic. She's not trying to arouse me for pleasure. Instead, she's measuring my strength, testing my defenses, and cataloging my responses.

I try to pull away, but her grip is firm, her expression serene, almost clinical, as she continues her assault. However, there's no malice in it, no petty satisfaction. Just the focused attention of a strategist gathering intelligence.

"Fight her," whispers Obis in my mind, and I understand. This isn't bullying. It's an assessment.

I imagine my skin as an impenetrable barrier, visualizing walls of steel between us. The sensations end without warning, and for the first time, Marla's composure shifts, her eyebrows rising in genuine surprise.

"Impressive," she murmurs on releasing my hand. "Most manage only seconds of resistance. You held that barrier for a full minute."

The other goddesses have gone quiet, watching this exchange with new attention. Even Cuprum looks wary rather than hostile.

In contrast, Marla smiles, her expression one of approval. "In the coming ceremony, there will be forces that make what I

just did to you feel like a gentle breeze. If you couldn't defend yourself against me, you'd have no hope of surviving."

She pauses, her expression growing serious. "Our brother god cares for you. I needed to know if that care was misplaced."

"And your verdict?"

All I get in response is a slight tip of her head, leaving me unsure if I measure up. It's something that bothers me more than I would have thought possible. Everyone wants the approval of family, no matter how screwed up they are.

"Now," she says, returning to her earlier courtesy, "shall we continue?"

On reaching my chamber, I expect the goddesses to leave me in peace, but I'm wrong. A moment later and the only flat surface not covered in half-naked females is the floor. Well, to hell with this.

"Out!" My voice is loud enough to cut through the crap the goddesses are spouting. It also garners me more than a few filthy looks. Determined not to back down this early in the proceedings, I plaster a no-nonsense expression on my face and cross my arms.

When they don't move fast enough for my liking, I help them to their feet and steer them out into the tunnel.

Aura, Alexis, and Vyra go without too much trouble. But when I go to pull Cuprum to her feet, the look she skewers me with has me yanking my hand back. I'm relieved when she uncoils herself, stands, and sashays out into the tunnel without further prompting. I also breathe a sigh of relief when the Goddess of Silver follows.

"You too," I say to Marla, who's making herself at home on the fur-strewn bed platform.

"But I am to oversee your preparation for the ceremony," says the Goddess of Iron, as though speaking to a child.

My sigh echoes around the cave, bouncing back at me and confirming how over all of this I am.

"How long before the ceremony?"

"Until the moon is at its zenith."

"And how the hell are we supposed to know when that is?" I say, reaching up and touching the solid rock above my head. This, in turn, has me realizing how much I want the sun on my face and how claustrophobic this place is. The last time I'd left here, it had been with Marla's brother. What if I can't escape this place on my own?

I take several calming breaths, fighting to get my panic under control, but it's no good. My breathing gets faster with every lungful until the spots in my vision let me know I'm getting more oxygen than I can process. That the walls appear to be closing in only adds to my escalating terror.

"Calm yourself!" shouts Obis inside my head, and loudly enough I'm surprised Marla didn't notice. "Here is your precious sunshine."

No sooner had these words finished ringing inside my head than the roof of my chamber disappeared and the space was flooded with blessed sunlight and fresh air. My breathing slows and so does my heartbeat, leaving me relieved it's no longer thumping inside my head.

"How, how did you do that?" says Marla, her voice unsteady.

"Not me," I say with a shrug.

I'm about to elaborate when I hear Obis's urgent instruction. "They are not to know of our connection. It is not something I share with any of them. There are those among them who don't deserve our trust."

Before I can analyze this, my senses are assaulted by Marla keening, the raw tones working their way up my spine like nails on a chalkboard.

"You need to close it," I whisper to Obis, not that Marla would be able to hear me even if I were shouting.

The roof of the cave has only just sealed when the other goddesses crowd back into my chamber en masse. Seol soon has her arms tight around Marla, calming her with surprising speed.

"What did you do to her?" says Cuprum, her eyes narrowed, her face ugly with suspicion.

"I did nothing," I say, holding my hands up in mock surrender

"Then why is our sister like this?" says the Goddess of Copper. "She is not one to allow her emotions to rule."

"I'm not sure. I asked her how we were supposed to tell when the moon rose, and she started carrying on. I'm not sure what set her off."

I feel mean about making Marla out as being unhinged, but Obis's constant warnings to keep our connection secret has left me with no option. I'm not sure what the dire consequences are that she's hinted at, but I'm not willing to see for myself.

In the end, Marla, still shaking, is taken away and the goddesses trail off one by one until I'm left alone with Cuprum.

"Do not think your borrowed power will last, little human. Praedytus grows bored with every female at some stage—and when he does, all that strength fades away. I have seen it happen before. I am unsure how you escaped the Fields of Obadyn, but you will return, and this time, you will stay."

She's close enough when she finishes hissing this threat that it's not a big stretch for her to slap her hand on top of my head.

"Oh, for fuck's sake!" I can't believe she's got me again. She doesn't even bother gloating when we materialize next to Seolfer and his mother. Instead, she mutters an incantation, gives me the evil eye and then disappears a second later.

"Well, screw this!" I spit at the God of Silver and his mother, who have yet to say anything, although their expressions speak volumes.

"Can you believe this crap?" I say to Obis inside my head, hoping for help to escape the fields yet again. But there's no response other than the mental equivalent of chirping crickets.

I know I need to get back to the Isle of Obis if I'm to continue getting ready for the ceremony, and with no guiding voice inside my head, I haven't got a clue how to get there.

I'm racking my brains for a viable solution when Seolfer opens his damned mouth, but I don't let him say more than a few words before holding my hand up.

"Zip it, silver boy. I'm thinking here."

His mouth drops open, him not being used to being told to shut up. Wanting to maintain the silence, I keep my hand up before closing my eyes to further block him and his mother out. Only then does an answer come to me, popping into my head as though by divine intervention.

This sees me focusing on the Goddess of Copper, imagining myself standing next to her, and a second later I know I've followed her successfully.

The only hitch is that she hasn't returned to the Isle of Obis.

2

From his spot on the bed in the master cabin of The Metal Beast, Ben devours me with his eyes. “Wow, you look amazing.”

From my spot behind Cuprum, I see her stand taller, and if the clenching of her ass muscles is any sign, she's jutting her sex in my boyfriend's direction.

Not that they stay clenched for long after I respond to Ben. “Thanks,” I say, gathering my improved boobs together with my hands and showing them off.

Cuprum spins so fast she has to take a step to stay upright, but I don’t give her time to do more than gape. Instead, I drop a boob and slam my hand on top of her head. “Say hi to Seolfer for me."

It’s a long shot, but it works. At least I think it does. Either way, she disappears a millisecond after I finish speaking. Not one to rest on my laurels, I instead wait, poised, ready for action, but after five minutes she’s still a no-show.

Meanwhile, Ben has been lying on the bed watching me, and I can tell by the growing bulge in his jeans that he likes what he sees. Dammit, I vaguely recall the God of All Desire saying something about me not seeing my human lover before the ceremony, but hell, Ben looks so good.

And if it was all that important, then Praedytus shouldn't have wiped my memory of the time I'd spent training with him, now should he.

"You're looking a little overdressed," I say to Ben while turning to display my new and perkier body to him.

“You have a point.” He bounds off the bed and, while kissing me, unbuttons his shirt.

“All of it,” I say, snapping my fingers. With no idea how much time we've got together, I don't want to waste a minute.

Thankfully, I get no arguments from Ben, with him soon naked, and me on my back in record time. He’s never been this frantic with me before. Keen, yes, but not as hyped up as he is now unless it's when I've interrupted him doing the dirty with that redheaded bimbo I've just sent packing. Maybe it’s my demigod status or the effects of the pale blue gel. Either way, I’m not complaining.

When he closes his mouth over my sex, I'm not sure which one of us gets the bigger shock. So much for all my training with Marlo, with my orgasm being instantaneous.

I'm thinking it's a fluke, but then it's followed by another and another. My body is now vibrating with waves of pleasure that fan out from my clit to every extremity. I’m no longer on the bed but floating above it.

This might be why Praedytus didn't want me anywhere near my human lover.

I grab Ben’s head and stop him mid-lick. It’s only once I’ve got his attention that I speak.

"I need all of you."

I can't manage any more than this, but I thank the gods he knows what I mean. This sees him flipping me onto my stomach and dragging me to the very edge of the bed in a move reminiscent of one of my earliest sessions with Vyran. It's also one that leaves me wet with longing.

After spreading me wide, he slides in, allowing me to enjoy every blessed inch of him. It's only when he's jerked himself into me as deep as he can that he reaches around and caresses my breasts.

I'm mesmerized by the nipple rolling and don't even notice he's withdrawn. But oh boy, do I notice it when he squeezes my nipples hard at the same time as ramming himself home.

"Yes. That. More."

"You sure you're ready?" says Ben, withdrawing again.

My need is now so great that all I can do is whimper yes over and over. He doesn't hold back, seating himself repeatedly until all I can focus on is the pleasure.

The climax, when it arrives, is dramatic enough that I come close to fainting, my body no longer my own, Ben having marked it as his. Only after my spasms have died away do I realize he's still right where I want him and still rock hard.

He's been practicing without me, that's for sure. I twitch my much-improved Kegel muscles and am rewarded with him sucking in his breath. Guess he likes it.

I let him have it, clenching and rippling my muscles until he's a shuddering wreck on my back. Soon enough, he's pumping himself in and out of me without control.

It doesn't take long for him to come, his seed filling me as it never had before. It's primal, especially when compared to the scant amount of cum the gods I've relieved of their fettyrs can produce.

I'm still enjoying the postcoital glow when I hear Obis's voice inside my head. "You must return."

I'm about to beg for a few more minutes when I comprehend I'm lying on my bed on the Isle of Obis. While Ben is no longer deep inside me, his presence is still strong.

"Is there anywhere I can wash?"

After following Obis's directions, I find myself in a chamber that's dominated by a large, crystal-clear pool. Of immense relief is the hole in the rock above it that allows sunlight to flood the water. "What does it do?" I say, looking down into its sparkling depths.

"It cleans you," says Obis, before laughing with delight.

Given my experience with liquids and gels, I don't think it was that stupid a question. I'm abusing her inside my head when I remember she's also in there.

"Sorry."

I'm squeaky clean and floating in the water, enjoying the sun shining down on me from overhead, when Alexis, the Goddess of Nickel, storms into the chamber. I can see her lips moving as I peek through my eyelashes, but the water has rendered her mute.

And that's just perfect, even if she has to resort to waving her hands around. However, when it looks as if she'll join me in the pool, I acknowledge her presence.

"Come! Your ceremonials are ready for you." She doesn't wait for a reply and instead leaves me to follow.

Obis directs me back to my chamber, although I stop dead when I see the paraphernalia spread out all over the bed.

"Holy hell." After picking up what looks to be a silver chain mail corset, I go to hold it against my torso, but the silver fills me with revulsion. Instead, I settle for holding it up and

spinning it around so I can examine it. Not that there's a lot to it. The missing bits must weigh twice as much as anything that's been left behind. "Why even bother?"

"You should be ready by now," says Seol from right behind me, causing me to drop the corset in a heap on the floor. Sneaky bitch. I hadn't even heard her come in.

"Ready for what?" Because of the sun that had been pouring down into the cave pool just a moment ago, I know it's too early for the ceremony to start.

"For us to purify you." While saying this, she picks up what appear to be a couple of bracelets. That they're for me is confirmed when she snaps them around my wrists. I go to remove them, but they won't budge. While I continue fighting with them, Seol repeats the process with anklets.

"Good, you are almost ready," says Marla, Goddess of Iron, close enough that her breath tickles the back of my neck. Damn, these women are light on their feet. I'm glaring at her over my shoulder when Seol slaps a silver collar around my neck.

"Are all these necessary?" I say, turning to face the Goddess of Silver.

"Yes. They are." Her curled top lip says she's not happy about being part of whatever this is. Well, that's just tough. I can't say I'm keen on a relative of Seolfer's being this close to me either, never mind all this silver.

"You will need the Phrenyr as well. Hurry," urges Seol.

"Phrenyr?" I say, although it's to her back with her already disappearing through the archway of my chamber, close on Marla's heels.

"The Phrenyr is for your protection," says Obis inside my head.

I'm about to grill her on exactly how it protects me when Seol returns, her body language shrieking her annoyance. “If you do not come soon, you will miss the ceremony. You will die.”

Talk about being crap at pep talks. Still, the Goddess of Silver has a point, with me wasting no time grabbing the Phrenyr off the floor and following her through a maze of tunnels to an enormous cavern.

This one is lit by a multitude of tapers, their smoke hanging heavy in the air. It gives the cave a soft focus that goes some way toward helping cloak the device that sits in the middle of the space.

“What the hell is that?” I say to the goddesses in general. However, none were forthcoming, with Obis even less reticent.

“It is the Throne of Obis. You must be clean to receive the gods.”

“What the fuck, I’ve just had a bath,” I mutter under my breath.

"You will need to be cleaner still for the ceremony," says Obis, my stomach dropping fast.

“It’s never bothered them before,” I whisper, conscious the goddesses are now looking at me like I’ve lost it.

"Ceremonial Nysa is different," says Obis, not bothering with further explanation. Then, following a loud pop, I know she’s no longer inside my head.

“Come,” says Vyra. “It’s not as bad as it looks, with many finding it pleasurable. Even now, there is a daughter of the mist who would take your place.”

As I look around the chamber, there's no missing the goddesses' discomfort. However, I don't think it's out of concern for me, but at having to perform what they see as

menial work on a mere human.

The only plus in all of this is that it looks like Cuprum has decided she can't stomach getting me ready for the festivities. Unless she's still stuck at the Fields of Obadyn? No, that can't be right.

Even with her absent, it's with reluctance that I stand before the throne while Vyra takes the Phrenyr from my nerveless fingers. Thereafter, she puts it down on the small table next to her. It's what I see crowding the rest of that surface that gives me pause.

Unable to make out what any of the implements are, I instead glance at the throne. On closer inspection, I can see that what I'd taken for leather padding is in fact a silvery white metal, and my eyes narrow. There is no way I'm putting my ass near anything connected to Seol or her creep of a brother.

I touch one of the footplates. "Is this silver?"

There's no need for me to turn to know which goddess has just sucked in more air than her flared nostrils are designed for. Well, that's just tough.

"No," says Marla, now over her earlier shock. "The Throne of Obis is made of ceremonial electrum, as is the Phrenyr."

"Electrum?" That's a new one. I'd ask Obis more about it, but the goddess is still missing from inside my head.

"Come, we must proceed," says Marla, nudging me toward what looks like it will be a ceremonial pap-smear. Fuck it all. I wish there were another way.

There's a loud pop inside my head followed by the Goddess of Obis all but yelling at me, "There is not!" She then returns to wherever the hell it is she hangs out when she's not cluttering up my head.

"Fucking hell!"

"We will be as gentle as we can," says Alexis.

Great, the Nyphrazi version of "this won't hurt a bit," no doubt meaning it'll be as uncomfortable as hell. It's with reluctance I turn my back on the device, enduring a flashback to the hollowed-out statue of Obis when I sit on the lattice-style seat.

The least they could have done was provide a cushion. I'm still giving thanks that the metal isn't cold when my back is flattened against the upright. Rather than being a lattice, it's like a rib cage. I'm still trying to make myself comfortable when the goddesses crowd around me.

As disturbing as this is, what's worse is when the bracelets, anklets, and collar that Seol had slapped on me earlier meld themselves with the chair. It would appear I'd been wrong about their being made of silver. Either way, I don't even need to struggle to know I'm trapped in place.

"Is this necessary?" I say to Obis as much as to the goddesses surrounding me before remembering my own personal goddess has popped out for a cup of sugar or something.

"It is better if you don't move," says Vyra, picking up what looks like a metal bottle brush off the table.

"What are you doing with that?" I check the strength of my restraints, but despite them looking ethereal and me being a lot stronger these days, they're like steel and I can't move an inch. This is the last time I get into or sit on any contraption in this realm.

Damn it, you'd think I'd know by now.

Even so, I shriek in surprise when the whole contraption flips back and the footplates—sorry, make those stirrups—swing out to the sides. As often seems to happen with the Nyphrazi, my bits are up for general comment.

And comment they do, but rather than talk about my

anatomy, it's more like, "If you clean the prize, I'll take care of her depths. Marla, the nadir first." It's like roommates allocating housework, with Alexis taking on Cuprum's duties, albeit with much grumbling.

Not that this everyday approach stops my sex from clamming up and my flesh shrinking away from the hands prodding and poking it. However, my reticence does me no good. I'm at their mercy.

Just how much is shown when Marla shoves a bristled butt plug—make that nadir—up my ass. Once the shock dies off, I'm surprised by the rush of pleasure that engulfs me when she twists it around.

There's nothing I can do about my moan of pleasure, even if Marla appears surprised by my enjoyment. There's no mercy shown when she yanks the nadir free and drops it in a nearby basket.

And if I was in any doubt, when she leaves the chamber, her back is stiff with tension. Was I not meant to enjoy her rough treatment? If I were a betting woman, I'd say no.

And then there were four.

Next, Vyra and Alexis close in on either side of me, their hands encased in mitts that appear to be made of fine rope. Not that it's fine when they scrub away at me.

"Careful! You'll take a nipple off if you keep that up!" I yell at Alexis, who is the more vigorous of the two. So much for this not hurting.

"Pffft, they are fine," she says, her tone dismissive. "Human flesh is more resilient than it appears." The way she says "human" makes it sound like something she'd scrape off her dainty sandal. Then, as if to prove her point, she squeezes my bud hard through the mitt. "See, no harm."

No, no harm other than my poor nipple being on fire.

Meanwhile, Vyra is gentle, although only compared to her goddess sister, leaving my skin sensitive and red thanks to her ministrations. I'm therefore relieved when they finish scrubbing every inch of me.

That is, apart from my girly bits, my nerves are already ramping up at what this will involve. If my body has been left stinging from their rough treatment, I dread to think how my sex will cope.

I'm still wondering when the pair ditch their rope mitts and step back, their hands clasped in front of them. However, rather than leave, they remain where they are, telling me they still have duties to perform.

When Aura moves to take her place between the stirrups, I know what's coming next, and it won't be me. On seeing the state of the cloth she's holding, I know my dread has been well-founded. I've scrubbed pots with pads that looked to be less abrasive.

Sure enough, her treatment is anything but gentle, looking to have more to do with retribution than cleanliness. She's being rough on purpose. However, the abrasive qualities of the cloth don't help. The bitch even smirks when she's rough enough that I wince in pain.

I grit my teeth and lock eyes with her, unwilling to satisfy her need for revenge by reacting. All this results in is her scrubbing even harder. Again, I grit my teeth, but this time, rather than hiss in pain, I moan as if in the throes of release.

While manufactured and sounding like something out of a B-grade porno, it has the desired effect. As if realizing she's met her match, the Goddess of Gold tosses the used cloth to one side before storming out of the chamber, her top lip curled in disgust.

At a sign from Seol, Vyra and Alexis retrieve the Phrenyr

and drape it over my torso before snapping it into clips down each side. No wonder there isn't any back to the damned thing. It isn't necessary.

Without another word, they leave the chamber, their silence unnerving me far more than any amount of threats or chatter.

And then there is but one.

Seol doesn't allow me a moment to ready myself before she shoves what looks like a metal bottle brush deep inside me. It's not as bad as I thought it would be.

Never mind that. It's amazing. Each of the metal bristles moves of its own accord, stroking and brushing my insides until there's not a speck of me that isn't compliant.

The climax curls deep inside me, swirling and building in strength. It's as though my very essence would fly free if it weren't for the Phrenyr pulling tight around my abdomen. Could that be what it was designed for?

I'm moaning for release when the Goddess of Silver wrenches the metal brush from me, shocking my soul back into my body and my climax into submission. This leaves me with a devastating sense of loss, no doubt on purpose.

On hearing the brush being dropped into the basket, followed by Seol's retreating footsteps, I know I've been left hanging on purpose, and I'm furious. Here I am ready to pop, and those bitches have all up and left me strapped here like a science project and unable to attend the ceremony.

"Obis, are you there?"

Nothing.

I take to calling her name over and over until she responds, her "What now?!" on arrival, letting me know she isn't happy to be summoned in such a manner.

Well, that's just tough. It wasn't as if I asked for any of this.

"What the hell do I do now? I can't stay here like something out of the natural history museum."

"This is not right," says the goddess, stating the obvious. "You should have achieved Nysa with the Inspicyre and been freed by now. Ready for the ceremony."

"I am so fucked," I say, also stating the obvious. I now know why those little bitches had been rough with me on purpose. For whatever reason, they hadn't wanted me to achieve my release. To achieve Nysa.

"Lie there and see if you can bring it on with your mind and muscles," says the goddess, her voice edged with panic. "You need to find your release prior to the ceremony in order for everything to work as it should."

Unable to hop up and leave, I lie there doing as she's told me, while wondering what good it is to be ready when I can't attend because I'm trapped. That is, unless my absence is noted by the gods and they come looking for me.

With the problem resolved, at least in my mind, I concentrate on running the sensations from earlier through my head over and over. Desperate to achieve my release, I think of Ben and ripple my muscles.

It's working, a coil of lust building deep inside me. However, I'm brought around with a start when someone pinches the insides of my thighs, hard.

I snap my eyes open to find Seolfer looking down at me from his spot between my outstretched legs. The hate in his eyes has me struggling against my restraints, but there's nothing I can do. I'm trapped.

Well, screw lying here while Seolfer gets his revenge.

I think hard about The Metal Beast and Ben, and when I open my eyes, Seolfer is still looking at me, a manic grin now pasted on his face.

"You cannot traverse while you are secured to the throne," says Obis, her voice full of sadness.

"Well, isn't this just great?" I spit out.

"Isn't it just," says Cuprum, the Goddess of Copper, from somewhere behind me.

3

It doesn't take a rocket scientist to know what Seolfer has in mind. The chain holding his fettyr snug around his waist is soon released, allowing his cock to slap against my wide-open and sparkling clean sex.

"Isn't there something you can do?" I say to Obis, my voice strained because of my escalating nerves.

"I thought I was," says Seolfer, looking at me in confusion.

"He must not know of our connection!" says Obis, stopping me from voicing my concerns again.

Not that I held out for long, with Seolfer's fingers soon rooting around deep inside me. "Do something, or else," I say to Obis while fighting against the response my traitorous body is offering to the God of Silver. I'm not sure what I've got in mind with my threat of "or else," but I'm getting desperate.

"Eager, isn't she?" says Cuprum, coming around to stand next to me. I'm then as confused as Seolfer when she undoes the clips that hold the Phrenyr in place. In answer to his questioning expression, she says, "If she achieves Nysa while

on the throne and without the Phrenyr in place, she will join the fallen."

I'd heard the expression about your blood running cold before, but never understood it until now. She'd consign me to a fate worse than death, and all to get her mitts on Ben? What a complete and utter bitch.

I wait for Obis to intervene, but it looks like she's abandoned me. Meanwhile, Seolfer is making the most of my being tied down. When he mashes his finger back and forth over my clit, I'm unable to stop my breath from hissing out.

Much as I hate him with a passion, the bastard knows what he's doing. And if I achieve Nysa without the electrum corset in place, I'll be worse than dead.

"Have patience," says Obis, once back inside my head and sounding almost as freaked out as I am.

For a start, I think I'm imagining it, but no, Seolfer is flickering like a lightbulb on the fritz. And then, after regaining his true form a few times, he disappears for good.

"What? How?" The Goddess of Copper isn't able to articulate further, but it's obvious that what has happened has shocked her. I'm awestruck myself.

I'm wondering what has happened when I hear screaming from the distance. It's making its way in our direction and bouncing off the walls of the tunnels that honeycomb the Isle of Obis.

"What did you do?" I say to Obis, although it's Cuprum who answers.

"I did nothing!" She stumbles back, distancing herself from the God of Silver's last known location.

Meanwhile, the source of the screaming is getting ever closer. Most of it's unintelligible, but then the words "She's risen!" pop out of the cacophony. Before Cuprum or I have

time to process this, Vyra runs into the chamber, her hair askew, mouth wide and once again wailing like a banshee.

Cuprum moves to intercept the Goddess of the Woods, who is now running in circles around the throne. It's only by throwing her arms around Vyra in a death grip that Cuprum stops the distraught goddess. This is made more difficult by Vyra struggling against this restraint.

I'm then distracted when one of the most stunning women I have ever seen glides into the chamber. A flame-colored gown hugs her curves like a living thing, while an intricate crown fashioned out of jet-black braids gives her a regal air.

But there's something about her that gives me the creeps. Perhaps it's the savage power that oozes from every pore? And I'm not alone in my reaction to the new arrival, with Cuprum dropping to her knees, taking a still incoherent Vyra with her.

The weirdest thing is that despite her unsettling presence, I long to join them in their supplication, and I would but for being stuck like a display butterfly.

Whoever the new arrival is, I get that she's senior to the other two. It's not that she looks older, but more to do with the raw power emanating from her. Even without that, Cuprum and Vyra's groveling would be a dead giveaway.

Still, she looks to be the only one capable of helping me and so I'm hoping the proverb about my enemy's enemy being my friend is right. I cough, hoping this will have the desired effect.

"Let me release you, child." Her voice is as beautiful as her face and instantly recognizable, though different now that it's no longer rattling around inside my head.

"Obis?" I whisper once she's between me and the two goddesses, still slumped in a heap. Her nod of response is such that none but myself can see it.

"Cuprum, Vyra, why is Jasmine still restrained after the

purification ritual?" says Obis, her voice loud and menacing, unlike the tone she'd used when speaking to me.

Much gibberish ensues, and I'm thinking Obis has blown it by using my name, but this appears to be the least of the younger goddesses' worries.

"It was Seolfer," says Cuprum, sacrificing the God of Silver to save her own ass.

"And how did Seolfer escape the Fields of Obadyn?" says Obis, in a take no-prisoners tone. The coldness of her voice is in contrast to the dancing flames in her eyes, giving them an unearthly orange glow.

"He, ah, he forced me to bring him here." Cuprum's delivery sucks, and Obis appears to know the redhead is lying through her teeth.

While this interrogation is going on, Obis removes the bracelets and anklets that are holding me down. That she does so simply by touching the metal and melting it freaks me out.

Not freaked out that she can melt things, but that I don't feel any heat from the metal as it drips onto the floor around the chair. Once I'm free, she swings the throne forward, allowing me to stagger to my feet.

"Go. You may take Seolfer's place in the Fields of Obadyn until I decide what to do with you."

I've only just processed that Obis isn't speaking to me when Cuprum disappears, her wails of anguish echoing around the chamber long after she's gone.

"Please, Obis, not that," says Vyra, cowering at the goddess's feet. "The others forced me."

What! It would appear they were all in on it, as I'd suspected. The question remained why.

"You may stay on the Isle of Obis for now, but any others standing against Jasmine will feel my wrath. With Cuprum

otherwise detained, let the others know I will stand in for her at the ceremony. Now, go!"

This final shrieked command has Vyra jumping to her feet and running before she has proper control of her legs. She crashes into the wall next to the archway twice before escaping.

Only after the sounds of Vyra's departure have died away does Obis speak again, although not until she's finished laughing.

"It is so good to be free."

"Free?"

"For many of your centuries, I have been trapped in the Sundering."

"The where?" I ask, my mind already filling in the blanks.

"The Sundering. It is an existence that belongs in neither space nor time," says Obis with a full-body shudder. "An in-between."

She then surprises me by laughing again, though there is no humor in her expression. No joy.

"But the Sundering is no mere prison. I could observe everything in this realm. I've watched every manipulation, every lie Praedytus has told. While the Sundering may trap, it does not blind."

"Hang on a second." While I know I shouldn't interrupt her, time isn't on our side. "Is that where you sent Seolfer?" With Obis having said Cuprum was to take his place at the Fields of Obadyn, I knew he was no longer hanging about with his mom.

"The Sundering is no place for the likes of him."

"So, if not the Sundering, where is the silver jerk?"

Obis laughs again. However, this time there is no faking her amusement. "I thought some time among the fallen would help

him learn humility. It is rare for males to join their ranks. The novelty of having a god among them has the attendants quite... eager for their duties."

For a second I'm appalled, but it doesn't take me long to think back to the God of Silver's treatment of me over the preceding year and only minutes earlier. "Can I go see him?"

"Most assuredly," says Obis, putting a motherly arm around my shoulders. "The Temple is our domain and is closer than you think."

A moment later, we materialize in a beautiful room, which is a surprise after all the caves I've visited. Central to the marble-lined room is an immense bed on which the God of Silver lies, his fettyred cock pointing at the ceiling.

"You should take your ease," says Obis. "None will interrupt you. This child of silver is here by my grace and therefore beyond his father's reach."

"You can't expect me to ..." I jerk my head in Seolfer's direction, incapable of finishing my sentence. While thinking about sex with the God of Silver would have had a dark part of me aroused a few months back, this is no longer the case. And I have Ben to thank for that.

"You were supposed to find your release on the throne that carries my name. You need to do so before the ceremony. If you achieve Nysa before any of the gods, the ceremony will not work as it is supposed to. But if you lay with Seolfer now, under no circumstances is he to achieve Nysa. If he does—"

I hold my hand up to cut her off yet again. "Yeah, yeah, I know, the ceremony gets derailed." Despite my then falling silent as the enormity of what I need to do hits me, I'm not quiet for long.

"But if Seolfer is stuck here, how can the ceremony go

ahead? Don't I have to lie with all six brothers to regain my human form?"

This time, Obis's smile doesn't reach her eyes. "Nowhere in our writings does it say that there have to be six brothers, only that there have to be six gods."

It doesn't take me long to work out who the sixth god will be. Praedytus, father of them all. My stomach sinks as I realize there isn't a chance I can hold back on achieving Nysa. Not with the God of All Desire in the mix.

He only has to think about touching me and I go off like fireworks that have been stored improperly. Damn it. I'm screwed before the ceremony even starts.

I'm halfway through explaining all this when Obis shakes her head. "There is a way to salvage the ceremony, child. One that may benefit you and many others."

She holds nothing back when describing her time in the Sundering, and how she'd ended up there. "The ceremony is my only chance to liberate those left behind. The other gods believe we... disappeared. Only the God of All Desire knows the truth of it."

"Jasmine, he plans on imprisoning them for eternity, and to achieve that, he must make a special offering to the gods who've gone before. His plan is to corrupt the ceremony. To use your divine power to seal the veils between our realms for all time. You would survive, but be trapped in luxurious servitude."

On her glancing at Seolfer on the other side of the room, there's no missing where I'd be imprisoned.

She pauses, letting the horror sink in. "He's been grooming you from the beginning, daughter. Every encounter, every accident that strengthened you—it was all to make your sacrifice, your fall, more potent. For Praedytus to lock the veils

for all time, the gods who've gone before would demand nothing less than perfection."

"WHAT?!" I scream, my voice echoing off the marble walls. "You're telling me this has all been a setup? That it was never about me regaining my human form?"

My hands are shaking with rage, and my body is flooded with terror. "I trusted him! I trusted them!" I pause in my tirade only long enough to glare at Seolfer. "Well, not all of them."

I pace back and forth across the marble room, my steps short, every muscle tight. "Well, to hell with him," I spat out. "I'm not doing any ceremony. I don't care if I die. Praedytus can go fuck himself!"

Rather than try to calm me, Obis lets me rage until I'm spent. "Jasmine, understand that running now will only ensure your death, and it won't stop what's already been set in motion. Your only hope of returning to your own world is to move forward—but with a knowledge of what's happening."

Her logic hits me like ice water. I stop pacing, my mind racing through the implications. If I run, I die. If I stay and do nothing, I'll be dead inside. But if I go through with this ceremony, knowing what Praedytus intends, then there's a chance...

"You're saying the only way out is through," I grit out, the full weight of my situation settling on my shoulders. "That I have to play along with his sacrifice plan to have any chance of turning it against him."

"Yes, child. If you are to survive, you must appear to cooperate while we work to subvert his true purpose."

As I think about what she's said, my pacing takes me ever closer to the bed, and as I move, Seolfer's gaze follows me, the venom in those two silver orbs enough to poison me. "I had nightmares about this asshole." On realizing how close I am to

him, I stumble backward. "He can't just... wake up and grab me, can he?"

"Not unless I allow it, child. In the Temple of the Fallen, the goddesses hold absolute authority. He is powerless as any mortal here. You may safely lie with him. He cannot hurt you, but he can help. You must achieve Nysa before the ceremony if you are to—"

"Yeah, I know," I say, holding up my hand, "if I'm to have any hope of survival."

As if finally understanding my reticence as regards being intimate with Seolfer, Obis picks up a piece of silken fabric from the small table next to the bed. "Would this help?"

"You want me to blindfold myself?!"

"No!" says Obis, her expression now as horrified as my own. "I thought you could cover his face."

It's not long before both of us are laughing hard at Seolfer's expense, and I know that if he weren't paralyzed, I'd be dead. Still, after hearing that latest snippet about the blasted ceremony, my tension abates somewhat. I suspect that, true to form for the Nyphrazi, I'll find out as we go along, with some elements never revealed.

"I will leave you to it," says Obis, handing me the piece of cloth. She then leaves through a curtained doorway, giving me a brief glimpse of a sun-drenched marble patio that is lush with palm trees in enormous pots and tinkling fountains.

I'm thinking about whether I can go near Seolfer by choice when her voice comes back to me. "But time is short, Jasmine. You must hurry."

The pressure in her voice reminds me of what's at stake. Not just my life, but Ben's safety, because if Praedytus locks the veils when Ben's in the Nyphrazi realm, he'll be trapped until such time as he pays the ultimate price.

There was also the freedom of those trapped in the Sundering to consider. I can't let my personal revulsion of Seolfer derail the only plan that might save us all.

Sheesh, no pressure. But if fucking the God of Silver is what it takes to get close enough to destroy Praedytus's plans, then I'll stomach it.

Upon looking down at him, it doesn't take long for me to know there isn't a snowball's chance in hell that I can achieve Nysa, even if I cover his face. I don't bother deliberating but instead walk over to the doorway just used by Obis and pull the curtains tight.

If I need to find my release before the ceremony, there's only one person who can help me achieve it. And if our time together might end soon, I want to make every moment count. I think of the place. I think of the time, and bam, I'm there. Dammit, I'll miss having all this power.

"Wake up, lover boy, I need you."

My timing is perfect on many levels. Not only is Ben sporting his usual daybreak erection, but he'll also be well-rested after a night's sleep. He'll need both with what I've got in mind.

As soon as I'm in his arms, I think of the opal lake and that large rock of Axel's. I don't know what shocks me more. That I've transported us both there, or that we're still aboard The Metal Beast. The Goddess of Obis is right. I am strong.

"Wow," says Ben, squinting in the strong sunlight that is now pouring through the hatch above our heads. "How long do we have?"

I don't answer thanks to my attention being caught by his now white-blonde hair, with him no longer resembling a certain British prince. Instead, he's all surfer dude, and I couldn't be happier.

And why? That would be because it let me know the Goddess of Copper's hold over Ben has been shattered by Obis banishing her to the Fields of Obadyn. All I can hope for is that Cuprum stays there.

Sensing he's getting impatient for my reply, I say, "How long do you want?"

"A weekend would be nice with what I've got planned for you."

And just like that, my attention is back on his body and off his new hair color. He pulls me closer, further reminding me why I'm here, before running his hands over my breasts and down my torso.

It's not long before he's sliding a couple of fingers deep inside me and smiling like a kid at Christmas. That he then uses my own juices to slick my pearl into a tight little bundle has me so aroused that I'm thinking a weekend won't be enough.

Also playing on my mind is that this is the second time I've gone against Praedytus's vaguely remembered instructions and visited Ben when I shouldn't. I'm hoping it won't make any difference, but if the ceremony goes haywire, then there isn't much time left, if at all.

This has me wriggling out of Ben's arms and straddling him. If our time together is soon to be over, then I want to make the most of it.

I glance at him while sliding myself backward and forward over his cock, enjoying his expression of pleasure and the power of having him under my control. Not that I'm in control for long, when he lifts his hands to my breasts, kneading and tweaking them until I'm purring.

This has me scooting further up his body, with him soon nudging for entrance. There's nothing timid about how I

impale myself on his gorgeous length. I want my memories of him to be with me forever.

This has me grinding against him, desperate to take as much of him as possible. My resultant sigh when he's as deep as possible is one of pure bliss and melancholy.

As always, we fit together like pieces of a puzzle, with me lifting and dropping a few times, loving the feel of his rock-hard length deep inside me. But there's something about it that's bugging me. I can't work out what it is until the visual of Seolfer lying back on that bed flickers to life inside my head.

"This isn't working. Much as I want to fuck you, I want you to fuck me more."

He takes a moment to understand what I want, but then wastes no time in rolling to the side until he's pressing me down into the mattress.

"Is this better?" he says, driving himself into me.

Enjoying it as I am, I'm only able to moan in response.

He takes my feet and puts them up over his shoulders. "What about this?"

"Oh, God, yes. This I like," I gasp out between his thrusts that are now deep enough to be nudging at my womb.

"You know what I'd like even more than this?" muses Ben.

Unable to speak, I shake my head, although my gaze is locked with his for the entire time.

"I love closing my lips over that perfect clit of yours and licking and sucking on it until you scream my name."

That he said this while looking deep into my soul and continuing to fuck my brains out is a turn-on beyond belief. It's also enough to have my body tightening in readiness for release.

"Hold on, not yet," says Ben, letting me know I must have a tell that lets him know I'm on the brink of orgasm.

He drops my feet from off his shoulders and then wraps them around behind his back. When I lean back, he pulls me up until I'm once again straddling him, but this is different. He's no longer prone, and when he tugs our bodies close together, he's able to drop his head and close his mouth over a nipple.

He sucks on it hard enough that it hurts, but then he runs his tongue over it, taking away the sting. After pulling back, he blows on it and my nipple puckers as if commanded.

Happy with my response, he moves onto the other breast and repeats the process until I'm arching my back to help him get better access.

"Lean back on your hands," he says, reinforcing the request with a twitch of his hips.

I do so, letting my head drop back as the sensations he's evoking with his quick thrusts pulse through me.

"Don't you want to watch me fuck you?" he says, his voice thick with passion.

He's right, I do. I lift my head with my neck more noodle than not and am in time to see his cock swallowed by my body. Knowing he's got my attention, one of his hands drops to where our bodies join at the same time as he withdraws.

His beautiful cock is slick with my juices, and he uses these to wet his fingers. This time, when he pushes himself deep inside me, he massages my clit into a froth. The sensation soon has me in a sensual haze because as well as sensing it, I can watch it happening.

He flicks my clit hard and fast, and it's a second later my body catches up and I'm flooded with sensation.

"Again?" he asks, urging me to be an accomplice.

"Yes," I gasp.

I'm thinking he means the flick, but he goes through the

entire sequence again with me on a knife edge waiting for that final rap to my pearl.

"Faster?"

I nod my response, unable to take my eyes off his fingers.

This time, rather than repeat, he starts with my breasts. Then he flicks my clit three times, one after the other. Every time he strikes, my neurons go off in a series of bursts.

"Time to take things up a notch," says Ben, leaning forward until he's hard up against my breasts.

He reaches behind me, and I can hear him rummaging around on the ledge that sits above the bed.

"Ah, here we are. I think you'll like this."

4

I take a moment to focus on the small clip in Ben's hand. The sunlight bouncing off the deep blue stone that is at the heart of it is spectacular, as is the sensation when he slides the jeweled clit clip into place, leaving my pearl on display and open to him.

"It's beautiful." That my voice catches doesn't go unnoticed.

"Come here, you," he says, dragging me into his arms to soothe me.

That this drives him back inside me and has his pubes tickling my now exposed clit soon rids me of maudlin thoughts.

Ben slides his lips over mine, slips his tongue inside my mouth, and then replicates the motion of his cock. He fills me with each drive, nudging my clit and mashing my breasts against his chest. I've never felt as cherished, ever.

As focused on my feelings for Ben as I am, the orgasm takes me by surprise. It washes over me, consuming me in a wave of

energy that's extreme enough to have my scalp prickling and my body a mix of electricity and pure raw power. For the first time in my life, I'm involved, flooded with the physical sensations. I'm also flooded with love of the growing-old-together kind.

It's wonderful.

But it's too much for me, and I burst into noisy tears while wrapping my arms around Ben and squeezing him hard enough that he groans.

"Sorry, sorry." I release my grip a little, but still keep us nice and close.

Ben's having none of it, though. He unhooks my arms and holds onto my hands so he can put enough space between us to look me in the eye.

"You want to tell me what's going on?"

I don't, but I don't want to keep dealing with this on my own, either. Sure, I've talked to some of the gods about it, but they're lacking in empathy, deeming my human emotions more of a weakness than anything else. And despite being a woman, Obis is perhaps the least empathetic of them all.

"It's the ceremony. I, ah, I haven't told you everything."

"This looks like it'll take a while," says Ben, relaxing down onto his side and taking me with him.

Once we're comfortable, I start but don't get far, with the words jamming tight in my throat. Ben rubs my back in circles, but all this does is release more tears.

"Perhaps if you bullet-point it?"

I think about this and decide it may be the only way I'll get the words out.

"Without the ceremony, I'll die."

"What? Are you fucking kidding me?"

Even with my face mushed against his chest, I can tell I've shocked him. Maybe I should have left that bullet-point until last?

"Unless all the gods achieve Nysa, I become one of the fallen."

Ben pulls back and stares at me. "The what?"

"The fallen maidens. They live in this... temple. It's supposed to be this incredible honor—luxury, pleasure, everything you could want." My voice breaks. "Except you can never leave. You become an eternal plaything of the gods."

It's only after a calming breath that I'm able to carry on, knowing that if I don't get this out, I never will. "If anything goes wrong during the ceremony, I join the ranks of the fallen." My voice has dropped to a whisper when I add, "Forever."

He's grinding his teeth now, and I know it's only a matter of time before he explodes, with this having me rushing on. "I think I'm already beyond demigod status, and I don't know if that will affect the ceremony or not."

However, Ben surprises me when, rather than explode, he drags me into a crushing embrace. "I can't let you go like that," he says, before his lips close over the pulse in my throat.

"You don't have a choice," I say before a hiccup of tears stops me from saying anything else.

The rest of the week is bittersweet as we savor every second. The lovemaking—it's too sweet to be called sex—is spectacular, with my responses increasing in intensity as the days pass.

Ben, however, is looking haggard to the point that I suggest

we stop, but he'll have none of it. It's as though he's imprinting me on his soul in case things don't go according to plan.

My heart belongs to him now to a degree I've not experienced before, not even with Vyran. As I lay in his arms, savoring the end of our time together, I knew by Ben's breathing that he's deep asleep. I've been fighting it myself.

After a featherlike kiss, I think of the berth at the harbor in Sitka, timing our arrival, complete with The Metal Beast, to be a fraction of a second after our departure. Not even the busybody on the boat next door will notice anything out of the ordinary.

The predawn light, the drop in temperature, and the sounds of boats clinking around us tell me I've succeeded. It's with reluctance that I extricate myself from Ben's arms and get up. I drag a blanket over him to protect him from the cold and look down at him for a few minutes, enjoying the simple pleasure of watching him sleep.

Hell, I hope the ceremony works.

Before I can give it any more thought, I envisage Seolfer's room in the Temple of the Fallen and am there a second later. Rather than be standing as I had been when I'd left The Metal Beast, I'm lying on the bed next to him.

Even though he's essentially paralyzed, I'm upright before my legs are ready to support me, and I stumble, landing hard on my knees. The pain cuts through any residual grogginess, and I get to my feet before going outside.

With my heart breaking at the thought of perhaps never seeing Ben again, I join Obis and the large group of women she's addressing. There are all shapes and sizes, ages, and races.

The one common thread is that they're all dressed in rags, with their hands chapped, their nails broken. This identifies

them as peasant stock, or whatever the equivalent is in this world.

"Yes, yes, you may all enjoy the pleasures of the newest fallen," says Obis, her announcement greeted by cheers from the women.

"And we can breed from him?" says one haggard old lady who I would have thought was well past her child-bearing days.

"No!" say Obis and I in concert, causing the group of women to turn in my direction.

"Bad blood," I stammer out. "But that doesn't mean you can't enjoy him."

"My daughter is right," says Obis, leaving me stunned that she's claimed me as family. Meanwhile, the women crow with delight. If there's one thing for sure, it's that Seolfer is about to have his silverware polished in a big way. No less than the jerk deserves either.

"Come, we must get to the Plateau of Gneiss," says Obis, after walking through the labor force. She then takes my hand and, a moment later, we're there. Although where the hell "there" is, I wouldn't have a clue. It's no longer daytime, with the drop in light leaving my eyes feeling as though they've been bathed in cool water.

The plateau is huge and glowing in the bright moonlight, which makes it easy enough to see. The moon is also huge, as though we're a lot closer to its surface than is possible from anywhere on Earth. Upon shuffling in place, I revel in the plateau's smooth surface.

It's only on looking at it closer that I realize it's one giant slab of marble with no joins I can see. It's also warm enough that it must have the Nyphrazi equivalent of underfloor heating installed, and I wiggle my bare feet in delight.

"Don't tell me there's a God of Stone I've yet to meet," I say, as an aside to Obis.

"Terra," she whispers, without going into further details.

It doesn't matter, with me filling in the blanks for myself. Terra, God of Stone—although when I think about it, God of Rock has a better ring to it.

Then it's all I can do not to double over in nervous laughter when I wonder if he's got moves like Jagger. This, in turn, has me thinking how much Ben would enjoy the joke, with tears soon welling up in my eyes.

Obis squeezes my hand hard enough to crunch a couple of my knuckles.

"You need to concentrate," she says, and for once her tone isn't kind. I know without looking at her that her eyes will once more be lit from within. It works, though, with her curt tone cutting through what I suspect would have been the start of a major meltdown. Something new to me.

I do as she instructs and start off by taking in my surroundings in more detail. The plateau must be high because its edges are shrouded in clouds, obscuring any views.

It's not only the view that's missing; there doesn't appear to be an altar either. Instead, in the center of the space, there's a large metal dish that has to be at least fifteen feet across. The metalwork appears ancient, with intricate runes carved around the rim that seem to pulse with their own dark energy.

Looking closer, I realize the dish's purpose isn't for ritual bathing, as I'd suspected. Rather, it's designed to contain something. The thought sends a chill through me, especially when I notice the channels carved into the metal that lead to a drainage hole in the middle.

It would appear I was wrong about there not being an altar. I just hadn't expected it to be of the sacrificial variety. I'm still

freaking out about this when Vyran and his brothers materialize around the enormous metal dish, but their formation is incomplete.

Rather than appear next to his sons, Praedytus materializes with his back to us, his gaze locked on this anomaly. "Where is Seolfer?" His voice carries across the marble expanse, sharp with irritation. "The moon will soon reach its apex, and we cannot delay the ceremony. That worthless son of mine chooses now to disappear!"

Rather than be naked, as was his preference, the God of All Desire is wearing armbands, shin guards, and a crown. They look to be made of a ceremonial electrum, marking him as an overseer and not a participant. In his hands, he holds an ornate scroll—doubtless instructions on how he is to run the ceremony.

"Uncle," says Obis, already on her way to join him, leaving me to follow in her wake. However, when Praedytus spins toward her, and the scroll tumbles from his nerveless fingers, I stop where I am.

Sometimes it's fun to be up close and personal, so you miss nothing, but that's not the case this evening. I'm especially glad I've held back when Obis stoops and retrieves the scroll, with Praedytus's face having drained of color.

Then, as if realizing the goddess isn't a figment of his imagination, his eyes widen in what I can only describe as fear. It's the first time I've seen him unsure of himself.

"Impossible," he breathes, staggering back a step. "The Sundering cannot be breached. How are you...?"

I watch his mask of control crumble, revealing the truth beneath. For all his careful planning, he never considered that his corruption of me might provide the key to Obis's escape. The irony is written across his face—

his moment of triumph has become the instrument of his downfall.

"It would appear it wasn't as secure as you believed," Obis replies with serene confidence. Her satisfaction is on display as she surveys his shock. "Though I must thank you for creating the perfect opportunity. Your beautification of Jasmine provided the exact power conduit I needed."

Her comment has Praedytus's gaze landing on me before it strays to his sons, who have all turned to witness this unexpected reunion. Meanwhile, the moon hangs low in the sky, huge and brilliant, the pressure of time bearing down on us.

"The ceremony requires six participants," Obis continues, stepping even closer to her stunned uncle. "You must take Seolfer's place. There is no time to find another."

"No," says Praedytus, but his voice lacks conviction. "I am to oversee proceedings, not—"

"The moon will not wait for your convenience," Obis interrupts, gesturing toward the brilliant orb that's already higher in the sky than it was moments earlier. "Would you have the ceremony fail because of your son's absence?"

She then pauses for effect before adding, "Would you risk Jasmine's life by delaying?"

It's something that has Vyran, Marlo, and even Ciprus voicing their objections to this scenario. Though there's no mistaking Aurum standing mute, his expression is resigned rather than shocked.

Unlike his brothers, who seem stunned by Obis's appearance and the ceremony's disruption, Aurum looks like a man watching a play he's already seen.

When our eyes meet, I see something that might be guilt

flickering across his features before he looks away. He's known all along what his father planned for me.

On turning back to watch the exchange between Obis and Praedytus, I realize she isn't just solving a problem. Rather, she's maneuvering the God of All Desire right where she wants him. But he's too shocked by her presence, too rattled by this deviation from his plans, to see the trap closing around him.

"This is... this was not..." he stammers, his mind racing to adapt his strategy to this development, but coming up empty. For the first time since I've known him, the God of All Desire appears to have been caught off guard.

"Come, uncle, would you see the veils removed in their entirety? Isn't that what you've always fought against?"

She doesn't give him a chance to respond before lifting her hand and gesturing in a way that is both casual and heavy with power. I'm wondering what was supposed to happen when I see Praedytus's cock is encased in a metal fettyr.

"You forget, Uncle," Obis says as his ceremonial crown disappears, only to reappear atop her head, "that you taught me the value of long-term planning. I've had centuries in the Sundering to prepare for this moment."

After staring at his niece with what I can only describe as grudging admiration mixed with fury, his gaze drops to the metal sheath. "This is not what I'd expect from a goddess," he admits through gritted teeth. "Though this does nothing to change the human's destiny."

"The ceremony must proceed," says Obis, her tone brooking no argument. Even so, I still catch the flash of triumph in her eyes. "And who better to lead proceedings than she after whom the festival is named? Take your place with your sons."

Praedytus moves like a man in a dream, still struggling to process what's happening. As he steps into the circle, I see him

tugging at the fettyr, his movements awkward. It's clear he's not worn one in a long time, if ever.

The other gods watch with confusion, but none dare question what's happening. The pressure of the approaching lunar apex, combined with Obis's commanding presence, keeps them silent.

"Come," says Obis, beckoning me to join her. "Let us complete the first round."

She then leads me over to the circle of gods, although she doesn't slow until we're passing them in a counterclockwise motion. I stare at each of them in turn, able to see they're all wearing electrum facsimiles of their usual fettyrs, even Vyran.

But it's when Praedytus comes into view that I'm most struck by the change. This is the first time I've seen him wearing a fettyr, and his discomfort is as obvious now as when Obis had first imposed it on him.

The other difference is that his fettyr lacks the brilliant shine of those worn by the other gods. Nor does it match his armbands and shin guards. It's only when I recognize the pattern that the truth reveals itself.

Praedytus's covering is fashioned from silver.

How does Obis expect me to help the God of All Desire achieve Nysa when the fettyr he wears is a constant reminder of Seolfer's torment? Throw in his planning to sacrifice me, and arousal is the last thing on my mind.

"You planned this," he hisses at Obis when we pass, his voice low. Despite this, there's a dawning realization in his tone that he's been bested, mixed with respect and perhaps shock.

The next time we pass, he says, "Seolfer?" to her.

After the merest of nods, she murmurs, "Fallen," with him grimacing in response.

The next time we complete a circle, rather than keep going, Obis stops dead in front of Praedytus. "We are ready."

"We are?" I'm not sure I'm as ready as Obis seems to think. The thought of going anywhere near that silver fettyr and the god who was planning on trapping me in eternal servitude has my girly bits scrambling for cover.

However, I don't get to stall, with Obis reclaiming my hand. Once again, we're circling the gods and the enormous dish they're guarding. The only difference now is that we're walking in the other direction.

"Why does it have to be silver?" I mumble when we again pass Praedytus.

As if understanding my misgivings, Obis gently squeezes my hand. "His alone must be silver for the ceremony to work as it should. Otherwise, his would be of electrum like the others, with it more precious than gold."

That she says this right when we're in front of Aurum isn't the best timing. I'm unable to stop a snort of laughter at the God of Gold's sharp intake of breath.

This, in turn, has Obis glaring at me, her eyes aflame.

"Sorry, stage fright," I whisper. Despite all the training and my having become somewhat immune to the unusual ways of the Nyphrazi, I'm entering the unknown here.

What if Obis is unable to reclaim the ceremony and I end up trapped as one of the fallen? And what if Praedytus is still able to use my power to lock the realms forever? Either scenario is enough to have me pinching my thigh hard to send my thoughts off in another direction.

Obis and I continue circling the gods, trudging away on the marble until my bare feet hurt. There's no way I'm complaining, though, because she'd more than likely bitch-slap me or incinerate me or something.

Each time I pass Axel or Ciprus, I'm caressed by their gaze, their eyes full of longing. I receive this plus more in the case of Marlo and Vyran but don't allow myself to think too much about what it means. Praedytus seems torn between looking at me and Obis, his eyes flickering between the pair of us with growing wariness.

The only god who doesn't regard me with pleasure is Aurum. Guess he's still pissed that his skin got all fucked up when Ben and I removed that gold C-string bikini the bastard forced on me.

This has me turning away whenever we pass him, preferring to concentrate on the licentious looks I'm getting from the other four. One thing I'm not sure about is what all the walking is supposed to achieve, because from what I can see, nothing's happening.

I haven't changed as far as I can tell, with my irritation escalating at the futility of it all. My temper is close to getting the better of me when I notice droplets of what appear to be liquid metal forming on the edge of the dish.

Obis and I are between Praedytus and Vyran when one of these droplets breaks away from the lip. Rather than fall to the marble below as I'm expecting, it floats up into the air. This keeps happening until there's a halo of spheres hovering at head-height over the edge of the dish.

I mutter an oath when one of these balls floats in my direction. Soon enough, they're following along in my wake. I keep looking back until I trip over my own feet, and Obis once again has to hiss at me to concentrate.

The sphere pops against my back, wetting my skin, and I'm flooded with well-being and a burst of strength. No sooner had this first bubble burst than I'm surrounded, with them popping against my skin one after the other.

Soon enough, my insides ripple with sensations, and while my skin looks as it did before, it doesn't feel that way. Not that I could explain the difference if I were asked. The sensation is too tenuous.

"It is time," says Obis, putting a stop to our long march.

"What now?" I ask, knowing only in general terms what is supposed to happen.

"Now you enter the sacred Circle of Obadyn," says Praedytus, holding his hand out to me. But there's uncertainty in his voice, a hesitation that doesn't inspire confidence.

I'm about to place my hand in his when the name of the disc cuts through the clutter in my head. "Obadyn? As in the Fields of Obadyn? Oblivion? That Obadyn?"

"Yes," says Obis inside my head, before Praedytus can respond. It's the first time she's communicated with me this way since she arose from her fallen state. I hadn't even realized it was possible. "You may relax. Not everything to do with Obadyn is bad."

While this clandestine communication has been taking place, Praedytus has taken hold of my hand, and once again I'm eaten up by an all-consuming lust. I try to think of my skin as a barrier, but it's no good. I'm not strong enough to resist the God of All Desire.

Mind you, as soon as I surrender to the sensations, I no longer care. At this stage, Praedytus could be coated from head to toe in silver, and I'd be okay with it.

The other thing helping to distract me is the warm breeze now blowing over the surface of the plateau. It's one that has my nerve endings clamoring for attention, but it's not enough.

On stepping onto the disc, I leave the ground, floating on the breeze like a leaf. On leveling out, I bob up and down

above the surface in a way I was not expecting, but that is comforting.

The warm zephyr spins me around, first in one direction and then the other, brushing my sensitive skin like feathered kisses. Soon enough, I'm aroused to the point that rational thought is beyond me.

All I want to do is roll around to increase the sensations, reveling in them until I achieve Nysa. It doesn't take long to see that as much as I want to move, my body is no longer under my control.

I'm at the mercy of the breeze that glides first over my pelvic mound and then up and over my breasts. This has me arching my neck, with a moan of enjoyment soon escaping my now wide-open lips. This tells me that at least my face and most of my neck muscles are still working fine.

I come out of my sexual haze when Obis claps her hands to signal the start of proceedings. But instead of the gesture being confident, there's something hesitant about it, as if she's not sure what comes next.

Please don't tell me she's winging it?

This hesitancy has me once again taking in my surroundings, noticing Praedytus has taken his son's place outside the circle. However, rather than looking inward as I'd expected, he looks out over the plain. As do all the other gods. It would appear the only divine creature slated to observe the ceremony is Obis.

I'm still wondering about the reason for this when Aurum turns and steps over the edge of the dish, but rather than float, he keeps both feet planted on the hard metal surface.

But that's not the strangest development. That would be the hush that settled over us like noise-canceling headphones the moment he entered the circle.

Unlike the filthy looks he'd been giving me earlier, he smiles with cold satisfaction while unhooking the chain that holds the electrum fettyr tight against his abdomen.

Just like his gold one, this fettyr is also unadorned apart from a luster only achieved through lots and lots of polishing. Sad as this is, my body still responds, my soul essence trying its best to move in his direction, but it stops in its tracks when he speaks.

"I'll fuck you until I achieve Nysa, even if it kills you. Father's plan requires a sacrifice, and I intend to deliver."

5

Aurum's lethal promise cuts through the carnal hypnosis that had been in danger of overwhelming me. If I could move, I'd be taking this bastard out in a big way.

Instead, I wait for the gods who are standing sentinel to turn and come to my aid, but it's as though Aurum hasn't spoken. Damn it, that strange hush I'd noticed when he first joined me.

In contrast, Obis appears rigid with fury, but when I look at her for help, she shakes her head. It's subtle enough that I almost miss it. However, it's only when she frowns that I realize I can hear her speak as clearly as if she were right next to me.

"Patience, my daughter. You will not come to harm while I am here," she says. This lets me know that while the gods can't hear what's going on inside the soundproof bubble, she knows what's happening because of our connection.

Her words are more than comforting, too. There's a warm

energy that flows with them, settling into my bones like liquid strength.

Aware that I'm looking off to the side, Aurum's gaze follows mine. "Don't expect that old crone to help. We're on our own for now, as Father intended."

Wrong, I think to myself. If only you knew how connected Obis and I are. She knows what's happening in here, you arrogant ass.

He's unaware of this when he slides his hands up my calves before holding my legs and positioning them to his liking. I'm spread wide enough that the persistent breeze airs my very core.

Aurum pushes his thumbs deep inside my sex, smearing me open, and riding my clit hard in the process. It might be the residual horniness left after Praedytus was done with me, or it the effects of the breeze and all that electrum.

But either way, I'm no longer thinking about the death threat I've just received. All I want now is to enjoy his slick length plunging deep inside me.

He doesn't worry about foreplay, and to be honest, I don't need it. Instead, he angles my whole body and plunges me down onto his fettyred cock until I can go no further.

He then lifts me up and down, filling me over and over, and while I'm enjoying it, I've had better. It must be something that shows because he doesn't appear to be having a good time, either, with his frustration building as the minutes pass.

"Use your muscles," says Obis inside my head.

"Will they work with the fettyrs?"

"What will work?" says Aurum, making me realize I've spoken aloud.

"Yes. Your muscles are powerful, and the metal this vainglorious creature favors is thin."

Right, let's get Aurum off and out of my life. I grip my Kegel muscles and am rewarded by his eyes dilating. Huh, Obis is right. I squeeze my muscles a little tighter.

"Not so hard," says Aurum, his voice squeaky and his eyes wide with fear.

"Jasmine, while tempting to teach him a lesson, to do so will not help the ritual," says Obis, stopping me from panel beating Aurum into submission.

I'm stumped about how to proceed, but then I remember Aurum's narcissistic tendencies.

"Oh, Aurum. You are the best of all the gods," I say, hoping he swallows my blatant lie. When it becomes obvious that he's as stupid as he is shallow, I don't hold back, telling him there's no comparison between him and the others.

He preens under my flattery, letting me know I'm on the money shot. I don't bother using my muscles again and instead stroke his ego until he achieves Nysa.

It doesn't matter that I'm nowhere near climaxing myself. The raw energy that races through me a second after Aurum's release fills me with enough power and light that I must appear as if I've done so.

Outside the circle, Obis is frowning, her head tilted as if trying to understand something that makes little sense. This has me worried that I've somehow messed up. Despite not having achieved Nysa, I was sure I'd gotten as much out of the exchange as the God of Gold. Maybe even more.

The moment Aurum pulls free, the sound barrier dissolves, allowing us to hear the other gods again. As disconcerting as this is, is the God of Gold leaving me like an inflatable love goddess with my sex still spread wide.

It's not the only thing that's exposed. Aurum's cock is now

missing the electrum fettyr, and there's no mistaking that he's okay with this development.

As I watch him rejoin his brothers and father, I wonder if he's now on an equal footing with the others who've achieved the same. Or does he think he's better than they are? His stance and smug grin suggest he knows something the others don't, with this leading me to believe it's the latter.

While waiting for him to return to his position and face away from the circle, I give thought to how I can get even with him for threatening to kill me. Then I come to my senses. After the ceremony is over, I'll either be human, one of the fallen, or dead. No matter the outcome, revenge will be impossible.

The other thing I'm having trouble accepting is that instead of looking out over the plain, Aurum's gaze is locked on mine, even as Axel enters the circle.

How the hell am I supposed to focus on the God of Nickel with that golden asshole eyeballing me? Not that it appears to bother Axel, who speaks the moment the sound barrier forms around us.

"Let's continue where we left off, shall we?" He runs his hands up the insides of my thighs, reducing me to an oversexed and quivering wreck in seconds. Despite this, the sense of power still swirls deep inside me.

Left off? Where the hell did we leave off? It takes a moment before I remember my last time I was with him.

"Yes, let's," I say, hoping my pause hasn't been too long.

Luckily, Axel has been too busy looking at my core and hasn't noticed. He pulls forward on my thighs, bringing me hard up against his electrum fettyr.

My bits buzz in recognition at the raised pattern he'd used with those little magnetic pebbles, although now the bumps

are fashioned out of precious metal. Not that I care either way when he tilts my pelvis, twists his hips and bam, my G-spot receives the most satisfying juddering.

"More of that please," I say, no longer giving a damn that Aurum is watching. Strange as it is, it might even be a bit of a turn-on. It might also be a way to exact some revenge.

It's something I work on when Axel next sheaths himself. After throwing my head back as much as I'm able, I open my mouth wide, as if screaming in ecstasy.

Sure enough, when I loll my head to the side and slit my eyes, I find Aurum standing rigid, his face a mask of impotent rage. It's then all I can do not to smile.

"Jasmine, stop the theatrics and use your muscles before we lose the moon," says Obis, her tone brooking no argument.

Oh, yeah. I keep forgetting not all of me is paralyzed, and the moment I flex my core muscles, it not only doubles my pleasure, but Axel looks to be enjoying himself, too.

This has me experimenting with different rhythms until I settle on something that's mind-blowing when combined with Axel moving me back and forth.

I'm settling in to work toward a climax when Obis interrupts my pleasure. I know she means well, but it's getting annoying.

"If you're having trouble fighting Nysa, think of Seolfer," says the goddess, killing my climax in its tracks. "Remember, you court great danger if you achieve your release before all of them have done so. Everything must proceed as planned for there to be any hope of success."

OMG, she's right. There's a big old chunk of me still in denial about the fatal—or worse, fallen—nature of my current state. It isn't something I can keep doing.

I get back to rippling my muscles, urging Axel over the finishing line. Again, although I don't climax, the wave of raw energy that floods my system right after he's achieved Nysa leaves me stronger than ever.

However, this time there's something different about it. Not just the surge of power, but the echo of ancient strength that's layered beneath it. I've come to no conclusions when Axel pulls free and the sounds of the others come through loud and clear.

"You did not achieve Nysa," murmurs Axel so that the others don't hear him. This lets me know he hadn't noticed the power and light that flooded my system not long after he'd achieved his release. Maybe I'm dealing with it better now?

Rather than show up his performance, I whisper back, "Ah, Obis said it would be safer if I didn't." With his masculinity intact, Axel, minus his electrum fettyr, joins the others outside of the dish, though he's now facing me like Aurum.

Ciprus is next and as much fun as I remember, but by using my muscles I have him achieve Nysa before he knows what's hit him. He looks crestfallen and then a little embarrassed.

But when the familiar surge of power crashes through me, my groan is guttural, no doubt letting him think I've also achieved Nysa. This seems to take the sting out of what he thinks was a poor performance.

I'm still processing the surge of ancient energy thrumming through my system when Marlo joins me in the dish. However, rather than pounce on me like the others, he looks at me in a way that says he's checking if I'm okay.

When he says, "Halfway, Princess, let's give them a show," it confirms I must look as good as I feel, with him soon flipping me over so I'm floating on my stomach. A heartbeat later, and he slips between my legs.

It's not until I've come to terms with Ciprus, Aurum, and Axel staring at us like we're pay-per-view that I notice movement in the distance. "Where the hell did all those people come from?"

"The People of the Mist are from below the clouds," says Marlo, his hands moving from around my waist to cover my breasts. "They serve the realm - farmers, builders, artisans. They witness all ceremonies of power, as is their right."

After using my breasts to steer me where he wants me, he drives his impressive length deep inside my core. Every riveted inch of him clatters against me as he slides home. There's also a visual element to the sensation when I see the crowd stand and wave their hands in jubilation.

Even though the sound barrier muffles their voices, I can see they're pleased about me being nailed by Marlo. The same can't be said for the three gods who've gone before, still watching from their positions.

Ciprus leans forward, checking out how close Marlo is to achieving Nysa, and I sense that the sooner this happens, the better. Anything to take the focus away from the God of Copper's own very short display.

Aurum is still furious. What? Did he think I'd turn away from the others after his amazing feats? Ha! Get real. Time to have some more fun at the asshole's expense.

The perfect opportunity comes when Marlo pushes me off his cock before pulling me back snug against his balls. I exaggerate my pleasure for the God of Gold's sake. I can't hear what he's saying, but I bet it's not very complimentary.

Meanwhile, Axel's attention is locked on my face, as if to check my reactions to his brother screwing me. He lifts an eyebrow in question before licking his lips in a way that leaves me in no doubt what he'd rather be slurping away at.

Marlo must be able to see this sideshow too, because he leans over my back and whispers in my ear. "I would run my tongue through your slit until you begged for mercy, but it's forbidden in the Circle of Obadyn."

Not that this rule stops him from running his tongue up the back of my neck and coating it with those magic enzymes of his. This has a wave of desire sluicing through my system with a whirr of pleasure growing deep inside me.

"You must not!" screams Obis inside my head, killing the pleasure for me. Still, she's reminded me yet again of my part in the ceremony.

"Do you enjoy that?" says Marlo, twisting my body around and around on his cock with the rivets on his fettyr tweaking me as he does so. I'd nod in response, but my neck muscles are now as hard as his cock as I battle the climax that's fighting for supremacy. Despite my willing it away, it gains momentum, but again Obis warns against giving in to the sensations.

Marlo pulls free, spins me around and then plunges me down hard on his length. It's then all I can do to keep myself from tipping over the edge when I see the bliss that fills his face when his hips jerk out of control.

I have to think of Aurum and Seolfer doing me together to blunt my senses. I've only just gotten it under control when the familiar surge of transferred energy crashes into my solar plexus, leaving me panting to catch my breath.

"Thank you, Jasmine," says Marlo, holding me tight before disengaging himself. It's with regret that he leaves me floating before exiting the dish to regain his place. When he turns to face the circle as protocol demands, I can see he's back to his full, unfettyred glory.

Vyran is next, announced by his turning and stepping

inside the dish. The second both his feet touch the surface, the sound barrier forms, giving us some semblance of privacy, despite us being watched by his four brothers.

I'd forgotten how gorgeous my God of the Woods is, his beauty taking my breath away. Not that my feelings for him are what they once were. While I might have been confused about whom I preferred between Ben and Vyran, now there's no doubt in my mind at all. Not that sex with the God of the Woods would be like screwing my brother or anything. Far from it.

"Are you all right?" he says, running his hands over my body, checking for injuries, but still having my skin singing in the process. "You must be tired."

Before I can disabuse him of this notion, I hear Obis inside my head: "Do not let him know you have been holding back. It's better the gods not be reminded of their ignorance at such a time."

Luckily, Vyran takes my lack of response as a sign of exhaustion. I know I've lied to him by omission, but I'm hoping he won't notice from my responses that I'm energized rather than exhausted.

He keeps running his hands over my body, kneading and teasing until there isn't an inch of me that isn't both relaxed and aroused in equal measure. My body is liquid, and boiling hot liquid at that. I'd forgotten how well this god knows me.

My pearl is the last piece of me to receive his undivided attention and oh boy, does she like it. He takes his time licking his fingers, and with the attention he gives each digit, having my senses stretched tight in anticipation.

By the time he slides his fingers over the hood and teases my nubbin out to play, I'm screaming inside. He flicks my clit

and, without warning, an orgasm overwhelms me in league with Obis screaming "NO!" inside my head.

I'm still shuddering from my release when I notice something different about Vyran's face. It's reminiscent of when we were kids and scared each other by holding a flashlight under our chins. Except this is no flashlight, and the source is scarier than anything we managed on Halloween.

Rather, my clit is glowing like some erotic night light, and bright enough that there's no missing the shock on Vyran's face. Of concern is that outside the circle, Obis looks to be every bit as horrified.

“What?” I say, as much to Obis as to Vyran. I don't give a damn who answers me as long as someone does. I'm sick to death of always being the last to know what the hell is happening.

"I've heard about it but never seen it," says Vyran, not answering my question.

“This should not be possible,” says Obis, also not answering my damned question.

“What?” I say again, hoping to get something more concrete in response.

"Things are not as they should be," says Obis, her voice tight with tension. "The ceremony will need to be adapted."

Damn it, I knew it. The blasted woman is winging it.

She's not told me how the ceremony is to be adapted, when Vyran says, "I need to achieve Nysa with you, and soon, if you are to return to your true form."

“Well, what are you waiting for?!”

He wastes no time, sliding deep inside me and holding me tight while pumping himself into me with short, fast thrusts. On taking in the reactions of his four brothers, I realize a couple of things at once.

They're as shocked as Obis and Vyran that my pearl is glowing like it is. And that's not the only surprise. I can move my head now, the paralysis weakening with each energy transfer. It's as if something is unlocking my body's constraints, which, in turn, reminds me I have other muscles I can already move.

This has me again feathering my core muscles, with Vyran groaning in pleasure. When I increase the speed and intensity, I'm rewarded when he roars his release as he achieves Nysa in double-quick time.

He's still groaning when the most intense energy surge yet pounds through me, strong enough that it comes close to blowing the top of my head off. Strong enough that I'm on the brink of passing out, and only by taking slow, deep breaths do I dissolve the black at the edges of my consciousness.

I'm still dealing with this when the sound barrier drops. But rather than be bombarded by nervous chatter, we're met by a stunned silence that is as deafening in its own way.

Even Vyran appears lost for words, his distraction obvious when he gives my clit one final rub, seemingly for luck, before returning to his allotted position. I'm still checking him out when I'm once again overcome by white noise.

This means Praedytus has joined me in the dish, with me twisting around to stare at him, and telling me the paralysis that had affected my upper body has eased.

It also allows me to see his shock, confirming he wasn't as up-to-date as the others about how off the rails the ceremony had gone. One of the drawbacks of looking out over the Plain of Gneiss instead of at the action.

There's something else in his expression, too. A dawning comprehension that he's not just lost control of the ceremony,

but that he was never in control in the first place. That someone else has been pulling the strings.

I expect him to say something, but I'm disappointed. Instead, he pulls on my feet while pushing my legs to each side and is deep inside me moments later. My body is soon awash with satisfaction, my nerve endings singing in pleasure and my clit on fire with want. Wanting to grow, wanting to disintegrate, wanting to glow enough to blind him.

The sensations build until I'm ready to detonate, but I don't. Instead, I hover on the edge, ready to fly, ready for freedom, but still a prisoner of my own body.

Praedytus soon achieves Nysa, yelling his lungs out as spasm after spasm roll over him. The only change in me is that I'm closer to exploding because of the power he's just pumped into me.

But there's something else building too—a reservoir of strength that feels both familiar and ancient, as if it's been waiting inside me all along. It's as if I'm about to experience the mother of all Nysas.

Instead, I imagine myself bursting into a million pieces and taking my place in the night sky, having to shake my head to rid it of this fanciful thought.

But then I see the sorrow on the faces of Obis and the others, and reality washes over me like lukewarm tea. As if sensing what is to come, Praedytus leaves my side, perhaps to avoid being collateral damage.

I don't get to focus on their pitying looks for long. The moonlight beaming down on the dish intensifies to the point I have to close my eyes against it. The vibrating of my pearl soon becomes the entire focus of my being. It's to the point that once again sounds are muffled, confirming I'm cut off from those outside the dish.

"Obis? Can you hear me?"

Nothing

While the vibrating of my clit continues unabated, I notice the moonlight shining on my eyelids has dimmed. I open my eyes a slit, my first instinct being to slam them shut again. Tight.

I'm no longer alone, that's for damn sure.

6

I can tell the guy standing naked and unfettyred next to me is a god by the way reality seems to bend around him. The air itself grows heavy with age—not his, but the weight of eons he's witnessed.

He's god-like in stature, too. And I mean everywhere. Yikes. He even makes Marlo seem a little on the small side, and my eyes widen as I take in the size of that veined and hooded beast. Whoever the hell he is, he can't expect me to...

His laughter echoes with ancient law, drawing my attention to his face. What I see there makes my breath catch. Not because he's ugly, but because his terrible perfection tells me he's never known doubt, never had his supremacy questioned. His beauty is absolute, but cold as marble, and looking at him feels like staring into the face of judgment itself.

"I cannot play with your kind," he says. Each word seems to resonate not just in my ears but in my bones, as if the universe itself is speaking through him.

Around us, the dome of moonlight flickers, responding to

his presence. I don't know whether to be relieved or insulted by his tone, but the compulsion to defer to him—to agree with whatever he says—is so strong I have to fight it.

"You have failed," he says, shaking his head in what I take to be the intergalactic sign for "you've fucked up bad." While my heart hammers in my chest, dread settles in my gut.

This has me fighting the sensations that threaten to overload my system, allowing myself a moment to process his presence before speaking. "Can't you do something about it?" I leave out the "if you're so powerful," but it still hovers in the air between us, and he stiffens in response.

"Why should Obadyn bother with this?" he says, and the way he speaks his own name makes it sound like a force of nature rather than mere identification. The temperature in the bubble drops several degrees, and I notice frost beginning to form on the edges of the moonlight dome.

Something about his perfect stillness, the way he never seems to blink, makes my skin crawl even as every instinct screams at me to kneel.

Luckily, after my dealings with Seolfer and Aurum, I know how to go for the jugular with his kind. With no let-up in the assault on my sex; I let him have it.

"Oh, I didn't realize... you weren't... capable. Perhaps one of the... others..." It's only by shallow breathing of the Lamaze variety that I get the words out around the pain of my delayed Nysa.

Again, I leave the rest unsaid, letting his ego fill in the blanks. But even as I think this, his eyes seem to look straight through me, as if he can see not just my thoughts but all futures branching out from this moment. The sensation makes me want to confess truths I didn't even know I was hiding.

"There is one way," he says, jutting his oversized cock out

even further, its rosy glow letting me know there's no blood north of his navel. I hope to hell he falls for it.

"Yes?" I say, hoping he's not somehow involved.

"You need another in order to attain Nysa. You were supposed to achieve this after you'd bestowed your gift on all the gods—not halfway through."

Crap! He interprets my horror correctly, reiterating he's not going anywhere near me. But my relief is short-lived because the only other I can think of is Seolfer, and I don't think he'd let me achieve Nysa. Not even if his life depended on it. He'd die in the process just to spite me.

"Does it have to be a god?" I grit out.

"You may not achieve Nysa with the People of the Mist. It is forbidden."

"Not them. Another."

Obadyn nods—a movement so slight I wonder if I might have imagined it. Then, unexpectedly, he reaches out and flicks my glowing clit with his forefinger. After an extra bright flash, the light dims, while the crushing pain that's been building around it eases to a manageable throb.

"You will need clarity for what comes next," he says simply.

Either way, it's enough for me, and rather than give him the opportunity to ask me what I'm planning, I go for it."

It's not as if I've got anything to lose. However, just because I'm technically strong enough to pull it off doesn't mean I'll be able to.

"Ben! Come to me!" I put everything I can into the summons. But for all I know, this damned dome of moonlight we're stuck under might stop my request from getting through.

Nothing happens, but I'm not giving up because I know if

someone doesn't take the edge off my stalled climax soon, it won't be pretty.

"Ben! Help me. Come to me now!" This last word is screamed as the pressure in and around my clit builds to the point of pain.

He flickers into being, but it takes longer than usual, and I worry he'll end up stuck in limbo. I release my breath only when he's materialized and is floating next to me. That he's wearing a suit is concerning, but before I can ask him about it, he grabs hold of my hands, drawing the two of us closer. This shows me I'm on my own when it comes to being paralyzed.

"What has he done to you?" he says, his gaze swinging between my glowing pearl and Obadyn.

"He's done nothing, but you need to make love to me fast and make it good." Ben doesn't move, forcing me to add, "If you don't, we all die." I'm not 100 percent sure about this, but I sense that if I go off with as big a bang as I suspect, we're all toast.

Unfortunately, the threat of imminent death is lousy when it comes to foreplay, and Ben remains clothed. That is until I get Obadyn to strip him.

"What the fuck?" says Ben, looking at the pile of tattered suiting on the disc beneath him. "I was in the middle of a job interview down in Phoenix."

He's muttering about not getting it now when I interrupt him.

"A job interview? Phoenix? Well, screw you if you can get over me that fast."

"Jasmine, I'd given up hope. I kept having these dreams you'd return. Dreams where someone was telling me to wait, that you'd need me for something. But it's been six months. I thought I was going crazy, but now... with this ...?"

His voice breaks, and I see the man I've put through hell. The nights he must have spent wondering if I was alive or dead. The way he must have questioned his own sanity when the dreams felt more real than waking life.

In the end, it's his pain that gets through to me, not just his words, but what my absence has cost him.

"Wait, six months! I've been gone six months?"

Rather than speak, he nods in confirmation.

"Ben, I'm so sorry. I thought it was only days." The guilt hits me like a physical blow, but my clit beginning to tingle reminds me we don't have time for this conversation.

"Then don't do it again!" he says, his words fierce. "Whatever power you have now, whatever this ceremony does to you—don't leave me behind again. I can handle gods and magic and impossible things, but I can't handle losing you."

"Can you give us some privacy?" I say to Obadyn, not sure I can go down on Ben with this motherfucker staring at us. His gaze is fixed on me with the patience of stone. Despite his turning away from us, his presence fills the dome like a held breath.

Can't you leave?" I grind out as the spasms attacking my clit build to painful levels again. "I may only leave when you achieve Nysa," says Obadyn, facing away but still monitoring our progress.

Sheesh, nothing like a little pressure. Still, if it'll get us out of the crap, I'll deal. Ben maneuvers us until my lips close over the end of his cock.

No sooner had my mouth touched him than the pressure eased off my sex. After groaning in relief, I put my heart and soul into getting my boyfriend hard enough to bounce quarters off.

I'm into it when out of the corner of my eye, I notice

Obadyn has turned and is watching us. His focus is such that he may as well be carved from marble, yet there's a gluttony in his perfect stillness. He's like an apex predator that's spotted prey and is deciding whether to strike.

It's something that has the surrounding air humming with power. With nothing to be done about it, I shut my eyes to blot Obadyn out and go back to blowing Ben's mind. Given how much he's moaning, I know I'm on track.

It isn't long before Ben grows inside my mouth. And keeps growing, to a size he's never achieved before, until I'm unable to take him any longer, letting me know it's now or never. However, it doesn't take long to understand that with both of us floating, it'll be difficult to make the best of things.

"A little help?" I say to Obadyn, having to repeat myself given that the only blood left in his body is now engorging his enormous cock.

In the end, he lets go of it to take me in his arms. This has my back pressed hard against his chest and my legs held up in each of his arms. I'm yet again left vulnerable, and this sensation only increases when his cock nestles between my ass cheeks, holding me in place.

"Fuck me, baby," I say to Ben. "Love me."

He swims through the air to join me, before grabbing one of my feet and pulling himself in the rest of the way. But he's so much bigger that without help, I can't see how it will work.

That is, until Obadyn reaches between my thighs and peels me wide, allowing Ben to drive his way in, with me adoring every inch of the man I love.

"Oh, hell, that's so..." Ben's incomplete avowal mirrors my thoughts, with the power and pleasure we're experiencing now anything but fatal. Rather, I'd call it life-affirming. And yet, I still need, want, and crave more.

As if understanding this, Obadyn tucks my legs around Ben's waist before holding me in place by closing his large hands over my breasts.

I can tell by Ben's expression that he's enjoying seeing my nipples being squeezed and tugged, and I arch my back, giving myself over to Obadyn. Doing so confirms my body is almost back under my control thanks to the accumulated power from six gods. Soon enough, Ben's burying himself to a point where I'm feverish and a slave to the emotions and sensations threatening to overwhelm me.

That Obadyn is grinding his hips against my ass only bolsters the sensations that are consuming me. There's something unsettling about how his ancient power translates into such calculated intimacy, as if he's performed this exact sequence across countless eons.

Our combined coitus goes from smooth and sensual to feral in a flash. With the slightest change, Obadyn goes from gliding his cock between my cheeks to nudging for entrance.

It's something I'm not keen on, but when he runs his tongue up the back of my neck as Marlo had earlier, it's like a switch has been flipped. Now, rather than be unwelcome, I've never wanted something this much in all my life.

My wish is his command, and when he pushes himself deep inside me, I'm glad of Marla's overzealous use of that ceremonial butt plug earlier. With Obadyn pumping into me from behind and Ben sheathing himself in my core, I'm flooded with bliss and a sense that I've found my place in the universe.

Whether by design or coincidence, each of their thrusts is timed, filling me to overflowing before retreating and leaving me hollow. The next time they ram home, I grip them with my muscles and hold on tight so they can't withdraw all the way.

This leads to a series of deep thrusts that push me over the edge.

I'm still screaming my release when Obadyn jerks free, Ben soon following suit. Then, with shocking speed, the walls of moonlight fade, and the three of us drop in a tangled heap in the middle of the dish.

However, that's not what has my face burning. That would be our postcoital dog pile, being visible to the six gods, Obis, and the People of the Mist.

While I'm expecting a reaction, it's not the one I get. All of them except Obis and Praedytus, drop to their knees. Even the People of the Mist follow suit, though I get the distinct impression they have no choice in the matter. Their service to the realm binds them to acknowledge power when it manifests.

After threading her way through the kneeling gods, Obis steps inside the dish and over to Obadyn's side. "Father, it is good to see you again."

"Likewise, daughter," says Obadyn, jumping to his feet and planting a fatherly kiss on her forehead. "You have done well."

"I was worried I had failed when Jasmine did not follow my instructions," says Obis, giving me a reproachful look. Then her expression softens. "Forgive me, child, but I could not tell you the truth. Every time we spoke, every moment of our connection—I was imbuing you with the power you'd need to survive."

Ben and I have only just made it to our feet, and wrapped our arms around each other, when she continues.

"Praedytus created the perfect conditions for me to strengthen you, never realizing he was helping me forge the

key to our freedom. Your power didn't come from his conditioning or the gods' touch alone. It came from me."

Wait, what? The bitch not only hijacked my ceremony, but she's also been pumping me full of goddess power? No wonder I feel so strong. Damn it, despite her beauty, she's every bit as devious as any other Nyphrazi.

However, on seeing how angry Marlo and Vyran are, I revise this. Even Ciprus looks furious at having been an unwitting pawn in what he thinks is her power grab. I wonder the three gods would think if they knew what Praedytus had really been up to? Would they be as angry as I am now? Angry enough to leave without a by your leave?

I don't think about it twice. Rather, I hold Ben tight and think of The Metal Beast. I want both of us as far away from here and whatever's about to go down as possible. But nothing happens other than Obadyn turning to face me and saying, "Not until I say so."

"Forgive us, brother. I was not aware you wanted to be awakened," says Praedytus, failing to hide his anger to any great degree. Other than him, the other gods have remained quiet.

It's as though they've been silenced. I hope those who are my friends are okay. Aurum can choke on his words for eternity for all I care, but what Obadyn does to him is much worse.

The change in Aurum's skin tone is gradual enough that it's hard to detect until I see he's more pewter than gold. By the time his skin is a dull gray, there are tears streaming down the God of Gold's face.

Make that the God of Lead.

Whoa, that's harsh.

"Harsh?" says Obadyn, once again turning to face me and

confirming he was also privy to my thoughts. "He would have killed you during the ceremony, ensuring Praedytus's sacrifice succeeded."

"Good point," I say, with any regrets I have on Aurum's behalf soon obliterated. The glee that replaces it is an emotion the gods would be proud of.

My self-analysis is soon interrupted when Obadyn claims one of my hands and squeezes it. " Now that the ceremony is complete, and you have reclaimed your human form, you must return to your own kind."

He then waves a hand in Ben and my direction, resulting in my body tingling like the worst case of pins and needles ever. We're on our way home but not so fast that I miss seeing Obadyn wink at me.

Even with my eyes closed, I know we're on the back deck of the Beast, and it's freezing, the wind biting my exposed skin like a swarm of mosquitoes. But I don't care, because being cold means being home.

"Are you okay?" says Ben, lifting me before allowing me to once again settle onto his still-hard cock. He runs his hands all over my body and gives his hips another small jerk. "Jasmine. Are you okay?"

Before I can ripple my muscles for his satisfaction, a pointed cough from the guy on the boat next to us lets us know he's not keen on our PDA. We waste no time getting below decks, although Ben won't let us separate to do so.

Safe in the master cabin, I do my own exploration of Ben's body. He's fine too, though a little different. Different in a good way, especially in the size department.

"It's great having my human babe back," he says, lifting me free of his cock before lowering me onto it again an inch at a time.

"Yeah, about that," I gasp out as I take his full length.

"What?" says Ben after he's lifted his mouth from one of my nipples.

"This," I say, before wrapping my arms and legs more tightly around him, with us materializing a second later on the Greek-style island that Marlo had once taken me to. At least I think it's the same island, because nothing was a given when it came to the Nyphrazi.

"I thought the ceremony was supposed to have you reverting to your human form," says Ben, his brow wrinkled in confusion as he takes in our surroundings.

I've not answered when Obadyn appears with a deafening clap of thunder that scares the crap out of both of us. What an asshole. I know full well there's no need for this showmanship, his having joined me in the Circle of Obadyn whisper quiet.

A second later and Praedytus materializes next to him, his face a mask of blind fury. "You ruined everything!" he yells at me, his ferocity such that Ben and I take an involuntary step back.

"Every moment after your accidental crossing was my design. I guided each of my sons to you at the right moment. You weren't stumbling through random encounters, Jasmine. You were following a crafted path to accumulate the divine power I needed. Your transformation into one of the fallen would have provided the energy to seal the realms for all time."

His hand moves toward me, but Obadyn steps between us. "You will not touch her, brother. Your plans have failed. The old order is restored."

"This isn't over," Praedytus snarls, backing away. "She's too dangerous to live. Too powerful. She'll upset everything we've built."

"Everything *you've* built on lies and manipulation," Obadyn corrects. "That ends now."

Praedytus looks between his brother and me, calculating. Then, with a sound of pure wrath, he vanishes in a cloud of steam.

"He'll be back," says Obadyn, turning to face us. "My brother doesn't accept defeat without a fight. But for now, you're safe. The power you've both gained through your connection to our realm will protect you."

"We're gods?" splutters out Ben.

Obadyn shakes his head.

"Demigods?" says Ben, his tone less sure.

Again, Obadyn shakes his head.

"Then just what in the hell are we?" I spit out, sick and tired of the mystic crap these gods are so keen on.

"You are whatever you want to be," says Obadyn, before disappearing in a multicolored flash. This leaves us none the wiser and has me missing my chance to kick him in those over-sized testicles of his.

While incensed at being manipulated not just by Praedytus, but also Obis, I welcome the power to travel wherever and whenever I want. Ben, however, is grinding his teeth to the point that I'm worried he'll crack a tooth. I'd speak to him, but his anger blinds him to my presence.

In the end, I grip hold of his cock with my core muscles, holding him tighter and tighter until I get his attention.

"How about we work it out between us? I'm as much in the dark as you are."

"I want to get as far away from those Nyphrazi assholes as possible," says Ben, his thoughts a perfect match to mine.

"So, what are you waiting for?" I say, and can see when he

realizes the potential. "All you need to do is think of where you want to take us."

"Let's give this a whirl," says Ben, after making sure my legs are secure around his back. There's a new confidence in his voice that wasn't there before—not just acceptance of our situation, but ownership of it. He's not just along for the ride anymore; he's choosing this adventure with me.

He slides his cock even deeper inside at the exact moment we dematerialize, and I realize this is Ben's moment of transformation, too. From a man trying to cope with losing me to a partner embracing whatever we're becoming together.

Even with my eyes closed, I know we're back aboard The Metal Beast. But there's something wrong with the light and the iciness of the master cabin. On hearing the clinking of rigging on masts, I know what it is. Only a heavy coating of snow can muffle the world in this way.

"Wait," I say, understanding flooding me. "What if we can control when we arrive, not just where?" This has me concentrating, thinking not just about the boat, but about arriving only hours after I left. To a time before my parents thought I was dead. When life was ordinary and boring.

Soon enough, the world shimmers around us.

When it settles, the early morning light has the right quality, and the sounds from the harbor match. I've reclaimed our lives.

But even as I think about it, I know this isn't true. While we can go back to our jobs and routines, we can't pretend we're just ordinary people.

Because we're not. Not anymore.

This has me examining Ben, waiting for him to come to the same conclusion as I did. Soon enough, I'll see when he accepts what I already have.

"We can travel anywhere," he whispers, his voice filled with wonder. "Any time. To any place we've ever dreamed of visiting."

"The whole world," I agree, feeling the power thrumming beneath my skin. "Or any world, for that matter."

He grins for the first time since I summoned him from that job interview, and it's the same mischievous expression that first made me fall for him. "So, where do you want to go first? Paris? Tokyo? Maybe somewhere with better weather than Alaska?"

I laugh, but then grow serious. "Ben, are you sure about this? About us? Because there's no going back to ordinary now. We'll be living between worlds, dealing with gods and magic for the rest of our lives. That's not what you signed up for when you moved to Alaska."

"Jasmine," he says, framing my face with his hands, "I signed up for you. Everything else is just details." His smile is soft but determined. "Besides, ordinary was overrated anyway."

"Even when I'm glowing and manipulating time and space?"

"Especially then," he murmurs against my lips. "You've always been extraordinary. Now the outside just matches what I've known all along."

I know that whatever comes next, ordinary will never be enough for us again. But more importantly, we'll face it together.

EPILOGUE

PRAEDYTUS

The silence in my domain is deafening. For the first time in centuries, I stand on my own in the crystalline chamber that once was the seat of absolute godly power in the Nyphrazi realm.

The walls that have witnessed countless supplications, the throne where gods kneeled before me, the altar where I shaped the very fabric of desire itself—all of it now feels hollow. Empty. Meaningless.

I flex my fingers, watching the silver light dance across my knuckles. My power remains intact, but what good is dominion over desire when lesser gods no longer fear me? When my own brother can strip my authority with nothing more than his presence?

"The old order is restored," Obadyn had said, as if his words could erase everything I had built. But I am not some petulant child to rage at failure. I am Praedytus, God of All Desire, architect of a realm that has thrived under my guidance for

countless ages. If the old order is restored, then I will adapt. I will wait. And I will plan.

I will reclaim what is mine.

Moving to the viewing portal overlooking the vast expanse between our realm and the human world, I survey the damage Jasmine's crossings have wrought.

The veil separating our worlds hangs in tatters, reality bleeding through the gaps like wounds refusing to heal. Each rift pulses with unstable energy, growing wider with every passing moment.

This is the price of allowing humans to gain divine power. I had crafted Jasmine's transformation so carefully—each encounter with my sons designed to accumulate just enough divine energy to make her the perfect sacrifice.

The power I'd gifted her was supposed to guarantee the sealing of the realms for all time, a permanent barrier that would have cemented my authority forever.

But Obis interfered, pumping the human full of her own essence until Jasmine blazed with enough power to guide Obadyn home.

The moment my brother latched onto that glowing pearl, my carefully laid plans had crumbled. Jasmine had become too powerful to sacrifice, too connected to the old bloodlines to control. It was her fault my new order had failed, and consequently why I was forced to kneel before the old order.

Humans are chaos incarnate, taking divine gifts and perverting them, using them without understanding, destroying without thought of consequence. Hadn't Terra, my brother in name only, found that out for himself?

But as I trace the rips in the veil, something else catches my attention. Energy signatures not belonging to Jasmine or her

lowly mortal lover. Fresh crossings that began after the ceremony's chaos. Those that should not exist.

My hands freeze on the crystal surface of the portal. Someone else has been traveling between realms. I splay my fingers, sending my senses out, searching for and finding—multiple someones. And they are not random breaches caused by weakened barriers—these are deliberate, controlled passages. The kind requiring knowledge of forbidden rubrics.

I expand my awareness, following the energy trails like a predator tracking scent. The signatures are familiar yet wrong, carrying a distinctive Nyphrazi resonance but tainted with something weaker. Something that has me clenching my jaw. The divine feminine.

My daughters have been crossing into the human realm. The first signature I isolate belongs to Cuprum. Her copper-bright energy has been bleeding through the veils since before the ceremony's disruption, each crossing leaving traces of her presence in the human world.

Obis freed her from the Fields of Obadyn after everything calmed down, having decided the Goddess of Copper posed no threat. And in so doing, she'd again proved why the females in our realm would always be weaker.

But as I trace Cuprum's energy signature deeper, following it to its destination, my blood turns to ice. The human she has been visiting, the one whose energy clings to her divine essence like a lover's touch, is Ben. Jasmine's Ben.

But that is not what I fear most. Even before her temporary banishment, the energy signatures showed she was returning with her power intact. As if her time in the human realm hadn't drained her divinity at all.

The very concept violates every law of divine physics, as they are written. Humans are supposed to drain goddess

energy, which is why crossing to their realm is forbidden. That is why the hierarchy exists. Only gods may claim goddess energy as their own, never a mere human.

But Cuprum's energy signature tells a different story. And worse, I detect residual traces of male human energy clinging to it. It is one thing for a god to bring his plaything through to the Nyphrazi realm; it is quite another for a goddess to do so.

With growing fury, I trace yet more signatures from before the ceremony's disruption. Seol made several crossings, each resulting in the same impossible preservation of power. My silver-bright daughter has also maintained her strength despite intimate contact with humans, defying every natural law.

But it is the final signature that has my chest tightening with something approaching panic. Vyra, the Goddess of the Woods, whose crossings began only after the ceremony's chaos, didn't just maintain her power. Rather, her energy grows stronger with each journey—a phenomenon that defies explanation.

Her crossings have escalated rapidly since the ceremony, with longer stays, more frequent trips, and power increases that defy every natural law. In mere weeks, she has accomplished what should take centuries. And underneath her divine signature, I detect something else. Human energy!

Not just one source, but multiple. A constellation of human power that orbits her presence like planets around a star. I yank my hands away from the portal, my mind racing through the implications.

If goddesses can maintain their power after human contact, the careful balance I've built will be compromised. And if one of them is gaining power, as I suspect, there's a risk everything I've built could be destroyed.

A hierarchy where goddesses depended on gods for sexual

fulfillment, their energy drained when their partner achieved Nysa. Under my rule, intimacy came at the cost of power. With them able to sate their desires without paying that price, what need did they have for gods?

Unlike my systematic oppression of the goddesses, Obadyn always believed in their equal place within our hierarchy. His "old order" never sought to diminish their sexual autonomy or drain their power through intimacy.

If anything, he encouraged goddesses to find their own strength. It was the reason Obis was so powerful, and motive enough for me to banish her along with her father. Her innate strength allowed her to subvert the ceremony without help from her sire.

My brother would see these human connections not as a threat to divine authority, but as a validation of his belief that goddesses deserve the same freedoms as gods. Another reason I must investigate this phenomenon myself, before he discovers what opportunities his restored order has created.

I pace, energy crackling around my feet with each step. Obis's escape and her sabotage of the ceremony was a catastrophe, but it also presents me with an opportunity.

With Jasmine and her lover gone and my brother's attention focused on reestablishing his authority over the Nyphrazi realm itself, I have an opportunity. Obadyn is too occupied with restoring the old order to notice what his goddesses are doing in the human world.

This leaves me free to investigate without interference, determine the scope of the threat, and plan a response. But I must be careful. Subtle. If I don't plan with care, Obadyn will intervene. After his display of power during the ceremony, I am not yet ready for another direct confrontation with my brother.

No, this requires finesse, patience, and long-term manipulation, all of which I've perfected over millennia. Returning to the portal, I focus on Vyra's energy signature. Her crossings are the most frequent, the most brazen, and the only ones showing actual power growth.

If any goddess has discovered something new about human contact, it is the Goddess of the Woods. I trace her most recent journey, following the energy trail to a forested region in what the humans call Alaska.

There, her divine signature mingles with four individuals whose energy resonates with ancient bloodlines. Nyphrazi bloodlines. My hands clench into fists as understanding dawns.

These are not random humans Vyra has encountered. They are descendants, distant relations carrying diluted but genuine divine heritage. A bloodline that allows for power amplification rather than the usual drain or the simple preservation of divine energy.

I trace the bloodline deeper, following its genetic echo back through generations until I find its source. Terra. The God of Stone has left his mark on their family line through a human grandmother, creating a legacy that has remained dormant until Vyra's touch awakened it.

Of course, it is Terra's bloodline. The god who vanished so long ago that most have forgotten he ever existed, banished to the Sundering in the earliest days of my rule.

Another reminder of how the past refuses to stay buried. A bloodline that could have a goddess addicted to human touch. "Fascinating," I murmur, though the word tastes bitter on my tongue.

Vyra is not just breaking laws—she is tapping into a power source that could strengthen her more than any goddess has

been in millennia. Even stronger than some gods. If word of this phenomenon spreads, if other goddesses realize some humans can amplify their power...

I need more information. I need to understand what is happening in that forest, what these humans can offer, which divine males cannot.

Most importantly, I need to determine whether this development can be contained or if more drastic measures will be required. The solution crystallizes in my mind with perfect clarity.

I'll visit the human realm myself. Not to confront Vyra—that would only alert her to my interest and drive her underground. No, I need to observe. To study. To learn what forces are at work.

Only then can I decide whether these goddesses represent an opportunity to be exploited or a threat to be eliminated. It matters not to me that the goddesses are of my loins. Power will always win out over family.

Moving to my private chambers, I begin the preparations for crossing between realms. It has been centuries since I last walked among humans, but the techniques remain unchanged.

A simple matter of projecting my consciousness across the veil while maintaining enough divine essence to manifest there. Unlike the complex rituals the goddesses require, my power allows for direct translation between worlds. One of the advantages of being male.

As I gather energy, my thoughts turn to Vyra. The Goddess of the Woods has always been more impulsive than my other daughters, more willing to take risks. If she has indeed formed a bond with these divine humans, she might resist my attempts at separation. However, that could prove useful, depending on

how events unfold. Hadn't I used the very power of heartache to my own benefit in the past?

I'm thinking back on this when my form shimmers and I feel the energy building around me. Soon I will walk in forests that have never known my divine presence, and breathe air that carries no trace of my Nyphrazi heritage.

I will see firsthand what temptation has drawn my goddesses away from their proper place. And if necessary, I will remind them why the natural order exists. The portal opens before me, revealing glimpses of towering evergreens and snow-capped mountains.

Somewhere in that wilderness, Vyra has discovered powers that could threaten everything I have built. Powers that need to be understood. Controlled. Or destroyed. A moment later, I step through the veil between worlds, leaving the crystal silence of my domain behind.

The game is far from over, with patience being the key to long-term victory. After all, I am the God of All Desire. And desire, when coerced and manipulated, can motivate any action. Especially betrayal.

THANK YOU

If you've enjoyed this story, we'd be thrilled if you could take the time to give it a rating or review at the online store you purchased from, or your favorite review site.

www.thepapersparrow.com

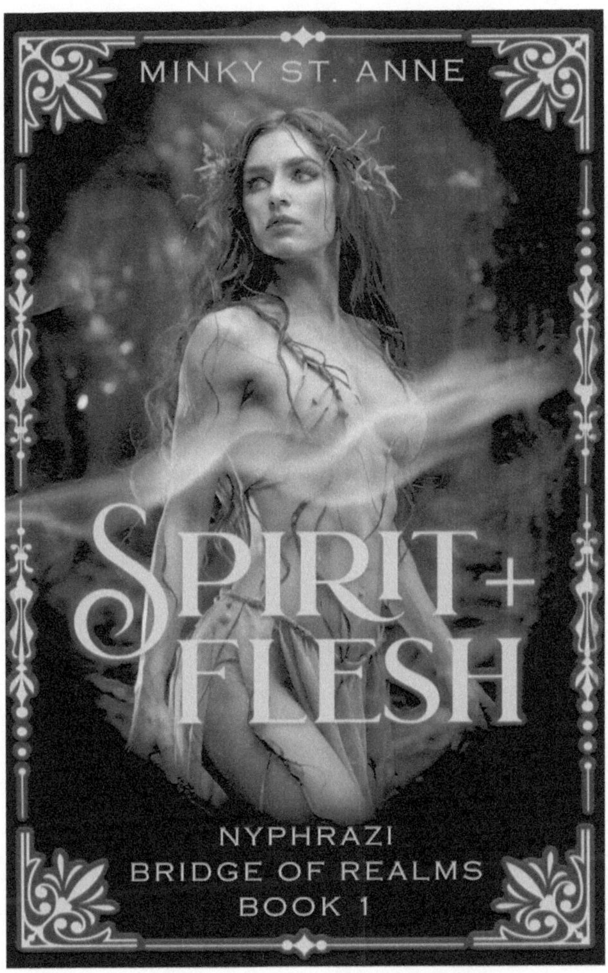

What happens when a goddess discovers the power of human touch with the very men whose god-blood could destroy her world?

Nyphrazi laws about goddesses not entering the human realm were absolute. And yet I'd not thought twice about crossing the portal into the Alaskan wilderness where Mason and his logging crew worked.

One glimpse of the four Hadley men, one brush of calloused fingers against divine skin, and I had no regrets. An unimaginable hunger arose, crying out to their mortality and the Nyphrazi fire in their veins, their touch awakening powers I struggled to control.

Now I'm addicted to my stolen moments with them, every one rendering me ever stronger. But as with all addictions, mine comes at a terrible cost.

Get caught breaking our sacred laws and watch the ritual sacrifice of the men I love, before those in power force me to join the ranks of the Fallen.

Or fight back, because they don't know what I've become.

What we've become together.

ABOUT THE AUTHOR

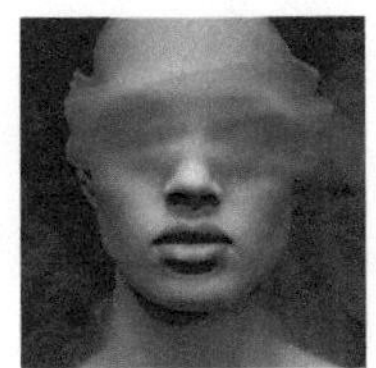

Minky St Anne writes smutty paranormal romance with a healthy dose of mythological mischief. She firmly believes that the best fantasies involve equal parts mythology, steam, and just enough scientific accuracy that you're tempted to experiment, or possibly invest in rechargeable batteries.

Her motto: Life's too short for vanilla romance and too long for boring gods and goddesses.

www.ingramcontent.com/pod-product-compliance
Lightning Source LLC
Chambersburg PA
CBHW021843010726
47493CB00005B/1524

* 9 7 8 1 9 9 1 3 2 1 2 3 7 *